Marble Hall Murders

Also by Anthony Horowitz

Sherlock Holmes
The House of Silk
Moriarty

James Bond
Trigger Mortis
Forever and a Day
With a Mind to Kill

Susan Ryeland
Magpie Murders
Moonflower Murders

Detective Daniel Hawthorne
The Word is Murder
The Sentence is Death
A Line to Kill
The Twist of a Knife
Close to Death

ANTHONY HOROWITZ

Marble Hall Murders

C
CENTURY

CENTURY

UK | USA | Canada | Ireland | Australia
India | New Zealand | South Africa

Century is part of the Penguin Random House group of companies
whose addresses can be found at global.penguinrandomhouse.com

Penguin Random House UK,
One Embassy Gardens, 8 Viaduct Gardens, London SW11 7BW

penguin.co.uk
global.penguinrandomhouse.com

Penguin
Random House
UK

First published 2025
001

Typeset by Jouve (UK), Milton Keynes
Printed and bound in Great Britain by Clays Ltd, Elcograf S.p.A.

The authorised representative in the EEA is Penguin Random House Ireland,
Morrison Chambers, 32 Nassau Street, Dublin D02 YH68

A CIP catalogue record for this book is available from the British Library

ISBN: 978–1–529–90434–5 (hardback)
ISBN: 978–1–529–90435–2 (trade paperback)

Penguin Random House is committed to a sustainable future for
our business, our readers and our planet. This book is made from
Forest Stewardship Council® certified paper.

Marble Hall Murders is a stand-alone novel — but it is also the third book in a series that began with *Magpie Murders*. Readers should be aware that the solution to *Magpie Murders* is revealed in this book.

THE CRACE FAMILY TREE

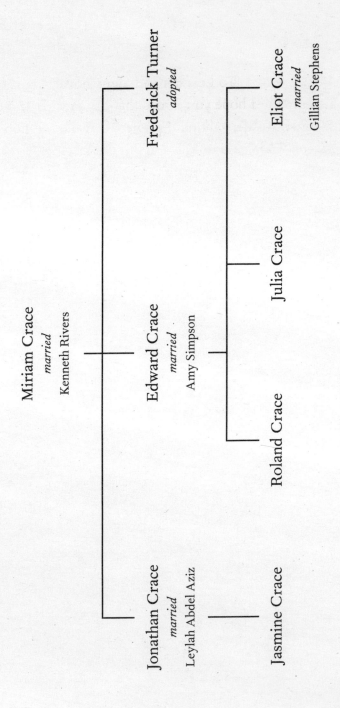

Miriam Crace
married
Kenneth Rivers

Jonathan Crace
married
Leylah Abdel Aziz

Jasmine Crace

Edward Crace
married
Amy Simpson

Roland Crace

Julia Crace

Frederick Turner
adopted

Eliot Crace
married
Gillian Stephens

To Leander and Cosima.
I hope you'll read this one day.

A New Start

Is there really such a thing as a happy ending?

When I think about the books I've loved throughout my life, it's always the final chapter that has left me with a sense of completeness, that has made the whole story worthwhile. I can still remember the relief I felt as a very young girl when Black Beauty found comfort and safety at Birtwick Park, or when Mary and Colin were discovered playing together in their perfect secret garden. Later on, I was feverishly turning the pages when Emma finally realised she was in love with Mr Knightley, and again when Jane Eyre gave birth to her first son with Mr Rochester.

Happy ever after? Of course they were! How could there be any question that they would be otherwise? It was a certainty that nurtured my love of literature and it never occurred to me that Mary and Colin would grow up, bicker and go their separate ways, or that Black Beauty would inevitably share the same fate — at the knacker's yard — as Boxer in *Animal Farm*, another book I devoured in my teens. How long would it be before Emma went back to her old ways or Mr Rochester came to resent being an invalid, in Jane's care?

The great joy of fiction is that no matter how problematic the journey, the resolution is somehow inevitable. Even when the main character dies – think of Sydney Carton's sacrifice in *A Tale of Two Cities* or Michael Henchard's pitiful departure at the end of *The Mayor of Casterbridge* – you realise it's exactly how it was meant to be and in that you find comfort. 'But there's no altering – so it must be,' as Hardy said.

Real life, with all its nuances and complexities, isn't the same, and this is especially true in the twenty-first century. Bad people prosper. Good people go bust. Read the newspapers or social media and it's easy to believe that there is no justice in the world and nobody is happy at all.

I had thought that Andreas and I were going to be together for ever. I loved him and although there were occasions when we wanted to strangle each other, I really believed I'd come to terms with Crete and had surrendered myself to the Aegean Sea, olive groves, the hollow tinkle of goats' bells, perfect sunsets and dinners with friends on long trestle tables beneath the bougainvillea. It was my own happy ending – or it would have been if my life had been a book.

But Crete never worked for me. I could have stayed there for a week, a month, even a year . . . but my whole life? I saw the very old ladies sitting outside their houses dressed head to toe in black and I thought, is that what I'm going to become? The Wednesday market, the olive harvest at the end of October, name days with cakes and biscuits, weddings and baptisms, always with the same box of fireworks. It just wasn't me. There were times when I almost resented the beauty of the landscape for keeping me its prisoner, and I found myself wondering just how much life I was missing on the other side of the mountains. I was, after all, on an island. Every morning, I went swimming in the dazzling blue water and came back with a vague sense that I hadn't swum far enough.

Against all the odds, the Hotel Polydorus, which Andreas had bought and I had helped to get running, was doing extremely well. We were booked out the entire season, the seafront terrace was jammed day and night and Andreas was even considering the purchase of a second property on the other side of Agios Nikolaos, near Ammoudi beach. This had brought his cousin and business partner, Yannis, back into the fold and the two of them never seemed to be out of each other's company . . . which only left me feeling more and more like an outsider. I was now working as an associate editor (freelance) with a new publisher, Causton Books, finishing the third in a series of very good Nordic noir mysteries. Did it really make sense to be doing the work on my bedroom's balcony, sending my notes via email and meeting on Zoom? What was I doing? My head was in London while my heart was no longer in Crete.

Oh dear. This all sounds like a long moan, which is not what I intend it to be. I'm just trying to explain why it was I'd decided that enough was enough and it was time to go home. Andreas drove me to Heraklion airport and although we had a last, fond embrace outside the departures lounge, we both knew it was the right decision and that although we would always be friends, we were no longer in love. At least, not with each other. Even as the plane climbed to thirty thousand feet, I thought about all the wonderful times we'd had together and there was an almost physical pain as the memories were swept away in the airstream behind me. But I knew I was doing the right thing. I was fifty-five years old and I was starting all over again.

I went back to Crouch End, in the north of London. That was where I'd been living when Andreas and I first met and I felt comfortable there. I knew lots of people in the area and it was convenient for Suffolk if I wanted to drive up and see my sister, Katie. I'd sold my old flat to buy the hotel, but I hadn't done too badly out of it. Andreas paid back my initial investment with interest and once I'd thrown in my savings and persuaded the bank to provide me with a mortgage I could just about handle, I had enough to buy a flat a few streets further down the hill from where I had been before. My basement flat was spread over a single floor with two bedrooms (one of which I would use as an office), a decent-sized kitchen/living room and a small bathroom tucked under the staircase that led to the two flats above me. The joy of the place was the patio garden on the other side of a pair of French windows, with flagstones, an ivy-covered wall and enough greenery to give the illusion that I was living in a tiny part of the countryside. A rickety door closed it off from the street, making it my own secret garden. There was even a murky pond with two goldfish. I named them Hero and Leander.

The next three months whizzed past. I'd arrived in time for the spring sales and threw myself into a shopping spree that included furniture and furnishings, kitchen equipment — pots, pans, glasses . . . everything including the sink. I found a team of local builders to put in a new bathroom and repaint some of the rooms. As for myself, I had to buy a completely new wardrobe as nothing I'd been wearing in Crete was any good in London, and then I went out and bought a completely unnecessary antique wardrobe to put it all in. I tussled with plumbers and electricians and spent hours on the phone waiting to speak to internet providers and insurance brokers. Best of all, I rescued my old M G B Roadster, which I'd never got round to selling, perhaps because I knew I would need it one day. It was only as I drove it out of its absurdly expensive home in King's Cross, cheerfully overtaking a police car on Highgate Hill, that I realised how sensible I'd been to hang on to it and how much it had become a part of my life.

I revisited friends and went to a couple of book launches, announcing to the world that I was back for good. I drove up to Suffolk and stayed with Katie, who was now divorced and, like me, living in a new home. She was going out with someone from the garden centre where she worked and I had never seen her happier or more self-confident. She persuaded me to adopt an adult cat I didn't want and which I only took when the rescue centre promised me it wouldn't eat the goldfish. I started reading James Joyce, something I had been trying to do since I left university. And I finished the edit I was working on, rearranging a few pieces of information in what was otherwise a perfect triumph for Politisjefinspectør Heidi Gundersen of the Norwegian Police Service.

I woke up on a Monday morning in June with the sun blazing in and Hugo (the cat) watching me from the small armchair that he had made his permanent home. I read twenty pages of *Dubliners*, glanced at the newspaper on my iPad, then showered and ate some breakfast. That was the time when I always missed Andreas. It was strange but for some reason getting out of bed alone was always more dispiriting than getting into it. I put the kettle on and was just reaching for the coffee beans when my mobile rang.

It was Michael Flynn, the publisher of Causton Books and effectively my boss. I knew him only from Zoom and could easily visualise his round face, thinning hair and glasses hanging on a cord because, he told me, he was always losing them. He usually wore a jacket and tie, but for all I knew he could have been naked below the waist when we spoke online. I didn't even know if he had legs.

'How are things going?' he asked. I'd told him I was back in London, but we'd only spoken a couple of times since I'd arrived.

'I'm fine, thank you,' I said.

'And the new house?'

'Well, it's a flat. But I'm very happy here. It suits me perfectly.'

'I'm glad to hear it. Look – I know this is a bit sudden, but could you come in today?'

'You've got the Gundersen book I sent you?'

'Yes. It's fine. But something else has come up and I have to say, you're perfect for it.'

'Can you send it to me?'

There was a pause at the other end of the line. 'It's not as easy as that. I think we should have a talk. If you come in at midday, we could have lunch.'

'I'm intrigued, Michael. I can be with you at twelve. But aren't you going to give me an idea what it's about?'

Another pause.

'Atticus Pünd,' he said, and rang off.

To Be Continued

Causton Books had offices on the edge of Victoria, not an area known for its literary associations. It occupied a modern office block, spread over four floors with an airport-style entrance, a cafeteria on the ground floor and lifts that demanded an electronic pass. As I walked into the reception area with book covers flashing up on television screens but no actual books in sight, I was reminded how much of my career was behind me. Gone were the days of the independent publisher tucked away in a quiet mews with a solid front door and bay windows. I'd spent eleven years at Cloverleaf and had grown used to the narrow corridors with bad lighting and offices that seemed to have been built deliberately so the more senior you were, the more difficult you were to find. On the other hand, when I'd been lying half-conscious with the flames leaping up and devouring everything in sight, it had dawned on me that the wooden panelling, dusty carpets and curtains that had been so much the character of the place, and which I had always liked, were now going to be, quite literally, the death of me and if I survived, it might be time

7

to have another think. Open-plan areas with line after line of desks separated by glass dividers, identikit furniture and lighting designed to enhance employee well-being may not be quite in the spirit of T. S. Eliot or Somerset Maugham, but at least they won't kill you.

Anyway, it's not the architecture or the furnishings that separate one publisher from another. It's the people. And as I walked into Causton Books just before midday, it was Jeanette, the receptionist who had never met me but knew I was coming and greeted me like an old friend, who made me feel at home. She provided me with the inevitable lanyard, opened the airport-style security gates and even managed to programme the lift to take me where I needed to go.

Michael Flynn was waiting for me on the fourth floor, minus the tie but, happily, with trousers and legs. Although we'd never actually met, we weren't exactly strangers and there was a brief hesitation as we hovered between a hand-shake and a more modern embrace, finally falling into the latter. With this ritual over, he led me along a passageway with shelves of books on one side and, on the other, a crowd of people in jeans and T-shirts hunched over computer screens, little white earbuds plugged into their heads, all of them at least twenty years younger than me.

He had booked a conference room and we sat on opposite sides of a table that was far too big for two people, surrounded by empty chairs. I noticed at once that as well as a coffee flask, milk and biscuits, he had a typescript waiting for me with a notepad resting on top, obscuring the title and the author's name . . . deliberately, I assumed. This was the reason he had wanted to see me.

'It's good of you to come in, Susan,' he began. 'Will you have some coffee?'

'Thank you.'

The coffee might have been sitting there for an hour, but it came out steaming. I already liked the real Michael Flynn more than his screen image. There was a steely quality to him. After all, he was high up the ladder in a company employing over a hundred people. But at the same time, he was quieter and perhaps more humane than he had seemed in our conversations. That's the worst part of Zoom. It provides pictures and sound but sucks out pretty much everything else.

'How does it feel to be back in London?' he asked. He had the clipped tones of a BBC newscaster sometime around the Second World War.

'Strange.'

'Is it a permanent arrangement?'

'I think so.'

'Well, that's good news for us. You've been doing a terrific job for us out in Crete, but I think there will be much better opportunities for you, having you closer at hand.'

'Does that mean I can start working for you full-time?' I asked. As a freelancer, I was being paid by the hour – or perhaps by the word – and I had no benefits or security.

Michael's eyes narrowed and I wondered if I'd annoyed him, being so upfront. 'I'm afraid that's not possible right now,' he said. 'But, as I mentioned on the phone, we do have a project for you – and if it goes well, we could be open to negotiation.'

'Atticus Pünd,' I said.

'Exactly.' He had made it clear that he was the one calling

the shots – which was how he wanted the relationship to work. 'As you know, Orion Books picked up the nine novels Alan Conway wrote and republished them. They did surprisingly well, considering it was public knowledge that Alan had no respect for the character he had created – or for his readers.'

'That's putting it mildly.'

'Well . . . yes.' He gave me a sympathetic look. 'I know you didn't have much fun working with him.'

'I didn't have any fun working with him. But I'm still glad the books were a success.'

It was strange to think how a chance meeting almost thirty years ago should have led to what had become, by any standards, a publishing phenomenon. Alan had started life as an English teacher in the private school where my nephew and niece happened to be students. He was unpopular even then, which should have warned me. Ten-year-olds have a way of knowing which way the wind is blowing. I sometimes think that Katie only introduced him to me in the hope that I would persuade him to leave the school.

That was exactly what happened. I read his manuscript and although it needed work, *Atticus Pünd Investigates* was an instant bestseller and launched a series that would sell eighteen million copies worldwide, making Alan a fortune in the process. He was translated into about thirty languages and, along with several literary awards, had been presented with a silver medal and the freedom of the city of Heidelberg. He had left Woodbridge School and bought himself a mansion outside Framlingham, changing its name to Abbey Grange, which happens to be the title of a Sherlock Holmes short story and tells you something about his self-image. The BBC had been on the brink of filming an eight-part series they were going to call *The Atticus Adventures*, and apparently Mads Mikkelsen had been signed up to play the lead – but that had all gone south when Alan had died, pushed off the tower of his expensive home.

Alan had never invited me to Abbey Grange, but then the two of us hadn't got on. I've met writers who mistrust their editors, but I've never come across one so resolutely opposed to them. Every suggestion I ever made, every cut, every question had invariably led to an argument, but it was only later that I realised it wasn't me he disliked. It was the books he felt he was being forced to write. Put bluntly, he wanted to be Salman Rushdie, not Agatha Christie – but that was never going to happen. He was stuck with himself.

'Anyway, we've stolen a march on Orion,' Michael went on. 'Someone here at Causton Books had the bright idea of commissioning a new Atticus Pünd novel.'

'Without Alan,' I said.

'Exactly. A continuation novel.' He went on quickly before I could interrupt him: 'It worked out very well for James Bond and Sebastian Faulks. I'm sure you know that *Devil May Care* was the fastest-selling work of fiction after Harry Potter . . . at least until Richard Osman came along. Then there are the new Hercule Poirot novels, Sherlock Holmes, Jeeves and Wooster, *Hitchhiker's Guide* . . .' He smiled. 'The simple truth is that nobody gives a damn about Alan Conway and Atticus Pünd can get along fine without him.'

He may have put it a little coldly, but he was right. It's strange how characters can become bigger than their authors, but popular fiction is absolutely crowded with them. It was one of the reasons Conan Doyle threw Sherlock Holmes off the Reichenbach Falls: a sense that his real talents were being overshadowed by his popular hero. Both A. A. Milne and his son Christopher Robin came to hate Winnie-the-Pooh, and Peter Pan left a trail of dead bodies in his wake. What do Mary Poppins, Tarzan, the Wizard of Oz and Dracula all have in common? Half the world knows them but would quite probably be unable to name the authors who created them.

'We got in touch with James Taylor six months ago,' Michael told me. 'I think you know him. He was Alan's live-in partner and he inherited the house, the money and the literary estate. We made an offer for an option for three new books. I'm amazed the idea hadn't occurred to Orion, but we persuaded James that we'd do a better job anyway. Have you seen the new covers they put on their reissue? Utterly drab and boring, I must say. Not that James gives a damn about such minor issues as style and presentation. All he's interested in is the bottom line. We made him a very generous offer and he's also come on board as a consultant. He couldn't be happier.'

None of this surprised me. I'd known James well, first when I'd arrived in Suffolk searching for the last chapter of *Magpie Murders* and later when I'd returned to England, trying to find the clue to an eight-year-old murder that had been concealed in *Atticus Pünd Takes the Case*, the third book in the series. In his twenties, James had been working as a male escort in London. He had been introduced to Alan, who had been married and very much in the closet at the time, and to be fair, James had helped him come to terms with his sexuality and had probably brought out the best in him. He had certainly been well rewarded. He had moved into Abbey Grange with Alan and, just as Michael said, had ended up inheriting everything. James was rude, brazen, unfaithful, self-absorbed and licentious – and I couldn't help liking him. The last time I'd seen him, we'd had lunch at Le Caprice and, as well as picking up the bill, he'd provided me with some of the clues I'd needed to solve the murder of Frank Parris and the disappearance of Cecily Treherne. I'd be happy to meet up with him.

'We certainly don't need Alan Conway,' Michael concluded.

'That may be true,' I agreed. 'I couldn't have worked with him again anyway. But even so, he'll be a hard act to follow. His plots were clever. He had a good ear for dialogue and I liked his characters. As much as I hate to admit it, he was a terrific writer . . . at least, when he wasn't trying to create the next Penguin Modern Classic.' I glanced at the typescript. The title and the author's name were still concealed. 'I take it that's the new book,' I said.

'It's the first thirty thousand words. Very much a work in progress.'

'I see you've printed it up for me.'

It was something of a joke between us. I suppose I'm old-fashioned, but Michael knew that I preferred working on paper. These days, everything is done via the computer screen, but I've always felt that a manuscript has a closer affinity to the finished book and I enjoy the physical contact when I'm making my changes. Even when I was in Crete, I'd bought a rickety printer that seemed to take half the morning to grind out a hard copy before I felt able to start work.

Michael smiled. 'Yes. It's all ready for your red pen.'

'So are you going to tell me who's writing it?'

'Of course, although I'm going to ask you to keep it confidential for the time being. As a matter of fact, you know him.' He paused for effect. 'Eliot Crace.'

For a moment, I was lost for words . . . all thirty thousand of them. It was the last name I would have expected.

'You published him when you were at Cloverleaf,' Michael reminded me.

'That's not entirely true,' I said. 'I saw him twice, but I didn't deal with him myself. It was Charles who recommended him. Charles worked with him, not me.'

'Did you like him?'

'The first time I met him, he was drunk. The second time, he was covered in blood. He said he'd fallen off a bus.'

'Yes. I have had reason to ask myself if it was a good idea commissioning him, but of course we were buying into the name, and part of your job will be to keep hold of the reins. The book is important to us for a great many reasons and we don't want him going off-piste. That said, hopefully his bad boy days are behind him. He was only – what? – in his early twenties when you met him. He's married now. I think you'll find he's settled down.'

'What's his writing like?'

'Well, that's for you to tell me.' He poured himself more coffee. 'You know a great deal more about murder mysteries than I do. But from what I've read, I'd say Eliot has done a very good job. It certainly feels like the originals.'

'When is it set?' There was a reason why I asked this. In the last book, Atticus Pünd had been diagnosed with a brain tumour. This was his Reichenbach Falls. Alan had only given him months to live.

'It follows on from *Magpie Murders*.'

'It would have to follow on very quickly.'

'It does. Atticus Pünd is not at all well. He runs into an elderly lady he happens to know and she invites him to her home in the South of France. Her name is Lady Chalfont . . .'

I recognised the name. She was a character in *Gin & Cyanide*, the sixth book in the series.

'She tells him she's overheard something and makes it sound as if she's afraid for her life, and sure enough she's killed. She has a rather ghastly family, but it's her husband – her second husband – who's the main suspect. I was hoping you'd have a read of it and then help Eliot finish the rest of the manuscript. We want to publish early next year.'

It's one of the strange rules of publishing that deadlines are always too close and there never seems to be enough time to get everything done. I made the necessary calculations. 'That's tight,' I said.

'Eliot was slow getting started.' Michael must have seen my face fall because he moved straight on. 'It wasn't his fault. We wanted to get the story right and he spent ages structuring.' He smiled at me a second time. I felt he was turning it on and off like an electric light. 'The moment I heard you were coming back to the UK, I thought it was a match made in heaven, Susan. After all, you discovered Alan Conway. You were intimate with his prose style, the various tricks he used. I'm not saying this is perfect, but with your input it could be very commercial. Everyone loves Atticus Pünd and Eliot's name is well known to the public . . . his surname, anyway. I really think we could have a bestseller on our hands.'

'The two books Eliot wrote for us at Cloverleaf didn't do too well,' I remarked. I wouldn't normally have been so negative, but I had plenty of reasons to keep away from this project. And what I said was true. It was the reason why there hadn't been a third book in his series.

'I've read them,' Michael said. 'I enjoyed them. It may be that they weren't properly marketed.'

'We did the best we could.' His criticism irritated me, but I tried not to show it. 'All right,' I went on. 'I'll read it and get back to you. Where is Eliot living now?'

'West London . . . Notting Hill Gate. For what it's worth, I mentioned I was seeing you and he was very excited. He remembers you from Cloverleaf and he's very aware of what you did for Alan Conway.'

'That's very nice of him.' I glanced at the typescript. 'So do I get to see the title?' I asked.

'Of course.' He swung it round and lifted off the notepad. And there it was in black and white.

PÜND'S LAST CASE
Written by Eliot Crace

The tenth book in a nine-book series.
'An anagramp,' I said.
'I'm sorry?'
It was a private joke. I didn't explain.

Thoughts

Alan Conway didn't enjoy writing murder mysteries, so he amused himself by playing games with his readers. He hid things in his books: puzzles within puzzles. The mention of Lady Chalfont had reminded me that, for no good reason, all the characters in *Gin & Cyanide* were named after London Underground stations. Lady Chalfont herself had come from Chalfont and Latimer on the Metropolitan line, and there had also been a butler called Hillingdon, Adam and Artemis Perivale – two socialites – and a Detective Inspector Stockwell. I was surprised he hadn't thrown in Lord Edgware for good measure.

And then there were the word games: the acrostics, the anagrams, the cryptograms, the codes. These had the effect of deconstructing the books, so that instead of focusing your attention on the characters and the plot, you were invited to consider the very building blocks he used, the letters on the page. This was one of the reasons why my time as Alan's editor was so difficult. I might ask him to take out an extraneous detail or reorganise a sentence because it didn't land comfortably on the ear and he would explode in anger. Over time, I came to realise that there were secrets in the book and although no reader would ever be aware of them, I was spoiling his fun.

Charles Clover, the CEO of Cloverleaf Books and the editor of Alan's last four books, had first-hand experience of this when he was publishing *Magpie Murders*. The two of them were having dinner at the Ivy restaurant when Charles referred to Alan's latest novel as '*The Magpie Murders*'. Alan had hit the roof. The title was '*MAGPIE MURDERS*', he yelled. There was no THE involved. It was only later that we discovered the titles of all nine Atticus Pünd novels had been deliberately chosen so the first letters would form an acrostic. *Atticus Pünd Investigates*, *No Rest for the Wicked*, *Atticus Pünd Takes the Case*, *Night Comes Calling* – and so on. What they spelled out was AN ANAGRAM.

Not an anagramp.

By adding a tenth title, *Pünd's Last Case*, Eliot Crace had spoiled Alan's joke.

I went straight back to Crouch End after my meeting with Michael Flynn. He had offered me lunch, but I had nothing else to say to him and wanted some time on my own. I had the typescript with me, although I wasn't ready to read it. In fact, as much as I needed the money, I didn't want to do this job at all.

To begin with, I had no love of continuation novels. Even the name put me off. There can be historical novels, romances, science fiction stories. All of these give you an idea of the authors' interests and what inspires them. But who wants just to continue? What exactly is the point?

I remember when the trend began – and perhaps it was

Sebastian Faulks who lit the blue touchpaper. His Bond novel was a big success, but suddenly it felt as if every publisher was trying to connect a well-known author with a much-loved character in the hope of a quick profit. I remember someone trying to pitch me Val McDermid doing a sequel to *Dr Jekyll and Mr Hyde*. She hadn't ever been approached, though if she had been interested, I suppose I would have gone along with it because I would have loved to work with her – but otherwise my views hadn't changed. Take the originality out of fiction and what's left?

My reservations about *Pünd's Last Case* went much further than that.

Alan Conway had been nothing but trouble for me almost from the day we met. I'd thought his books were entertainments, but it turned out they were more like dangerous weapons, loaded with malevolence and launched to cause maximum damage.

Take his habit of putting people he knew into his stories. Lots of writers do that. Charles Dickens drew many of his most famous characters – Bill Sikes, Mr Micawber, Fagin, Scrooge and others – from real life. But Alan deliberately set out to distort and caricature those closest to him. His sister became a jealous spinster, his boyfriend an idiot, one of his students a paedophile gardener. It was an ugly thing to do and, in the end, it led to real tragedy: to the disappearance and death of Cecily Treherne, who had recognised the identity of the killer concealed in *Atticus Pünd Takes the Case*. Twice, I had been called in to pick up the pieces and, on both occasions, had come close to being killed myself. I was in no mood to try my luck a third time.

It wasn't as if I'd come out of all this unscathed. I'd lost my livelihood when the business had burned down with me inside it. My eyesight had been permanently damaged to the extent that reading, always my greatest pleasure, now had to be rationed to one-hour doses. Worse than that, the whole of the London publishing scene had turned its back on me once Charles Clover had been identified as the killer. There was a feeling that Alan had got only what he deserved, but it was thanks to me that a successful indie had gone out of business, with its CEO ending up in jail. I no longer had a job, nobody wanted to employ me and I'd had little choice but to sell my flat and move to Crete, an adventure that hadn't ended happily either.

In the long run, I would have been much better off if I had never heard of Alan Conway, and if I had any sense at all, I would have nothing more to do with him. It seemed almost unbelievable that Michael Flynn should have thought up this new novel in the first place and that he was attempting to foist it on me. It was like one of those horror films that come with a number six or seven after the title, where the leading lady, despite having changed her name, gone through therapy and moved to the other side of the world, still finds herself being chased along the corridors by the same maniac with the black robes, the disfigured face and the fifteen-inch kitchen knife.

So why was the typescript sitting on my kitchen table? Why had I even taken it with me from Causton Books? The answer to that was all around me. I had saddled myself with a mortgage that needed to be paid off each month and even the chair I was sitting on had put a strain on my credit card. Quite simply, I needed the money — and more than that,

Causton Books was the one place in town that might offer me a permanent, senior job. Michael Flynn had said he was open to negotiation. Turn him down and I'd have nothing to negotiate with.

I hadn't even looked at it while I was on the tube train, but finally I allowed my eyes to settle on the title and my first thought was that it would have to change. In every title of the series so far, the main character had appeared either as Atticus or Atticus Pünd. Pünd felt too abrupt on its own. It didn't work. I also wondered if his fans would want to follow him round the South of France while he was in the last throes of terminal cancer. Anyway, Michael had said that he was commissioning three new books, meaning that he was expecting Eliot Crace to come up with at least two more cases after this one. By the time he got to the third in his series, poor Atticus would be on his back, attached to a saline drip.

It was two o'clock in the afternoon, far too early for alcohol, but I went to the fridge and poured myself a glass of wine, adding a plate of cottage cheese and salad to reassure myself that it was just a late lunch. The cat appeared the moment the fridge door opened and began to rub itself against my leg, much to my annoyance. A woman in her fifties living alone in a cosy ground-floor flat is perfectly fine, but the moment you add a cat, it somehow turns into a cliché. I bit into a stick of celery, grimacing at the creature at the same time.

I thought about Eliot Crace. I had to admit that choosing him had been a smart decision on Michael's part.

Eliot was the grandson of one of the UK's most successful authors, a worldwide phenomenon who dwarfed even Alan Conway. Miriam Crace had never written detective fiction, but that was what Michael wanted: the famous name without the comparisons. The last thing he'd want to hear was '*Not as good as Granny.*'

Miriam was a children's author who had produced sixty-three books during a career that had spanned about as many years. She was the author of *The Little People*, a fantasy about an ordinary family of do-gooders who were only two inches tall (in later editions this was changed to five centimetres, much to her dismay). At one stage, it was estimated that 95 per cent of homes in the UK had at least one of her books on the shelves and 40 per cent had ten or more. She had sold an astonishing billion copies worldwide – not quite putting her in the *Guinness World Records* but certainly outselling it – and had made the word 'little' comprehensible in forty-seven languages. Miriam had insisted that the family's name should not be translated. So there was never *Les Petits Gens* or *De Små Menneskene*. About half the children on the planet had grown up with Grandpa Little, Grandma Little, Mr and Mrs Little, Harry, Jack, Jasmine and Rose Little . . . and, in the late nineties, Karim and Njinga Little, who had both been adopted.

Although she was a much-loved public figure, a household name, very little was known about Miriam Crace as far as her private life was concerned. She had been the subject of two biographies, but she had worked closely with the authors and the one I'd skimmed through had portrayed her as nothing less than a saint. There had also been a third, unauthorised biography commissioned by HarperCollins that had hinted at darker things, but the Crace Estate, working with a ferocious team of lawyers, had threatened to sue both the author and the publisher and the book had been withdrawn before it got anywhere near the shelves.

Miriam had given interviews reluctantly and only when she was promoting a new book or raising awareness for the two charities she supported: the St Ambrose Children's Home and Orphanage in Salisbury and the Miriam Crace Libraries Trust. She came from a religious background – her father had been a deacon in the Catholic Church – and she kept her faith throughout her life. This may have been the reason why she never divorced her husband, Kenneth Rivers. (Like Margaret Chalfont, she had never taken her husband's name, but more peculiarly had insisted that her children should follow suit.) There had always been rumours that her marriage was not an entirely happy one and, sure enough, the couple did separate for a year. In 1955, she had a nervous breakdown – caused by overwork, according to her biographers – and spent six months recharging her batteries in a private clinic in Lausanne. It was on her return to England, the same year, that she had bought Marble Hall, near Devizes, along with fifty acres of Wiltshire countryside. At the time of her death, forty-eight years later, she was still living there with Kenneth, her two sons and their wives, and four grandchildren. Marble Hall was now open to the public.

Today, she was still a major force in publishing, selling millions of books a year, much to the annoyance of many living writers who felt she'd had more than a fair innings. The Miriam Crace Estate continued to be a full-time business, managed by her elder son, Jonathan Crace, who was of course related to my new author. He was Eliot's uncle. *The Little People* had been turned into graphic novels, a cartoon series on ITV, a hugely popular musical at the Bridge Theatre, three feature films, a ride at Universal Studios and a vast range of merchandise that included stationery, stuffed toys, biscuit tins, board games, computer games, clocks, calendars and children's clothes. It had recently been announced that Netflix had agreed a deal for two hundred million dollars for the TV rights and were planning a major new drama series to run for five seasons. It was Jonathan Crace who had negotiated the deal.

And what of Eliot Crace?

I'd seen him two or three times when he came into Clover-leaf Books and I remembered him as a very handsome, angelic young man, with long fair hair and an elfin face. He had all the charm and self-confidence that comes with a private education and a wealthy upbringing, although, unfortunately, they had arrived with a measure of arrogance too. He always seemed to be in a hurry, talking too fast, flitting from subject to subject, lurching out of his chair and over to the nearest open window to light a cigarette.

As I'd told Michael, it was Charles Clover who had discovered him and who looked after the two detective stories he wrote for us. But I'd been understating it when I'd said they hadn't done well. They'd barely sold at all. Eliot wasn't a bad writer, but he'd been unwise in his choice of detective: a time-travelling alchemist from the court of Queen Elizabeth I let loose on the twenty-first century. His books had fallen between too many stools. I wasn't sure if they were adult or teenage fiction, real or fantastical, to be taken seriously or to be laughed at – and the book-buying public obviously couldn't decide either. Charles had worked with

24

Eliot's uncle and had known Eliot since he was a child, so he was particularly upset when I put my foot down and refused to go ahead with a third Dr Gee mystery. But it had made no sense to publish books that nobody wanted and anyway, Eliot was a liability: high on drugs, drink, parties and anti-depressants that seemed to be working too well. Charles was sure that Eliot would succeed as a writer once he grew up and he insisted that the door would always be open at Cloverleaf Books. But Eliot never came back.

Until now. I wondered how Michael Flynn had got hold of him and how he'd had the idea in the first place. Suddenly, I regretted not staying for lunch.

Instead, I carried my plate and my glass of wine over to the kitchen table and sat down with the typescript in front of me. I had already decided that I was going to read it. I had nothing else to do that afternoon and I thought it would be interesting to see how Atticus Pünd had turned out in a different author's hands.

At the end of the day, what harm could it do?

PÜND'S LAST CASE

by
Eliot Crace

CHARACTERS

Atticus Pünd	The detective
James Fraser	His assistant

THE FAMILY

Lady Margaret Chalfont	The wealthy widow of Henry Chalfont, the 6th Earl Chalfont
Jeffrey Chalfont	Son of Henry and Margaret Chalfont, now the 7th Earl
Lola Chalfont	An actress and singer, married to Jeffrey Chalfont
Cedric Chalfont	Jeffrey and Lola's eight-year-old son
Judith Lyttleton	Daughter of Henry and Margaret Chalfont. An ethnologist.
Harry Lyttleton	Married to Judith. A property developer.
Elmer Waysmith	An American art dealer, now married to Lady Margaret Chalfont
Robert Waysmith	Only son of Elmer Waysmith from his first marriage

OTHERS

Frédéric Voltaire	A police officer with the Sûreté
Béatrice Laurent	Housekeeper at the Chateau Belmar in Cap Ferrat
Estelle Dubois	Director of the Werner-Waysmith art gallery
Jean Lambert	Solicitor with an office in Saint-Paul-de-Vence
Alice Carling	His secretary
Harlan Scott	A private investigator
Hector Brunelle	A pharmacist in Nice
Dr Benson	A Harley Street doctor

ONE

London, 1955

The rain was lashing down, cold, grey rain that slicked the pavements, hammered at the windows and spat into ever-widening puddles. Rain dripped out of guttering and penetrated the brickwork. It felt as if it had rained all of May, and although June was just around the corner, there was no escaping it. Everyone was in a bad mood as they scurried along the pavements, still in their winter coats. The summer should have arrived by now, but it was as if the rain had beaten it back.

Atticus Pünd made his way down Harley Street, his hands in his pockets, drawing his trench coat closer to his body, trying to keep out the rain. It was a journey he had made several times since the shock of his diagnosis six weeks ago, and he was surprised how quickly everything had become familiar to him, even the certainty of his own death.

He had a brain tumour. Nothing could be done about it and in just a few months it would kill him. This visit to the doctor was little more than a formality. Dr Benson would examine him, ask questions about his physical well-being, his sleep, his appetite, his state of mind – and then send him home with a smile and a few words of comfort. The two of them had developed a strange rapport, something more than doctor and patient. They were partners in a process that was universal, beyond their comprehension, and one that neither of them could change.

Dr Benson's clinic was on the ground floor of a tall, narrow building, identical to its neighbours on either side. Fifteen years ago, there would have been railings separating it from the street, but these had been removed along with all the other metal in London, repurposed for the war effort. It reminded Pünd of the times he had lived through, the world tearing itself apart, so many millions of deaths while he had languished behind the barbed wire of a Nazi concentration camp that he should not have survived. Even when Dr Benson had told him the bad news, Pünd had thought of himself as fortunate. He had never expected to live this long.

He reached the front door and rang the bell. Almost immediately, it was opened by a young woman whose face he recognised but whose name he had never learned. She was the clinic's receptionist. She knew every patient who came to the building and remembered those who didn't return.

'Mr Pünd,' she said, with a smile that suggested they were both delighted he was there. 'What a beastly summer we're having! Do come in.'

She showed him into the waiting room with its flock wallpaper, antique floor lamps and mahogany table on which rested the usual pile of magazines: *Country Life*, *Punch* and *Reader's Digest*, none of them up to date. Four doctors shared the building and all of them had patients arriving at the same time. Pünd recognised a foreign-looking man sitting in the corner. From his appearance and his posture, he had to be ex-military. Sure enough, a nurse in a white coat came in a moment later.

'Major Alcazar . . .'

The man stood up stiffly and followed her out.

Pünd took his place on a sofa and reached out for one of the magazines, not because he intended to read it, but because it prevented the two other people in the room from questioning him. He flicked it open and glanced at a picture of a country estate in Wiltshire. It reminded him of the case he had just solved in the village of Saxby-on-Avon. His last case, probably.

Outside, in the corridor, he heard a woman speaking, high-pitched and a little querulous, someone who was used to being obeyed.

'I think I left it in the waiting room. It must have dropped out of my bag.'

Pünd had already recognised the voice before Lady Margaret Chalfont appeared in the doorway. There could be no mistaking it. Lady Chalfont spoke in the same way she lived her life: imperiously and with every intention of being noticed. The figure who now stood before him was a tiny bird of a woman who seemed to be shrinking even as she stood there, but who was fighting it with every inch of her being. She was in her mid-sixties, but illness had added ten years to that. Her hair, which had been dyed silver and mauve, was carefully coiffured to disguise how thin it had become, and she had dressed purposefully in bright colours with a green jacket, ballooning maroon trousers and an exotic headband missing only the feather, but none of this could disguise the truth of her condition. She was holding a Gucci clutch bag in one hand, a single glove in the other.

As she came into the room, she was already searching for its companion. Her eyes darted over to the sofa where Pünd had chosen to sit and he saw the expression on her face change as she noticed him.

'My dear Mr Pünd! What a surprise. You are the last person I'd expect to see in this awful place. Are you ill?'

It was just like her to be so direct. Pünd rose to his feet. 'I am waiting to see the doctor,' he replied non-committally.

'They don't know anything!' Lady Chalfont sighed. 'They look you in the eye and tell you, take this pill and that pill and you'll be fine, but you're not. You never are. When the Grim Reaper comes calling, the doctors can only sit there, hiding behind their charts and their X-rays. Charlatans, the lot of them!'

'You seem unchanged, Lady Chalfont.'

'An illusion, Mr Pünd. Anyway, "*Nichts ist höher zu schätzen als der Wert des Tages*,"* as Goethe so rightly said. And nothing has brightened up this one more than bumping into you.'

Pünd smiled. He had met Margaret Chalfont in Salisbury nine years ago, when she had been one of the main suspects in the murder of George Colindale, who had been poisoned at a New Year's party to which they had both been invited. At that time, she had been single. Her husband – Henry Chalfont, the 6th Earl Chalfont – had been killed by a V-2 rocket in the last months of the war. Pünd recalled that there had been a son and a daughter, both married, and later he had spotted the arrival of a grandson, announced in *The Times*. He had liked Lady Chalfont immediately. She might be loud and

* Nothing is worth more than today.

outspoken, but she was also cultured, well meaning and, as it turned out, the one who had made the single observation that led Pünd to solve the case.

It seemed remarkable that they should have met now and in this place, and he was wondering what he should say next when his eye fell on something he had noticed the moment he had entered the room but which he had until now ignored. He leaned down and retrieved a single calf-leather glove from underneath the sofa where he had been sitting. Only the fingertips had been visible.

'I believe this is what you are looking for, Lady Chalfont,' he said.

She took it, beaming, and pressed it against its partner. 'You really are a marvel, Mr Pünd. You don't miss anything, do you!'

She was about to go on when there was a movement at the door and a much younger woman presented herself; not a nurse and quite possibly not a patient either. She looked uncomfortable, in a hurry to be out of there. She was very much stouter than Lady Chalfont, with the face of a woman who took herself seriously. She wore heavy glasses and her almost colourless hair was tied back in a bun. Her clothes, like her manner, were businesslike. There was something of the prison warden about her as she stood there, upright, in her ungainly leather shoes.

'Have you found it, Mother?' she asked impatiently, then stopped, seeing that she had company. Pünd bowed to her. So they were related! It was said that Lady Chalfont had been a great beauty in her youth, but her daughter looked nothing like her.

'This gentleman found it for me, Judith. In fact, we're old friends. This is Atticus Pünd. I'm sure you've heard me talking about him. He is quite probably the best detective in the world.' She turned to Pünd and continued without taking a breath. 'My daughter. Judith Lyttleton as she is now. She drove me here.'

'It is a pleasure to meet you, Mrs Lyttleton,' Pünd said.

'Actually, it's Dr Lyttleton,' Judith replied with impatience rather than rancour, as if this was something she was used to explaining – which indeed it was. 'I have a postgraduate degree in ethnology from University College, London. I've written several papers about Peru. You may have read them.'

'I'm afraid I have not.'

Judith nodded, disappointed but unsurprised. 'We really ought to be on our way, Mother. We must pick up the cases and get to the airport.'

'We're heading back to the South of France,' Lady Chalfont explained. 'My late husband, Henry, bought a house in the Côte d'Azur and I spend the whole summer there. I remarried, by the way. Did you know that?'

'I did not,' Pünd said.

'Technically, I'm now Margaret Waysmith, but I've kept my old name. I like being Lady Chalfont. Why should I lose my title along with everything else?'

She had both her gloves and her daughter was waiting for her to leave. But something held her back. 'It's extraordinary I should have bumped into you today,' she went on. 'Something has happened that I would very much like to discuss with you.'

'Mother . . .' Judith said impatiently.

'There's no need to hurry me, dear. We've got plenty of time to catch the plane.' She examined Pünd with eyes that were bright and intense. He could see her mind working as she came to her decision. 'I wish to consult with you on a matter of the greatest urgency,' she said. 'Are you still at the same address?'

'I regret that I am not taking on any new cases, Lady Chalfont.'

'I shall write to you anyway. I believe that everything has a purpose, Mr Pünd, and you were sent here today for a reason. We were meant to meet. The truth is that there is nobody else in the world who could help me in my hour of need. Would you be so good as to give me your card?'

Pünd hesitated, then produced a business card, which he handed to her. She glanced at it before slipping it into her handbag.

'Thank you, Mr Pünd. I cannot tell you what a relief it is to know that there's someone I can trust and believe in. Even if you can offer me nothing more, I will appreciate your advice.'

Judith Lyttleton looked more uncomfortable than ever. She glanced at her mother, and for a moment their eyes were locked and something – perhaps an unspoken warning – was exchanged between them. Then the two of them swept out of the room. Pünd heard the front door open and close.

The nurse reappeared. 'The doctor will see you now, Mr Pünd.'

She led Pünd down a corridor that had already become familiar and through a door at the far end. Dr Benson was waiting for him, sitting behind his desk in his stuffy office with the radiators turned up too high. It had been six weeks since the examination that had told both men the worst news possible and now their meeting was brisk and businesslike. Dr Benson took Pünd's pulse and blood pressure, listened to his heart and examined his eyes. Then came the questions.

'How are the headaches?'

'They come, but not too often. And the pills that you prescribed are very effective.'

'Are you sleeping well?'

'Yes, thank you.'

'Appetite?'

'I am eating less, I think, but I would have said it is by choice. My assistant has complimented me on my loss of weight.'

'Have you told him yet?'

Pünd shook his head. 'He knows I am not well. He has seen the various medicines. But I have not told him the full seriousness of the situation.'

'You're worried he'll leave you?'

'No, Doctor. Not at all. But James is a sensitive young man. It is better, I think, to keep the worst from him. He is also helping me continue with the book I am writing. It is my hope that *The Landscape of Criminal Investigation* will one day take its place in the British Library, the Criminal Records Office and anywhere else it may help future investigations.'

Dr Benson nodded and reached for his pipe. He did not light it. 'Well, Mr Pünd, you're doing very well. Much better than I had expected. You can call me any time, of course, but I don't think we need to meet again until next month.'

Pünd smiled to himself. He had recognised the moment when Dr Benson reached for his pipe. It was his way of announcing that the meeting was over, and he liked to end with a note of optimism. Next week. Next month. Next time. He always looked to the future, reassuring his patients that they still had one.

But Pünd did not move. 'I wonder if I may ask you something,' he said. 'Just now, before I came into your office, I met an old friend, Lady Margaret Chalfont.'

'You know her?'

'Indeed so. We met on an earlier case of mine. I was sorry to see her here and wondered if you could tell me something of her condition.'

'I'm not sure I should share information about my patients, Mr Pünd. Why do you ask?'

'Because Lady Chalfont has requested my assistance in a matter she described as urgent, and because although we only spoke for a few moments, it seemed to me that she was afraid.'

'Afraid of dying?'

'Perhaps. But not as a result of her illness.'

Dr Benson considered. 'Well, as it's you, Mr Pünd, I can't see any harm in telling you, in confidence, that Lady Chalfont is suffering from mitral stenosis. This is a narrowing of the mitral valve which controls the flow of blood to the heart, and regrettably I have had to inform her that, given her advanced age, I do not believe surgery is worth the risk. I'm afraid she has limited time.'

'How limited?'

'Hard to say. But months rather than years.'

Pünd nodded. It had been typical of Lady Chalfont to be so defiant, scornful of doctors and modern medicine, having been told there was nothing they could do for her. 'Thank you, Dr Benson.'

He got to his feet.

'Has she asked you to join her in the South of France?' the doctor asked.

'She did not go so far.'

'That's a pity. I understand she has a very beautiful house on the coast at Saint-Jean-Cap-Ferrat. I would have said it would do you good, a week in the Mediterranean sun. This blasted weather here in England makes even the healthiest and fittest of us feel run-down.' He looked at his window and the water buffeting the glass. 'I've never seen so much rain. Perhaps you should think about it anyway!'

Pünd considered what Dr Benson had said. It had never occurred to him that he might travel again, at least not further than the south-west of England, where his most recent case had taken him. But why not? It was not just a question of feeling the warm sunshine on his skin one last time. There was something else.

He remembered the way the mother and the daughter had looked at each other just before they left. Lady Chalfont had already spoken of urgency, the need for help, but it was Judith Lyttleton who had attracted Pünd's attention.

From the moment she had heard his name and understood who he was, Judith had wanted to get her mother out of the room and away from him. She had heard Lady Chalfont asking him for help, but she had made no comment herself, as if it had nothing to do with her.

The doctor of ethnology hadn't just been uncomfortable about the meeting.

She had been afraid.

TWO

Four days had passed since Atticus Pünd had visited the clinic in Harley Street and he was up bright and early in his office in Clerkenwell Square, working through the most recent pages of his book, which James Fraser had typed for him. *The Landscape of Criminal Investigation* had become the main priority in his life and, given the slow progress of his illness, he was beginning to think there was a chance he could finish it, even if he might not have the time to correct all his assistant's typing errors and spelling mistakes. Well, a publisher would see to all that. It was the content that mattered.

He drew a page towards him and began to read. He knew that he had to be careful. If he worked non-stop, after a couple of hours the typescript would give him a headache that would knock him off his feet. He had to measure himself. Thirty minutes of concentration, then either a walk in the fresh air or a cup of tea, perhaps with a piece by Brahms or Schubert on the gramophone. But the section he had just completed was a fascinating one. It was in a chapter called 'The Killer Tells All'.

He read:

> Just as a poker player has what is called a 'tell', so the murderer will give himself away by involuntary

41

behaviour, particularly when he is under pressure.
I have named this phenomenon 'The Tell-All' and
it once manifested itself in two quite different
ways during the same investigation. I have already
discussed the case of Eileen Marino, a very attractive
and intelligent woman with two children and a
career in journalism. She had attempted to persuade
me that she very much loved her husband, Paul, a
successful lawyer, even though, as it later became
clear, she had stabbed him to death on their return
from the theatre.

I was interviewing her in the sitting room of their
Chiswick home and for thirty minutes she had been
completely relaxed. During our conversation, her pet
dog pushed open the door and came into the room
and it was from that moment that I noticed a marked
difference in her attitude. She was nervous and ill
at ease. This was her first 'tell'. What was it that had
made the difference? For a long time, I assumed that
it must be something to do with the animal (which
had curled up in front of the fire). Could it be that the
dog had been a silent witness to the crime? There
was, incidentally, nothing outside the door – not that
I could see.

The answer only became apparent to me when
I placed myself in her position and realised that,
because of the angles, when she looked into the
mirror that was in front of her, she was confronted
by a full-length portrait of her husband, hanging on

the wall of the corridor outside. When the door was closed, it had been out of sight, but when she was forced to look at him, she had been overcome by guilt and shame.

Mrs Marino later admitted that she and her husband had argued over the family's savings, most of which she had spent. She still insisted she had had nothing to do with his murder, but it was now that her second 'tell' came into play. Why did she repeatedly dab at her eye as if she were on the edge of tears? It was always the left eye, I noticed, as if she had some strange medical condition that allowed her to weep only on one side of her face.

After I had re-examined the photographs taken at the scene of the crime, the solution to this curious behaviour became quickly apparent. When Mrs Marino had stabbed her husband to death, a few drops of his blood had splattered into her left eye, and it was not remorse I had been witnessing but disgust. Recalling what she had done, in the manner of a modern-day Lady Macbeth she was trying to wipe away the memory of her crime.

Pünd turned the page and was about to continue reading when the door opened and James Fraser came in, carrying a tray with a cup of tea, a folded copy of *The Times* and about half a dozen cards and letters. He had dressed optimistically in cotton trousers, a white shirt and a V-neck sweater, as if the summer had finally arrived. It was true that no clients ever called at the office now and Pünd had agreed that a jacket and tie were unnecessary, but it still seemed to him that his assistant was taking informality a touch too far.

'Good morning, Mr Pünd.' Fraser was as cheerful as ever, as if he was determined not to acknowledge Pünd's illness. 'How are you today?'

'I am well, thank you, James.'

'I see you have the new pages.'

'I think they read very well,' Pünd said. 'I'm hoping to complete the chapter before the end of the day.'

'Well, I've brought your tea, the newspaper and the morning post.' Fraser carefully set the tray down on Pünd's desk. 'A couple of bills. I'll sort those out. A note from Detective Inspector Chubb wondering if you'd care for lunch next week.'

'I'm afraid not.'

'That's what I thought. I'll send your apologies. An invitation from the Police Orphans Fund asking you to be the guest speaker at their autumn conference. Again, I'll tell them no. Oh – and you've had a letter from France.' Fraser smiled, pleased with himself. 'I can tell from the stamp.'

'That is indeed good detective work, James.' Pünd reached for the envelope and tore it open. 'It is something I have been expecting,' he added.

'A case?'

'A lady who perhaps requires my help.'

He took out a single sheet of paper. The letter was handwritten in green ink, the words looping and leaning into each other, fighting for space on the line.

44

Chateau Belmar

Sunday, 28 May

My dear Mr Pünd,

I was so surprised to see you in Harley Street that I am not sure I enquired properly after your health. I very much hope that you are in better shape than me. You may recall that I was having problems with my heart when we met all those years ago. Unfortunately, it looks as if the beastly thing is about to give up altogether. I am on borrowed time.

So I hope you are well enough to consider this request, which I am making to you with . . . well, all my heart. I need your help. And I only hope that you will receive this before it is too late.

You never met my first husband, Henry. After he died – at the very end of the war – I thought I would never be happy again, but then I met Elmer Waysmith and we hit it off from the very start. We have been married for six years now and he has become my best friend and confidant: someone in whom I have complete trust.

But the day before I left for London, sitting on my balcony with the Mediterranean so beautiful in front of me, I overheard something that shocked me to my core and which I find impossible to believe. I was thinking of approaching the police, although I dreaded doing so. And then, against all the odds, I ran into you.

If you will come and stay with me at the Chateau Belmar (it is a beautiful place and we have an excellent chef), I will explain

45

everything. I must know the truth, Mr Pünd, and there is nobody else who can help.

Sincerely,
Margaret Chalfont

Pünd read the letter, then handed it to Fraser, who did the same.

'She sounds a bit desperate,' Fraser observed. 'Will you go?'

Pünd took the letter back and gazed at it for a long time, not rereading it – he had already memorised every detail, down to the last comma and the double crease in the middle of the page where it had been folded into the envelope. *I must know the truth, Mr Pünd.* Those were the words that most troubled him. He had spent much of his life in a search for the truth and if there was one thing he had learned, it was this.

The truth can be dangerous.

He looked out of the window. It was not raining today, but the sky was still grey, the clouds threatening. He reflected that he had spent many hours sitting in the same chair in the same room, and although it was true that he had made good progress with his book, he was beginning to feel almost a prisoner . . . of both his illness and his work. Dr Benson had suggested to him that sunshine and a change of scenery might do him good. Pünd had never believed in coincidence, but he had to admit that the letter was remarkably well timed.

'What is your opinion, James?' he asked.

'I'd love to know what she overheard,' Fraser replied. 'And it would be fascinating to find out what's going on. It's just a

46

shame that you've decided to hang up your hat. Shall I write to her that you're too busy to make the trip?'

Pünd thought for a moment, remembering what Dr Benson had said to him. He came to a decision. 'On the contrary, James, you can send her a telegram to say that we will arrive the day after tomorrow.'

'You mean, you're going to take the case?'

'A little sunshine will do me no harm, and Lady Chalfont is a friend. How can I refuse?'

'That's absolutely marvellous!' Pünd could hardly believe how quickly his assistant cheered up again. 'I haven't been to the South of France since I was a boy and my parents sent me on one of those French exchanges. I spent six weeks with a family in Provence. The Duponts. They were very nice people, although they were always shouting. Dinner time was like being at the storming of the Bastille.'

'How is your French?'

'Rusty, but it'll soon polish up. Do you want me to get plane tickets?'

'I do not think I am quite well enough for the demands of air travel, James. I would prefer to take the train. You can book two first-class sleeper compartments on Le Train Bleu to Nice. Can you also inform Lady Chalfont that we shall be staying at the Grand-Hôtel?'

'She's offered to put you up at her chateau,' Fraser reminded him.

'It is most thoughtful of her, but I will be more comfortable in my own domain. I will need privacy and somewhere to rest. The gardens are very beautiful, I believe, and they have a swimming pool which I am sure you will enjoy.'

'Right-ho. I'll get on the phone and book two rooms.'
Fraser sprang to his feet, then turned round before leaving.
'It's not my place to say this, Mr Pünd, but I'm ever so glad
you've decided to take this case. You really haven't been
quite yourself these last few weeks, and although I know the
book is terribly important and all that, I think you'll be much
happier sniffing out a crime. That's what you do best!'

The door closed as Fraser headed off towards his own
small office next door. Atticus Pünd stayed where he was, his
work forgotten, the letter in front of him. Had he made the
right decision? He had no doubt of it. The thought of what
lay ahead had awoken something in him. Already, for the first
time in a long time, he felt alive. And there was something
about the letter that alarmed him – even more than the words
themselves. Lady Chalfont was in danger. He was certain of
it. He was leaving as quickly as he could. He would ask Fraser
to start packing straight away.

Still, he wondered if he would arrive too late.

THREE

The sun was rising on another perfect day in the South of France – but then, when was the French Riviera anything but perfect? Swiftly, the shadows were pushed away. The sea glittered. The palms and olive trees seemed to wake up and stretch out their arms. The first fishing boats appeared, skimming across the surface as they returned to the harbour, and the seagulls hung expectantly in the air, hoping there had been a good catch.

The Chateau Belmar had been constructed on a promontory overlooking the Bay of Villefranche, a front seat in this glorious natural theatre. It was a splendid building, designed in the belle époque style with the emphasis on geometry and elegance. It was painted in that deep yellow which can only be truly appreciated in tropical climates, with white shutters and porticos and a terracotta roof that extended over two wings connected to the main body of the house. It was surrounded by nine acres of gardens designed by the great Achille Duchêne so that the view from every bedroom would have at least one unique feature: a fountain, a statue, a gazebo, the swimming pool or the beehives.

It was not a huge chateau, nowhere near the size of its near neighbour, the Villa Ephrussi de Rothschild (also created by Duchêne). But with its seven bedrooms spread over three floors, its two *salons*, its banquet-sized dining room, the patios and terraces, it was certainly spacious enough. It had been bought by Henry Chalfont, who had been born rich and had multiplied his fortune by creating the private bank that carried his name. He had expressed the hope that the chateau would remain in the family for generations to come.

Tucked away in a small bedroom on the top floor, Béatrice Laurent was woken by the sound of hammering at the door.

It happened often and she knew even before she opened her eyes that it was only a dream. As always, she had heard the cars arrive, the shouting in German, then the men pouring into the house, a series of confused images that made no sense to her nineteen-year-old eyes. At the time, she had been a kitchen maid working for a wealthy family in Paris – the Steiners. It was 16 July 1942, the first day of the mass arrests that came to be known as the Vel d'Hiv after the sports arena where the prisoners would be held. Béatrice had seen Monsieur and Madame Steiner and their three children taken away. It was something she would never forget. She had liked the family. They had always been kind to her.

The soldiers had told her to pack her bags and leave, along with the other servants. The house on the Boulevard Haussmann was to be requisitioned, but already it was being emptied. The last thing Béatrice witnessed was the family's silver being swept off the sideboards and the painting – a vase of red tulips on a table – that had always hung over the fireplace in the living room being lowered from the wall . . .

Now, thirteen years later, Béatrice shook off the memories that sleep had brought and forced herself to get out of bed. Her room was small, built into the roof of the chateau, with a slanting ceiling and a skylight that offered no view. There was a shower and toilet on the other side of the corridor and once she had washed, she dressed in the grey and white uniform of the *femme de ménage*. A service staircase, invisible to the rest of the house, led all the way to the kitchen and she made her way down as quietly as she could, the stairs creaking beneath her feet.

Béatrice had a morning routine, starting with the dining room. The supper had already been cleared away, the plates and dishes washed, but often the family would stay drinking port and Cointreau until late and there would be glasses and ashtrays (all four men liked cigars) to deal with. Then she went into the *petit salon*, where the family would take breakfast overlooking the rose garden and the steps down to the sea. The baker's van would arrive soon with fresh croissants and brioches still warm from the oven, and in the meantime, Béatrice would lay the table, then cut up and squeeze oranges in the kitchen, filling a jug that would go into the fridge. Finally, she would make coffee for Lady Chalfont. Madame Claudel, the cook, did not live in the chateau and would not be in until ten.

She heard the crunch of tyres on the gravel and knew that the boy had arrived on his bicycle with the morning newspapers. He would never have rung the doorbell at this early hour, but she was standing outside the front door as he pulled in and took them from him.

The newspapers had come from London, Zurich and New York and their stories might be several days late, but what did time matter in a house where nothing ever seemed to change? People died, politicians argued, the queen of England did

51

this, the weather did that. None of it seemed at all relevant in the Côte d'Azur. The newspapers went onto the big table in the *grand salon*. Béatrice arranged them neatly, then fetched the dustpan and brush to clean the grate. It was the first week of June and the days were warm and sunny, but the evenings could be cool, so Lady Chalfont had asked for a fire to be lit. The cinders were still warm as Béatrice swept them into a metal bucket, all the while keeping her eyes fixed on her work. She had to be careful not to look up. Never once did she allow herself to glance at the chimney breast.

Monsieur Waysmith had hung the new picture there three weeks ago. It would eventually be put on sale in his gallery in Nice, but he often liked to display the art in his own home first. He was particularly pleased with this new acquisition, *Spring Flowers*, by Paul Cézanne.

Béatrice could not look at it. Turning her back on the brightly coloured tulips in their Delft pottery vase, she walked out of the room.

*

Lady Chalfont had the largest bedroom in the house, a magnificent suite that her second husband had once called the Lounge of Nations on account of its Venetian marble floor, its Chinese silk curtains, its French mirrors and furniture and its collection of German porcelain. To this, she had imported an English walnut bed manufactured by Waring & Gillow. It had belonged to her mother and gave her comfort, perhaps in the thought that the two of them would soon be reunited.

She never drew the curtains. Three slender archways stretching from the floor to the ceiling led out onto a white marble balcony. From here it was possible to see the entire garden and the sand-coloured path leading down to the magnificent Hippodamia fountain – a riot of centaurs, soldiers and wedding guests, with a naked woman (the bride) being stolen away, water exploding all around her. It was, in part, a copy of a work by Michelangelo and of uncertain provenance.

The sun had not risen fully and Lady Chalfont shivered slightly in the cool morning air, even though she was well protected by two thick blankets and a hot-water bottle still generating a little heat behind her neck. Propping herself up on the pillows, she looked out to sea, enjoying the sound of splashing water and the warbling of *les chardonnerets* – the goldfinches – which had built their nest under a loose tile in the roof. Every year, she had watched the father flying in and out with grubs for the newly born chicks. She had scolded Bruno, the gardener, when he had suggested removing the nest and mending the roof. Nothing gave her greater pleasure, she told him, and it was true. Very soon, she would see the whole family take flight.

For the last time. She had to face up to the fact that she would not be here for another spring. She was unlikely to live even until the winter. Looking past the colonnades, she gazed at the flowers bursting into colour: deep red poppies, white peonies, Spanish broom in clumps of brilliant yellow and a great carpet of mauve lavender. All of life continuing without her.

There was a knock at the door, interrupting Lady

53

Chalfont's train of thought, and Béatrice came in carrying a tray with a steaming cup of ginger and lemon tea, as she did every day.

'*Bonjour, madame,*' she said, laying the tray down on the side of the bed.

'*Bonjour, Beátrice. Comment ça va?*' Lady Chalfont spoke a little French, but she did so in the manner of an English aristocrat, with little interest in accent, rhythm or even sense.

'*Très bien, merci, madame. J'ai votre thé – et un télégramme est arrivé hier.*'

'Why did you not give this to me yesterday?' Lady Chalfont demanded. She was too annoyed to continue in a language that was not her own.

'I am sorry, madame. I did not see it. Someone had placed it with the newspapers . . .'

The housekeeper fluffed up the pillows and removed the lukewarm hot-water bottle, then left as quickly as she could. The moment the door closed, Lady Chalfont reached for the telegram, ignoring the tea. She picked up the envelope and pulled out a single sheet of paper.

> DEAR LADY CHALFONT. ARRIVING FRIDAY
> 3 JUNE ON LE TRAIN BLEU. HAVE BOOKED
> ROOMS AT GRAND-HÔTEL. WILL CALL AT
> YOUR CONVENIENCE. ATTICUS PÜND

At her convenience? What time would that be? Lady Chalfont had taken Le Train Bleu often enough to know that it would have left Paris, Gare de Lyon, at eight o'clock in the evening, travelling through the night to arrive early morning in Marseille. It might be there now. Then it would continue along the coast, through Toulon and Saint-Raphaël to Cannes and on to Nice, the nearest station to Cap Ferrat. Mr Pünd would be at his hotel by lunchtime. Why had he chosen not to stay at the Chateau Belmar? That wasn't important. All that mattered was that he had come.

Lady Chalfont put down the telegram and rested her head against the pillows, relieved. The cup of tea was still steaming on the tray that Béatrice had left on the bed, but she didn't drink any of it. She was aware that something was wrong. She thought back to what had just happened: the knock at the door, the entrance, the message. She picked up the envelope a second time and examined it. Yes. That was what it was. She hadn't torn open the envelope. It had been open when it was delivered to her. She could see where the knife had been drawn across.

Someone had read the telegram before it had been delivered to her. They had taken it and then put it back in the wrong place. They knew that Pünd was here, which meant they would also know she had invited him.

But who?

*

'Are you getting out of bed?' Lola Chalfont asked her husband.

'What time is it?' The voice came from under the covers, disembodied and tetchy.

'Almost half past eight. You know Elmer hates it when we're late for breakfast.'

'Why should I care what Elmer thinks? This isn't his house and I'm not his damn servant. You go down. I need to sleep.'

A hand with a gold signet ring appeared, pushing back the sheets and revealing a pockmarked face with a sprawl of bright red hair that almost made it seem as if his head was on fire, sideboards slicing into his face, a flat nose and puffed-out lips. Jeffrey Chalfont, now the 7th Earl Chalfont and aged thirty-seven, was running to fat, his thick neck and fleshy shoulders resting against a mountain of pillows. He had begun to resemble his father – but, unfortunately, when Henry Chalfont had been twenty years older than Jeffrey was now. He was short-tempered. He seldom smiled. When Lola woke up, it sometimes took her a few moments to remember she was married to the man lying beside her. They had been together for ten years and had an eight-year-old son, but saw less and less of each other as the days went by.

The 7th Earl was not completely at home in the South of France. He would much rather be in the 11,000-acre estate he had inherited in Norfolk, rattling around in his trusty Massey Ferguson, barking orders at workers who had been with the family for generations. He liked to dress in a flat cap, tweed jacket and waistcoat and would march along country lanes surrounded by his four dogs, two Labradors and two Pinschers, forming a pack around him. He was the master of the local hunt and at weekends he would invite friends over for a shooting party. By the following Monday, not a single bird would be seen in the sky. He enjoyed fishing too. A river ran for half a mile through his estate and fortunate the salmon or perch that would make it from one end to the other.

'What hour did you get in?' Lola demanded.

'Damned if I know. I don't remember. About twelve o'clock.'

By which he meant one or two o'clock in the morning. Lola had learned to adjust any answer Jeffrey gave her, adding or subtracting as necessary. He had gone out after dinner, supposedly meeting some chums in Nice. He had met them, of course, at the casino – not that she had asked him that. Why invite another lie? But now, in the light of the morning, she couldn't resist challenging him.

'How much did you lose?' she asked.

'What makes you think I lost?'

'Old habits die hard,' Lola muttered, reaching for her eau de toilette.

Lola Chalfont was already dressed and sitting at her dressing table, in front of an antique mirror that unfolded like a triptych on a church altar. The three reflections in their separate panels showed a woman who was still beautiful but who was fighting her thirty-three years and the disappointments of her life. She and Jeffrey had met at the Theatre Royal in Norwich. He had been in the audience, she on the stage, in the lead role, performing as the exotic spy Mata Hari. When she had found a young and enthusiastic Jeffrey Chalfont at the stage door with an impressive bouquet of flowers, she had been swept away, particularly when she had found out about the title he would one day inherit along with his Norfolk estate. Lola Chalfont, countess! That was a part she could certainly play.

It was only after their marriage that she realised she had made the mistake of her life. She had swapped glamour and greasepaint for bridge parties and long, muddy tracks. The title role for a supporting part. Nor could there be any going back. Producers and directors were nervous of her. She was a member of the aristocracy now, not one of them, and they didn't even return her calls. She knew she had nobody to blame but herself. Even so, she blamed her new husband and quickly came to despise him.

'So how much?' she demanded a second time.

'How much what?'

'You know what I'm talking about, Jeffrey. The casino.'

Jeffrey grunted. 'A couple of hundred francs,' he admitted at last.

He meant three or four hundred, then. It had been the same the night before – and the night before that. Lola had a sick feeling in her stomach. Where was all this money going to come from? Their bank manager, Mr Spurling, had been on the phone several times – and with every call he'd become less deferential, more demanding.

'Who were you with?' she asked.

'Harry and Charley and Algy . . .' All Jeffrey's friends had names that ended in 'y'.

'I suppose they all lost.'

'You're wrong. Charley had a fantastic run of luck on the roulette wheel. Champagne all round.'

'Good old Charley!'

Lola picked up the hairbrush and adjusted the jet-black locks that tumbled over each other, crowning a face that was at once vulnerable and imperious. Born and brought up in Seville until her parents moved to London, she felt completely at home next to the Mediterranean. Her reflections in the mirrors showed intense eyes, a slender neck and a smile that could dazzle across a room, even if that room contained six hundred people. It's not over yet, she thought to herself. If the producers wouldn't ring her, the solution was simple. She would become a producer herself.

Grab Me a Gondola was going into rehearsal at the end of the year and hadn't yet been cast, but Lola had read the script and listened to the songs, played for her by a rehearsal pianist she had hired out of her own pocket. She was certain the show was going to be a hit and the part of Virginia, a starlet at the Venice Film Festival (where the musical was set), could have been made for her. She had met the writers at a cocktail party at the Dorchester and when she had mentioned she was thinking about investing money, they had shown an immediate interest. She had told them how much she loved the story of *Grab Me a Gondola* and all the wonderful characters – particularly Virginia Jones. Did they think there was any chance that she might audition for the part? And how much was she thinking of investing? How about two thousand pounds? Suddenly it seemed to be a perfect fit.

She'd had to tell Jeffrey, of course – he was the lord of the manor – and of course he had objected. Had she forgotten who she was, what she had become? A return to the stage would be utterly demeaning, to him, to her, to the family name. She should have realised she had left all that behind her.

But just for once she had stood up to him and he had been shocked by the vehemence of her resistance. He would never have understood, of course, but Lola had come to a realisation. It was as if her two worlds had swapped places.

The Chalfont estate, her title and Norfolk society were just an illusion. It was her life on stage that was real.

'I'm going to call Dino today,' she said. Dino Wolfe was the manager of Strand Productions, who were mounting *Grab Me a Gondola*. 'I thought I might ask him to join us here.'

'At the chateau?'

'Why not?'

Jeffrey said nothing. Lola twisted round and saw that her husband had disappeared back under the bedclothes.

For a brief moment, Lola was angry. This was not the man she had met. She thought of the champagne and caviar, long drives in his SS Jaguar 100, that visit to the estate in Norfolk, how enthralled she'd been by the beauty of the landscape – so much land, all owned by him. Everything had seemed so perfect at the time. Was that what marriage and motherhood always did? Carve out the joy and ambition of young life and replace it with this . . . emptiness?

Lola put down the hairbrush, took one last look in the mirror and got to her feet. Right then, she could imagine herself in her dressing room, about to go on stage. The orchestra was warming up. The audience was murmuring excitedly. In a few moments, the lights in the auditorium would go down.

It was going to happen. She was going to make it happen. She had a plan and if it all worked out, everything would change.

There was just one problem. Where was she going to get two thousand pounds?

*

The sunlight was streaming in through the double windows of the *petit salon*, glinting off the glass and silverware and turning the tablecloth into a blaze of pristine white. There were six people sitting around the antique dining table, which dated back to the seventeenth century and the time of Louis XIV, and it would have been easy to imagine them posing for a classical painting with perhaps Vermeer or Boucher standing in front of an easel, brush in hand, on the other side of the doorway. Béatrice had served the coffee and the breads, still warm from the bakery, along with honey (made by their own bees), toast, fruit and yoghurt, and quietly excused herself.

Elmer Waysmith had taken his usual seat at the head of the table with his son, Robert, on one side of him. Judith Lyttleton – Lady Chalfont's daughter – was on the other, with her husband, Harry Lyttleton, next to her. Lola Chalfont had come in with her eight-year-old son, Cedric, who was staring out of the window, moodily swinging his legs.

It was not a comfortable scene. There was a distinct yet undefined tension in the air, as if they were all characters in a play, not quite sure of their lines and waiting for the curtain to come down so that they could all go their own way. But for the time being they were going through the motions, each playing their own part.

Elmer was sixty-seven, two years older than his second wife and still handsome, although his hair had turned a premature white and no longer matched his eyebrows. He had the physique and bearing of a military man even though he had never seen action, having spent much of the war in Washington, overseeing the vast export programme supplying

61

thousands of tanks, planes, weapons, uniforms, chemicals and food to the beleaguered Soviet Union. He had been a personal appointment of President Roosevelt: he claimed that the two of them had been close friends.

Elmer had come to the breakfast table in an ivory-coloured suit and bow tie with a pair of gold half-frame glasses balanced on a connoisseur's nose. He was reading an edition of the *New York Times* that was spread out on the table beside him. He didn't seem to have noticed that the news was out of date, but nor did it matter to him. 'So I see Churchill's back,' he muttered, spreading jam on his croissant and examining the front page at the same time. Sir Winston Churchill had resigned as prime minister in April.

'I didn't know he'd been away,' Robert Waysmith said.

'He was at the opening of Parliament. Everyone cheering him to the rafters.' Elmer read another paragraph before making his next pronouncement. 'The trouble is that these people never know when to stop.'

'Well, he's still very popular . . .'

Robert Waysmith, Elmer's son from his first marriage, had inherited his father's good looks. Slim and athletic, he had the waywardness of a poet, an adventurer or a Lothario, with a full head of hair and dark eyes that sparkled with intelligence. He had been educated at Winchester and Oxford and spoke with a perfect English accent, unlike his father, who had been born in New York and might never have left. Hearing what Elmer had just said, he smiled as if at some private joke. It was so typical of his father to stir up trouble for no reason at all.

'I think Winston Churchill is quite wonderful,' Judith said. 'We certainly wouldn't have won the war without him.'

'You wouldn't have won the war without *us*,' Elmer corrected her.

'Oh come on, Pa. Don't start that again.' Robert never called him 'Daddy' or 'Father'. The two of them had lived together in New York and subsequently in London ever since the death of Elmer's first wife, Marion. Tragically, she had taken her own life when Robert was just eleven. There were no other children and the two of them had the closeness that comes from years of living within the same walls. As a child, Robert had dreamed of becoming an artist, but that had never happened. His father had insisted he should train as a lawyer in his twenties, but that hadn't suited his temperament either and, in the end, Elmer had taken pity on him and brought him into his business, putting him in charge of the day-to-day running of the two galleries in London and Nice. He was now thirty-two and still unmarried.

Judith Lyttleton's husband, Harry, had overheard Elmer's comment. 'If he starts going on about Lend-Lease one more time, I'm going to chuck myself into the Med,' he whispered to his wife.

Judith ignored him. As usual, she was studying a book she had brought with her to the table: *Geoglyphs from the Paracas Phase in Peru and South America*. It was a dusty volume, at least two inches thick. She picked up a pen and made a note in one of the margins.

'What did you say?' Elmer snapped.

'Nothing, Elmer,' Harry Lyttleton exclaimed, with a smile. 'Can you pass the marmalade?'

The Lyttletons made a decidedly odd couple. Judith was shorter than her husband but she was also stouter, more

masculine. Slightly built and elegant, Harry took great care
with his appearance. Today he was dressed in white trousers,
an oyster pink jersey and the white tennis shoes he often
preferred. He was a keen cricketer as well as a member of the
Wimbledon tennis club, which, along with his visits to the
South of France, might have accounted for his year-round
tan. He had wavy fair hair that tumbled down in a way that
looked careless but which was almost certainly the result of
careful grooming. His eyes were a piercing blue, full of life if
not quite intelligence.

His first connection with the Chalfonts had been with the
older son, Jeffrey. The two of them had been best friends at
Eton, sharing a study, and there had been some wags who
had joked that he had only married Judith because it was the
next best thing to marrying her brother. The two men still
spent as much time as they could together. In Norfolk, they
went hunting and shooting. In the South of France, they
ate good food, drank too much wine, gambled and smoked
cigars until the early hours of the morning.

Harry had been an only son with four sisters sharing the
family home in Essex and he alone had been sent to boarding
school. He had never been very wealthy, but marrying Judith
had put him on an almost equal footing with the 7th Earl.
She was, after all, a future heir to her late father's considerable
fortune, which included houses in London and Cap Ferrat
and part ownership of Chalfonts, the exclusive bank in the
City of London. At least some of this money would come
to her and, frankly, Harry needed it. He was a developer,
building a hotel between Cap Ferrat and Beaulieu that he
insisted would rival even the Grand-Hôtel itself for luxury

and comfort, but after three years of construction only a skeleton stood in place, disfiguring the landscape.

'Where's Jeffrey?' Elmer demanded, noting his absence for the first time.

'He's not up yet,' Lola said. 'He was out late.'

'Out where?' Elmer demanded scornfully. 'Beaulieu, Monte Carlo or Le Palais?' He had named three casinos.

'You know perfectly well. Jeffrey works very hard when he's in England.' Lola might not approve of her husband's gambling habits, but there was no way she was going to let her stepfather-in-law criticise him in front of the family, particularly with Cedric at the table. 'He's on holiday now. He's allowed to let his hair down.'

'If he lets his hair down, how does he see?' Cedric asked.

'That's not what it means, Cedric,' Lola explained. 'It just means he's enjoying himself.'

'Can I go with him?'

'No. You're too young.' Lola glanced out of the window. 'It looks like it's going to be a gorgeous day. Why don't we all go to the beach for a picnic?'

'I hate the beach,' Cedric announced. 'Sand in the sandwiches and melted ice cream.'

'I'm going into the gallery later on,' Elmer muttered. He turned to Robert. 'Is the Sisley being delivered today?'

'Yes, Pa. I thought I'd take it myself. You know what Dorfman is like.'

Alfred Sisley was an Impressionist painter who, although British by birth, had lived in France until his death at the end of the nineteenth century. Dorfman was an avid collector with a handsome villa in Antibes, further down the coast. He would appreciate the personal attention and it might be an opportunity to talk about further purchases.

'Good idea.' Elmer didn't smile. He only offered praise reluctantly. 'Just don't forget we're meeting at the gallery at half past twelve. Don't be late.'

'I'm never late.' It was true. Elmer Waysmith hated unpunctuality and in all their years working together, Robert had learned to keep a careful eye on the clock.

'I say, Elmer. I was wondering if you might have time for a quick chat.' Harry Lyttleton sounded nervous.

'What about?'

'Well . . .' He hadn't wanted to have the conversation here, not in front of everyone else, but realised he had no choice. 'Actually, it's about the hotel . . .'

'I don't want to talk to you about the hotel. How often do I have to tell you that? I warned you at the time that it would never come to anything. A bad business plan, bad associates and a bad idea. Anyway . . .' Elmer turned back to his newspaper. 'I don't discuss business at the breakfast table.'

'Why do you have to be so unpleasant?' For the first time, Judith lifted her eyes from her book and fixed them on her stepfather. 'Harry was only asking to talk to you. He wasn't asking for money.'

'Although there are still a few investment packages available, if you're interested,' Harry added, hastily.

Judith pretended she hadn't heard him. 'Ever since you married our mother, nothing has been the same,' she said. 'And quite soon she won't be here any more either. It doesn't bear thinking about.'

Elmer scowled at her. 'I love your mother,' he said. 'I would do anything for her, and that includes protecting her from all of you.' He'd had enough. He folded the newspaper shut and got to his feet. As he left the room, he glanced briefly at Robert. 'Twelve thirty,' he reminded him, then walked out of the room.

'Eurgh! A seagull just did its business on the window!' Cedric exclaimed, half repulsed, half amused. Lola looked at him disapprovingly, although it occurred to her that in some respects what he'd said was an appropriate comment on everything that had passed.

*

After he had left the *petit salon*, Elmer Waysmith climbed the stairs to the first floor. He had a suite at the front of the house: a bedroom, a bathroom and a study where he was putting together a new catalogue of Impressionist paintings. It was his habit to work here every morning until eleven o'clock, when he would drive into Nice and visit his gallery tucked away beneath the arches in the Place Masséna.

First, however, he turned the other way and knocked twice on the door of his wife's bedroom. There was no answer. Thinking she might be asleep, he opened the door gently and saw at once that the bed was empty, the tray with her breakfast untouched. He continued into the room and found her sitting outside on the balcony, wearing the crêpe de Chine dressing gown he had bought her in Paris. She did not seem to have heard him. Her eyes were fixed on the garden and, in particular, the fountain with the water splashing around its throng of stone figures.

'Margaret?' he called out.

She turned and smiled. 'Elmer. Come and sit by me.'

She gestured to the empty seat beside her. There had been a time when they shared the bedroom and they had often sat together on the balcony, particularly at night, when they would each have a glass of cognac and Elmer would smoke a cigar, listening to the dying fall of the cicadas and watching the stars.

Margaret Chalfont had first met Elmer when he had been invited to Chalfont Hall in Norfolk to advise on the family's extensive art collection. Many of the paintings had hung on the walls for more than a century and he had identified the artists, researched the history of the works and, most importantly, provided valuations. The two of them had quickly become friends and it was hardly surprising that, after the death of Margaret's husband, this should have developed into a romance. They were similarly aged and both had lost their first partners in tragic circumstances.

Margaret's children had never forgiven them for daring to get married. Elmer was an American. He was an outsider. He might be working in the rarefied world of nineteenth- and twentieth-century art, but he was still a merchant – after all, a gallery was only another name for a shop. What right did he have to ingratiate himself into the sphere of an English family with five hundred acres in Norfolk and a history that went back to the time of Queen Elizabeth I? And then there was the memory of Henry Chalfont, a war hero who had helped bring Jewish refugees into Britain, killed by a bomb as he walked through Whitechapel. Nobody had ever believed that Margaret would marry again, and the fact that she had kept her old name suggested she wasn't entirely serious about the new relationship, that she was still living in the past.

'How are you feeling today?' Elmer asked the same question every morning, although he tried to find different ways to formulate the words.

'I'm very well.' Margaret had never answered otherwise, even after a bad night. 'It's lovely of you to look in and see me. What are you doing today?'

'I'm still working on the catalogue.'

'I thought I might take tea in the gazebo. Will you join me?'

'I'm afraid I can't. I have lunch with Robert in Nice and then I must work.'

'Well, I'll ask Judith and Harry.'

Elmer scowled. 'They're still asking me for money for that damn hotel.'

Margaret reached out and rested a hand on her husband's arm. 'Maybe you should help them a little, Elmer. Just a little. Harry means well and he's not as clever as you.'

'I warned him against it, Margaret. He didn't listen to me. If I help him now, it'll just be throwing good money after bad. And what about the rest of them? Lola's investing in a musical – as if that isn't the fastest way to lose money on the planet. Judith wants to spend thousands preserving a desert in Peru. And Jeffrey's worse than any of them, throwing cash away at the casino.'

'I do worry about them, I admit it. You will look out for them, won't you, after I'm . . .' She didn't finish the sentence, but she loosened her grip and her hand fell away.

'My dearest, that's all I've ever tried to do – from the minute I walked into your life.' Elmer took hold of her, his face close to hers. 'To look after them if they'll listen to me, which sadly they never do. But I'll never stop trying and I promise you, you don't need to worry about any of them.' He tried to smile. 'Anyway, I don't like this talk about you leaving me or going anywhere. Right now you look as beautiful as the day we met. The sunshine down here does wonders for you, and who knows, maybe you'll prove the doctors wrong and live to be a hundred. The important thing is to enjoy every minute we have together, and that's what we're going to do.'

'You still haven't got time to have tea with me.'

'You know how much work I have.' He sighed. 'Why don't we have an early supper together, just the two of us? I can ask Béatrice to lay a table out here on the balcony and we can watch the sun set.'

'I'd like that.' Margaret tried to smile, but Elmer could see she was uneasy. There was something holding her back.

'What is it?' he asked. 'What aren't you telling me?'

She turned away. 'I had a bad dream last night,' she said. 'I didn't want to tell you, Elmer, but sometimes I'm afraid. It's so beautiful here, but I feel the shadows closing in. I'm not talking about my illness. It's something else. Don't you feel it too?'

She shivered. Elmer gazed at her, his eyes full of concern. 'You're cold,' he said. 'Maybe you should come inside.'

'No. Please. Let me sit here.'

'I'll fetch you a blanket.'

Elmer got up and went into the bedroom. As soon as he

had gone, Margaret Chalfont allowed one hand to drop to her dressing-gown pocket and felt for the single sheet of paper that she had placed there and which she knew would bring her comfort. It was the telegram from Atticus Pünd. He had said he was arriving on 3 June. That was today. So where was he? When was he going to come?

FOUR

The Place Masséna was one of the busiest squares in Nice, mainly thanks to the art deco bus station that had been built to one side, its neon sign – GARE MUNICIPALE D'AUTOBUS – blazing out the fact that it had been given pride of place. Without all the attendant traffic, buses, coaches, taxis and cars, the square might have been beautiful. There was a thick border of trees on one side and a row of classical colonnades on the other, with several old-fashioned shops and boutiques tucked away behind. This was where the Galerie Werner-Waysmith was located. It was at the very heart of the old town, surrounded by cafés, easy to find for dedicated art buyers and perfectly placed for passing trade – not that casual tourists often looked in. The gallery was too austere, lacking anything of the colour and life that tourists would find just a few minutes away on the Promenade des Anglais.

It was also far too expensive for anyone except a dedicated collector. Very little that was sold there cost less than five thousand francs and there were pieces priced at twenty times that amount. A single work would be displayed in each of the two windows on either side of a forbidding, iron-rimmed door and the absence of any price tag was more than enough to suggest that what was on sale here would probably be out of most people's reach.

Those who passed through the door would find themselves in a dark, expensively carpeted room with an antique table and two chairs surrounded by a small selection of paintings and sculptures exquisitely displayed. Very little daylight entered the gallery. The artworks were picked out by carefully placed spotlights that lifted them out of the shadows.

Visitors would find themselves confronted by the gallery's *directrice*, a woman in her late sixties, usually dressed in dark colours. Madame Dubois had no first name that anyone knew and had worked there both before and after the war. She had never explained what she had done during the hiatus, but had turned up for work on 28 August 1944 (a Monday), three days after the liberation of Paris.

Tourists or passers-by were dealt with swiftly but politely. Madame Dubois had a way of dismissing them that somehow never gave offence. If the caller seemed serious or came with the right credentials, she would look after them with perfect efficiency. Finally, if they had purchased an artwork from the gallery in the past – and Madame Dubois never forgot a name or a face – then she would offer coffee or a *coupe de champagne* while she went to the back office to summon the younger Monsieur Waysmith or his father.

Robert Waysmith was sitting in the back office now. He had entered through a door that opened into a narrow street behind the gallery and taken his place at one of the two desks that faced each other across the room. Given that both father and son were in the business of selling art, the office was surprisingly bare. There were many canvases, framed and unframed, leaning against the walls but none on the walls themselves. A single window would have given a view of the square but even this had been blanked out by frosted glass. A long shelf ran from one end of the room to the other. It contained a series of box files, colour-coded and dated. An old-fashioned safe stood in a corner. It didn't look as if it had been opened for years.

Robert was holding a framed oil painting that showed a stream on a summer's day. A woman, holding a parasol, was walking along one of the banks. This was the work that his client, Lucas Dorfman, had purchased and which he was about to deliver. He examined the image one last time, marvelling at the play of light and colour, the perfectly captured landscape, the delicate brushstrokes. Not for nothing had Alfred Sisley been called the purest of the Impressionists.

And now it was going. Robert wrapped it carefully in thick brown paper, which he secured with string. He had already prepared a copy of the invoice and had written a detailed description of the work that included its subject matter, the medium (oil on canvas), the size and the provenance. It had been purchased from the Fischer Gallery, a highly respected arthouse in Lucerne. Before that, it had been in a private collection. Finally, Robert had provided reports by two art experts attesting to the painting's authenticity, condition and artistic significance.

Carrying the picture under one arm, Robert left the office and went into the gallery. Madame Dubois was on her own.

'I'm driving to Antibes,' he told her. He spoke in English. Madame Dubois was fluent in three languages and would have been offended if he had used his faltering French. 'I'll be back at half past twelve. I'm meeting my father for lunch.'

Madame Dubois glanced at her watch. 'The traffic may be difficult,' she sniffed. 'All this construction! This new autoroute they are going to build . . .'

'It'll make life easier in the long run,' Robert said.

'It will destroy the region. You mark my words, Monsieur Robert. Hotels, apartments, new houses, motorways . . . One day there will be nothing left.'

Carrying the painting, Robert exited the gallery by the front door and crossed the square to where he had left his car. He did not notice the silver Peugeot 203 parked nearby, nor the driver, watching him intently through the front window. The man was alone in his car and as Robert emerged, he lifted a German-made Voigtländer 35 mm camera and adjusted the lens. The sun had clouded over and he wanted to be sure that the images would be as clearly defined as possible. He took several shots.

Satisfied, he placed the camera on the passenger seat beside him and waited until Robert had driven off.

Then he followed him.

*

The Pharmacie Lafayette was named after the street in which it was located, about a twenty-minute walk from the Place Masséna. It was a small, old-fashioned establishment in a narrow street hemmed in by flats that rose five storeys on each side, with a run-down café at one end and a family-run hotel at the other. The only other shop anywhere close was a grocery full of bottles and cartons that looked years out of date. The pharmacist who ran the shop and spent seven

75

hours a day behind the mahogany counter was a man called Hector Brunelle. He had inherited the business from his father. His wife nagged him. His children ignored him. This was all he had.

Approximately two hours after Robert Waysmith had left the art gallery, the door opened, jangling a bell on a metal spring, and an elderly man walked in. It would have been difficult to tell his age from his appearance. He was wearing sunglasses and a panama hat and moved slowly, supporting himself on a stick. There were tufts of white hair showing under the hat, and when he spoke, his voice gave away his advancing years. He was also a foreigner. His French was good but heavily accented. He was surely American. The man was wearing a crumpled pale blue suit that was a little too big for him. There was something else that Brunelle noticed: a smell, perhaps of surgical spirit.

'*Bonjour, monsieur.*' Brunelle spoke no language other than his own. Both his eyes had a cloudy, white sheen to them, evidence of cataracts. He gazed uncertainly at his customer. '*Comment puis-je vous aider?*'

'I wish to buy two grams of aconitine,' the man said. He used the French word, *aconit*. The pharmacist recognised it at once. If used very carefully, aconitine could act as a painkiller – for the relief of headaches or toothache, for example. Too large a dose, however, would simply kill.

'I'm afraid I cannot help you, monsieur.'

'You do not have any?'

'I do. But you will require a prescription from a doctor. May I ask what it is for?'

The bell clanged a second time and another customer

came in, a young woman wearing a light raincoat and clasping a handbag. She was evidently in a hurry and looked annoyed to find that she would have to wait.

'I am a doctor,' the man said and Brunelle nodded. That might explain the smell of surgical spirit. 'I have a patient in Nice who is suffering from gout.' As he spoke, he had taken out a document with his name, address and other details, dated and marked with official-looking red and blue stamps.

'What age is your patient?'

'He is in his fifties. An Englishman. I have prescribed the same medicine in the past.' He was beginning to sound annoyed.

The woman, too, had been listening to all this with growing impatience and edged forward. '*Pardon,*' she said. She addressed the customer in front of her. '*Je suis un peu pressée. As-tu l'heure?*' Excuse me. I'm in a hurry. Do you have the time? She was obviously French.

The pharmacist was wearing a watch, but his eyes weren't up to the task of reading it. The man who had introduced himself as a doctor answered for him. '*Il est midi quinze, madame.*' Twelve fifteen.

With an apologetic glance, she addressed the pharmacist. '*Je cherche le shampooing Dulsol.*'

'*Je ne l'ai pas, madame . . .*'

He didn't have the brand she was looking for. The woman turned and left. Throughout all this, the man in the sunglasses had done his best to keep his face out of sight.

'Two grams, *monsieur le docteur*?' he said. 'I can do this for you. But you will have to sign the register.'

'Of course.'

The pharmacist put on a pair of glasses with thick lenses and perched them carefully on his nose. Then he unlocked a display cabinet and took out a small, sealed flask containing a white powder. He unscrewed the lid and carried it over to a set of scales. Meanwhile, the man who claimed to be a doctor laid a ten-franc note on the counter and watched, expressionless, as the poison was weighed out.

*

Thirty minutes later, Elmer Waysmith and his son were having lunch at a restaurant close to the gallery. Le Poisson d'Or was a typical bistro, cosy and unpretentious. It specialised in seafood but was set back from the Promenade des Anglais, with no view of the sea. This was one of the reasons Elmer liked it. As he often said, move it twenty steps further south and the prices would double and it would also be a lot more crowded. He liked the simplicity of the decor and the fact that the manager and waiters knew him well. They didn't fuss around. For Elmer, lunch was just another part of the business day, even when he was eating with his son, and he wanted to get on with it.

They had been given their usual table in the corner and had both ordered the fish of the day – red mullet – with pommes frites and salad. There was a chilled Pouilly-Fuissé on the table; the half-empty bottle had been returned to the fridge after Elmer's last visit. They would have no more than one glass each and perhaps half a glass of red wine with the cheeseboard, which they preferred to dessert.

'Did you see Dorfman?' Elmer asked.

'Yes, Pa. I told you I was going over.'

'You told me you were going over, but that doesn't necessarily mean he was there.'

'Yes, I saw him,' Robert said, with a visible sigh.

'Did you talk to him about the *View of Louveciennes* or the *Bridge at Saint-Martin*?'

Robert hesitated. These were two other paintings by Alfred Sisley that had been in the gallery for some time, but his father hadn't mentioned them recently. 'No,' he replied. 'Mr Dorfman was very happy with *Woman with the Parasol* and I didn't think he was in any mood to talk about anything else.'

'That's a pity.' Elmer had a particular expression when he was unhappy, a sort of petulance that didn't suit him at all. Back at the gallery, Madame Dubois knew it well. She called it his bad-weather face. 'Maybe you could see him next week.'

'Why?'

'I might be able to offer them to him at a special price. You could tell him we're having a summer sale.' He did a mental calculation. 'Thirty per cent reduction.'

'Why would you want to do that?' Robert was genuinely surprised. A thought occurred to him. 'Did you get them from Mr Werner?'

Werner was Elmer Waysmith's business partner and the other half of the gallery's name. He lived in Zurich and these days the two of them seldom saw each other.

'No. It's got nothing to do with Werner!'

'Then why do you want to get rid of the paintings?'

Elmer glowered at his son. 'I need the cash. I've told you – I want to buy those Kleins.'

'The blue canvases . . .'

79

'That's not what they're called, Robert. Give them their proper name.'

'The *propositions monochromes*.'

'Exactly. If we move quickly, we could get all eleven of them. It's the sort of opportunity that never comes twice.'

'I don't understand, Pa.' Robert paused, not wanting to annoy his father. 'The Sisleys are beautiful. They're his best work and you've always said that when he's at his best, he's better than anyone. But Klein! He doesn't paint anything! They're just blue squares.'

'Klein creates colours that have never been seen before.'

'But they're only colours! His paintings have no subject.'

'The colours *are* the subject.' Elmer threw down his fork and picked up his glass of wine. 'The trouble with you, Robert, is that you have no understanding of this business. Even if you're too blind to appreciate the work for yourself, you might ask yourself why Colette Allendy has agreed to exhibit all the works in Paris next October . . .'

'In the sixteenth arrondissement. It's hardly very central.'

'But she is central to everything that's happening in modern art right now.' Elmer emptied his glass in one swallow. 'It's no wonder you didn't succeed as an artist. You have no vision. You're looking backwards. Believe me, Robert. Impressionism is over. Yes, Sisley will continue to fetch high prices . . . like Monet and Pissarro and all the rest of them. But if you want to make real profits, you must look to the unknown, and trust me, one day everyone in the world is going to know Yves Klein.'

'I didn't succeed as an artist because you stopped me,' Robert said dully.

'I did you a favour, son. You didn't have the talent. You weren't going to get anywhere. I put you into law school and when that didn't work out, I brought you into my business. I won't be running Werner-Waysmith for ever and I'd like to see you at the helm, but maybe it's time you started pulling your weight. Go and see Dorfman!'

Elmer picked up his knife and fork and continued easing the flesh off the skeleton of his red mullet. Robert sat in silence. He was used to being treated this way. It had happened often enough. But there were also times when he hated his father, when everything in his life – the failure of his career, the death of his mother, the hours wasted in a world that meant nothing to him – came to the boil and he would do anything – anything – to break free.

It was just such a time right now.

FIVE

At four o'clock that afternoon, Margaret Chalfont went downstairs for tea in the garden. It was her favourite time of the day. Some of the heat would have gone out of the sun, but for the past six hours the chateau and its grounds had been bathed in its warmth and the air would be thick with the smell of roses, lavender and pine.

The gazebo was tucked away from the main house, on the edge of an ornamental lake. It was circular, with eight Corinthian pillars holding up a limestone cupola faced with marble and decorated with semi-precious stones that took the form of a garland of flowers, continuing all the way round. Lady Chalfont loved it here. There was a small island in the middle of the lake and she had left instructions that she would like to be buried here if she died in France. It was strange, but as she made her way, fully dressed, along the corridor that led to the stairs, she had a premonition that the end might be coming very soon. It wasn't that she felt ill. In fact, the week in Cap Ferrat had done her a power of good, just as Elmer had said. But she was having bad dreams. She had not yet heard from Atticus Pünd, although she was sure he must have arrived. She wished she had seen him today and wondered when he would come.

As she reached the staircase, she heard the sound of

typing coming from her husband's study. She thought of knocking on the door and asking if he might not change his mind and join her for tea, but quickly decided against it. She knew he was trying to finish the catalogue for his next exhibition. He would hate to be disturbed.

Instead, she followed the stairs down to the *grand salon*, a space that stretched from the hall and main entrance all the way to the floor-to-ceiling glass doors that opened onto the garden. A line of pillars separated the house from the grounds: they supported the balcony in front of her bedroom where she sat for much of the day.

Lady Chalfont felt almost lost as she crossed the room, making her way outside. It wasn't just its size; it was also filled with so many gorgeous things – antique tables and sofas, a desk, a grand piano, a gaming table with a chessboard said to have belonged to Victor Hugo (although Elmer insisted it had been crafted at least fifty years too late), pedestals and pictures. Much of this had been bought by the 5th Earl Chalfont, her late husband's father, but Henry and then Elmer had also added to the collection to the extent that she sometimes felt as if she was living in a museum or a very high-class bric-a-brac market.

She was about halfway across when Béatrice appeared as if out of nowhere. The housekeeper had an extraordinary ability to hear any movement in the house and to make herself available like a genie out of the lamp.

'Good afternoon, madame. You take tea?' she asked.

'Yes, Béatrice. I'm joining Harry and my daughter at the gazebo.'

'You would like me to walk with you?'

'No. I can manage on my own, thank you. Will you bring out the tea?'

'I make it now.' Béatrice stopped to tidy the magazines on an ornamental table, then walked back towards the kitchen.

Lady Chalfont continued out into the garden, following the path that led past the fountain and then on to the lake and the gazebo. Harry was already waiting for her, but there was no sign of Judith. Instead, he had been joined by Jeffrey. Cedric was also visible in the distance, prowling around the herb garden. Margaret worried about her grandson sometimes. He spent too much time on his own and he wasn't like any other children she had ever met. What was he doing now, for example? Cedric had recently developed an unhealthy interest in poisons. Only the week before he had brought a clump of *Atropa belladonna* to the dining-room table. Deadly nightshade. Béatrice had removed both the plant and the boy from the room, only allowing Cedric to return after he had thoroughly washed his hands.

The two men stood up as she approached. Jeffrey greeted her with an embrace and a kiss on both cheeks.

'Hello, Mama. How have you been today?' he enquired.

'Much the same as usual, Jeffrey dear.' She accepted the kisses with a certain stoicism. Since her illness had been diagnosed, she had come to dislike close contact such as this. 'Where's Judith?' she asked.

'You know what she's like,' Harry replied. 'It's these wretched lines in the Peruvian desert. She won't leave them alone. She sent her apologies and I came instead.'

A table had been laid in the centre of the gazebo with china cups and plates and an ornamental stand, three tiers high, laden with sandwiches and madeleines. 'Is Cedric going to join us?' Lady Chalfont asked as she took her place.

'I have no idea, Mama.' Jeffrey sat next to her. 'That boy lives in a world of his own.'

'The same could be said about you,' Lady Chalfont remarked caustically. 'Couldn't Lola look after him?'

'She's learning her lines.'

'Do you think she's going to get this part in the play?'

'It's a musical – and she hasn't been cast yet. She's hoping to meet the producers soon, and meanwhile she's working on her Italian accent. And singing! She won't stop singing. Right now, it's like living with Maria What's-her-name. You know. That opera woman.'

'Callas.' Jeffrey's father had loved classical music and opera. Lady Chalfont often wondered how their only son could have grown up so uninterested.

'I'm starving,' Harry said, delicately pinching a sandwich between his forefinger and thumb. He hadn't thought to offer Lady Chalfont one, but he knew she would have no appetite. 'Where's Béatrice with the tea?' he asked.

At that moment, Béatrice was pouring milk into a porcelain jug, which she then placed on a tray. She went over to the sideboard where she had set out two teapots: one with Fortnum & Mason's Royal Blend, the other with lemon and ginger, which Lady Chalfont preferred. As she drew nearer, she stopped, puzzled.

She was quite sure that she had left the lids on both teapots. It was her usual practice. She made the tea and then she left it to brew for exactly three minutes, the way Lady Chalfont liked it. But although the larger teapot with

85

the Royal Blend was still closed, the lid of Lady Chalfont's
pot was lying on the counter. Béatrice was certain she had
replaced it after she had poured in the boiling water. Could
someone have come into the kitchen while she had been in
the *grand salon*? But why would anyone want to touch the tea
things?

Béatrice dismissed the thought. She replaced the lid, then
loaded the pots onto a tray along with the jug of milk, a dish
with some neatly arranged lemon slices and a bowl of sugar.

Looking around her and checking that everything was as it
should be, Béatrice carried the tea out into the garden.

*

Twenty minutes later, a grey Citroën Traction Avant pulled up
in front of the house. There was a man sitting in the front, in
the passenger seat. He was in his fifties, bald and unsmiling,
dressed in a dark suit and black tie – and this, along with the
colour of the car, gave him something of the appearance
of an undertaker. His name was Jean Lambert and he was a
solicitor – or an *avocat*, as it is called in France. He worked for
both Lady Chalfont and her husband and had also advised
Harry Lyttleton on many occasions as he had continued in
his struggles to build his hotel.

Monsieur Lambert could not drive. It was his secretary
who was behind the wheel, a young, quite plain woman with
her hair tightly drawn in a bun, wearing a cropped jacket
and a smart dress. Alice Carling had an English father and a
French mother, both in their sixties. Her parents had moved
into a small house in a village close to Saint-Paul-de-Vence

after they married and had been there ever since. Tom Carling, a former mechanic who had met his wife in a French field hospital, had never learned a word of French, but his daughter was bilingual. Monsieur Lambert's office was inside the town and she had been with him for four years.

Monsieur Lambert was the first out of the car, picking up his briefcase, which had been resting on the back seat. Now that he was on his feet, it could be seen that he was several inches shorter than his assistant. They made an odd couple as they made their way to the front door without speaking.

Alice rang the bell, then stepped aside so that Monsieur Lambert could introduce them. It took a long while for anyone to arrive, but just as she was about to ring again, the door opened and Béatrice stood in front of them, a look of puzzlement on her face. It was possible that she did not remember who Monsieur Lambert was – she had only met him a couple of times. Either that or she knew who he was but had no idea why he was here.

'Good afternoon,' Lambert said, in French. 'I have an appointment with Lady Chalfont.' He gestured with his watch as if it was proof of both his punctuality and his permission to enter. 'She asked me to call on her at half past four.'

'Lady Chalfont is having tea, monsieur.'

'Excellent. Then we will be happy to join her.'

'You are . . .?'

'We have met before. I am Maître Lambert. My assistant, Mademoiselle Carling. We have spoken with Lady Chalfont in this house many times and she has invited us today to discuss some important business.'

Béatrice seemed unsure what to do but came to a decision.

ELIOT CRACE

'You can follow me, monsieur,' she said. 'I will take you through to the garden.'

Lambert and his secretary exchanged glances and entered the house, the solicitor walking ahead. They went through the *grand salon* and out the other side, and it was only as they passed underneath the balcony that they heard shouting and saw a man in a blazer and cravat running towards them, his long fair hair flying in disarray. As he drew nearer, they recognised Harry Lyttleton. His cheeks were flushed red, but it was the look of terror on his face that struck them most. His eyes were wide and staring, as if he was being pursued by something terrible. Which, in a way, he was.

'You have to call a doctor. And the police!' His voice was high-pitched.

'What has happened?'

'Lady Chalfont . . .! It's ghastly! I can't believe it. It happened in front of my eyes.'

'Is she unwell?'

'No. No.' Harry had reached them as if he had just made it to the wicket with the cricket ball inches behind him, closing on the stumps. He doubled over, his palms resting on his thighs, gasping for breath. It took him a few moments to recover. 'She's not ill,' he wailed. 'She's dead!'

SIX

Atticus Pünd woke up late the following morning and it took him a moment to remember where he was. He was lying in bed in a large room with a window opening onto a private balcony and views of the hotel grounds. The carpet, pink and patterned, might not be to his taste and the wallpaper was certainly far too busy, but the bed was unquestionably comfortable, piled up with more pillows than he could possibly need. Lying there, he thought about the journey he had just made. It had exercised him more than he would have believed.

It had all begun well. The sea had been calm on the crossing to Calais and the famous Blue Train had been waiting for him at the platform, swathed in a cloud of white steam, the famous LX Wagons-Lits assembled one after another, a wall of sapphire blue scored by a single gold line. Smartly uniformed porters carried the luggage and more of them stood at the doors, waiting to greet the passengers on what was intended to be not just a journey but the experience of a lifetime.

Pünd had been astonished by the almost absurd luxury of the enterprise. It was as if the designers had taken the world's greatest restaurants, cocktail bars, hotels, theatres and gentlemen's clubs and stretched them until they were impossibly long and narrow but still afforded every comfort to those lucky enough to be on board. His oak-panelled sleeping compartment – there were only ten in each carriage – was a perfect home in miniature. The sofa folded into a comfortable bed. There was a table, an upholstered chair, even a small sink in the corner. James Fraser had been beside himself with excitement.

'They serve a five-course meal in the dining car,' he said. 'The food is said to be sensational. Would you like me to reserve a table?'

'No, thank you, James.' Pünd was already beginning to have his doubts about the journey. 'I think I shall retire early to my bed, once we have left Paris. Perhaps, after all, it would have been simpler to have taken the plane.'

It was true. There were five hundred and sixty miles between Calais and Nice, and twelve hours later, Pünd was beginning to feel the strain of the journey. All the comfort in the world could not diminish the rattling of the wheels, the noise of the engine, the smell of cinders and steam, the sense of captivity. His head began to ache and the pills given to him by Dr Benson seemed unable to combat the seemingly deliberate attacks on what was left of his health. Much to his assistant's dismay, he ate only a few slices of dry toast and drank nothing more than tea. Soon, he was forced to travel with the blinds drawn, not even enjoying the view, and by the time they arrived at their destination, he was sure that the entire trip had been a terrible mistake.

This was the reason he had not visited Lady Chalfont on the Friday, when he had arrived. He had not even felt capable of telephoning her. He was sure she would forgive this brief delay. He would see her over the weekend.

There was no question that he was already feeling much better. He got out of bed and pulled open the shutters, allowing the sunshine and the Mediterranean air to flood into the room. He stood there for a few minutes, feeling his strength returning. All in all, he decided, an airplane would have been just as exhausting but in a different way. The important thing was that he had arrived.

An hour later, dressed in a lightweight summer suit, he joined James Fraser at the breakfast table in the vast dining room with its soaring columns and windows opening onto the terrace that ran along the back of the hotel. There must have been at least seventy people eating breakfast, spread over the various tables, and yet apart from the occasional clatter of a knife or fork against a plate, the room was almost religiously quiet.

James was less formally dressed in a polo shirt and V-neck pullover. He stood up as Pünd took his place, then handed him a menu.

'How are you feeling today?' he asked. 'I have to say, you were looking a bit done in when we got the taxi at the station.'

'It was a long journey,' Pünd agreed.

'Well, this place is marvellous. It's almost lunchtime, but they're still serving breakfast. Which one are you going to have?'

'I'm sorry?'

'Breakfast or lunch?'

'Breakfast, I think.'

'Right.' James studied the menu. 'Would you like some eggs? I can't remember if *brouillés* is scrambled or boiled.'

'No, no, James. I think a croissant and a coffee will be enough for me.'

'You don't mind if I dig in, do you?'

'Not at all. You can have whatever you wish.'

Ten minutes later, Pünd was enjoying his croissant, a glass of orange juice and *un grand crème*, while his assistant had gone for boiled eggs, ham, cheese, a length of baguette and a silver jug filled with hot chocolate.

'So when are we off to the Chateau Belmar?' James asked.

'I will telephone Lady Chalfont as soon as we have finished breakfast,' Pünd replied. 'You must arrange a taxi for us.'

'Maybe she'll send a car.'

'That is indeed a possibility.'

They were interrupted by the approach of a waiter, who looked not just apologetic but indignant, as if something unprecedented had occurred. He was being followed by a man in his thirties or forties: it was hard to be sure. The visitor was dressed in a dark, crumpled suit that did not fit him well. The collar of his shirt was unbuttoned and his tie was loose. His choice of wardrobe would in itself have been inappropriate in the dining room of a luxury hotel, but it was not the reason why the guests greeted him with brief looks of surprise and dismay as he passed their tables. One of his eyes was covered with a black patch and the entire side of his face was a mass of scar tissue. He was clasping his right arm with his left hand as if he was in constant pain. Or perhaps the entire limb was a prosthetic. He might

once have been handsome. It was very hard to see past his
disfigurement.

The waiter stopped at Pünd's table. 'I apologise for the
interruption, monsieur—' he began.

But the new arrival did not wait for him to continue. He
stepped forward. 'Herr Pünd?' he said.

Pünd nodded.

The man turned to the waiter. 'You may leave us.'

The waiter managed to reach another level of indignation
but didn't argue. He bowed briefly and walked away.

'My name is Frédéric Voltaire,' the man introduced
himself. 'I am with the Sûreté. Do you mind if I join you?'
Without waiting for an answer, he drew up an extra seat and
took his place at the table.

'You have travelled down from Paris?' Pünd asked.

'I took the overnight train.' Voltaire spoke excellent
English, although with the formality and accent of a student
at the Sorbonne.

'For what purpose?'

By way of an answer, Voltaire reached into his jacket
pocket, withdrew a piece of paper and laid it on the table. It
was a telegram. Pünd glanced at the words and recognised the
message he had sent to Lady Chalfont.

'Where is Lady Chalfont?' Pünd asked, although he already
feared the answer.

'Lady Chalfont is dead.' Voltaire made no attempt to
soften the blow.

'What? Are you saying she's been killed?' James Fraser
stared at the man from the Sûreté.

Voltaire turned, as if noticing him for the first time. 'Do

you think I would have come all the way from Paris if she had been run over by a bus?'

'What were the circumstances of her death?' Pünd asked.

'She was having tea yesterday afternoon in the gazebo which stands in the garden of her chateau here in Cap Ferrat. There were two members of her family with her: her son, Jeffrey Chalfont, and her son-in-law, Harry Lyttleton. She became ill and died very suddenly.'

'You are aware, Monsieur Voltaire, that Lady Chalfont was seriously unwell. She had a heart condition. According to her doctor, she might have been brought down at any time.'

'The doctor told you this?'

'He did. I spoke to him shortly after he had examined her.'

'This was when you met Lady Chalfont?'

Pünd considered. There was something quietly aggressive about the way the man from the Sûreté was interrogating him, a sense of something unsaid. It was almost as if he suspected Pünd might be involved in the way Lady Chalfont had died. 'I was at the clinic for a routine examination,' he explained. 'Lady Chalfont and I had a brief conversation in the waiting room. She was with her daughter, Judith Lyttleton.'

'What did she say?'

'She wanted to consult with me on a matter of urgency and shortly afterwards she sent me a letter asking me to come to France. I will of course make it available to you, as I am sure you will wish to see it, Monsieur Voltaire, but once again it impressed upon me the urgency of my attendance.'

'She was afraid?'

'She had overheard a conversation that almost certainly

related to her husband, Elmer Waysmith. It had clearly upset her, but, as you will see, she did not describe exactly what was said. Nor did she state at any time that she felt herself to be in danger. So I would be interested to know what reason you have to believe that there may be suspicious circumstances surrounding her death.'

'You are the main reason,' Voltaire replied. 'A very wealthy member of the British aristocracy summons a world-famous detective to her house. Almost immediately, she dies. You do not see a connection?'

'Many clients have called me to their houses. Not all of them have been murdered.'

'There is something else. Just before she died, Lady Chalfont remarked that her tea had a strange taste. She had drunk about half the cup when she complained of a burning sensation in her throat. She became short of breath. Then she died.' Voltaire paused. 'This does not sound like a heart attack to me, Herr Pünd.'

'I am inclined to agree, Monsieur Voltaire. I will ask my assistant to retrieve the letter from my room. I assume you are returning to the Chateau Belmar?'

'That is my intention.'

'Then perhaps you will allow me to accompany you. Lady Chalfont was not a client – at least, not formally. But we had met before and I would say we were friends. As you can see from the telegram, I was intending to meet her yesterday, but I was not well enough to make the journey to the chateau. If it turns out that you are correct and that she was indeed the victim of foul play, I will not be able to forgive myself. I have let her down.'

'You were in no shape to go anywhere,' James muttered from the other side of the table.

'Even so, I feel a duty towards her and would be happy to help you with this investigation.'

Frédéric Voltaire was sitting very straight in his chair and the look on his face suggested that this was the last thing he wanted. However, finally he nodded. 'I will be honest, Herr Pünd. I would prefer to work alone. I do not think I need your assistance and I find it frankly offensive that you should suggest otherwise. However, the matter has been taken out of my hands.

'When I reported to my superiors that you were here in Cap Ferrat and that Lady Chalfont had communicated with you, I was given the direct order to involve you in the case. The Commissaire wishes this matter to be dealt with as quickly as possible. Do not think for a minute that this has anything to do with Lady Chalfont or her family – or, for that matter, yourself. The Côte d'Azur is becoming increasingly important to the economy of the whole country. We need tourists, and not just that. Wealthy tourists. We already have enough problems with Corsican drug gangs, as well as corruption and vice. If people with wealth and influence think they cannot come here without being murdered in their own homes, it could place the entire area in jeopardy.

'In short, my hands are tied. The Commissaire sends his compliments and formally asks for your help in this matter. If you have eaten your breakfast, I have a car outside. Despite my own considerations, you will be given complete freedom to pursue the investigation as you see fit.'

'You are very direct, Monsieur Voltaire.'

'Would you wish me to be otherwise, Herr Pünd?'

Pünd examined the other man curiously, wondering about his injuries, the manner in which the detective had approached them, and what it was that made him so hostile. But this was far from the right time to start asking questions.

'I'll get the letter,' Fraser said.

'Thank you, James.' Pünd smiled at the Frenchman. 'I shall finish my coffee and then we shall go.'

SEVEN

There was a police driver waiting outside the hotel for Frédéric Voltaire, who grabbed the front seat, leaving Pünd and Fraser to squeeze together in the back. The Frenchman had not spoken a word since they left and sat in hostile silence as they drove along a narrow lane, following the coastline towards the port of Saint-Jean-Cap-Ferrat.

James Fraser alone seemed relaxed, his face pressed against the window, enjoying the brief glimpses of dazzling blue water in the gaps between the ancient villas and the abundance of foliage and trees. The lane climbed upwards, taking them above the port, and now he saw dinghies and sailing boats dotted haphazardly around the jetty. Everywhere he looked, there were signs of new building – cranes, scaffolding, cement mixers and clusters of workmen – as the sleepy village was rapidly transformed into a holiday resort that would attract millionaires and celebrities from all over the world.

'What a lovely place!' he exclaimed, as much to himself as anyone in the car.

Pünd smiled at him. In the front of the car, Voltaire and the driver behaved as if he wasn't even there.

They took another road that crossed over to the western edge of the promontory, surrounded by sea on three sides.

98

After a short drive, they came to a driveway that ran between two rows of poplar trees with a handsome pair of gates at the end. It was only as they slowed down that James realised they had arrived at the Chateau Belmar. The gates were open. They drove through and parked on the gravel drive next to a pair of Renault 4CVs painted black and white, with only the single word POLICE, written in small letters, revealing to whom they belonged.

The driver turned off the engine.

'I am still leading this investigation,' Voltaire said. He spoke without turning round. 'And you will share with me any information that you receive.'

'We are here to assist you, Monsieur Voltaire,' Pünd assured him. 'Not to get in your way.'

Pünd and Fraser stepped onto the driveway and waited for the French detective to join them. Whatever had happened to him, presumably a war injury, it had affected his whole body, making it difficult for him to manoeuvre himself out of the car. It was obvious that he was in constant pain. Finally, the three of them stood in the sunshine, looking up at the handsome façade of the house and the three white marble steps leading up to the front door. A gendarme had been positioned outside and saluted Voltaire as he approached.

They walked through a vestibule with an elaborate tiled floor and into the *grand salon*. In the far distance, a plump, red-faced man was sitting with his legs splayed out, gazing around him impatiently. There was a second, fair-haired man with him, his hands on his knees, wearing a lilac jacket and white trousers. They were side by side on a gilded chaise longue with another gendarme watching over them. Voltaire provided their names: 'Jeffrey Chalfont and Harry Lyttleton.'

Jeffrey Chalfont looked at his watch, clearly agitated. 'We've been here for the best part of an hour, Mr Voltaire,' he grunted. 'Is this really necessary?'

'You do not think your mother's death is worth an hour of your time, Monsieur Chalfont?'

'It's Lord Chalfont, if you don't mind, but right now I suppose that's beside the point. There are a lot of things I must do following my mother's death. I may have to go back to Norfolk – assuming I'm allowed to leave this wretched country.'

'That will not be possible until my investigation is complete,' Voltaire said.

'Why? It seems to me there's no chance that she was murdered and so this extensive police presence is both boring and unnecessary.' Jeffrey Chalfont had done his best to make himself look more presentable. He had shaved and smoothed down his red hair and he was wearing a jacket and tie. But there was still something apish about his appearance. He didn't want to be here and he didn't care if Voltaire knew it. So far, he had shown no interest in Pünd at all.

'Can you describe what happened in the garden?' Pünd asked.

'This is Herr Pünd,' Voltaire explained, still using the German form of address. 'He is a well-known detective who met Lady Chalfont in London when she was last there. She asked him to come to France.'

'Herr Pünd? You're a Jerry?'

'My family emigrated from Greece,' Pünd told him, ignoring the insult.

'Well, my mother never mentioned you to me,' Jeffrey Chalfont remarked gruffly.

'Nor me,' Harry Lyttleton added.

'And yet your wife was present when we met,' Pünd said. 'She did not say anything to you?'

'You mean – Judith? No. Not a word.'

James Fraser had taken out his notebook and had written down everything that had been said so far. He put a question mark beside this last statement – but only because he had noticed that Pünd seemed surprised.

'Your mother also wrote to Herr Pünd,' Voltaire explained. 'I have seen the letter and although she does not say as much directly, it could be implied that she was in fear of her life.'

'She was ill!' Jeffrey said. He made it sound completely obvious. 'She knew she was going to die.'

'But not from poisoning.'

'There's still no proof of that,' Harry Lyttleton cut in. 'She died immediately after drinking tea and Jeffrey agreed we should call the police. Wouldn't you have done the same? It was his mother, after all.'

'You told the police that she complained of a burning sensation in her throat,' Pünd said.

'That was true.' Harry reached forward and opened a silver and ivory box on the table in front of him. He took out a Gitanes cigarette and lit it, coughing as the smoke hit his lungs. 'She did say that.'

'A burning throat is not usually a symptom of a heart attack, Mr Lyttleton.'

101

'She could have just scalded herself. I mean, isn't that a possibility? The tea was rather hot.'

'How far is the gazebo from the house?'

'Oh . . . it's miles away,' Harry answered and scowled. In the space of five seconds he had managed to contradict himself.

'And so the tea could not have been of a scalding temperature by the time it reached you.' Pünd made the obvious conclusion.

Jeffrey Chalfont managed a thin, humourless smile. 'But who would want to kill a woman who had only months to live? Why risk hanging when the end was so near anyway?'

'It would not be hanging but the guillotine,' Voltaire remarked coldly. 'We are fortunate to have the contents of the teapot from which Lady Chalfont took her tea. They have been sent for analysis in Marseille and we will have the results very soon.'

Harry Lyttleton had gone pale at the mention of the guillotine. Jeffrey Chalfont was unmoved.

'Can you describe for me what occurred?' Pünd asked. 'Was it always your practice to take tea with your mother?'

'Not always,' Jeffrey replied. He took a breath. 'She spent a lot of time in her room, but she liked to come out to the garden for afternoon tea and given how ill she was, we always made sure there was someone to sit with her.'

'So you and Mr Lyttleton were in the garden. Who else was in the house?'

'My stepfather was in his study. He spends all day there sometimes, writing one damn catalogue after another. He'd had lunch in Nice and he got back at three o'clock. I know

102

because I was on the terrace and heard the clock strike in the *petit salon* just as his car pulled in. Béatrice was in the kitchen, I imagine. I'm not entirely sure where Cedric was. He's my son. He's only eight years old. He was mucking around somewhere in the garden. He does that a lot.'

'And his mother?'

'Lola was in her bedroom, learning her lines.'

'She is an actress?'

'She used to be. That's how I met her. She was playing Mata Hari at the Theatre Royal in Norwich. She was a gorgeous young woman, I have to say. And she got the voice and the look absolutely right – but this is something rather different: a comedy musical. It's called *Where's My Gondola?* A complete waste of time. It'll probably sink.'

Harry Lyttleton smirked, but it seemed to Pünd that Jeffrey hadn't intended to make a joke. 'Was there anyone else?' he asked.

'My wife was in Peru,' Harry said. 'Which is to say, that's where she always is in her own mind. She'd have been at her desk, writing about the Nazca desert.'

Jeffrey thought for a moment. 'That just leaves Robert,' he said. 'Robert Waysmith is Elmer's son by his first marriage. I only saw him when the police were here and I didn't ask him where he'd been. I imagine he was working at the gallery, in Nice. That's his business. He sells art.'

'Are the two of you close?'

'Robert and me? We don't have many shared interests, but we get along. I like him. I'd say we all do.'

'So you had tea with Lady Chalfont in the gazebo. How did she seem to you?'

The two men glanced at each other as if wondering who should speak. It was Harry Lyttleton who answered. 'She seemed to be in jolly good spirits,' he said. 'She hadn't been at all herself recently, not since she got back from that trip to London. But Jeffers and I both thought she was on top form.'

'Maybe that's because she knew Mr Pünd was coming,' Fraser remarked.

'You were aware that Lady Chalfont had approached me?' Pünd asked.

Jeffrey shook his head. 'Judith didn't tell us that you'd met. As a matter of fact, I'm quite annoyed with her. If we'd known there was something preying on Mama's mind and that she felt she needed a detective, we might have been able to talk to her.'

'That's how she was,' Harry added. 'We didn't even know the old girl was ill until a month after she'd been diagnosed. She kept everything close to her chest.'

'But she was not anxious at the time of the tea,' Pünd reminded them. 'You said just now that she was in good spirits.'

'That's right. She was.' Jeffrey picked up the story. 'We talked about the garden and some of the new houses being built in the area, local gossip, that sort of stuff. Mama seemed on good form. Then Béatrice brought out the tea.'

'Did all of you drink from the teapot?'

'Margaret had a pot of her own,' Harry said. 'It was a lemon and ginger concoction, supposedly good for her health. Jeffrey and I shared the other one.'

'The two pots were similar?'

104

'Not at all. Hers was pink. Ours was blue. And hers was much smaller.'

'We already told Mr Voltaire all this,' Jeffrey said. 'She complained that her tea had an odd taste. We were about to call Béatrice, but before we could do anything, she started coughing and pawing at her throat. She said the tea was burning her. Then she sat back in her chair and let out a gasp and – we had no idea what was happening – she jerked back. And then . . .' his face fell '. . . she died.'

'It was hideous!' Harry's eyes were filled with horror as he recalled the last moments in the garden. 'I mean, she'd been so alive one minute and now she wasn't breathing. Her eyes were staring and I somehow knew . . . I could tell at once that she was dead. But how could it have happened just like that, sitting in the sunshine, drinking tea?'

'Did you think she might have been poisoned?'

'No! No! No! That thought never occurred to me. I still don't believe it now.'

'So why, then, did you call for the police?'

'Isn't that what you do when someone dies? We both agreed it was the right thing to do. Jeffrey stayed with his mother. It didn't seem decent to leave her alone. I ran to the house and called for help.'

'Who was there?'

'Well, I was looking for Béatrice. I don't speak French. I had lessons at school, but I never understood a word of it. All this *le*, *la*, *les* stuff. Why do the Frogs need so many words for "the"?'

'Please, Monsieur Lyttleton,' Voltaire said. 'Stay to the point.'

'Yes. I'm sorry. I was going to explain things to Béatrice and get her to make the appropriate telephone calls. But she wasn't on her own. Mr Lambert and his assistant had turned up out of the blue. Apparently, Lady Chalfont had invited him to the house. But it couldn't have been worse timed.'

'Who is Lambert?' Pünd asked.

'He's the family solicitor,' Jeffrey explained. 'We have two solicitors. One in London, one out here. Jean Lambert deals with all legal matters relating to the chateau and to the gallery in Nice. He's also advised Harry about his new hotel. And he drew up my mother's will.'

Voltaire picked up on this. He leaned forward. 'Had he come here to discuss the will?' he asked.

'I have no idea, Monsieur Voltaire. He stayed until the ambulance arrived, but I was too upset to talk to him. He said he had an appointment. That's all. He was the one who called the police and the hospital in the end. He took over the situation. Maybe you should talk to him.'

'We will,' Voltaire assured him.

EIGHT

From the *grand salon*, Atticus Pünd, Fraser and Voltaire passed through to the L-shaped kitchen, where they found Béatrice sitting at the table, polishing the silver. It was obvious that she had been crying. Her eyes were red and there were several balls of tissues in front of her. She had already met Voltaire earlier that morning, but the sight of two more strangers had her trembling in her seat.

Pünd sat down opposite her. 'You are Mademoiselle Béatrice?' he asked gently, trying to put her at her ease.

'Béatrice Laurent, monsieur.'

'This must be a very difficult time for you.'

'You have no idea, monsieur. Lady Chalfont was always so kind to me. I know that she was ill, but I did not expect this. And I hear them saying that maybe she was poisoned! That is impossible! I will not believe it!'

She reached for another tissue and Pünd waited until she had wiped away fresh tears.

Béatrice spoke no English, so James Fraser had been translating everything that was being said. Pünd waited for her to calm down. 'You live here in the villa?' Pünd asked.

'She lives here for six months when the family is in residence,' James translated. 'During the winter months, she comes in twice a week and lives with her brother just outside

107

Nice.' He frowned. 'I didn't quite catch the last part, but I think she said he's a bastard.'

'Miss Laurent and her brother live in a stone house,' Voltaire cut in. 'The French word for a stone house is *bastide*.'

'Oh. Sorry.' Fraser blushed.

'Would you like me to take over the translation?' Voltaire asked.

'That will not be necessary, Monsieur Voltaire, thank you. But if you could point out any other misunderstandings, we would both be very grateful.' Pünd turned back to the housekeeper. 'You made the tea yesterday afternoon.'

'Yes, monsieur. Lady Chalfont liked to take tea in the garden with her family. I made sandwiches and cakes and took them out, as she had instructed. One pot for madame, another for the two gentlemen.'

'You took everything together?'

Béatrice shook her head. 'No, monsieur. I waited until Lady Chalfont went into the garden. Then I took out the fish.'

'The drinks,' Voltaire muttered. '*Boissons*. Not *poissons*.'

'Sorry,' Fraser said.

Pünd chose his words carefully. He didn't want to upset the housekeeper any more than she had been upset already. 'You realise, mademoiselle, that if Lady Chalfont was deliberately poisoned at the gazebo, it could only have been in the tea.' Before she could react, he went on. 'Can you tell me how you prepared it? Of course, you boiled the kettle. You added the leaves. What I am asking is, did you leave the kitchen at any time during the preparation?'

'I did. Yes. When Lady Chalfont came down, I spoke to her in the *grand salon*.'

108

'How long were you with her?'

'For about a minute.'

Béatrice had more to say. Pünd saw her start, then hesitate. 'There is something else?' he asked.

'I do not wish to make false accusations,' she began.

'You must tell us everything you know, mademoiselle,' Voltaire said sternly.

'Well, it was something I saw at the time. I'd taken two teapots from the cupboard and I placed them over there.' She pointed at the sideboard. 'I put in the tea leaves and filled them with boiling water and then I replaced *les couvercles* . . .'

Fraser looked to Voltaire. 'The lids,' Voltaire said.

'That was when I heard Lady Chalfont outside and went to speak to her. I met her in the *grand salon*. But here is what I do not understand, monsieur. When I returned, the lid of the smaller pot, the pink one, had been removed. That was madame's! But I am sure the teapot was closed. It is not like me to be so clumsy.'

Pünd considered. 'Can you tell me, Mademoiselle Laurent, how many ways there are into the kitchen?'

Béatrice had to think for a moment, looking around her to be sure. 'There are four,' she exclaimed eventually. 'You came in through the main door to the house. The door over there connects directly with the *petit salon*. There is a third door into the garden.'

'And the fourth?' It was Voltaire who asked.

'There is a service staircase that leads all the way to the top floor. You cannot see it from here. It is hidden round the corner. I have a room at the top of the house and I use the stairs at the beginning and the end of every day.'

'So someone could have been waiting for her to leave,' Fraser said. 'The moment she left to have a chat with Lady Chalfont, they could have crept in and added something to the teapot.' He turned to Béatrice. 'Did you hear anything?'

'No, monsieur. I heard nothing.'

'I would like to see for myself these hidden stairs,' Pünd remarked. He bowed to the housekeeper. *'Je vous remercie, mademoiselle. Vous m'avez beaucoup aidé.'*

James Fraser stared at him as they made their way to the back of the kitchen. 'You speak French!'

'Only a little, James. A few words. You did an excellent job.'

What looked like a cupboard door opened to reveal a narrow wooden staircase, uncarpeted, rising between two plaster-covered walls. The steps creaked as he began the climb upwards, followed by Fraser and a struggling Voltaire. After a short while, he came to a door and opened it to emerge onto a wide, richly decorated corridor that ran the full length of the first floor with eight or nine doors leading off it. The door to the staircase itself virtually disappeared into the wall. Looking around him, Pünd recognised a Chagall painting nearby. In fact, there was so much art and fine furniture that he could have been standing in a museum.

'You think someone entered the kitchen by the service stairs?' Voltaire asked.

Pünd shrugged. 'To come in from the garden – that is to take a great risk as they might have been seen from the gazebo. The main doorway also was in full sight of Mademoiselle Béatrice and Lady Chalfont. The *petit salon* is possible, but why would they have been in there in the first place? This would seem to be the most likely.'

'Well, where do you want to start?' Voltaire pointed to a door. 'That's Elmer Waysmith's bedroom and office suite at the end of the corridor. He's in there now, I would imagine, although I would doubt that he is ready to talk. I saw him this morning and he was so upset, he couldn't say a word. His son, Robert, has the room opposite.' He turned round and pointed. 'Lady Chalfont slept at the back of the house.'

'Not with her husband?' Fraser asked.

Pünd smiled at his assistant. 'It is quite common for members of the British aristocracy to sleep in separate rooms,' he explained. 'Also, you must remember, Lady Chalfont was unwell.'

'Judith Lyttleton and her husband have a room round the corner,' Voltaire explained. 'And Jeffrey Chalfont and his wife are next door.'

'I would like, I think, to speak to Dr Judith Lyttleton,' Pünd said. 'Her husband said that she did not discuss our meeting in London. I must ask her about this.'

'You think he was lying?'

'Somebody is most definitely lying, James. It seemed to me at the time that Dr Lyttleton was unhappy that her mother had approached me and I would be interested to know why she did not mention the encounter.'

'All right,' Voltaire said. 'Let's start with her.'

*

In fact, Judith Lyttleton had company. When Pünd knocked and entered, he found himself not in a bedroom as he had expected, but in a comfortable living room with a sofa and

111

three armchairs and a highly ornate, gilded cassone to one side. An archway opened into a second space with a four-poster bed, only partly visible.

One corner of the room was taken up by an antique globe, spun round so that South America was uppermost, next to a monumental desk piled high with books and black-and-white photographs. Glancing at them, Pünd saw a desert landscape with symmetrical lines and shapes dug into the sand. There were also representations of different animals: a condor, a monkey and a spider. He realised that he was looking at the Nazca Lines, which Dr Lyttleton seemed to have made her life's work. They were certainly spectacular.

Lola Chalfont was sitting with her. The two women had been deep in conversation when they were interrupted. Lola appeared entirely composed, sitting with her legs crossed, a cigarette in one hand, a cocktail glass cradled in the other. But Judith was still in shock, her face haggard, her eyes empty. The shutters were half closed but the early-afternoon light was still streaming in, giving the room the feel of a church or a sanitorium.

Once again, Voltaire introduced the two arrivals. Lola had not met Pünd, but Judith recognised him and started, as if he was the last person she had hoped to see. Pünd noticed this, but said nothing as he took his place on the sofa. Voltaire and Fraser remained standing.

'May I offer you my condolences on the death of your mother,' Pünd began. 'I met her many years ago and we were friends.'

'Yes. She told me.' Judith could barely manage the four monosyllables.

'This is ridiculous,' Lola weighed in. 'As if it isn't bad enough having Monsieur Voltaire from the Sûreté, now we have a private detective from England? Margaret was not murdered, and forgive me, Judith, but Harry was an idiot to call the police in the first place.'

'It was Lady Chalfont herself who invited me to come here,' Pünd replied. He glanced at Judith. 'You were present when we spoke.'

Judith nodded. 'Yes.'

'You will recall that she wished to consult with me on a matter of the greatest urgency. Those were her words, and she asked me for my card so that she could write to me.'

'It's true.' The words came out breathlessly, as if forced. Judith turned to her sister-in-law, apologetic. 'I should have said,' she muttered miserably.

'I am a little surprised that you do not seem to have mentioned our meeting to your husband or to anyone in the family,' Pünd continued.

'I . . . I didn't think it was important.'

'When a woman approaches a well-known detective and asks for him to investigate and then, just a few days later, is found murdered, of course it's important,' Voltaire said. Unlike Pünd, he had not even tried to be kind.

'She was just asking for his advice!' Judith took out a handkerchief and wiped her eyes. 'Of course it was important. In the taxi on the way to the airport I asked her several times what she was going on about, but she waved me away and I didn't think any more about it. I know it sounds awful now, but I had other things on my mind.'

'Your work.'

113

'Yes. I'm making a study of the Nazca Lines. They really are one of the wonders of the southern hemisphere, Mr Voltaire. They are mathematically precise drawings in the desert that cover an area of almost one hundred and ninety square miles, but they've been calculated to the nearest inch. Nobody understands why they were put there or how. They can only be seen by air. But the worst thing is that the wretched Peruvian government is refusing to look after them. They've already built a highway across the desert—'

She stopped herself, realising that she had allowed her enthusiasm to get the better of her. A moment before she had been mourning her mother. Now she had forgotten her.

'You say she was murdered,' Lola stepped in, as if to defend her sister-in-law. 'But that's ridiculous. You don't kill a woman who is already so very ill. And all this intrusion . . . the very idea that there might have been poison in her tea! It's nonsense. It's only making everything worse.'

'You believe I'm intruding, madame?' Voltaire growled. 'You should be grateful that the Sûreté took this matter seriously enough to send me here.'

'We will find out soon enough if there is a need for you to be here, Monsieur Voltaire.' Pünd was trying to be conciliatory. 'The tea that Lady Chalfont drank is being analysed even as we speak,' he explained. 'But until the results are known, there are still questions to be asked.' He turned back to Judith Lyttleton. 'Your mother wrote to me of a conversation she had overheard. In her letter, she suggested that she had come upon something criminal and that it might be a matter for the police. She never discussed it with you?'

114

'What sort of crime are you talking about?' Lola was scornful. 'What do you take us for, Mr Pünd? My husband is the seventh Earl Chalfont, in case you hadn't noticed. This is a respectable family. Do we look like thieves or murderers to you?'

'It is astonishing how many thieves and murderers do not resemble thieves and murderers,' Pünd replied.

'That's true!' Fraser agreed.

'I didn't know she'd written to you,' Judith said. 'She must have posted the letter without telling us.'

'Where is the nearest postbox?' Pünd asked.

'It's in the port,' Lola replied. 'But she wouldn't have needed to walk there. If anyone wants to send a letter, they just leave it on the table beside the front door. Béatrice takes the mail in every morning to catch the midday post.'

'There is still the possibility that somebody in the house might have seen my name on the envelope.'

'And recognised it?' Lola raised an eyebrow. 'Until Monsieur Voltaire introduced you, I didn't have the faintest idea who you were.'

It was difficult to say if Lola was being purposefully insulting, but Pünd was unperturbed. 'It is strange,' he said. 'When I first met Lady Chalfont – it was in Salisbury, when I was investigating the death of George Colindale – she was a most courageous woman. She was also someone I would describe as forthright. She spoke her mind. She held nothing back. And yet the woman you describe, who does not tell you why she has summoned me or the nature of the crime she has supposedly discovered, she appears secretive. Perhaps even afraid.'

115

'It may be that my mother had changed since you met her, Mr Pünd,' Judith said, adding in a low voice: 'Since she married Elmer.'

'You do not approve of your stepfather?'

Judith flinched. 'No. That's not what I meant at all.'

'But it must have been difficult for you when your mother decided to remarry.'

'We were all surprised to begin with. Elmer had only come into our lives to advise on the art collection at the Hall, but whatever we may have thought of him, my mother adored him. She would have done anything for him. And if he made her happy, that was all that mattered.'

'You say "whatever we may have thought of him".' Pünd paused. 'What did you think of him?'

'When he first turned up, we thought he was a gold-digger,' Lola said. 'He had her round his little finger and he still does – at least, he did until yesterday afternoon. She never did anything without asking him first. But Judith's right about one thing. He didn't need her money. He'd inherited more than enough when his first wife died.'

'How did she die?' Voltaire asked.

'She threw herself under a train.'

'How awful!' Fraser muttered.

Lola glanced at him. 'Maybe it was better than living with Elmer.'

There was a brief silence, broken only by the sound of Fraser's pen scratching against the surface of his notebook. Then Pünd continued. 'You were not expecting to meet Maître Lambert yesterday.'

'I couldn't believe it when I saw him here,' Judith said. 'He

116

insisted that Mother had asked him to come to the house at half past four, but she'd never said anything about it to us.'

'Could it be there was something that she did not wish you to know?'

'I suppose that's possible. But if it was important, I'm sure she would have asked Elmer first.'

Voltaire had been listening to all this with growing impatience. It seemed to him that Pünd had learned nothing of any importance and that his questions seemed to have been fired at random, none of them coming close to the target. Voltaire's way of doing things was more straightforward. 'Can you tell me your movements yesterday?' he cut in.

'I had breakfast in the *petit salon*—' Lola began.

'I am referring to the afternoon, madame,' Voltaire snapped. 'Did either of you go down to the kitchen at around four o'clock?'

'I stayed in my room.' Judith was the first to answer. 'I was reading and I was very much immersed in my book. The next thing I knew, I heard Harry in the hall and he was shouting. That's when I came down.'

Voltaire turned to Lola.

'I was also in my room.' Lola waved a languid hand. 'You might like to know that before I married Jeffrey, I was an actress. A well-known actress, as a matter of fact. Right now I'm considering taking a part in a production that's opening later this year. I'll be meeting the producers quite soon, so I was looking at my lines.'

She paused.

'There is something else?' Voltaire asked.

'Well, since you ask, I did hear someone go down to the

kitchen. Don't ask me the exact time, but it must have been around four o'clock. They went down the service stairs. They're right next to my room and they creak. Béatrice sometimes wakes me up in the morning when she goes down to do the breakfast. I've told her a hundred times to make less noise, but I suppose it's not her fault.'

'Do you know who it was?'

'How could I know who it was, Monsieur Voltaire? I heard them. I didn't see them.'

'How can you be quite certain that they were not climbing the stairs?' Pünd asked. 'It could have been someone coming from the kitchen or perhaps even climbing up to the top floor.'

Lola thought about this. 'I suppose you have a point,' she conceded. 'I heard the door open on the landing, so they must have started from there. But I suppose they could have gone up, not down.'

'Only Béatrice has a room on the top floor,' Judith said.

'And Béatrice was serving the tea,' Lola added.

'Where was the younger Mr Waysmith?' Pünd asked.

'He went into Nice for lunch with his father. I don't know what time he got back.'

'I didn't see him until after the police arrived,' Judith said. 'He was probably at the swimming pool. He likes to keep himself fit.'

'You should ask Bruno,' Lola added.

'Bruno is the gardener?'

'Yes – but he does the pool too. There's a sort of Swiss chalet thing next to it and Robert uses it to get changed. It's quite possible Bruno will have seen him.'

'But whether he did or not, your questions are ridiculous!' Judith scowled. 'Robert would never have hurt Mama, not in a million years. None of us would. Mama died of natural causes and your presence here is both intrusive and irrelevant.'

There seemed to be nothing more to say. Pünd stood up and, with a brief nod of thanks, Voltaire moved to the door. Pünd followed, James Fraser close behind.

'Well, that wasn't very helpful,' James said, glancing at the notes he had made once they were back in the corridor.

'I am not so sure, James.' Pünd shook his head. 'Do you not see how it all begins to fit together?'

'But Judith Lyttleton does have a point. We still don't know if Lady Chalfont was really poisoned!'

Pünd turned to Voltaire. 'When do you expect the results of the analysis, Monsieur Voltaire?'

'This afternoon.'

'Then let us continue.' Pünd looked up and down the corridor, past the gold-framed mirrors, oil paintings and engravings. 'I would very much like to see Lady Chalfont's room.'

'Follow me.'

The French detective was moving more slowly than ever, as if already exhausted by the investigation. He led them to the back of the house and through a door that opened into a magnificent suite of rooms: a bedroom, a bathroom, a dressing room and a small sitting area, all of them exquisitely furnished. But more glorious than any of this was the panoramic view of the garden on the other side of the three Romanesque arches. This was a room to wake up in. It would be impossible to start the day without a sense of inspiration.

119

There was a brown envelope on a table beside the bed and Pünd recognised it at once. The envelope was empty now, but it had the words POST OFFICE TELEGRAMS printed in red above the royal coat of arms. He showed it to Voltaire. 'You left this here?' he asked.

'I left it where I found it,' Voltaire replied. 'It was here when I arrived. I brought the telegram with me when I came to the hotel.'

Pünd ran a finger across the top of the envelope, feeling the edge. 'I wonder who opened this telegram,' he muttered, almost to himself. 'I do not believe it was Lady Chalfont.'

Voltaire scowled. 'It has been severed with a knife,' he said. 'I think it's quite likely that Lady Chalfont would have had a paper knife in her possession.'

'Then where is it, Monsieur Voltaire? And if you look at the way the paper has been cut, you will clearly see that the knife that was used had a serrated edge. That would suggest to me that it was a bread knife or perhaps a fruit knife, and it is unclear to me why, if she opened the telegram in this room, Lady Chalfont would have had either such implement anywhere near her.'

'But if someone had cut it open before it was given to her, she would have known.'

'If that person was certain that she would be dead within a few hours, it would not matter.'

Voltaire was about to reply when Pünd held up a hand for silence. He could hear voices coming from outside and, gesturing at Fraser to accompany him, he stepped out onto the balcony.

In the distance, he could hear the fall of water from

the fountain, but much closer two voices were raised in argument.

'I don't like it here. I want to go back to Norfolk.' It was a child who had spoken and Pünd knew at once that this must be Cedric, Jeffrey and Lola's son, talking to someone in the *grand salon*.

'We can't go back yet.' Jeffrey Chalfont's voice was unmistakable. 'Even if we wanted to, it wouldn't be allowed.'

'Because Granny's dead?'

'Exactly, Cedric. And you could try to show a little more sympathy.'

'I didn't kill her! The police don't want to talk to me. They probably think you did it.'

'That's a dreadful thing to say, Cedric. I think you should go to your room.'

'I hate it here. I've got no friends. The food's horrible. It's boring. And nobody speaks English.'

'We're not leaving yet and that's the end of the matter. Now go to your bloody room!'

'Maybe you'll be next. Or Mummy. Or Uncle Harry. There's lots of poison in the garden. Lots and lots of it. I know. I've seen it.'

'Cedric!'

But there was no reply from the child. Only the banging of an unseen door.

NINE

Elmer Waysmith was sitting slumped behind his desk in the study that adjoined his bedroom. The energy seemed to have drained out of him. There were bags under his eyes. With his white hair, he had already looked older than his sixty-seven years, but the sudden death of his wife might have added another ten. He was wearing a grey cotton blazer with a silk handkerchief poking out of the top pocket, although from the look of him, he would have been more comfortable in a morning suit. But who brings black to the South of France?

The study was a square room with a single window, which even when fully open did not allow enough air to circulate. Much of the space was taken up by an ornate Mazarin bureau piled high with papers, newspaper clippings, photographs, receipts and certificates. Three of the walls were covered by bookshelves that only added to the sense of claustrophobia. The books largely related to the world of art, with monographs and biographies in several languages, but there were dictionaries, encyclopaedias and reference books covering a wide range of subjects. Elmer had a fountain pen in front of him. He had been working on his new catalogue and there were several pages covered in turquoise ink.

A silk-covered divan with scroll legs had been placed

under the window and this was where Robert Waysmith was sitting. He, too, looked exhausted. He had not shaved and a dark shadow seemed to be spreading across his face. He was examining his father with watchful eyes, waiting to hear what he might say next, nervous of what it might be.

'We'll have the funeral in England.'

'In Norfolk?'

'Of course it will be in Norfolk. Where do you expect it to be? Paddington Station?'

'Whatever you say, Pa.'

Elmer wiped a hand across his brow as if to excuse his bad temper. It was grief, of course. Robert knew that he had to make allowances. His father had been married to Margaret Chalfont for six years and although she had never taken his name, the two of them could not have been closer. 'Madame Dubois will make the arrangements,' he went on. 'She'll know what to do.'

Robert nodded, something almost like a smile touching his lips. Madame Dubois had shipped paintings and sculptures all over Europe. Now she would do the same for his stepmother. 'I can't believe this is happening again,' he muttered, almost to himself.

'What?' Elmer looked up sharply, his grey eyebrows rising.

'Nothing, Pa.'

'I heard what you said. "Again". What do you mean by that? Are you suggesting that Margaret . . .?'

'The police are saying that someone poisoned her. But isn't it possible that she could have killed herself?'

'No, Robert. It is not possible! She would never have done that! She was ill. She knew her time was limited. But she lived

123

every day to the full and she loved every minute that was given to her. She had no reason to take her own life.'

'Unlike my mother.'

Elmer gazed at his son with barely controlled fury in his eyes. 'Your mother was a sick woman, Robert. She didn't know what she was doing. You know that.'

'So what's the alternative, Pa? That someone in the family deliberately killed Margaret? One of us?'

'I never said that. And the simple truth is that this damn fool detective from Paris has got it wrong. Margaret's heart gave out exactly as the doctor said and exactly as we knew it would. It was only a matter of time.' Elmer picked up the fountain pen and clipped it into his pocket. 'Unless you think I had something to do with it . . .'

'I didn't say that.'

'You don't need to. I can see it in your face. You're not married. I sometimes wonder if you're even capable of falling in love. But Margaret and I were perfectly suited. I loved everything about her. I know it was difficult for you, Robert, losing your mother, and maybe you never forgave me for marrying again. There's nothing I can do about that. But I saw a chance for happiness and I grabbed it. I make no apology. And now – now that she's gone – I don't know what I'm going to do.' There was a break in Elmer's voice and his eyes clouded over. 'I have nothing left to live for.'

'You have the gallery. You have me.'

Elmer said nothing. The room felt hotter and more airless than ever.

'The police are going to want to talk to you,' Robert said. 'This man – Voltaire.'

'I have nothing to hide from him.'

'What about Herr Werner?'

Elmer looked up as if he had just been stung. 'Erich Werner?'

'You know what I'm talking about, Pa.'

'We've already been into this. Erich Werner is seventy-three years old and retired. For thirty years, he was a respected art dealer in Zurich and he has got absolutely nothing to do with what has happened here.'

'Are you sure of that?'

'How stupid can you be, Robert? This misunderstanding with Erich is completely irrelevant, and if you have any sense at all, you won't mention any of it to Voltaire – or to anyone else who comes here asking questions.'

'I wasn't going to.' Robert felt bruised. 'Why do you treat me this way, Pa? It's always the same. Why do you have to be so hard?'

'Hard?' Elmer sounded genuinely surprised. 'The trouble with you, Robert, is that you're much more like me than you think. You just haven't woken up to it yet. Things are going to change now that Margaret has gone and the next few days are going to be difficult. But we have each other. If we stick together, we'll come through this all right and maybe – who knows? – what has happened will bring us closer. It's up to you.'

He was going to say more, but just then there was a knock on the door.

'Come in!' Elmer called.

The door opened and Voltaire entered, followed by two strangers. The first was a man in his mid-sixties, elegantly

125

dressed in a light summer suit, his hand resting on a rosewood walking stick with a bronze handle. He wore thinly framed glasses and his eyes, behind the circular discs, managed to be kind and dangerous at the same time. He was accompanied by a younger man, perhaps thirty years old, fair-haired with a boyish face and the first dusting of a suntan.

Voltaire introduced them as briefly as he could. 'This is Atticus Pünd. He's come from England to help me with my inquiries. And this is his assistant, James Fraser.'

Elmer Waysmith had already met Voltaire earlier that morning, but he was clearly perplexed by the arrival of a second detective. 'What the hell is going on here?' he demanded. 'My wife dies of a heart attack and the Sûreté sends a man down from Paris. And if that isn't enough, now we have Scotland Yard. Who's going to arrive next? Interpol?'

'I am not with the police. I am a private detective.' Pünd took a chair opposite Elmer Waysmith. Voltaire sat at the end of the divan. Fraser remained by the door with his pen and notepad poised. 'I knew Lady Chalfont,' Pünd continued. 'You could say we were friends.'

'She never mentioned you.'

'We met most recently in London just a few days ago. She invited me to come to the South of France and that is why I am here.'

'Looks like you arrived too late, Mr Pünd.'

Fraser looked shocked. Pünd could only nod in agreement.

'This must be uniquely painful for you, Monsieur Waysmith,' Voltaire remarked. Despite his words, there was no sympathy in his voice. 'To lose not one but two wives in suspicious circumstances.'

126

'I see you've done your homework, Mr Voltaire,' Elmer said. 'And, yes, it is very painful. But I can assure you, there is no connection between the two deaths.'

'On the contrary, monsieur. You are the connection.'

'Perhaps it might help to tell us a little about your first marriage and the loss of your first wife,' Pünd said. He was trying to sound accommodating, as if to suggest that although he did not approve of Voltaire's directness, it would be impossible to ignore what had happened in the past.

'I think we should leave Marion out of this,' Elmer insisted.

Voltaire said nothing. Robert looked from his father to the French police officer and then back again.

'It's extremely painful for me to dig up the past,' Elmer continued. 'But I'll tell you what you want to know. Marion had a long history of mental illness. She suffered from what the doctors called "housewife syndrome", although God knows, she never had to cook a meal or change a sheet. That was all done for her by the servants. It was a sort of hysteria, which, you might like to know, is a condition known to many well-to-do women in the US. I was quite aware that she wasn't well when I married her and I spent a fortune on a top psychiatrist in Madison Avenue. I'm sure we can make Dr Bronstein's notes available to you if you so wish.

'But it was all to no avail. When Robert was just eleven years old, his mother took her own life by throwing herself under a train at Grand Central Station – and before you ask, I was on business in Europe at the time. I was devastated by the news. It was a week before I was well enough to travel home.'

127

Robert glanced up when he heard this, but still he said nothing. Voltaire had also lapsed into silence and Pünd took over, turning his attention to Robert for the first time. 'To lose a mother at such a young age must have been very hard.'

'Well, I had Pa.' Robert tried to smile. 'You're right, though, Mr Pünd. I adored my mother. We were alone a lot when Pa was away on business. There are days when I wake up and I still find it hard to believe she's gone.'

'But your father has cared for you.'

'Yes. He brought me up.'

'My son and I are in business together,' Elmer Waysmith explained. 'We run an art gallery here in Nice and there's a second gallery in London. We divide the year between the two.'

'You enjoy the work?' Pünd was still examining Robert as if there was something about him he didn't understand.

'To be honest, it wasn't my first choice, but I like it well enough.'

'Robert wanted to be a painter,' Elmer explained. 'That didn't work out, so he trained to be a lawyer.'

'I wasn't any good at that either,' Robert said. 'I'm glad I've found something I can actually do.'

'And what of Lady Margaret Chalfont? Again, it may not be something you wish to answer, but when your father announced that he intended to remarry, it cannot have been easy for you.'

Robert Waysmith shrugged. 'He was happy and that was all that mattered.'

'But what of your happiness, Robert?'

'Lady Chalfont was extremely kind to me from the day we met. She did everything she could to make me feel wanted. Jeffrey and Judith were the same.'

'How did you meet Lady Chalfont?' Voltaire asked Elmer Waysmith.

'I was introduced to her by a mutual friend who was arranging her insurance. She had a number of paintings at her home in Norfolk and she had absolutely no idea of their value. This was long after her husband had died. We became friends and shortly afterwards we married.'

'How did her children feel about that?' Voltaire asked.

'It wasn't easy for them.' Elmer lit a cigarette. 'Of course, we had our run-ins to begin with. They were both suspicious of me. Why wouldn't they be? I had to persuade them that I wasn't after their mother's fortune, that I had a successful business that would bring in all the money I needed. But I didn't care about them. Let me tell you something about me and Margaret.'

He paused, and when he spoke again, his voice caught.

'I would have married her if she hadn't had a penny in the world. She was a brilliant woman. Witty, clever, beautiful. We were both of us in our later years and we were going to make each day count – until this foul illness struck.' He lifted a hand and covered his eyes. 'Robert, do you mind leaving me alone with these gentlemen for a moment?'

'Of course, Pa. Are you OK?'

'I'll be fine.'

Robert glanced at Voltaire, asking his permission. Voltaire nodded. Robert got up and left.

Elmer waited until he had gone, then drew a breath. 'I hate my son to see me like this,' he said.

Voltaire and Pünd waited for him to compose himself. Fraser crossed the room and sat on the divan.

'I need to explain something about the Chalfont family,' Elmer continued. He had become less aggressive now that his son was no longer in the room. 'I didn't want Robert to hear it because it's not something we've discussed and I don't think it's appropriate that he should!

'You asked me about my relationship with Jeffrey and Judith just now and I didn't tell you the truth. The fact is, they resented me when I married their mother and they still do. The same goes for Lola and Harry. And it's a two-way street. All four of them were a cause of endless concern to Margaret. In fact, she was worried sick about them.

'First of all, there's Jeffrey. He's inherited the title and the land and – boy – he likes to let you know it! He has an estate manager, tenant farmers, groundsmen, servants, and he treats them all like dirt. I'm American. I can't pretend to understand how the British aristocracy works, but he's the seventh Earl and that seems to give him a licence to behave as badly as he likes. And there's another side to him that you need to know. He gambles. You ask at the casinos around here. He's well known to every one of them. He doesn't win, of course, and the sums he's losing are beginning to mount up. His father left him plenty of cash, but Margaret had no idea how much of it is left and he had no intention of telling her.

'Judith is extremely intelligent, but don't be fooled by that quiet ethnologist act of hers. She's a tough cookie and she'll do anything to protect her husband, which includes taking his side against me. And she's got her eye on the main prize, just like him. She wants money to fight the Peruvian government over some sort of South American Stonehenge in the desert. And speaking of Harry Lyttleton – he was at school with

Jeffrey. The two of them were in the first eleven cricket team. Harry has no money. Maybe that's why he keeps so close to Jeffrey. He calls himself a businessman and right now he's trying to develop a hotel, but so far it's brought him nothing but a truckload of trouble.

'He's a year behind schedule, way over budget and he hasn't even laid the first brick. Worse still, I understand he's managed to get himself involved with some pretty unsavoury characters. You might as well know that Harry has been demanding financial support from his mother-in-law – and from me.' Elmer shook his head. 'I looked into his accounts and it's just good money after bad, which is exactly what I told Margaret. She agreed. But that hasn't stopped him badgering us.

'Lola completes the pack. I like her. She's feisty and she doesn't want to sit around on her backside, which does her credit. But she's got this idea of going back onto the stage – she was an actress when she met Jeffrey, although she gave it all up to become a fully licensed countess. Well, she wants money too. She had this idea that Margaret would pay for her big comeback. Two thousand pounds – that's what she asked for to finance some musical set in Venice. She pays for the production, she gets the part and if things go wrong, they go down together.'

Voltaire considered. 'You might say that everyone in the household had a motive to kill your wife, Monsieur Waysmith. They all wanted money. Does that include you?'

'She was going to die anyway, Monsieur Voltaire. Or had you forgotten that little fact!'

Not for the first time, Elmer Waysmith sounded utterly cold-blooded, not like a grieving husband at all.

131

Pünd had chosen his moment. 'You have not asked why it was that I came here,' he said.

'You came here because of the murder.'

'No, no. I explained to you that your wife invited me. She wrote me a letter.' He drew the letter out of his pocket. He had already shown it to Voltaire. Now he unfolded it and read out loud. '"*We have been married for six years now . . . But the day before I left for London . . . I overheard something that shocked me to my core and which I find impossible to believe. I was thinking of approaching the police, although I dreaded doing so.*"' He slid the letter back into its envelope. 'She had clearly heard a conversation in which you had taken part. Can you explain what she might have meant, Monsieur Waysmith?'

'Can I see that?'

'I would prefer you to answer the question.'

He shook his head wearily. 'I have no idea what she was talking about. Does she say it was me she overheard and who I was supposed to be talking to?' Pünd didn't reply. 'Margaret spent most of her time in her room. You make it sound like she'd stumbled onto some sort of criminal conspiracy – but that's crazy. This is the South of France, not Shanghai. The only thing that's criminal round here are the restaurant prices!'

'And yet you remarked just now that your son-in-law, Harry, is involved with some unsavoury characters.'

'I didn't say they were crooks.'

'Could it be that she learned something that made her wish to alter her will?'

'No! She'd have spoken to me first.'

'Have you seen her will?' Voltaire asked.

'Of course. My wife and I discussed it at length. But if you think I'm going to tell you what's in it, you've got another thing coming. It's private. And I want the kids to find out first.'

'That's not a decision for you to make,' Voltaire replied. 'It is important that I know anything that is relevant to this investigation.'

'You know nothing, Mr Voltaire. You don't even know that my wife was poisoned.'

'We'll find that out very soon, Monsieur Waysmith.'

'I'm glad to hear it. I don't like having this sort of thing hanging over my head and the sooner it's cleared up the better. I don't suppose I can stop you coming to the reading of the will if you really want to, but until then it's my business and I'm not saying anything.'

Fraser glanced at the French detective. Voltaire clearly wasn't pleased, but, short of arresting Elmer Waysmith for refusing to cooperate, there wasn't much he could do.

'It was your solicitor, Maître Lambert, who drew up the will,' Pünd said.

'Jean Lambert. Yes. We have solicitors in London, but we've known him a long time and, frankly, he's half the price. Margaret and I talked to him last summer.'

'You are aware, I am sure, that Monsieur Lambert came to this house yesterday afternoon. He had been invited to a meeting by Lady Chalfont.'

'She never mentioned anything to me.'

'Could it be that she wished to speak to him about her will?' Pünd suggested.

'I don't think so.' Elmer Waysmith shook his head. 'The

will was signed and witnessed. Margaret knew exactly what she was doing. I have no idea why Lambert came here. There certainly wasn't anything left to discuss, and frankly, gentlemen, I don't think I've got anything more to say to you either.'

It was a dismissal. Pünd got to his feet and, moving with difficulty, Voltaire did the same. Fraser clicked the top of his biro and slipped it back into his pocket. But even as Voltaire opened the door to let them out, Pünd glanced back at the bookshelf. 'You have an interesting collection of books, Mr Waysmith,' he said.

'I need them for my work.'

'There is one volume in particular that has attracted my attention.' Before anyone could stop him, Pünd walked behind the desk and removed a single volume that had been left jutting out slightly, separating itself from the others. He laid it on the surface.

Fraser craned down so that he could read the title. '*Erskine's Toxicology*,' he announced.

'I have had reference to this very interesting book many times,' Pünd remarked. 'Dr Robert Erskine was a physician of the eighteenth century who became an adviser to the Tsar of Russia. He was an expert on the use and the misuse of poison and much of his knowledge is contained in this work. I would be interested to know why it was of value to you.'

'You think I poisoned Margaret? You can go to hell, Mr Pünd. If you look on the same shelf, you'll find a book about medieval weaponry. I didn't stab her either.' Elmer paused, allowing this to sink in. 'I have a great many interests,' he continued. 'Many of them relating to the art world. Did you know that Matisse and Gauguin had cadmium, a poisonous metallic element, in their paints? In the nineteenth century, William Morris used arsenic for the colours in his wallpaper. Caravaggio died of lead poisoning, and it may have been lead that drove Van Gogh mad.'

He had proved his point. Elmer picked up the book and returned it to the shelf. He was still standing there, watching them silently, as Pünd, Voltaire and Fraser left the room.

'Are you satisfied?' Voltaire asked as soon as they were on the other side of the door. His tone was scathing.

'I think I learned a great deal from both father and son,' Pünd replied.

'And what was that?' Voltaire demanded.

'Mr Elmer Waysmith was an extremely handsome man when he was young. You only to have to look at young Robert. It is surprising that he is still single. There is a definite tension between the father and son, although they are remarkably similar. In fact, I would say that there is a great deal of anger and hatred here at the Chateau Belmar.'

'But nobody hated Lady Chalfont,' Fraser said.

'Exactly, my friend. So why was she the one who had to die?'

TEN

'Are you sure you're up for this, Mr Pünd?'
      'I believe I am.'

'I just hope you're not overdoing it. If you don't mind my saying so.'

'It is most kind of you to be concerned, James. But we will return to the hotel after this visit and we can rest later in the afternoon.'

'That's marvellous. They've got this amazing pool I've discovered. There's a funicular railway going down the hillside. Maybe you'll join me for a dip.'

'I think I will remain in my room – but please go ahead.'

Pünd and Fraser were once again in the back of the Renault with Voltaire in the front seat and a police driver. They had followed the coast and then turned inland. Now they were climbing up a winding road into the hills. Saint-Paul-de-Vence was a medieval walled town that did not admit traffic. They parked outside the tower gate, which soared above them, its machicolations framed against the sky, and walked through the archway and into the main street. It was now mid-afternoon and the sun was at its hottest. Pünd took care navigating the steep pathway, while this time it was Voltaire who, brisk and impatient, strode ahead.

Jean Lambert's office was about halfway up. He occupied

just two rooms, one behind the other, with a discreet sign beside the front door and a bell. Voltaire rang and a moment later they were admitted by a plain-looking young woman with dark hair fastened tightly at the back of her head, pale skin and heavy glasses that did not suit her face. She was wearing a businesslike dress and thick leather shoes. It seemed to Pünd that she was a prisoner of her own wardrobe and perhaps of her job too. She was still in her twenties. He wondered how much time she spent tucked away behind the town walls.

'I am Frédéric Voltaire. This is Herr Pünd and his assistant.'

'James Fraser,' Pünd added. It was clear that Voltaire had felt no need to introduce him by name.

The young woman spoke a few words to Voltaire in French and then continued in perfect English. 'Do please come in,' she said. 'I'm Alice Carling. Monsieur Lambert is just finishing a telephone call, but you can wait here. Can I get you a coffee?'

'A glass of water, please,' Pünd said, exhausted from the climb.

'Of course.'

There was barely enough space for them in the anteroom, which was furnished simply with a desk, an assortment of not very comfortable chairs and a small fridge. She took out a bottle of Evian and poured a glass for Pünd.

'You are English?' Pünd asked.

'Half and half,' Alice replied. 'English father, French mother. My father was wounded at Ypres in the First War and she was the nurse who looked after him.'

Pünd smiled. It was a story he had heard before, although it was unusual for a young Englishman to leave his own country. 'He chose to remain in France?' he asked.

'He was very angry about the war. He still talks about it – the incompetence, the waste, the loss of so many young lives. He never wanted to go back to England.'

'And how many people had he killed before he came to that decision?' Voltaire asked.

Alice didn't answer, but Pünd glanced briefly at the French detective, beginning to understand him. 'How long have you been with Monsieur Lambert?' he asked, changing the subject.

'Four years. My father knew him because they played boules together in the Place de Gaulle and he said he was looking for an assistant.'

'Did you know Lady Chalfont well?'

'No. I hardly knew her at all.'

Alice was clearly uncomfortable, but she was saved by the opening of the inner door. Jean Lambert was suddenly standing there, dressed in an old-fashioned suit complete with pocket watch, wing collar and pince-nez, as if he was deliberately trying to model himself on a character in a novel by Dickens – or perhaps Zola.

'Gentlemen,' he said. 'I apologise for keeping you waiting. Please will you come into my office.' His English was excellent, if accented. 'Mademoiselle Carling, you will join us and take notes.'

Fortunately, the office was larger than the anteroom and more comfortable and cooler, with views looking out to the medieval walls as they curved round the back of the town.

Jean Lambert took his place behind his desk, with Alice to one side. Chairs had been arranged for the three visitors.

'How can I help you, messieurs?' he asked, although in a way that suggested there was very little he could do.

'You must have been saddened by the death of your client, Lady Chalfont,' Pünd began.

'A great shock. Yes. Although, of course, I was aware of her illness.'

'She had confided in you?'

'I had helped her with her affairs for many years. I also advised her late husband, Lord Chalfont, when he was purchasing the Chateau Belmar. As you may imagine, a large amount of my work is involved with property because of the amount of development that is occurring here. A great many wealthy Englishmen are purchasing homes in the Côte d'Azur, although rarely are they quite as splendid as the Chateau Belmar. I was most sad to hear that she was unwell, although I had not expected the end to be so soon.'

'It is my belief that Lady Chalfont may have been murdered,' Voltaire announced.

Alice Carling looked terrified. As usual, the man from the Sûreté had not minced his words. 'It's not true,' she whispered.

'Why do you say that, mademoiselle?'

'I mean . . . who would do such a thing?' All the colour had drained out of her face.

The *avocat* examined her, concerned. 'Are you all right, Mademoiselle Alice?' he asked.

'Yes, sir. I'm sorry. It's just so hard to believe.'

'I entirely agree with you!' He turned back to Voltaire. 'I

know the family intimately and I think you are making a grave mistake. Lady Chalfont was a kind and generous woman who was loved by everyone who knew her. Nobody could have had a reason to do her harm.'

'You are reading the will tomorrow.'

'Yes, Monsieur Voltaire. I hope you are not going to ask me to reveal the contents today.'

'There is no need for that.' Pünd took over the conversation and continued more gently. 'But there is something that I do wish to know. I understand you arrived at the chateau at exactly the moment that Lady Chalfont died. Can you tell me why you were there?'

'I can see no reason not to tell you, Monsieur Pünd. I received a telephone call from Lady Chalfont the day before she went to London for a medical appointment. She asked to see me at the villa once she got back and suggested a day and a time.'

'Did she give some indication of the reason?'

'She said only that it concerned her will. I had the sense that she did not wish to speak on the telephone.' Lambert hesitated. He was not the sort of man to overdramatise events. 'She was under a great deal of strain. She did not sound well at all.

'At any event, acting on her instructions, I arrived at the villa at the appointed time and was met by Monsieur Harry Lyttleton. I know him well.'

'He's a client?' Pünd asked.

'He was. I helped him with the purchase of land close to Cap Ferrat, where he was planning to build a hotel, and I also gave him my opinion concerning a number of loans he was seeking.' He paused. 'Sadly, Monsieur Lyttleton did not accept my advice and it was because of this that I felt I could no longer assist him.'

'You advised against the loans?'

'I had concerns about the people who were providing them.'

Jean Lambert seemed to have forgotten his earlier reticence. Or perhaps he was making an exception for Harry, owing to their having fallen out.

'And how was Mr Lyttleton when you met him?' Pünd enquired.

'He was in a state of considerable shock. Lady Chalfont had died as she took tea in the gazebo. He urged me to call for an ambulance – and the police. He did not speak French and felt he was unable to do it himself.'

There was a brief silence as Pünd considered what had just been said. Lambert had told him something that did not make complete sense. 'When exactly did Lady Chalfont call you?' he asked.

'I can't recall exactly. It was the middle of last week.'

'It was the Wednesday,' Alice said. 'She rang at half past one in the afternoon. I took the call and transferred it to Maître Lambert.'

Lambert smiled for the first time. 'You see how lucky I am to have Mademoiselle Carling as my assistant. I will miss her.'

'You're leaving?' Fraser asked.

'I'm getting married.'

'How marvellous. Who's the lucky man?'

Alice looked away, blushing. 'His name is Charles Saint-Pierre. He is a doctor in Grasse.'

141

'He is a very lucky man,' Lambert said. 'And for me, I will need not just a new secretary but a driver. Perhaps it is also time for me to consider retirement. I am fifty-eight years old. My wife has said to me that we should be spending more time together.'

He stood up, signalling that the meeting was over.

'You will be present tomorrow?'

'We'll be there,' Voltaire assured him.

The three men left the office and walked back down through the town and out to the car park where their driver was waiting. A second police officer had also arrived on a motorbike. As Voltaire approached, he saluted and handed him a folded slip of paper. Voltaire opened it and read. He dismissed the policeman with a flick of the wrist.

'Lady Chalfont did not die of a heart attack,' he said, turning to Pünd. 'The analysis from Marseille shows that at least two grams of the poison aconitine had been added to her tea. More than enough to kill her.'

He folded the paper and slipped it into his pocket.

'It is exactly as I told you this morning when we met. This was not a natural death. Lady Chalfont was murdered.'

ELEVEN

The following morning, Pünd and Fraser were joined once more at the breakfast table by Frédéric Voltaire, but this time, having commanded the waiter to draw up a chair, he sat down with them. Pünd had slept well, although he had risen early to work on the next chapter of his book. Fraser was fresh from the swimming pool, his hair still damp. Neither of them particularly welcomed the intrusion.

For his part, Voltaire was making it clear that he had not joined them by choice. He was even more stiffly formal than he had been the day before, as if his injuries had impaired his personality as well as his movement. He had already ordered a hot chocolate, which arrived in a silver pot with a bowl of sugar cubes and a porcelain cup. He used his left hand to pour the steaming liquid for himself.

'We do not need to be at the house until eleven o'clock,' he explained. 'That is when the will is being read.'

It was revealing that he had spoken only of the business at hand, without even so much as a '*Bonjour*' or an enquiry after Pünd's health. He knew, after all, that Pünd had been unwell. It was not unusual for police officers to feel threatened by the detective who had been sent to undermine them, but this was something different. Pünd felt certain that Voltaire's hostility stemmed from something unconnected with the investigation. It was more personal.

'Are you staying nearby, Monsieur Voltaire?' Fraser asked, trying to break through the cold atmosphere at the table.

'I am in a small hotel in Nice,' Voltaire replied. 'The Sûreté would consider an establishment such as this to be too extravagant for its officers.' He poured himself some more hot chocolate. 'I am perfectly comfortable,' he added hastily. 'And I do not expect to remain here long.'

'You believe the investigation will be over soon?' Pünd asked.

'I have already informed my superiors that I expect to be back in Paris early next week.'

Pünd showed his surprise. 'I wish I shared your confidence, Monsieur Voltaire. You really think that the murder of Lady Chalfont is so straightforward?'

'Where there's a will, Herr Pünd, there is often a motive for murder – and if there is one thing that we have learned, it is that this is a family in need of money. The son, Jeffrey, gambles and loses. His wife, Lola, hopes to launch her career by investing in a stage production. The son-in-law, Harry, supported by his wife, Judith, tries to build a hotel and does not choose his associates wisely. And then there is the husband, Elmer Waysmith. Lady Chalfont suspected him of deceiving her, of being involved in a crime that he may deny but which nonetheless prompted her to seek advice from you.

'We know also that she had summoned her *avocat*, Maître Lambert, to come to the house on the very day that she died. She had spoken to him about her will, and as night follows day it seems clear to me that she was thinking to change it. This is the oldest story in the world and does not merit the attendance of a second detective, in particular one who is working in an unofficial capacity.'

Pünd was unperturbed. 'I accept your analysis, Monsieur Voltaire,' he began. 'On the face of it, this crime does seem to be unremarkable. An elderly lady with a great deal of money has spoken to her solicitor about her will. She is killed before she can meet with the solicitor to inform him of her intentions. Her family hopes to inherit. Straightforward, yes – but even so, there are details which seem strange to me.'

'Such as?'

'Let us start with the letter written to me by Lady Chalfont. She devotes one paragraph to her second husband and the feelings that she has for him. Then she says that she has overheard something that has made the ground dissolve beneath her feet. Unfortunately, she does not say what it was she heard nor who was speaking. Even so, we can make the obvious inference. Let us say that she had discovered that Elmer Waysmith was engaged in some form of criminal activity and this had compelled her to reconsider her will. I had the very same thought when we were in the office of Monsieur Lambert in Saint-Paul-de-Vence yesterday, but almost at once I knew that something was wrong.'

'And what was that?'

'If Lady Chalfont feared that her husband had deceived her, she might have called her solicitor to discuss the will. Or she might have asked a detective such as myself to investigate what had occurred. But would she do both? It seems to me that one action fights against the other. If he is guilty, change the will, but do not summon a detective. If he is innocent, summon a detective, but do not change the will.'

'And if she doesn't know?'

'Then wait until the truth is revealed.'

'Perhaps she didn't feel she had enough time.'

'It is unfortunate that her actions certainly made this the case.'

Fraser nodded. He had taken out his notebook and began to fill a page.

'There is also the preparation of the tea in the kitchen,' Pünd continued. 'We know from the housekeeper, Béatrice, that she filled the two teapots, but then left them unattended. When she returned to the kitchen, she noticed that someone had removed the lid from the pink teapot, which was the one intended for Lady Chalfont and which would contain the aconitine. But the question I would put to you is – why did the killer do this? Why did they effectively draw attention to the fact that they had been in the kitchen?'

'That's simple,' Voltaire retorted. 'They slipped into the kitchen when Béatrice left and added the poison to Lady Chalfont's tea. However, Béatrice came back too soon and they didn't have time to cover up what they had done. They left the lid on the side and that was that.'

'You say it is simple. To me it is the work of less than two seconds to replace the lid, unless you are telling me that the killer was distracted or simply forgot. And I have another question. From where did this poison come?'

'This is France, not England, Herr Pünd. Our pharmacists are much more easily persuaded to prescribe medicines which may be lethal if misused. My men are already asking in every

146

establishment in Nice, Cannes and the surrounding villages to see if a measure of aconitine was recently sold.'

'But why use aconitine at all? Even with the strong flavours of lemon and ginger, Lady Chalfont tasted something in her tea. She displayed the symptoms of poisoning. There are many other substances that the killer might have chosen which would have more closely resembled a heart attack, and we overheard the child – Cedric – telling his father that the garden here has many toxic plants.'

'He's eight years old. He knows nothing.'

'It might still be worth asking him what he meant.'

'In other words, there's more to this than meets the eye.' Fraser had spoken without thinking. He glanced at Voltaire's disfigured face. 'Sorry!'

'We are not expected for another hour,' Pünd said. 'So I will return to my room, where I have work to do. You have your car, Monsieur Voltaire?'

'It's waiting by the door.'

'Then I will meet you there.'

*

No-one was in sight when they reached the Chateau Belmar, shortly before eleven o'clock. The sun was beating down on an empty garden where the fountain was splashing magnificently but a little forlornly at the centre. Nor was there any sign of Lambert's car. Given the splendour of the house and grounds, the tropical weather and the soft whisper of the sea, it was almost impossible to believe that less than forty-eight hours before, this had been the scene of a murder.

147

As they got out of the car, the front door opened and Robert Waysmith appeared, dressed in a dark suit for the reading of the will. He looked briefly over his shoulder, then moved down to join them.

'Monsieur Voltaire, gentlemen . . .' He drew a breath. 'I was wondering if I could have a quick word with you before you went in.'

'There is something that concerns you?' Pünd asked. He could see that Robert was worried. He had also taken care to make sure that he wasn't being watched or overheard.

'I just wanted to apologise to you for yesterday. The way my father behaved . . .'

'He was a man who had just received a great shock.' Pünd's tone was forgiving. 'I am quite sure he did not mean to give offence.'

'He was extraordinarily rude to you. I don't know what he said after he sent me away, but I just wanted to tell you that he's nothing like the man you met. He's looked after me ever since my mother died. Yes, he can be difficult if he doesn't get his own way. He likes to be in control. I was terrified of him when I was a child! But he's also a reasonable man and, underneath it all, he very much loved my stepmother. So I suppose what I'm saying is, please don't judge him too harshly. Once you get to know him, he's not quite the monster you think.'

There was the sound of a second car arriving and Pünd turned to see Lambert and his secretary arriving in their grey Citroën.

'You go ahead,' Robert muttered. 'I'd better see to them.'

They went their separate ways, Voltaire entering the house

148

with Pünd and Fraser close behind. There was no sign of Béatrice. They entered the main vestibule and walked towards the back of the house, passing the open door of the *petit salon*. Pünd heard a soft chiming and looked into the room. Sure enough, there was an oak grandfather clock, elegantly curved, standing against the far wall. He turned back towards the main entrance, now some distance behind him.

'Do you see Monsieur Lambert?' he asked.

Fraser turned round. There was nobody there. 'The solicitor? No. I think he's still outside.'

Pünd smiled. 'That is exactly my point.'

'Honestly, Mr Pünd. You really are quite unfathomable at times.'

Pünd smiled to himself. Voltaire was waiting for them and they moved forward to join him.

The *grand salon* had been prepared for the reading of the will.

Two wooden seats had been placed behind a heavy ornamental card table that had been pressed into service as a reading desk and faced the family, who were both actors in the drama that was to follow and its audience. They were already seated, spread across a variety of sofas and chairs.

Jeffrey and Lola Chalfont – both wearing black – were next to each other on one side of the room, an angry-looking Cedric leaning between them.

'Why can't I stay?' he was complaining with the face of every eight-year-old who can't get what he wants.

'Because this is for grown-ups,' Lola told him.

'But Granny may have left me money in her will.'

'If she has, we'll tell you.'

149

Harry and Judith Lyttleton were on the other side, and as Pünd entered, it seemed to him that Judith was as nervous as she had been when he met her at the clinic in London. Elmer Waysmith was sitting on his own in a straight-backed chair near the door to the garden, separate from the rest of the family, his eyes focused on something in the distance. In some ways he seemed to be in control of everything that was about to happen, but at the same time, he was on the very fringes, an outsider.

Three more chairs had been set out for Pünd, Fraser and Voltaire. These were in front of the fireplace and as he sat down, Pünd noticed there was a new artwork above the mantel. The vase of tulips painted by Paul Cézanne had been removed and replaced by a very ordinary landscape. He wondered when this had happened – and why.

There was a stir in the room as Robert Waysmith came in with the *avocat* and his secretary. Alice Carling nodded at Robert, then sat down at the table, next to her employer. She took out a series of typewritten documents, which she placed in front of him. For his part, Robert drew up a seat near his father.

The moment had arrived.

'Good morning,' Lambert began. As always, and despite the hot weather, he was wearing a formal suit. He took out his pince-nez and balanced them on his nose. 'I wish to express my condolences to all of you in this room . . . which is to say, Monsieur Waysmith and the family. We all loved and admired Lady Chalfont and although we had of course prepared ourselves for her loss, it is almost impossible to believe it has occurred and in such terrible circumstances. I will go so far as to say that I find it most upsetting that we have the police here today on this melancholy and private occasion. However, it makes no difference to my work, which is to inform you of Lady Chalfont's last wishes, so I will make no further reference to it. And I will be brief.'

He glanced at the first page in front of him.

'We must begin with the estate of Chalfont Hall in the county of Norfolk in England – the manor house itself, along with its contents and the five hundred acres of land, the various farm buildings, the tied cottages, the hunting lodge, the chapel and the two pavilions, all passed down to the seventh Earl, Jeffrey Chalfont, following the death of his father. This is a result of the male-only primogeniture system, which has been in place for many hundreds of years. As I am sure you are aware, there is also an entail which forbids the sale or division of the property. The income from the land and the tied cottages have also passed directly to the seventh Earl.

'We therefore arrive at the considerable fortune which Lady Chalfont inherited from her first husband. There is this property. The house in St James's, London. The private bank and funds. All of these together total approximately nine hundred thousand pounds sterling. I also have here the details of stocks and shares and other investments, which, when brought into consideration, will double that figure.'

'So when do we get it?' Jeffrey asked, his hands folded on his belly and a scowl on his face.

Lambert's eyes narrowed behind his pince-nez. It was as close as he allowed himself to come to contempt. 'I spoke at length to your mother last summer,' he said. 'She made certain arrangements that she wished to explain to you herself. To that end, she wrote a final communication witnessed by myself and Mademoiselle Carling in my office.'

Alice Carling had already produced a handwritten letter, a single sheet of paper, which she removed from an envelope. She passed it to the *avocat*, who read:

'"I have come to a decision with respect to my will and I want it to be known that it is, without any question, my decision and mine alone. I do this without malice and with only the best intentions. I am very fond of all the young people who make up my immediate family and wish to care for them, but I sometimes question their judgement. Wealth is a great blessing, but it is my opinion that it can be destructive, if placed in the wrong hands."'

There was an eerie silence in the room as Lady Chalfont's last words, spoken from beyond the grave and interpreted by the elderly solicitor, hung in the air. Nobody spoke. But Jeffrey and Harry were already frowning.

'"I am leaving the sum of twenty thousand pounds to my son, Jeffrey Chalfont, and his wife, Lola. I am leaving the same amount to my daughter, Judith, and her husband, Harry. Cedric will receive his parcel of twenty thousand pounds when he turns twenty-one, the money being held for him by Monsieur Lambert until he reaches that age. My stepson, Robert, will also receive ten thousand pounds.

'"Apart from a few small bequests, which are listed separately, I am leaving the rest of my estate to my dear Elmer, who has been my rod and my staff since the day we met, who has never left my side and who gave me new life after the tragic loss of my beloved Henry. It is not my intention to enrich him personally. He has no need of that. It is more to protect my family that I ask him to be the custodian of my wealth. I am relying on him to provide the guidance and financial support that are needed now I am no longer there, and I end my time in this world with the comfort that the ones I love will always be cared for."'

Lambert lowered the letter. 'That is the end of her personal communication,' he announced.

'Can I see that?' Jeffrey Chalfont had already got to his feet and almost snatched the letter out of the solicitor's hand. There were red blotches on both his cheeks and as he read his mother's handwriting, his eyes were bright with anger. It took him only a few seconds to gauge that the document was authentic. He turned and glared at his stepfather. 'Did you put her up to this?' he demanded.

'Your mother knew exactly what she was doing,' Elmer replied tautly.

'That's not true.' Harry leapt to the defence of his friend. 'You had her round your little finger, Elmer. You controlled everything she did. You probably only married her to get your hands on her money.'

'That's a disgusting lie.'

'I don't understand!' Judith complained. 'Twenty thousand pounds. Mother supported my work and what I'm trying to do. She promised me she'd help.'

'It is a considerable amount of money, Madame Chalfont,' Lambert assured her.

'You don't understand. I'm fighting an entire country. I can't do it on my own.'

'Why do I get half as much as everyone else?' Robert

asked, addressing his father. 'Is that how she saw me? Only half as good as the rest of this family?'

Elmer lost his patience. 'What makes any of you think you deserved anything! Look at you! She hasn't been dead forty-eight hours and you're already squabbling over her cash. Twenty thousand is more than many people earn in a lifetime, but it's not good enough for you. However much she left you, you'd want more.'

'Twenty thousand is one tenth of what you're getting,' Lola reminded him archly.

'I'm not going to argue with you . . . not with any of you.' Elmer got to his feet. 'The will is legal, signed and sealed, with Mr Lambert and Miss Carling as witnesses. I suggest you stop sniping and listen to the rest of it.' He suddenly swung round to face Pünd and Voltaire. 'Have you seen enough?' he demanded. 'I guess you wanted to be here to see for yourself what a pack of jackals we have in this house. Well, it should be more than enough for you. Maybe you can give us a little privacy so that we can continue tearing each other apart.'

Pünd glanced at Voltaire, who nodded briefly, once. With Fraser following them, they got up and left.

*

Once they were back in the sunlight, Voltaire took out a cigarette and a matchbook he might have picked up in Nice. Fraser noticed the words HÔTEL LAFAYETTE written on the cover. That presumably was where he was staying. Voltaire smoked awkwardly, his hand a claw, his fingers not quite up to the task of holding the fragile paper tube. 'This is a most horrible family,' he said. 'It is obvious to me that one of them killed Lady Chalfont for her wealth. As much as they complain, twenty thousand pounds is a huge amount of money. Any one of them could have added the poison to her tea.'

'But if she was about to change her will . . .?'

'Then Elmer Waysmith would be the obvious suspect.' Voltaire blew grey-blue smoke into the air. 'That still remains a strong possibility. Unfortunately, we have no proof that this is what she intended, as she was dead before her solicitor arrived.' He threw down the cigarette and ground it out. 'My driver will take you back to the hotel.'

'And you, Monsieur Voltaire?'

'There are one hundred and twenty-seven pharmacists in Nice, Cannes and the surrounding area. One of them must have supplied the aconitine. That is what I am investigating, Herr Pünd. Everything else is speculation.'

He walked away.

'May I ask something?' Fraser said.

'Of course, my dear James.'

'Well, it seems to me that it has to be Elmer Waysmith who killed his wife. After all, she did write to you saying that she suspected he'd been up to no good. That would have given her a reason to cut him out of her will and he could have overheard her calling her solicitor.'

'And what of the rest of the family?'

'Well, it's clearly the case that they needed the money. I wouldn't say no to twenty thousand pounds myself! But they were going to get it anyway. Maybe in a few days. Maybe in a few weeks. All they had to do was wait.'

Pünd smiled. 'Ah, yes. It is the question that comes up again and again.'

'Why murder a woman who is already dying?'

'Exactly, James. And I will give you the obvious answer, because it is, I believe, the key to everything that has happened.'

'Why, then?'

'Because, my friend, it does not matter.'

The First Anagram

That was where the manuscript ended.

The sun had sunk out of sight while I was reading and my little garden was cast in a bluish-green light. I could imagine Hero and Leander circling each other in the shadows. I would have to read the whole thing again before I met Eliot Crace, but already I was wondering if it would be a good idea to meet him at all. I remembered what Michael Flynn had told me. Eliot knew I was being brought in to work on the manuscript and he was 'very excited' and wanted to see me as soon as possible – but was he making a mistake?

I poured myself another glass of wine and considered.

Writers aren't like other people. All those hours spent alone, obsessing about every word, can make them neurotic, nervous, needy or – like Alan Conway – plain nasty. When you think about it, all the odds are stacked against them. There are around two hundred thousand books published in the UK every year (as many as a million in the USA), and how many of them do you really think are going to end up on the front table at Waterstones? According to the Authors' Licensing and Collecting Society, the average salary earned by a novelist is just seven thousand pounds a year, which makes a nurse or a librarian look rich. I've seen it often enough. The excitement of a new writer when they're told that their book is going to be published, followed by the dawning realisation that it's not the end of the journey or even the beginning. They've just been invited to stand on the platform and wait for a train that may never arrive.

This had been Eliot's experience. The two books he had written about his Elizabethan detective, Dr Gee, had both misfired. *Gee for Gunfire* and *Gee for Graveyard* had been well-enough written, they'd looked good, they had a semifamous name on the cover and we'd managed to get a bit of advance publicity – but they hadn't connected with the public. We'd tried to find excuses, but the sales figures had spoken for themselves. Six months after the second book appeared, it was all over. The shelves in the warehouses had been cleared. As for the books themselves, the covers would have been torn off and the pages pulped, chemically cleaned and recycled. This is the humiliating end for so many writers' dreams – to be turned into somebody else's. Crace hadn't written anything since.

My first reaction to what I'd read so far was that he stood a much better chance of success this time round. He'd certainly captured the voice of Alan Conway and there was a lot in the book that I liked. Naturally enough, I had plenty of thoughts – but was this the right time to be sharing them?

An editorial meeting with a young writer is like dancing with someone with three feet. You have to be so careful not to trip them up, not to shatter their confidence, which, like the pages of their manuscript, may be paper-thin. It's such a strange relationship. Who is in control? In those early days, it's the editor who offers experience and professionalism, who knows the market and can guide the book to the success it so obviously deserves. The author has dreams, but the editor has plans. And at the end of the day, it's the editor who chooses the book and who pays for it. If new writers have one thing in common, it's gratitude.

It's only when the books become successful that things change – and this was exactly what had happened with Alan Conway. As soon as he started selling in large numbers and had his awards and the freedom of the city of Heidelberg under his belt, he decided that Cloverleaf needed him more than he needed Cloverleaf. And the worst of it was that he had a point. I dreaded meeting him because he was so unpleasant to work with: I disliked him and needed him in equal measure. Charles Clover had to take over, and what good did that do? In the end, the whole business burned down.

I didn't think it was a good idea to meet Eliot before the book was finished for a whole host of reasons.

First of all, how can you possibly judge a whodunnit before you've read the end? Thirty thousand words in, it looked almost certain to me that Lady Chalfont had been murdered by her second husband. Elmer Waysmith wasn't a particularly pleasant character and he was the one who had the most to lose if she'd gone ahead and changed her will. He'd had to act quickly. His wife had overheard something and had telephoned Jean Lambert, the solicitor, who had turned up at the house on the very day she died.

But if Elmer did turn out to be the killer, I'd be disappointed.

It would be too obvious and it really wouldn't matter how well or badly the book was written. The whole thing would fall flat and that would get it a kicking on Goodreads and the other critical websites. From my experience, I'd say that people who enjoy crime fiction and who form communities all over the internet are the most discerning – and the most unforgiving – of all readers. Do you think *Murder on the Orient Express* would have become one of the greatest mysteries of all time if the train driver had done it?

That might be an argument for getting in early, before it was too late, but there was a real danger that if I started asking too many questions, I might accidentally tear up everything Eliot had done so far. I remembered the sensitive, unpredictable young man I'd met all those years ago. Michael had said that he'd settled down since then, but I didn't want to take any chances. There was an extremely tight deadline hanging over us. The book was wanted early in the New Year, which meant getting the proofs out by October at the latest. That was only four months away.

There was another question clouding my mind. Even before I'd accepted the manuscript, I'd had misgivings about editing it. Alan Conway might be dead, but his ghost lived on, as malevolent as ever. Reading *Pünd's Last Case*, I'd felt him standing at my shoulder and I'd begun to wonder if Eliot Crace wasn't playing exactly the same mind games that had got me into so much trouble before.

It had begun with an anagram. I'd spotted it almost immediately – it wasn't difficult. Eliot Crace's grandmother, Miriam Crace, had lived at Marble Hall.

Marble Hall.

The Chateau *Belmar*.

I wondered to what extent Eliot had based the characters living in the South of France on his own family. If I met him, I could ask him, of course, but I wasn't sure I wanted to know. If my experience with Alan Conway had taught me anything it was that I was better off keeping my distance from writers, especially the ones who wanted to get their revenge on the world.

My mobile rang.

I picked it up and glanced at the screen. It was Michael Flynn, still at work, even though it was after six o'clock.

'Hello, Susan. I was wondering how you were getting along with the book.'

'I've just finished it.'

'That's quick. What do you think?'

'I think it's very good. I mean, the characters are believable. It's great that we get to the murder after just a few chapters. That's when things start motoring. He's certainly managed to capture Atticus Pünd. I do have some questions, though . . .'

'That's the reason I'm calling. I just spoke to Eliot. I told him you had the manuscript and he's very keen to meet you to get your thoughts. He wondered if you'd be around tomorrow? We could give you a room in the office.'

'Well . . .'

'Will eleven o'clock work for you?'

There were so many things I could have said. I'd had enough of Atticus Pünd and never wanted to go near him again. I didn't even really want to work on murder mysteries. Couldn't he find a nice, cheerful historical romance set in nineteenth-century England with couples romping in hay wains or dancing the quadrille and nobody being killed? But I needed the job. I wanted to be taken on as a full-time editor. I didn't really have a choice.

'I'll see you then,' I said. And hung up.

Eliot Crace

It was half past ten when I walked into Causton Books the following day. I'd texted Michael Flynn and told him I was coming early and I think he understood why. It all goes back to the relationship between the editor and the writer. I needed Eliot to feel that I was part of the publishing house – or at least had its authority behind me. I wasn't sure to what extent we were going to talk about the manuscript at this first meeting. It might just be one of those getting-to-know-you encounters over coffee and biscuits in the canteen. But either way, it would make it much easier for me if I got there ahead of him and didn't look as if I'd just wandered in off the street. For the same reason, I'd asked Michael to set me up in an office, not a conference room. I didn't care if it was the size of a storage cupboard. I wanted Eliot to feel I belonged there.

I didn't see Michael, as it turned out. He was locked in meetings until lunchtime, but his PA – Sandra – showed me to a neat corner office on the same floor as last time. It had a table, two chairs, a sofa and enough books to feel lived-in.

They'd left me a couple of notepads and a flask of coffee on the side.

'Is there anything else you need?' Sandra asked with a bright smile.

'No. Thank you. Just let me know when Eliot arrives.'

An hour later, I was still waiting.

Eliot Crace was late. I wasn't quite sure what to make of this, but all in all I was bloody annoyed. So much for the new, reformed Eliot! He was the one who had asked for this meeting and it was quite a slap in the face to leave me sitting here on my own. I tried to ignore the various staff members passing and glancing in through the glass door, wondering who I was as I sat there twiddling my thumbs. I forced myself to stay calm. I'll give him another five minutes and then I'll walk away, I told myself. Five minutes passed. All right – five more minutes and that's it. I might have sat there like that all day.

But then Sandra appeared at the door. 'He's just coming up.'

'Thanks.' I hoped my irritation didn't show.

The lift doors opened and suddenly he was there, moving hurriedly through the open-plan area towards me.

First – his appearance. He'd been in his early twenties when I'd first met him and now he was thirty-two and married. He was still a striking figure, with thick fair hair reaching down to his collar and sculpted features, even if he had lost some of his boyish good looks. He had filled out a bit. I wouldn't have said he was fat, but he could certainly have done with a bit of time in the gym. He was wearing designer jeans and trainers, a shirt with a grandfather collar, the sleeves half rolled up. He had that mix of innocence and energy that I remembered, reflected in his intense blue eyes. I had to admit it was the sort of face that would look great on a back cover: a son to any mother, a star on social media, a serious thinker for anyone looking for an intelligent read.

'Oh God, Susan. I'm late. I'm sorry.' He was talking even before he'd come through the door. 'Someone's thrown themselves under a tube and the whole Central line is shut down. I had to get a cab and it took for ever.'

A small part of me wondered if he was telling the truth. After all, I had just read the same thing in the first section of his book: Elmer Waysmith's first wife had died that way. But Eliot was doing his best to be charming and I didn't want to set our relationship off on the wrong foot.

'Please don't worry about it,' I said. 'I'm very glad to see you again. It's been a while.'

'Yes. I heard all about Charles and what happened at Cloverleaf. I couldn't believe it.' He threw himself into the nearest chair, which swivelled round as it took his weight. 'Is it really true he tried to kill you?'

'I'm afraid so.'

'And he killed Alan Conway.'

'Yes.'

'It's incredible. Charles was so kind to me when I was writing the Dr Gee books, and when they didn't work, he couldn't have been more supportive. He and Elaine were almost like parents to me. I was always in and out of their house. And he was about the gentlest person I ever met. It's hard to believe he had it in him.'

'He put me in hospital, Eliot. And he pushed Alan off a tower.'

'I know. I know. I'm not doubting you. And I'm sorry. It must have been horrible for you. It's just that when you've known someone almost all your life, you think you have an idea about them. And when I heard he was going to prison . . . it turned my world upside down.'

He was already on the defensive. This wasn't at all how I'd wanted the meeting to go. 'I can understand that,' I said. 'Charles was kind to me too, and I was probably as shocked as you were. I hope all this past history won't make it difficult for you and me to work together, because I really liked the pages you sent.' A thought struck me quite suddenly. 'I didn't know you'd already met Charles when we commissioned your novels.'

'He worked with my grandmother in the last couple of years before she died. He often came to Marble Hall.'

That made sense. Charles had worked at Jonathan Cape, who had originally published *The Little People*. It was strange that he had never mentioned knowing Eliot Crace. Perhaps he'd been worried that I would question his editorial judgement, commissioning books from someone who was effectively a friend.

'So you liked what I've written so far?' Eliot went on.

'I think you've done a terrific job and I can't wait to read more.' It looked as if we were about to get down to the nuts and bolts, but I wasn't ready yet. I still hadn't quite got the measure of him. 'Would you like some coffee?' I asked.

'Yeah. Thanks. Black.'

'How long have you been working on the story?'

'Oh God. I started in March. It took me ages to think up the plot.'

'You've got it all worked out now?'

'I know who did it, if that's what you mean.' Eliot took out a vape and sucked on it, but I noticed that his fingernails were yellow, so he must smoke cigarettes too. 'You never really liked Alan Conway, did you?' he said, changing the subject.

'Did Charles tell you that?'

Eliot nodded.

'I tried to like him, but Alan hated writing murder mysteries and that made him difficult to work with. But I'd say that we got on well enough and that I helped make the books a success. You know he sold eighteen million copies.'

'Do you think I will too?'

'I think there's a good chance.' I had poured two cups of coffee. I brought them over to the table and sat down opposite Eliot. My copy of his manuscript was in my bag, but I didn't bring it out. I didn't want him to see the comments and the underlining. 'How far have you got?' I asked.

'I've done about another ten thousand words.'

'Are you enjoying writing it?'

He gave me a peculiar smile. 'Very much.'

'It shows. You've got a lovely lightness of touch and I liked some of the jokes. Fraser mistranslating things, for example. I think if Alan were alive, he'd be impressed.'

'If Alan were alive, I wouldn't have been given the gig.'

'That's true.' I paused for a moment. 'You were the one who asked to see me, Eliot. And I'm very happy that we're meeting face-to-face. I like to get to know all my authors. Have you shown the pages to anyone else?'

'Gillian has seen them.' I looked at him enquiringly. 'My wife.'

Michael Flynn had suggested marriage had helped Eliot settle down, but there was something about the way he spoke those two words, and the cold smile that accompanied them, that made me wonder how close the two of them were.

'She doesn't really read murder mysteries,' he went on. 'But she said it was good.'

'It is good and I'm looking forward to reading the rest of it.'

'Do you have any notes?'

'Notes?'

'Is there anything you want me to change?' He was completely good-humoured, sitting there, cradling his coffee cup, but still I wondered if he wasn't challenging me in some way.

'I'm not sure I really want to give you notes right now,' I countered. 'Of course, I have some thoughts, but I wouldn't want to interrupt your flow. Wouldn't you prefer to get to the end? Then we can look at everything in context.'

'Actually, I'd like to hear them now.' He paused. 'They'd really help.'

Again, there was something in that smile of his I found unsettling. It was on the edge of insolence, and remembering how long I had been sitting there, waiting for him, I was tempted to get up and walk out. But I wasn't the sort to throw in the towel and I decided that I wasn't going to be mucked around by a writer half my age, especially one who had never written a novel that had come anywhere near success. I remembered what Michael Flynn had told me when he gave me the job. He wanted me to hold on to the reins. Like it or not, we'd already reached the defining moment in what would be our working relationship. This was where I took control.

'All right,' I said. 'I'll give you my thoughts if you really want them – but they are only thoughts. You have to trust your instincts, Eliot. This is your book. I'm only here to support you.'

'Go on.'

'Well, let's start with the title.' I felt on safe ground here. '*Pünd's Last Case*. Are you sure you're happy with that?'

He shrugged. 'I don't see anything wrong with it.'

'I wonder if you've thought it through. You must know that Causton have signed a three-book deal with Alan Conway's estate. How are you going to write two more books if Atticus Pünd dies?'

'I thought he might get better.'

'Then why is this his last case?'

'He thinks it's his last case. That's all that matters.'

'OK. But I don't think you should break faith with your readers and I'm sure you can come up with something better. Also,' I quickly moved on, 'I did find the opening chapter a little depressing, if I'm going to be honest with you. Atticus is seeing his doctor about a fatal brain tumour. He meets a woman who has a fatal heart condition. They both have weeks to live. It's not exactly a barrel of laughs.' I smiled, trying to make light of it.

'That's the story, Susan. It's how they meet. If I take that out, I've got nothing left.'

'I'm not asking you to take it out, but there are plenty of other ways they could meet. You need to think of someone reading the first page in a bookshop. Do you want to depress them or do you want them to buy the book? All that rain! You mention the rain six times in the first two paragraphs. This is meant to be an entertainment. It isn't *Bleak House*.'

Eliot reached into his back pocket and drew out a notebook and a biro. He laid them on the table and wrote the single word: RAIN. 'OK,' he said. 'What else?'

This really wasn't what I'd intended, but now that I'd started, I couldn't stop myself. 'Well, this may sound like a huge note, but it isn't. It's more of a question. Are you sure about the South of France setting?'

That threw him. 'What's wrong with it?'

'There's nothing wrong with the way you've written it. I think you've described it very well. I love the Chateau Belmar and the descriptions of Nice and Cap Ferrat. But I do wonder if you aren't creating problems for yourself. For example, it doesn't make a lot of sense for Margaret Chalfont to use a French solicitor to draw up her will rather than someone in London or Norfolk. Elmer Waysmith dividing his time between art galleries in Nice and London doesn't feel completely realistic either. Are you saying that the gallery in Nice is closed for the whole of winter? I'm getting a sense of disconnection. The family is tied to England, but they seem to be spending a lot of time in France. Who's looking after the estate while Jeffrey Chalfont is away?'

'That's the whole point. He's not interested in the estate.'

'I understand that. But he doesn't have very much to do, lounging around in Cap Ferrat.'

'He gambles.'

'He's a good character, Eliot, and I like the gambling. But you have a lot of foreign characters and you're having to work in two languages. Sometimes that makes things complicated. Take the scene in the pharmacy, for example. You have a pharmacist who speaks only French, dealing with a customer who speaks English with an American accent. Then a Frenchwoman comes in and she also speaks in French, but she talks to the customer who's English, so you have to translate everything word for word. It seems quite a cumbersome way to get across the point, which I suppose is the time of day.'

'So where would you prefer me to set it? The Isle of Wight?'

'I think that would be a very good setting, since you mention it. It would certainly make life a lot easier for you.'

'That scene in the pharmacy only works *because* it's in French,' Eliot said, quite tetchy now. 'You may not have noticed, but the woman who comes in tutoyers, which is to say, she uses the informal "*tu*" form of address.'

'I hadn't noticed,' I admitted. 'And I wonder how many of your readers will have A-level French?'

'It's a clue.'

'Well, it doesn't matter now, but it may be something you want to think about.' I waved the conversation away. 'What's a cassone, by the way?' There was one in Judith's bedroom.

'It's a wooden chest.'

'And a Mazarin bureau?'

'It's nineteenth century, French, with marquetry.'

'You seem to know a lot about furniture.'

'I had a job in an auction house.'

'Well, they're nice details, but – again – they could be a bit confusing. There's absolutely nothing wrong with using

171

foreign words, but it's a bit like when Margaret Chalfont quotes in German on page four. Adding a translation as a footnote is a bit of a distraction.'

Eliot added a second word to his notes. GOETHE. 'Anything else?'

I'd said enough. 'I really think you should keep going, Eliot. You're doing a great job and the reason I came in today was to get to know you, not to start deconstructing the book. You obviously know what you're doing and I can't wait to read the next section, if you still want to show it to me. But my advice would be to get to the end before we meet again.' I stopped as one other thought occurred to me. 'There is something else I wanted to ask you, though,' I said.

'And what's that?'

'I noticed the name of the house in Cap Ferrat. The Chateau Belmar.' I waited for him to speak, but when he said nothing, I filled in the blank. 'It's an anagram of "Marble".'

He smiled at that, but not in a pleasant way. It was rapidly dawning on me that Eliot Crace – young, good-looking, talented, laid-back, wealthy – was, as I had expected, trouble.

'I see you've picked up a few tricks from Alan Conway,' I went on. 'Is there anything else hidden in the novel that I should know about?'

'I don't know what you mean.'

'Well, your grandmother lived in Marble Hall. I was wondering if you've partly based Margaret Chalfont on her.'

'What makes you think that?'

'Your Miriam Crace died of a heart attack and Margaret Chalfont has a heart condition. They also have the same initials. It's none of my business, and I don't want to dig into your family history, but I'm sure you'll understand that, after my experiences with Alan Conway, I'm not too keen on literary secrets.'

'Alan used anagrams.'

'And acrostics. I hate to mention it again, but that's why Charles pushed him off that tower.'

'Are you going to push me off a tower, Susan?' He smiled, as if to reassure me that he was only joking.

I leaned forward and looked him straight in the eye. 'You're a very good writer, Eliot, and I like the first part of your book. But I'm not prepared to go through all that again. If you're keeping secrets from me and from your readers, if there are nasty messages hidden between the lines, then I'm afraid you're going to have to find another editor. Life's too short.'

'Michael Flynn says you're the best.'

'That's very kind of him.'

'He says that you were the one who made Alan Conway successful.'

'Alan Conway made Alan Conway successful. But it's true that I helped.'

'I want you to work on the book. I mean – I'll be very grateful if you'll help me, and I'll think about what you've said.'

'Are you writing about your family?' I asked.

He reached for his vape and sucked in the steam and the nicotine. I saw the light glow between his fingers. 'I grew up in Marble Hall,' he said eventually. 'I hated it there. Yes, Lady Chalfont is inspired a little bit by my grandmother. And my father is in there too. You could say that Cedric is me. But doesn't every author base some of their characters on people they know in real life?'

'A few of them do. But not out of a sense of malice or because they want revenge.'

'Are you talking about me or Alan Conway?'

'I hope I'm just talking about Alan Conway. If you're using this book as a weapon, you're the one who could end up getting hurt.'

Eliot glanced at his watch. 'Do you mind if we talk about this another time?' he asked. 'I don't feel completely comfortable doing it here. And I'm meeting someone for lunch.'

'Fine,' I said. But I'll admit I was a little thrown. He'd cut short the time we had together by arriving so late and now he was on his way out.

He must have sensed he'd offended me. 'Why don't you come over for dinner next week?' he asked. 'You should meet Gillian – and if you're really interested, I can show you some stuff about the family.'

'I'd like that, Eliot.'

'Are you leaving now?'

'Yes. I've got nothing more to do here.'

'Then we can go down together,' he said.

We left the room and walked over to the lift. You needed an electronic pass to go up, but we pressed the button for the ground floor and the doors slid shut.

'You're right about France,' he said as we travelled down. 'I have no idea what the Grand-Hôtel looked like in 1955, although my mother once told me there was a funicular railway going down to the pool. I don't know what they'd have served for breakfast. I've looked up Nice on Google Earth, but I'm sure it's completely different now. I've made half of it up. Do you think I need to get someone to do the research?'

'Let's leave that until the book is finished,' I said. 'A copy editor will spot any major errors further down the line. But you really have done a good job. Just keep going.'

That pleased him. We were both slightly more at ease with each other by the time we reached the ground floor.

But then we walked through the security barriers.

There was a woman waiting for him on the other side, sitting on a sofa. She stood up as we approached and we recognised each other instantly. I stared at her, then glanced at Eliot, furious with him, knowing that for his own dark, Alan Conway reasons, he had done this on purpose. He had set me up.

The woman was Elaine Clover. It was her husband, Charles, who had tried to kill me and who was now in prison because of me.

Eliot smiled. 'I think you two know each other,' he said.

Old Friends

'Yes, we're old friends,' Elaine said, also smiling. 'How are you, Susan? I was wondering when I'd see you again.'

Standing there in the reception area of Causton Books, with Jeanette in the background and people passing in and out on their way to lunch or whatever, I was feeling so many conflicting emotions that I wasn't sure how to react. First and foremost, I was furious with Eliot. It was obvious that he had led me, quite deliberately, into a trap. He had suggested I come down with him in the lift. Why? He knew about my history with Elaine. Did he want to humiliate me or was this his way of putting me in my place? I was forced to re-evaluate everything I'd thought about him in our meeting. He'd had an edge to him – that much was sure. But I hadn't thought of him as deliberately malicious. This scene he'd set up was something that would have delighted Alan Conway.

And then there was Elaine herself. She must have known that I was on my way because she hadn't shown any surprise. So the two of them had planned this together. Again, I had to ask myself – why? I'd seen Elaine many times when Charles

176

and I were working together. I'd been to dinner at her house. The last time we'd been together, though, had been at the Old Bailey in London when I had been the star witness in her husband's trial. At that time, we had studiously avoided each other's eyes.

The last few years must have been traumatic and I could see it now in the heavy make-up she was wearing, which didn't quite disguise the lines that had insinuated themselves around her eyes and mouth. She had aged, certainly. Otherwise, she was much as I remembered her, smartly dressed, with a designer handbag on her arm, expensive jewellery and immaculate silver hair . . . although it had been light brown at the time of the trial. She was about ten years older than me, with two daughters who must be in their early thirties by now. I wondered how they had reacted to everything that had happened. It hadn't been my fault, but the truth was that I had destroyed this family and I was waiting for her to scream at me, to slap me, even to pull out a knife and stab me. If she had, I wouldn't have entirely blamed her.

She surprised me. Before I could say anything, she reached forward with both hands and took hold of my arms. 'Please don't be cross with Eliot,' she said. 'I asked him not to tell you I was meeting him here.'

'Why?'

'Because I knew you wouldn't want to see me.' Her grip tightened and to my astonishment I saw tears in her eyes. 'I am so sorry about what happened, Susan. I feel so ashamed. When they told me what Charles had done, at first I refused to believe it. You have no idea what this has done to the family . . . his parents, the girls, me.'

177

'You don't blame me for what happened?'

'You were the victim in all this. He nearly killed you!' Elaine took a deep breath. 'I saw you that day in court, but Charles's lawyers said I couldn't talk to you. Afterwards, I wanted to write to you, but you'd already left Crouch End and gone to Crete and I wasn't sure you'd want to hear from me.'

At the edge of my vision, I saw Eliot glance at his watch. It was a vintage Rolex on a leather strap – perhaps inherited and certainly valuable. I didn't think he cared about the time. It was a signal that he wanted to leave.

Elaine saw it too. 'I can't talk now,' she said. 'Will you come to the house, Susan? Do you still have your old MG?'

'Yes. I never got rid of it.'

'Then you could drive over. I feel we have so much to talk about. We were friends once and maybe we can be again. Or if you felt uncomfortable coming there, we could meet in a bar or a restaurant in town.'

'Are you still at the same address?' I asked.

Elaine was still holding on to me, as if she was afraid I would run away. 'Oh yes,' she said. 'I thought about moving. All the fuss. Reporters on the doorstep. Everyone in the street knows what Charles did and they'll never forget. But it's the family home. The girls grew up there and they didn't want me to leave.' Finally, she released me. 'Can I text you – maybe later today? You've never been out of my thoughts, Susan. It was terrible what he did to you.'

'Of course you can contact me,' I said, although I wasn't exactly happy about the idea. Did I want to be dragged back into a past I'd spent the last few years trying to forget?

But perhaps she was right. Perhaps, together, we could put everything behind us. 'You know how much I liked Charles,' I went on. 'I never wanted any of it to happen.'

'We should go,' Eliot said.

'Yes.' Elaine looked at me one last time, her expression somewhere between gratitude and dismay.

Then she let go of me and they left together.

*

I took the tube home and all the way there, rattling through the tunnels, I thought about what had happened.

Eliot first.

You might think that I'd been a little hard on him, questioning the first chapter and suggesting a complete change of location, but in fact I'd been very careful with my criticisms, effectively testing the water. I'd had other quite serious issues that I hadn't mentioned. The whole business of the will, for example, struck me as unoriginal. Agatha Christie must have used the device at least a dozen times and it had been done to death in pretty much every TV detective series I'd ever seen. The scene with the reading of the will was as much a standby of crime fiction as a final chapter with all the suspects gathered in the library. This was just one of the things I'd kept to myself.

There had been plenty of others, but that was hardly surprising. I've been doing my job so long that I find it almost impossible to read any manuscript without visualising the circles and crosses, the asterisks, the underlines, the carets and the brackets that are among the tools of the editor's trade. So, for example, I'd have crossed out the reference to the Nazi concentration camp on page two. I'm not sure a whodunnit is the right place for a casual mention of the Holocaust, and even Atticus Pünd generally preferred not to talk about it. I wasn't sure about the Nazca Lines either: they just seemed wildly out of place.

I was concerned by the characterisations of both Judith Lyttleton and Alice Carling, the first 'stouter' than her mother and the second 'plain'. I'd be the first to defend an author's right to free speech, but the fact is that it's not a good look for a male writer to body-shame his female characters. It just isn't. I also wondered how Dr Benson, who was treating Pünd for a brain tumour, could also be advising Lady Chalfont on her heart condition. How many specialities could one man have?

And so on and so on. At the end of the day, I couldn't order Eliot to make changes, but if I was going to work with him, I needed to find out how far I could push him before he turned against me. Alan Conway was a case in point. I should have known it was all over between us when he'd had a complete meltdown because I'd questioned his use of a semicolon.

How long would it be before Eliot went the same way?

He'd already kept me waiting forty minutes and then excused himself with a story that, frankly, I didn't believe. From the start, he'd been playing with me, and that was most certainly the case when it came to Elaine Clover and our encounter in the reception area. Eliot had set me up quite deliberately. '*Then we can go down together.*' Elaine might have asked him not to tell me she would be there, but he had been a willing participant in what could have turned into an unpleasant scene. Maybe he already knew that she was going to forgive me for her husband's disgrace, but it made no difference. He had played a trick on me and I had found myself in a difficult position. What with the two of them acting in concert, plus Atticus Pünd and Alan Conway watching from the wings, I wondered if there weren't too many shadows from my past closing in on me.

I heard the ping of a text arriving on my mobile.

I picked it up and glanced at the screen. I didn't recognise the number, but I knew at once that the message had been sent by Elaine Clover. I glanced at my watch. It was only two fifteen. Either she was still at the table or her lunch with Eliot must have been a short one.

> So glad we met, Susan. I need to talk
> to you – not just about us. I'm very worried
> about Eliot and Gillian. Will you come to
> supper on Thursday evening? 6 pm?
> Please say you will. Elaine.

Thursday was the day after next. I weighed my phone in the palm of my hand for a few moments, then texted back.

> Yes. Happy to see you and glad we're
> talking. Will see you then. Susan.

And there it was. With a wiggle of a thumb, my fate was sealed.

181

Parsons Green

Just walking up to the house two days later brought back memories. I'd had dinner here with Edna O'Brien, Stephen Fry, Hilary Mantel, Ian McEwan and many more – not all at once, mind you, but Charles Clover had loved to sprinkle famous names amongst his guests. On one occasion, Nigella Lawson had done the cooking. Charles had worked on her first bestseller, *How to Eat*, published in 1998, and also claimed that *Amsterdam*, which had won McEwan the Booker Prize, had been his idea, although he was almost certainly exaggerating about that. The conversation around the well-worn French fruitwood dining table embraced life and literature and it would usually be one or two o'clock in the morning before the first taxis arrived. Charles always served excellent wine and nobody ever drove home.

The house looked the same as I remembered: a neat, red-brick Victorian construction with bay windows, a front garden and four floors, standing at the end of the terrace. Like most of its neighbours, it had been knocked about with skylights above and a basement conversion below, although

I remembered that Charles had baulked at a conservatory. For old times' sake, I'd come by public transport, although I didn't think I'd be drinking heavily tonight.

I rang the bell and heard the opening bars of C. P. E. Bach's 'Solfeggietto'. Charles had recorded himself playing the piano and it must have been odd for Elaine, hearing him every time anyone came to the house. Just for a moment, I expected him to fling open the door, his jacket off, a tea towel tucked into his belt and a glass of wine in his hand. He liked to cook, unless he happened to have a celebrity chef on the guest list, and the meals he prepared were first class. *'Hello, Susan! Come in! Come in!'* I could almost hear his voice. Strait-laced in the office, he turned into a bon viveur when at home, and it was strange to think that he had morphed from that into a convicted murderer. There would certainly be no high-minded conversation or *champignons farcis* where he was now.

The door was opened just a few inches, then closed again. I heard the security chain slide and then it opened fully to reveal Elaine, now dressed in black trousers and T-shirt with a single gold chain around her neck. I was glad that I hadn't put on anything too fancy myself. I'd gone through all the new clothes I'd bought when I got back from Crete, but what do you wear for dinner with a woman whose life you've managed to destroy? I still felt uncomfortable about coming here, and although Charles had always forbidden his guests to bring anything to his dinner parties, I'd decided that I couldn't come empty-handed. I held out a bouquet of flowers and a decent bottle of wine.

Elaine took them with a smile. 'That's very kind of you, Susan, although there was absolutely no need.' She was less nervous than she had been in the office, perhaps because this was her home turf, but the fact that she wouldn't open the door until she knew who was on the other side told me a lot about her state of mind. 'Do come in,' she said.

Nothing had changed. The house was elegant, almost obsessively so. The furniture and lighting were modern eclectic, the colours easy on the eye, the artworks – mainly modern artists – arranged in galleries with very little of the walls left bare. The rooms were well proportioned, with the main living space taking up much of the ground floor and backing onto the garden. The kitchen and eating area were below.

She led me into the living room, with the baby grand piano that Charles had often played sitting in one corner. It was loaded up with family photographs. None of the sofas or armchairs matched. They were scattered around a coffee table and I saw that Elaine had already brought up four champagne glasses and a couple of bowls of olives and crisps.

Four glasses.

'I hope you don't mind . . .' Elaine must have seen the look on my face '. . . I've invited Eliot and Gillian to join us for supper. I'm afraid your meeting at the publisher's was cut short because of me and I thought it might be helpful to you to have some social time with him and his wife. They're not coming until seven, so we can be together a while, just the two of us. Is that all right? I don't want you to feel ambushed a second time.'

'I presume they know I'm here?'

'Oh yes.'

'It'll be nice to meet Gillian.'

184

'Would you like some champagne?'

'Thank you.'

She left the room and went down to the kitchen. I ran my eyes over the books on the shelves (plenty from Cloverleaf, but none by Alan Conway), then wandered over to the piano and examined the photographs, many of them showing Charles and Elaine in happier times: on their wedding day, on holiday, standing with their two teenaged daughters. There was a whole cluster of them, but right in the middle I spotted one of myself, Charles and Elaine, taken at the top of Arthur's Seat in Edinburgh. I remembered the occasion well. It had been the last day of the book festival and we'd decided we'd had enough of talks and signings, so we'd skived off and climbed all the way up in the late-summer heat, only to find ourselves surrounded by about a hundred thousand midges. *'They're even more irritating than the authors.'* It was Charles who had said that. We'd asked a German tourist to take the picture and then we'd climbed down as quickly as we could to find a pub.

I was still holding the photograph when I heard a footfall behind me and saw Elaine standing close by with an open bottle of Moët.

'Edinburgh,' she said.

'I was thinking about the midges.'

'I prefer to remember the Glenmorangie Lasanta.'

She was right. We'd found a pub with a vast range of single malts arranged on mirrored shelves and that was the one the barman had recommended.

'Sit down,' she said.

I perched on one of the sofas and she poured two glasses of

185

champagne. I watched the bubbles chasing each other up the side of the glass, but they did nothing to change my mood. What was I doing here? Did I even want to have dinner with Eliot and his wife?

I shouldn't have come. It wasn't Elaine's fault, but I felt an overpowering sense of guilt and even shame. I thought of Charles pleading with me in his office after he had confessed to the murder of Alan Conway. '*Alan is dead. He was going to die anyway.*' It was true. Alan had terminal cancer. It was one of the reasons he had decided to kill off Atticus Pünd, taking his much-loved detective with him. Charles had asked me to stay silent, not to go to the police – not just for him, but for his family and for everyone who worked at Cloverleaf Books who would lose their jobs when the business closed.

Maybe he'd had a point. It was something I'd never thought about, certainly not in the murder stories I'd edited, but was there any point in locking Charles up for twenty-plus years? It wasn't as if he was a career criminal. In a moment of fury, seeing his whole life's work threatened, he had pushed Alan Conway off the tower of his house, and if I'd been in his shoes, it's just possible that I might have done the same. He hadn't planned what he was going to do and you could hardly call him a danger to society: it was extremely unlikely that he would ever have killed anyone else. Would it have made such a difference to the world at large if I had stayed silent? Certainly, it would have improved my own prospects – considerably. Charles had been planning to retire. I would now be the CEO of Cloverleaf Books with complete editorial freedom and a healthy pay packet.

It would also have made me complicit in Alan Conway's

murder – but the reason I had insisted that Charles call the police and tell them what he had done wasn't as high-minded as that. I had been offended by him. He had been so arrogant, so coldly patronising. Frankly, he had disgusted me. In a way, I'd been as impulsive as he was.

It had done me no good at all. Charles had knocked me to the floor and set fire to the building. I still believe his attempt to kill me was more unforgivable than his attack on Alan because this time he knew exactly what he was doing. He was cowardly and cruel, but in retrospect, I have to say that I was stupid. Charles had given me the opportunity to go along with what he'd done. 'All right,' I could have said. 'Maybe you're right. I never liked Alan very much, he was already dying, and nobody could argue that the world would be a worse place without him. Let me think about it . . .' If I'd said all this, we could have gone down the road to have a drink together and I could have shopped him later. Instead, I'd blithely hoisted myself up onto the moral high ground and had pretty much invited the attack on me that followed. In some respects, I had to admit that I was partly to blame.

Sitting with Elaine in her living room with a glass of champagne warming itself in my hand, I found myself questioning everything I had done. Suddenly I saw an alternative future in which Charles would have been sitting there with us, all of us laughing like we used to, and this sense of emptiness and sadness would have been absent. It was his fault, I had to remind myself. He had brought this on all of us. I had done the right thing.

But I wasn't sure I believed it.

'How is Charles?' I couldn't avoid it. I had to ask.

Elaine shrugged. 'I see him twice a month. It takes quite a bit of getting used to . . . going into that place. Sometimes Laura comes with me, but Gemma finds it very hard.' Those were her two daughters. 'I'm not sure you'd recognise him, Susan. I'm not sure he quite believes what's happened . . . that he's taken it on board. He doesn't look like himself and although we only have an hour together, he doesn't have very much to say. Worse than anything, there's the terrible shame of it all, sitting there in the horrible tracksuit they make him wear, surrounded by disgusting people. And the smell!

'I'm not asking you to feel sorry for him – or for me, for that matter. That's not why I invited you here. I still love him. After he was arrested and he was waiting for his trial, they let him live here. He had to pay some money and surrender his passport, but we had a lot of time together and he said he wanted to divorce me, but I wouldn't have it. He was still my husband, whatever he had done, and although I can't forgive him – his behaviour has ruined all our lives – I hope you won't mind if I say this.

'I don't think he was in his right mind when he attacked you, or when he killed Alan Conway. I'd been married to him for thirty years and I can tell you that I'd never met a less aggressive man. He never so much as raised his voice to me and he wouldn't even watch violent films. You might like to know that he was thoroughly ashamed of himself. He'd wake up in the night, sobbing his eyes out. He wasn't a killer! My feeling is that it was just the pressure of work that made him go mad . . . first with Alan, then with you. He was fighting not just for his own survival but for the whole family, for everything he'd done. That doesn't excuse him. But I'm not going to lie to you and say that I hate him. For better, for worse, for richer, for poorer. I happen to believe in those words.'

'It does you credit.' I regretted the words even as I spoke them. I sounded like a vicar in a country village. I threw back some of the champagne. Perhaps it would be easier to get through the evening if I was drunk.

She noticed my reaction. 'I didn't invite you here to talk about Charles,' she said. 'Do you think we can be friends again, Susan? Not like the old days. Those are gone for ever. But maybe it'll help me to cope with all the changes in my life if I know we don't hate each other.'

I raised my glass. 'How many years have we known each other?' I asked. 'Of course we're friends. None of this was your fault and I completely understand why you still support Charles. Maybe they'll let him out sooner than you think.'

'I want to talk to you about Eliot Crace.'

She refilled both our glasses.

'You have to understand that I've always been very close to Eliot,' Elaine began again. 'When Charles first met him, he was already a very damaged child. That was the year before his grandmother, Miriam Crace, died. I'm sure you know Charles worked on her last two books: *Little Angels* and *Little and Often*. He often had to travel down to Marble Hall in Wiltshire and meet Eliot, who was living there with his brother and sister and their parents – Edward and Amy.

'Charles always used to tell me what a strange place it was. Miriam was in her early eighties, married to her husband, Kenneth, and not in good health. She had a heart condition. But she still ruled over that family with an iron fist. From what Charles said, she was quite a spiteful woman. She forced her family to live at Marble Hall. The children went to local schools. None of them had any choice. She wanted them close to her so that she could have them around her – and control them. She wasn't just a matriarch. She was a tyrant.'

'I'm absolutely amazed,' I interrupted. 'I didn't know any of this. *The Little People* must have sold a billion copies all over the world. If Miriam Crace was some sort of tyrant, you'd have thought that the truth would have come out by now. Charles never said anything – not even when he started publishing Eliot.'

'He wasn't allowed to. Anyone who worked with the estate had to sign an NDA before they were allowed near Marble Hall and I imagine Charles would have got into terrible trouble just for telling me! In fact, he never said anything until she died. Miriam Crace nearly separated from her husband. She dominated her children, bullied the grandchildren, and gave everyone who knew her a bad time. But the family was forced to hide the truth for the same reason they gave in to her demands. They needed the money! You probably know better than I do how much *The Little People* was worth, but if any one of them had gone to the press and blabbed about how much they disliked Granny, they'd have been cutting off their nose to spite their face.'

'What impact did this have on Eliot?' I asked.

'I'm coming to that now. Edward was her younger son and he and his wife, Amy, had three children. In the year 2003, when Miriam died, Roland was seventeen, Julia was fifteen and Eliot was twelve. The older brother, Jonathan, and his wife, Leylah, had one child, a girl called Jasmine. Later, sadly, there was an accident and she died in her twenties.

'Eliot doesn't like talking about his life at Marble Hall, but I do know that he worshipped his older brother and was very close to his sister. The three of them were like a gang or a fellowship.

'As soon as Miriam Crace died, the family went its separate ways. Charles said that they couldn't wait to get out. They had properties all over the country, so Edward and Amy moved with their children to a house in Notting Hill Gate. They sent Eliot to a local prep school and then to the City of London School near St Paul's, which was when things began to go wrong. It wasn't the school's fault. Eliot fell in with the wrong crowd. You know, he'd lived his whole life out in the sticks and maybe London was just too much for him to handle. There were drugs and alcohol, all-night parties and girls, and God knows what else. When he was sixteen, Eliot was expelled and his parents sent him to some sort of crammer in the hope that he would settle down and go to university, but there was never any chance of that. Things went from bad to worse. There was trouble with the police. His uncle Jonathan was running the estate by then and I have no idea how he managed to keep that out of the papers. Miriam Crace's grandson arrested! That would really have made the headlines.'

'Where are his parents now?'

'They're in America. Both his parents are in the art world. Edward was a curator at a gallery in Bath and then at the Wallace Collection here in London. His wife was quite a well-respected portrait painter. They didn't really know how to handle Eliot. Charles said that to start with they overindulged him and then they went too far the other way, trying to rein him in. In the end, Eliot didn't want anything to do with them and when Edward was offered a job at some sort of institute in Miami, he grabbed it with both hands. Roland and Julia were doing all right for themselves and they saw Eliot as a lost cause – so why not?

'Eliot wasted the next few years. He worked in an art gallery and an auction house, and I think he was an estate agent for a time. And then, when he was in his early twenties, he turned up at Cloverleaf Books with a novel he'd written.'

'*Gee for Gunfire.*'

'Yes.'

'Charles said he loved it.'

'He wasn't quite being honest with you, Susan. He remembered Eliot from Marble Hall and knew his story. He was still in touch with Jonathan Crace – for business reasons. He felt sorry for Eliot and wanted to give him a chance.'

'It was good of him.' That was the vicar talking again. In truth, I'd have been furious if I'd known then what Elaine had just told me. Cloverleaf Books had been a small, independent publishing house fighting in a fiercely competitive market for every single book we produced. Had Charles really diverted some of our limited resources out of a misguided sense of charity?

Elaine must have seen what I was thinking. 'He believed in the book,' she added. 'He showed it to me and I enjoyed it.'

'It didn't sell.' I was short with her, but I couldn't help myself. 'We did everything we could,' I went on. 'It just didn't seem to connect.'

'Eliot was in and out of this house quite often while he was writing both his books,' Elaine said. 'He was still a very troubled young man. He wasn't looking after himself at all. He didn't look good. He didn't shave and he was always smoking. There was one occasion when I told him to take a bath while I put all his clothes in the washing machine. It was hard to believe that he was twenty.' She paused. 'But he was also very charming and funny. He was the sort of person it was hard not to like and we became friends very quickly.'

'So why are you worried about him now?'

'You've seen him, Susan! I don't know what happened to him as a child at Marble Hall, but he still needs looking after now – and it doesn't help that his parents have dumped him and gone off to America.' She noticed that her champagne glass was empty. Mine too. She refilled both, then continued. 'Throughout the publishing process, Eliot was almost like a son to us. He behaved badly. Sometimes we were expecting him and he didn't show up. Sometimes he was late or drunk, or both. But we never gave up on him and it was strange how working on the Dr Gee books helped him. He told us that he'd always wanted to be a writer, but that he wasn't able to get started while his grandmother was still alive and even after she died he struggled to find his self-confidence. This was his big break.

'When the books failed, we were terrified he would go off the rails again, but by that time he was going out with Gillian and she gave him the one thing he'd never had in his life: stability. I'll tell you how they met, but you must pretend you don't know. Eliot took an overdose and ended up in hospital. Gillian was a nurse on the ward. She's the angel who saved his life, in more ways than one. They started going out together and then they got married – just the two of them and a couple of witnesses at Chelsea registry office. His brother, Roland, was the best man. From that moment, he seemed to change completely. Off the booze, off the drugs. Really trying to hold himself together. I was thrilled when I heard that he'd been asked to write three more books about Atticus Pünd. Maybe Dr Gee was a bad idea, but Eliot's a good writer and I'm sure you'll agree that this time he has a real chance of success.'

'I've read the first thirty thousand words and I think it's very promising,' I said.

'I know. He told me.' She paused. 'I'm just worried that this could be make or break for him. The last couple of times I've seen him, he hasn't been quite himself. Or rather, he's been a bit too much like his old self. He's smoking again, for one thing. I don't know about the rest of it, but Gillian is as worried as I am. She's told me.'

'I'm sorry, Elaine, but what's this got to do with me? I didn't commission him. I'm only his editor.'

'But you worked with the great Alan Conway. You made him into a star and you put Atticus Pünd on the map.' Elaine lowered her glass. Somehow the two of us had managed to polish off three quarters of the bottle of Moët. 'Eliot has pinned all his hopes on you and I'm not sure he has the resilience to fail a second time. That was the reason I wanted you to come tonight, Susan. Of course it matters to me that you and I have a relationship again, but this isn't about us. It's about Eliot. I want you to promise me that you'll look after him.'

'Can I be honest with you, Elaine?' I knew she was asking me to commit myself, but I wanted her to understand. 'It's not my job to "look after" my writers. I admire them. I try to like them. But I'm not their therapist. I may not be able to help him the way you want.'

'You don't have other writers like Eliot. If Charles were here, he could tell you so much more than I can.'

It was the mention of Charles that did it. Whatever my feelings about the past, I felt that I owed her something. I couldn't refuse. 'I promise you I'll be a friend to him,' I said. 'And I'll do everything I can to make this book a success.'

'That's all I can ask of you, Susan. And I'm sure—'

She didn't finish the sentence. The doorbell played its tune a second time. Elaine got to her feet.

Eliot Crace had arrived.

Grandma

I knew it was going to be one of those evenings the moment Eliot and Gillian came through the door. They had been arguing. It was obvious from their body language, the distance between them and the tears still visible in Gillian's eyes. It was sad because at first sight they made such an attractive couple: so young, so good-looking, smartly dressed, Eliot carrying a bottle of wine for Elaine – or perhaps for himself. He had been drinking. I could see that too. He wasn't quite drunk, but he was swaying on his feet, making every effort to keep himself steady.

'Hello again,' he said, a little too loudly. He was wearing jeans and a velvet jacket with an open-neck white shirt.

'Hello, Eliot.'

'Have you been here long?'

'About an hour.'

'Have you been talking about me?'

'Of course, Eliot. What else is there to talk about?'

He gave me a crooked smile. 'This is my wife, Gillian. Gillian, this is Susan Ryeland. My editor!'

My first impression of Gillian Crace was that she was a strikingly attractive woman, a little younger than Eliot — maybe twenty-eight or twenty-nine — and she could have been born to be a nurse. She had sandy-coloured hair, neatly parted in the middle, blue eyes and freckles. When she smiled, she radiated calm and kindness.

'It's lovely to meet you,' I said.

'Eliot has told me a lot about you.'

'We hardly know each other.'

'Well, he knows all about you. He was buzzing when he came back from your meeting the other day.'

'Let's go downstairs to eat,' Elaine said.

A flight of stairs led down to an open-plan area that ran the full length of the house, the kitchen at the front end and the French rosewood dining table at the back. The twelve chairs that surrounded it were a sad memory of former times. Tonight there would be just four of us to occupy them and, looking at the empty spaces, I was reminded of what life must be like for Elaine now that Charles was 'away'. There were bottles of wine already laid out, lit candles, serviettes neatly rolled inside silver rings, and as we took our places, Elaine served up the cauliflower soup that was to be our first course, adding a swirl of truffle oil to each bowl. There was something about the ritual, the formality of it all, that made me feel uneasy. It was like having dinner in a lepers' colony where nobody is allowed to mention the disease.

I had been placed opposite Eliot. Gillian was next to me, with Elaine making up the square on the other side. Eliot poured wine into his glass, not stopping until it had almost reached the brim.

We started off talking about *Pünd's Last Case*. That was what connected us and it was what mattered most. If Elaine was to be believed, Eliot had invested his entire future in its success – and now that I thought about it, the same was true for me too. Michael Flynn had hired me to make the book a bestseller. If it failed, I could kiss goodbye to any long-term employment at Causton Books.

'Eliot told me you liked the book,' Gillian said nervously. I could tell that she wanted me to be nice to him to make up for whatever had happened between them before they arrived.

'I liked it very much,' I said.

'I thought about what you suggested.' Eliot didn't meet my eye. He was stroking the edge of his wine glass, examining the contents. 'I'm going to change the title.'

'That's good. Do you have any other ideas?'

'I was thinking of *Another Man's Poison*.'

'I like that,' I said, although I wondered if it was a little too generic. 'It might be a good idea to have the name – Atticus Pünd – in the title, though.'

'You could call it *Atticus Pünd: Another Man's Poison*,' Gillian suggested.

Eliot ignored her. 'I'm going to set it one year before *Magpie Murders*,' he went on. 'That way, I can miss out on all that stuff about cancer.'

'As long as you're sure about it yourself, Eliot.' I was surprised he was being so accommodating. 'I was only making suggestions. You don't have to do anything you don't want to do.'

'I won't make any changes until the next draft. I'm going

to keep it in the South of France, though. I know there are problems, but if I changed it now, I'd have to go back to the start and I want to keep going.'

'Eliot's been working so hard since he saw you,' Gillian said. 'He hasn't stopped!'

'I'm really pleased. I'm just glad you're making progress and that you weren't put off by our discussion.'

'Actually, I can't wait to get to the last chapter. To the big reveal.' As he said that, he glanced at Gillian in an unpleasant way – as if she was the one who was going to be revealed as the killer. He drank half his wine. 'Isn't that the only reason to read a murder mystery? To get to the end?'

I didn't know if he was joking or not. I hoped he was. It was something Alan Conway might have said.

'Do you think it will be a bestseller?' Gillian asked me.

'Of course it will,' Elaine said. 'I know Charles would have given his right arm to publish it. It's going to be huge.'

It was the first time she had mentioned Charles since we had sat down. I realised everyone was waiting for me to speak, so I plunged in. 'If there's one thing that's certain in publishing, it's that you can't predict anything,' I began. '*Harry Potter* was turned down by a dozen publishers and when it was finally accepted, they only printed five hundred copies. That's how many they thought they could sell. Stephen King wrote a novel – *Carrie* – that was rejected thirty times. It's insane! When we published the first Atticus Pünd novel back in 1995, we had no idea it was going to do so well. Twenty-eight weeks on the *Sunday Times* Bestsellers List! It sold more copies than Nick Hornby or Barack Obama, who were both huge that year. And it just shows that nobody knows anything. You only realise you have a major success on your hands when the author rings to complain he can't find any copies in the shops.

'The most important thing is to get the book written and worry about sales and marketing and all the rest of it later.' I looked directly at Eliot. 'Causton Books couldn't be more behind you, and there's a huge audience waiting for the next outing for Atticus Pünd. Right now, everything's on your side . . . so let's just hope for the best.'

Eliot smiled and seemed pleased. Some of the tension went out of the air.

After that, the conversation zigzagged from books to theatre, Gillian's work at Charing Cross Hospital, Crete, politics and Parsons Green gossip. The soup bowls were cleared away and replaced by a bubbling coq au vin. Somehow, we had finished our first bottle of wine and started on a second. Gillian said nothing, although she was embarrassed by Eliot's heavy drinking and did her best to keep the bottle away from him. Elaine, on the other hand, didn't seem to notice. As for me, I remained stone-cold sober. I wasn't hating the evening. I just felt completely unconnected and was counting the minutes until I could make my excuses and leave.

It was as the pudding was being served that I asked the question that changed everything. It was stupid of me. I was trying to flatter Eliot, make him feel good about himself, when really I should have left well enough alone. 'Elaine told me you always wanted to be a writer,' I said. 'Was that because you wanted to be like your grandmother?'

Nearly all the successful authors I've worked with have claimed, quite sincerely, that they were born with a pen in their hand, and that was all I meant. But I knew at once that I should have left Miriam Crace out of it.

His face fell. 'God, no! I never wanted to be like that sour old bat. I hated her. We all did.'

His venom surprised me, even after all the wine. Elaine had already told me that Miriam was spiteful and domineering, but I hadn't thought his feelings would run this deep. 'I was thinking of her sales,' I said, back-pedalling.

'I wish she'd never sold a single bloody book. I wish her stupid Little People had died a death before they saw the light of day. Somebody should have stamped on them. They've been the curse of my whole bloody life.'

It was too late, I realised. He had come into the room with a sackful of resentment and I'd given him the excuse to release it.

'You have no idea what it was like at Marble Hall,' Eliot continued. 'You should go and visit the place, Susan. It's open every day of the week and it'll only cost you fifteen quid to have a snoop around. Of course, you won't see it the way I did. They've managed to get the blood out of the carpets. What you'll see is a lovely country house with chandeliers and wood panelling and lots of awards on the shelves.'

'Let's talk about something else,' Gillian suggested.

'What else is there to talk about? My grandmother is the reason we're all here. She's the reason why nothing – nothing! – has ever worked out for me. That venomous old cow!' He leaned towards me, as if drawing me into his confidence. 'She turned that place into a rat trap and kept every one of us locked inside. We weren't her family – we were her prisoners! My uncle Jonathan was the only one who didn't care, but he thought the sun shone out of her withered backside and couldn't wait to get his hands on her precious creation. It was always "legacy" with him. You know he even named his daughter after one of her characters? Jasmine Little – meet Jasmine Crace. How creepy is that? My parents hated Grandma just as much as I did, but they were too cowardly to break away. They stayed in Devizes and my dad worked in some third-rate art gallery and didn't dare write a word about art or artists because he knew what she would say. My mum wasted her time painting the local councillors and farmers who only ever complained that she made them look too fat or too old.

'Do you know what her power was? She knew exactly how to be cruel. She would find the weak spot in anyone and twist it until they screamed. Julia was overweight. Jasmine was useless. And as for me, when I told her I was thinking of being an author, she didn't give me a word of encouragement. She laughed at me! I was only ten years old! But she was the same with all of us. My grandfather never went near her unless he had to. My poor uncle Freddy – only he wasn't really my uncle – couldn't do anything right. Grandma was a patron of an orphanage in Salisbury and she'd adopted him, brought him in to live with us. Everyone applauded and said what a saint she was, but she treated him like a skivvy from the day he arrived. He was a second-class citizen. He didn't even eat with us!

'I'll tell you something that will amuse you, Susan. Roland, Julia and me – the three of us planned to kill her! We used to talk about it all the time. There was an abandoned cottage in the grounds and we used to meet there and talk about how we were going to do it. That was the game we played. Would it be poison from the garden? She always had a glass of lemon and ginger on her bedside table – it was the first thing she drank in the morning – and we thought we could put it in there. Or we could leave a roller skate at the top of the stairs and wait for her to take a tumble. We thought about setting fire to her bedroom or pushing her off the roof, like poor old Alan. Maybe that's why I became a murder writer – because I was already thinking of murder when I was nine years old.'

'It's just as well she died of natural causes,' I said.

He sneered at me. 'What makes you think that?'

'Did anyone ever suggest otherwise?'

'No-one would have dared.'

'I think we should go,' Gillian said. 'It's late and I'm on the first shift tomorrow.'

'No. I want to tell Susan about Roland. We all want to talk about Roland, don't we? He was my hero!'

Eliot drank some more wine.

'Grandma Miriam picked on Julia and me,' he continued, before anyone could stop him. 'I was the stupid one, the baby of the family. But my sister got it much worse. Have I already told you this? She was fat! That's all there was to it. She was very fat. It wasn't her fault. It wasn't as if she was stuffing food into her mouth. It was just something genetic, and anyway, what does it matter, what shape you are? She was a darling. We all loved her. She was so kind and gentle when she was a girl. She was always out in the garden. She loved flowers and birds and all that stuff. She's a teacher now, but I'm surprised she didn't become a garden designer or something like that. She knew all about plants.

203

'Anyway, Grandma used to make jokes about her, all the time.' Eliot fell back on the old lady's voice. ' "Fat Julia. Piggy Julia. How many chocolates have you had, Julia? We're going to have to get a stronger chair for you, Julia." '

He reached for the wine bottle, but Gillian stopped him. 'You've had enough,' she said firmly.

'Why would you care?' Eliot wrenched the bottle towards him and held it close. 'Roland protected us,' he said. 'Roland was the only one who stood up to her. He was only seventeen years old, but he was the bravest person in the house. Jasmine adored him. And for Julia and me, he was our knight in shining armour. Grandma was afraid of him. When he was with us, she never did any of her teasing.'

'Where is he now?' I asked.

'I don't know. In London, I think. I haven't seen him for a while.'

Gillian stood up. 'I have to go,' she insisted. 'You can stay if you want to, Eliot, but I want to go to bed. I'll call an Uber if you like.'

I came to her rescue. 'I ought to be on my way too,' I said. 'It's been a lovely meal, Elaine. Thank you for inviting me.' I turned to Eliot. 'Maybe you should write about your grandmother, now that she's dead,' I said.

He gave me a queer look, half smiling, half warning me.

'Maybe I already have,' he said.

Marble Hall

Marble Hall stood close to Salisbury Plain, surrounded by so much land that even if you climbed to the top of its highest tower you wouldn't see anything you didn't own. There were gardens, orchards, great swathes of pasture and broadleaf woodland. The house itself was a mishmash of different styles, mainly Tudor and Jacobean, knocked around by different owners until Miriam Crace bought it. Goodness knows what she must have been thinking at the time. She'd already made a ton of money, but this was a couple of years before her first child was even born. Why did she think she would need nine bedrooms, a dining room, a breakfast room, a library, a conservatory and a ballroom – not to mention the coach house, stables, tennis court, swimming pool, lodge house and gamekeeper's cottage in the grounds? Did she see herself as the Citizen Kane of children's authors, building a retreat from the world that would become a world in itself?

Less than half of the property was open to the public, but that was more than enough. It wasn't the carpets or the chandeliers that drew ten thousand visitors a year, it was the life of its famous occupant. Or, at least, her ghost. Her books, in forty-seven languages, including Latin and Welsh, filled the library. Her shoes, summer dresses, hats, gloves, the mink coat she wore to the premiere of the *Little People* musical at the London Palladium, were displayed in the bedroom. The twenty-three left-handed fountain pens she'd had specially made for her were laid out on the desk in her office, along with notebooks and manuscripts covered with her almost illegible handwriting.

Here was her CBE, resting on the grand piano she played for an hour every morning. Here was her favourite egg cup and a silver spoon, one of the dozen she had been given for her wedding by Lord Mountbatten, a huge fan of her books. And everywhere you looked there were the Little People themselves: models, photographs, cartoons, toys, framed newspapers and magazines, chocolate bars, dolls, games, jigsaws, key rings, cushions, beer mats and playing cards. After an hour or so, even the most ardent fan must have felt exhausted. It was lucky, then, that the stables had been con- verted into a café where you could enjoy Grandma Little's Cream Tea or a glass of Grandpa Little's Ginger Beer.

I had driven down from London a few days after my dinner with Elaine, although there were plenty of other things I could have been doing. Michael Flynn had surprised me by sending me a second manuscript to edit – another piece of Nordic noir. It was wanted by the end of the month, but it had been horribly translated and almost every line needed work. I couldn't focus on any of it.

My thoughts were all over the place. It looked as if I was stuck as Eliot's editor whether I liked it or not; certainly if

I was to have any hope of continuing my career at Causton Books. I had also promised Elaine that I would be a friend to him, which went against all my professional instincts. But she'd persuaded me that I owed it to her and, much to my annoyance, I'd decided she was right. And then there was Eliot himself. Every word he had said at the dinner table had come as a hammer blow, smashing all my preconceptions about his famous grandmother. Could Miriam really have been the horror he had described? How could she possibly have created the world's most lovable family when she'd been so hateful to her own?

I couldn't walk away, although I was tempted to do exactly that. I was already too committed. It was as if I'd tumbled into a web, only to discover that I was, in fact, the spider. If I was going to hold everything together, I had to be strong, which meant learning as much as I could about the house, the family, Eliot's childhood and, above all, Miriam Crace herself. I think Elaine was hoping that I would protect him, but in reality I was simply protecting myself.

And so I'd gone back and read as many articles as I could find about Miriam, including her obituaries, and they all told the same story: a major talent, the inspiration for a generation of children, a hugely wealthy, record-breaking British writer loved all over the world, who had devoted her life to charitable causes and had passed away in her early eighties. The queen herself had sent a note of condolence. I scoured the internet, but there wasn't so much as a whisper that there had been anything suspicious about her death. It had been the inevitable conclusion of many years of declining health.

'It's just as well she died of natural causes.'

'*What makes you think that?*'

It would have been easy enough to dismiss Eliot's insinuations. He was drunk. He'd just argued with his wife. But when I was lying in bed, trying to get to sleep, that last exchange had echoed over and over in my head. Eliot knew exactly what he was doing. He had spent the first twelve years of his life at Marble Hall and he had weaponised that experience. I knew now that *Pünd's Last Case* wasn't just a book. It was an act of revenge.

Marble Hall and the Chateau Belmar. Two old women, both with the initials M C, both with a heart condition, had died. At least one of them had been poisoned. And there were plenty of other parallels. Julia Crace and Judith Lyttleton. The first names of Eliot's sister and Jeffrey Chalfont's sister started with the same two letters. Both had an issue with weight, and from schoolteacher to postgraduate doctor wasn't too far a stretch. Jonathan Crace, married to Leylah, must find a reflection in Jeffrey, married to Lola. Eliot had told me that he had based the character of Cedric on himself and it seemed to me that Elmer Waysmith – who treated his son with such contempt – might well have been inspired by Eliot's own father.

Even the lemon and ginger tonic that Miriam drank every morning had its counterpart in the lemon and ginger tea that had killed Margaret Chalfont. Was that what Eliot was saying? Was that how he believed his grandmother had died?

I wasn't sure if I should be editing the book or persuading Eliot not to write it. I knew I was going to have to confront him about all this and it wasn't going to be pleasant. But when I woke up on a bright Sunday morning, it was clear to me what I had to do. Marble Hall was real. Marble Hall was two and a half hours away. Before I made any decision, I had to see it for myself.

It was an easy drive down and I'd chosen a beautiful day. It gave me a chance to put my old MG through its paces and once I'd come off the M4, I put the roof down and enjoyed the rushing green and the glorious fresh air of the Wiltshire countryside, Adele blasting out of the sound system.

The main car park was already close to full when I pulled in shortly before midday. I walked through the gardens up to the main entrance, looking out for a Michelangelo-inspired fountain and a Corinthian gazebo, and I was glad they weren't there. Architecturally, the very English house had nothing in common with the Chateau Belmar. It was darker, with smaller rooms – and more of them – connected by creaking corridors or tucked away in hidden annexes.

Miriam Crace had bought the hall in 1955 and over the next forty-odd years it had opened its arms – or perhaps its tentacles – to embrace three generations. First, there had been Miriam and Kenneth, still married but definitely not together. Jonathan and Edward had been born and grew up there. When they had married, their wives – Leylah and Amy – had moved in too. Then there had been four grandchildren: Jasmine, Roland, Julia and Eliot, arriving in that order. And let's not forget Frederick Turner, adopted in 1961. How had he fitted in to all this?

That was what I was asking myself as I joined the tourists and their children, some of whom were dressed up as their favourite characters from the books, following the arrows from one clutter-filled room to another. What would life have been like for the children here, rubbing shoulders with your uncles and your cousins, always kowtowing to whatever Grandma might demand? At some stage, Jonathan had moved his wife and daughter into a separate building in the grounds. But which room had been Eliot's? Where had his parents slept? Only Miriam's bedroom was labelled – with a red cord across the doorway to stop people from entering. I spent a long time looking at the bed with its two cabinets, one on each side. I was fixated by them. I could almost see the servant or a housekeeper placing a glass of lemon and ginger on one of them for Miriam to drink, the bright yellow liquid shimmering like something out of a Hitchcock film.

From what Eliot had told me, his parents couldn't wait to get out of Marble Hall and had left the moment Miriam died, taking their three children with them. After just one hour in the place, I knew exactly how they felt. There was something incredibly oppressive about the place. So many doors and staircases, so little natural light. And then there were the stuffed animals. Crows, foxes, rabbits, owls, just about every form of wildlife watched me with their incurious glass eyes as I strolled past. I was particularly struck by a kingfisher locked away in a glass cabinet, the glorious colours of its plumage somehow obscene given that it had been dead for perhaps a hundred years. Kenneth's workshop in one of the towers was open to the public. It was like Frankenstein's castle: shelves lined with flasks and old bottles, bits of bone and feather, wooden work surfaces still stained with decades-old dried blood. Seen through the eyes of an imaginative ten-year-old, it would have been like living in a bad dream.

And there would have been no escape. The house was so remote that Eliot would have grown up without seeing anyone from the outside world, and if he wanted to go anywhere, even to school, he would have had to be taken in a car. I had paid seventeen pounds fifty to get in. I could imagine that he would have paid a thousand times that to get out.

I bought a history of Marble Hall in the gift shop, mainly because there was a black-and-white photograph of Miriam Crace on the cover and I thought it would be useful to have it with me. Although born in 1920, she had the look of a character out of Sherlock Holmes. The black-and-white photography did her no favours, I thought, and there was something truly ghostlike about her: her head tilted to one side, her hair floating like clouds above her face, her eyes staring at something over the photographer's shoulder. She was not a beautiful woman, but nor was she ugly. She just looked . . . dead.

As I took out my credit card, I struck up a conversation with the woman behind the counter. Her name was Brenda. It was written on a tag pinned to her chest. I asked her about the stuffed animals.

'That was Kenneth Rivers,' she told me. 'He was married to Miriam Crace, although she never used his name. They are a bit creepy, I must say. Apparently, there are over two hundred of them scattered through the house. Sometimes they seem to be watching you as you walk down the corridors. All those glass eyes!'

'When did he die?'

'Two years after her, in 2005. He was ninety years old by then. He stayed in the house, although at the end he was on his own. A few years ago, they decided to open the property for people to visit. Are you a Miriam Crace fan?'

'Absolutely.' The staff at Marble Hall must have come in from Devizes and the surrounding villages. They had all been delightful, huge fans of the Little People, and I didn't want to say anything that might offend them. 'I understand the whole family lived here when Miriam was alive,' I said.

'That's right.'

'I know it's an odd question, but I'd love to know where everyone slept. Were any of them on the same floor as Miriam Crace?'

Brenda was happy to share her expertise. 'The three grandchildren all had rooms next to each other on the first-floor corridor, and you'll have seen Miriam's bedroom at the far end, next to the bathroom. I love the curtains – and what a view to wake up to! Part of the family was in the Lodge House and Mr Turner was up at the top. He was brought here when he was a boy and he still lives here now. If you'd come in the week, you'd have found him showing people round the house or working behind the ticket desk. He likes to pitch in. Unfortunately, he doesn't work on Sundays.'

'I'm sorry? Frederick Turner is still here?' I had to make sure we were talking about the same person. 'The boy adopted by Miriam Crace . . .?'

'That's right. It was such a kindness and he tells lots of lovely stories about her.'

'Is he in the house right now?'

'He might be. But it's his day off.'

It was too good an opportunity to miss. 'I wonder if you could call him for me?' I went on quickly before she could refuse. 'I'm working with Eliot Crace, Miriam's grandson. In fact, it was Eliot who suggested I come down here. He's writing a book about Marble Hall and I'm his editor.' She looked doubtful, so I pressed on. 'It would be hugely helpful if he could spare me a few minutes of his time – and if he's busy, he can always say no.'

'Well, I suppose there's no harm asking.' She didn't look happy, but she reached for the telephone and punched in a four-digit number, turning her back on me and speaking in a low voice so that I couldn't intrude. I heard a few words.

'. . . a lady who . . . she says she's working with Eliot . . . writing about the house. No. She didn't say.'

She turned back to me. 'What's your name?'

'Susan Ryeland. I work for Causton Books. Can you tell him I've driven down from London?'

This was transmitted down the line. There was a silence and I thought he must have refused, but then she lowered the phone. 'He'll be down in a minute.'

'That's wonderful. Thank you, Brenda.'

While I waited, I glanced through the other souvenirs and read a few pages of *Little Miracles*, which still hit the bestseller charts every Easter. There was something a little depressing about the gifts on offer, but it was only as I was thumbing through the postcards that I realised what it was. Andreas was in Crete. Charles was in prison. Katie was in Suffolk. I realised I couldn't buy anything because I had nobody to give anything to and that reminded me how much I'd made my work the centre of my life. It was a feeling that passed quickly enough. I had plenty of friends and none of them would have wanted any of this tat anyway, but it was still a reminder of the extent to which I had been cut adrift by the events of the last few years and that there was a definite fragility about the way I was living.

Then a door over to one side opened and Frédéric Voltaire appeared.

Of course it wasn't the French detective from Eliot's novel, but there could be no doubt that this was where he had found his inspiration. The man who was approaching me had one eye covered by a patch and moved slowly, as if in pain. I knew that Frederick Turner was Eliot's adoptive uncle and straight away I wondered what he had done to find himself in the novel, and hoped that this wasn't going to be another case of old scores being settled.

'This is the lady here, Mr Turner,' Brenda cooed. 'I hope you don't mind me disturbing you on your day off.'

'That's all right, Brenda.'

'Did you get any asparagus?'

'No. I'm afraid they're finished for the season.' He turned to me and smiled. 'Ms Ryeland?'

I tried to look past the injuries. The man who was standing in front of me looked to be in his late fifties, casually dressed in a paisley shirt tucked into baggy cords, with leather slippers on his feet. Unlike the character in the book, he was mixed-race, with African and white heritage. He was a handsome man despite the loss of his eye and the scarring on the side of his face. He had a quiet intelligence and a gentleness I found endearing. He spoke softly, as if afraid of giving offence.

'Susan, please,' I said.

'I'm Frederick Turner.'

'Thank you for coming down. I'm working with Eliot—'

'Yes. I know who you are. Would you like a coffee? We have quite a good tea room here – the Little Parlour. The ladies make all their own cakes.'

We set off together, leaving the house and heading for the stables. Frederick walked with a limp. 'You'll have to forgive my appearance,' he said. 'I have an allotment at the back of the house and I'd just finished lifting the early potatoes and was about to jump into the shower when Brenda rang. We had a marvellous crop of asparagus this year, by the way, but sadly the season is all too short.'

'You manage Marble Hall?'

'Yes. I hope you enjoyed your visit. Isn't it a marvellous place?' He pointed to a line of casement windows on the second floor. 'I have a suite of rooms up there. It's funny to find myself back where I began, but I love living here and there's absolutely no way I could do this job remotely. I've been here so long that probably one day I'll be part of the guided tour. I might even come back and haunt the place!' He smiled at his own joke.

The room was crowded, but we found a table and after I had declined both lemon drizzle cake and French fancies, he ordered tea and biscuits. The waitress was called Daphne and she fussed over him as if he was a schoolboy being given a special treat. In that respect, she was just like Brenda in the gift shop. Both were obviously fond of him, perhaps because of his injuries.

'Who told you about me?' I asked. I assumed it must have been Eliot. Nobody else in the Crace family knew I was working on the book.

'I met Charles Clover a few times,' he explained. 'He came

down here when he was working on the last books written by Miriam Crace and we stayed in touch after he set up
Cloverleaf. He often mentioned you. He spoke very highly
of you.'

I wasn't sure if this was a compliment or a rebuke. Frederick must have been aware of what had happened to Charles
and his company, but he didn't make any reference to it so I
decided I wouldn't either. 'I'm freelance now' was all I said.

'I'd heard Eliot was writing a book. Is it set here at Marble
Hall?'

I wasn't sure how to answer that. I knew I'd struck lucky.
Frederick Turner could give me a lot of the background
details I needed about Miriam Crace, Marble Hall and the
families who had lived here – but it might be difficult to
draw information out of him if I said that Eliot was using
the family as the template for a murder mystery set in the
South of France in 1955. At the same time, he seemed like
a nice enough man and I didn't want to lie to him. 'He's
writing a mystery story,' I said, keeping things vague. 'It's
a work of fiction, but it's partly inspired by his childhood
here.'

He smiled. 'I always thought Eliot would become a writer.
He was an odd little boy, always living in his imagination.'
He paused. 'Am I in it?'

'I've only read a few chapters. He won't be delivering
until later in the year.' Both statements were true, but didn't
answer the question. 'I understand you were adopted by
Miriam Crace.'

'That's right.' He paused while the waitress brought over
one of those silver pots that make such a business dribbling

out a measure of tea, and two gingerbread men on a plate, both based on characters from Miriam's books, their names – Harry and Rose – written in icing sugar. 'I first came to Marble Hall in 1961, when I was almost six years old.'

I did a quick calculation. He'd been born in 1955, which made him sixty-eight now, much older than I'd thought.

'If Eliot's writing a mystery novel, he should start with me. I never knew either of my parents. My mother died giving birth to me. We know very little about her. We think my father was an agricultural worker and she may have been a Traveller. Mary Turner was the name she gave at the Trowbridge Community Hospital, which is where I was born. Apparently, she said that she wanted me to be called Frederick if I was a boy, and it makes me sad to think she never found out that it happened. I ended up at the St Ambrose Orphanage and Children's Home . . .'

'In Salisbury.'

'That's the one. When no relatives stepped forward to claim me, I was put up for adoption, but that didn't happen. It may have been my ethnicity. Back then, in the fifties, down here in the West Country attitudes were different. Anyway, I was the lucky one. Mrs Crace was a patron of the orphanage. I'm sure you're aware, she did an enormous amount for children throughout her life and we all knew her. *The Little People* was the first book I ever read – and the second, and the third, and the fourth. When she came swooping in in that Bentley of hers, I couldn't believe what was happening. It was like a fairy story.'

'Were you happy at Marble Hall?'

'How could I not be?'

'Did you fit in with the family?' He looked puzzled, so I added: 'Eliot suggested to me that you all had quite separate lives.'

He laughed and poured tea for both of us. 'Forgive me for saying so, Susan, but if you're going to work with Eliot, you really mustn't trust everything he says. I was one hundred per cent happy here and Mrs Crace couldn't have been kinder to me.'

'You don't call her Miriam.'

'I wouldn't have dared when she was alive and it still seems wrong now that she's dead. She was one of the most famous writers in the world. Margaret Thatcher loved her work and invited her to Downing Street. There were Hollywood stars queuing up to meet her. Faye Dunaway, Paul Newman, Meryl Streep. She was a powerhouse of a woman and there were many people who were intimidated by her. I never thought of her as a mother. To me she was simply the person who saved my life.'

'Did you go to the same school as Edward and Jonathan?'

He frowned. 'Why are you asking me that?'

'I'm sorry.' I backtracked quickly. 'I don't mean to be personal, but Eliot has told me very little about his father – about either of his parents – and I suppose I feel a little protective towards him. Publishing a book can be a tough business and it's part of my job to make sure he's looked after.' This seemed to make some sort of sense to Frederick, although I wasn't sure it made any to me. Yes, I tried to support my writers, but this didn't usually involve digging into their family history. 'I'm sure you're aware that Eliot has had a few problems,' I added confidentially.

'I haven't really spoken to Edward since he went to America,' Frederick said. 'And since you ask, Susan, I did not go to the same school as Edward or Jonathan. They were educated privately and I went to a comprehensive in Devizes. That was fine as far as I was concerned. Mrs Crace had done enough for me. Why should she and Kenneth have to pay for my education? Maybe that's what Eliot meant by separate lives. All three of us were very different. Edward was the quiet one, interested in art and art history. Jonathan couldn't wait to take over the estate and build on what his mother had created. He's the one who employs me now. I was the oldest of the three of us, but of course things were different for me. I kept myself to myself. I moved to London in my twenties and qualified as an accountant. Mrs Crace paid for everything. I was thinking of going to America, but then I had my accident.'

'I'm sorry. What happened?'

'It was entirely my fault. I was driving to the airport. I had a bad head cold and I wasn't concentrating. I drove through a red light and my car was hit by a truck.' He paused and drank tea. 'I was quite badly injured and I came back to Marble Hall to recuperate.

'Jonathan was extremely helpful. By now he was running the family business and he suggested I take over the accounts. Once I was back on my feet, I worked in the London office, in Kingston Street. I was there until 2016, when Jonathan decided to open Marble Hall to the public. He asked me if I'd like to manage the house and I leapt at the opportunity.' He glanced down at his leg, stretched out beside the table. 'At least in so far as I was able.'

'So, as far as you were concerned, it was all one big, happy family?'

I'd done my best not to sound sarcastic, but I could see that Frederick was becoming impatient with me. 'Mrs Crace certainly liked having her children and grandchildren around her,' he said. 'There was plenty of space. Jonathan and Leylah were in the Lodge House with their daughter, Jasmine. You can see it as you drive out of here. It's set back among the trees, past the old swimming pool, on the left. Edward and Amy had a whole suite of rooms at the back of the house. That included a living room and kitchen.'

'And you?'

'I was up in the eaves. I loved it there. The roof sloped down over my bed, and lying on my back before I went to sleep, I could see the moon and all the stars. There was an owl in the rafters and sometimes I could hear it hooting. I presume you visited the rooms occupied by Mr Rivers and Mrs Crace on the first and second floors?'

'They didn't sleep together . . .'

'I'm amazed you're asking that.'

'I didn't mean to be intrusive, Frederick. Eliot told me they weren't close.'

'Well, it's none of my business and certainly none of yours, so I'm not going to make any comment. But I will say this.' He sighed. 'Eliot wasn't completely happy at Marble Hall, but that was his problem. It may be that he resented his grandmother for making him live here, but the truth of the matter is that once he left Marble Hall, his life fell apart.

'I'm not sure I should be telling you this, but I'm going to take you at your word that you've got his interests at heart.

220

Eliot was trouble pretty much from the day he was born. Neither of his parents could control him. He and his father used to have shouting matches when they were here, but once they moved to London, it only got worse. They were at each other's throats twenty-four seven, and according to Jonathan, Eliot was the main reason Edward Crace and his wife packed their bags and headed off to America. They'd both had enough. Drugs, alcohol, self-harm, theft, vandalism . . . Eliot even set fire to the house once. It all ended with a big blow-up one Christmas and a few weeks later they left – just like that. Roland tried to sort things out. He was always the peacemaker, a decent soul, but the decision had been made.

'I'm sorry, Susan. I really hope he manages to find himself with this book of his. Maybe it will act as some sort of therapy. But whatever he tells you about Marble Hall, I think you should take it with a pinch of salt.'

'He suggested there might have been something unusual about his grandmother's death.'

'I'm sorry?'

'He suggested . . .' I began.

But I could see I had gone too far. Frederick Turner was looking angry and upset – annoyed with himself for inviting me into the Little Parlour, with its triangular sandwiches and smiling gingerbread men. 'I don't know what you're implying, but it's complete nonsense,' he said. 'I was in the house the night Mrs Crace was taken ill. Actually, it was six o'clock in the morning. She had an alert necklace which she wore all the time and that was when she pressed it. There was a housekeeper living in and she summoned me.'

'You were the last person to see her alive?'

'No. We entered her room together. Mrs Crace was lying in bed, clearly in a bad way. She was barely conscious and breathing with difficulty. Mrs Rodwell – the housekeeper – called Dr Lambert. He was her personal physician and lived nearby. He set off immediately, but unfortunately she died before he arrived. He was the one who examined her and pronounced the cause of death: a heart attack. We'd all been expecting it, so it was hardly a surprise.'

'Was there an autopsy?'

'There didn't need to be! I can assure you, Susan, there were no suspicious circumstances surrounding her death, none at all, and I really think you should have a word with Eliot if he is going to suggest otherwise.'

'Could I talk to Dr Lambert?' It hadn't escaped me that, despite the English pronunciation, Miriam's doctor and Margaret Chalfont's lawyer had the same name.

'I really don't think that would be a good idea.' Frederick stood up, using the edge of the table for support. 'I don't mean to be rude, but I do get the feeling that you've been talking to me under false pretences,' he suggested. 'You said that Eliot was writing a work of fiction, but everything you have asked seems to be an unpleasant distortion of the truth. Miriam Crace made millions of people very happy. When I was alone in the orphanage, it was her work that gave me hope I might one day have a future, that the Little People would come and rescue me. You really should think very carefully before you allow Eliot to bring a wrecking ball to everything she created.'

'That's not what he's doing,' I said, also getting to my feet. 'His book is set in 1955 in France. It's a detective story.'

'Then why have you been asking me all these questions?' He leaned towards me, his hands balled into fists, resting his weight on the table. 'If you don't mind, I don't think it would be appropriate for me to speak to you any more. Do finish your tea. There won't be any bill. But please don't upset the ladies with more questions – and when you've finished, I really think you should leave.'

Dr Lambert

Who was I to believe? I had been given two completely different versions of the same story: 'Hansel and Gretel' vs 'Cinderella', if you like. For Eliot Crace, Miriam Crace had been the wicked witch, desperate to feed the children to the flames. For Frederick Turner, she had been the fairy godmother who had waved the wand so that he *would* go to the ball. What did that make Marble Hall? A prison or a palace? I had a two-and-a-half-hour journey back to London and I'd already decided that I wasn't going to start it until I had a clearer idea of what had really been going on all those years ago.

It was always possible that both of them might be right – speaking their own truth, as we're meant to say these days. Frederick had admitted that he'd been educated separately from the other children and no matter how pleasantly he'd described it, he'd been sent to sleep in the attic. To what extent had he really been part of the family? Miriam Crace had adopted him, but he had never called her 'Mother' – and now he was reduced to managing the house where he had once lived, limping around, glad-handing the tourists.

As for Eliot, he'd given me a version of events as seen by a twelve-year-old, and having visited Marble Hall, I understood how easy it would have been to be unhappy there. The dark corridors, the claustrophobia, the isolation, even the taxidermy . . . I wouldn't have wished it on any child of mine. It was also true that his parents had abandoned him at the first opportunity. The rapid exodus from Wiltshire, with Kenneth Rivers left behind to die on his own, certainly supported Eliot's recollections.

What I needed was a third perspective from someone who had witnessed events without being involved in them. An outsider. And luckily, Frederick had given me the name of just the man. Dr Lambert had been Miriam Crace's personal physician. Presumably he knew the family well. Frederick had also let slip that he lived nearby. It shouldn't be too hard to find him.

I took out my phone and tapped four words into the search engine: LAMBERT, MIRIAM CRACE and DEATH. Nothing has done more damage to modern detective fiction than the invention of the internet. Forget Sherlock Holmes and his ratiocination or Hercule Poirot's little grey cells. We have all the information in the world at our fingertips and there's no longer any need for deduction. Sure enough, within seconds I had found what I was looking for in the *Wiltshire Times*.

WORLD-FAMOUS AUTHOR FOUND DEAD AT HER DEVIZES HOME

Speaking from his surgery in Urchfont, Dr John Lambert described what had happened. 'I was called to her home at six o'clock in the morning, when she was discovered by the housekeeper. I had known Mrs Crace for many years and was aware of the fact that she had been suffering from heart disease, but still it was a great shock. My own children had been brought up on her books. Sadly, there was nothing I could do for her. She had passed away peacefully in her sleep.'

Urchfont was less than five miles away from Marble Hall. It was a beautiful place, a Wiltshire village bathed in the afternoon sunshine, centred on a handsome church and a duck pond that might have been purposely designed for jigsaw puzzles and chocolate boxes long before they were invented. I cruised along the high street in my MG with the roof down, looking for that more traditional search engine: the village pub. It was called The Lamb Inn and although it was past three o'clock, there were still drinkers sitting outside. I parked and went in.

A young man barely out of his teens stood behind the bar. I went over to him. 'Can you help me? I'm looking for Dr Lambert. John Lambert. It's stupid of me. My phone has gone down and I've lost his address.'

The barman looked at me blankly. 'Mum!' he called, never taking his eyes off me.

An older woman bustled in from a back room. 'Yes?'

'Do you know a Dr Lambert?' I asked. 'I'm trying to find his house.'

She looked me up and down. 'You don't look ill.'

'I'm not. He's a family friend.'

'Well, I don't know where he lives.'

'He's at Pynsent House, on the green.' The voice came from the other side of the room. A man in a flat cap, playing dominoes, had taken pity on me. 'That's two minutes from here. He's not a doctor any more, though.'

'She says she's not ill,' the man playing against him said.

'I know. I heard her.' The first man scowled. 'He doesn't need to work,' he went on. 'Him and his wife. They're doing all right for themselves.'

Around the pub, a few heads nodded in agreement. I got the sense that Dr Lambert and his wife weren't the most popular members of the community. Even the barman's mother seemed to have taken against him.

The village green was triangular, with three roads leading off. Pynsent House was a handsome brick building with three chimneys and a thatched roof, partly concealed by shrubbery. There was a classic car parked in the street outside, a Jaguar convertible with dark green panel work and gleaming chrome. It really was a museum piece and although it was an unworthy thought, I wondered how Dr Lambert had managed to afford it. Somehow it didn't quite fit with the image of a retired country doctor. There wasn't anywhere to park on the green, so I drove round the corner and found a spot nearby. Then I walked back and rang the bell.

The door was opened by a man in his seventies. He was still in good shape, but his thinning hair, drooping moustache and weathered skin gave away his age. If that was his car, he had spent too many hours with the roof down and the wind rushing into his face. He was wearing a cardigan, despite the warmth of the afternoon. He examined me with the sort of look he might have reserved for a door-to-door salesman or a Jehovah's Witness.

'Yes?'

'Dr Lambert?'

'Yes.'

'My name is Susan Ryeland. I'm a friend of Eliot Crace, Miriam Crace's grandson. I wonder if I might talk to you for a moment?'

'What is this about?'

'It's a bit difficult to explain, but I'm quite worried about him. He's writing a book that contains some allegations about his family, and obviously I don't want anything to come out in print that may be damaging to him or to anyone else. As the family doctor and the man who was there the morning Miriam Crace died, I'm hoping you can help.'

He blinked at me. 'You'd better come in.'

I'd stretched the truth when I was talking to Frederick, but this time I'd turned it on its head. My meeting in the tea room had taught me a simple lesson. If I introduced myself as Eliot's editor, I'd be implying that I was on his side. I'm not suggesting that Frederick – or Dr Lambert, for that matter – had anything they wanted to conceal, but a great deal of secrecy had always surrounded Miriam Crace and her life at Marble Hall, and anyone asking questions was bound to be seen as an interloper. I'd decided that Dr Lambert was more likely to talk to me if he thought I was preventing a book from coming out rather than publishing it, and so far it was a strategy that seemed to be working.

He led me through the hallway and into a living room

with a low ceiling, exposed beams and a heavily patterned carpet, all of which made the space feel even more compressed than it actually was. The furniture was comfortable and chintzy. The scent of retirement hung in the air. A woman in a floral dress was sitting in an armchair, reading a newspaper. She was the same age as him, very countrified, with a mauve tint to her hair and glasses on a cord running behind her ears. She seemed put out by my appearance.

'This is Susan Ryeland, dear,' Dr Lambert said. 'She's a friend of Eliot Crace.'

'We haven't seen Eliot Crace for a very long time.' This was her only observation. She returned to the article she had been reading, making no secret of the fact that she was annoyed to have been interrupted.

'You say you're working with Eliot?'

'I was an editor at Cloverleaf Books when he had two books published about ten years ago. Now he's written another book and he's asked me to help him with it. But I have some concerns about the content.'

'What is it he wants to write?' Dr Lambert asked. He was immediately nervous, his eyes blinking and his mouth turning downwards, following the curve of his moustache. 'What allegations is he making?'

'He seems to have quite a negative view of his grandmother,' I began.

'Miriam? Well, she could be difficult, it's true. But I suppose it comes with the territory. After all, she was getting on a bit. And there was a lot of pressure on her. She had millions of fans.'

'According to Eliot, she treated her family very badly.'

'That's nonsense. And I think you would be very ill-advised to suggest such a thing in public. Have you spoken to his uncle, Jonathan Crace? I can tell you, Miss Ryeland, Mr Crace won't be happy at all. I myself have signed a non-disclosure agreement with the estate and there is very little I can tell you about Mrs Crace or anything else. I'm surprised that Eliot didn't sign an NDA too.'

'Well, he was only twelve years old when he left Marble Hall.'

'That's exactly right, Miss Ryeland. I wouldn't have thought anyone would have any faith in the recollections of a child.'

'A very devious child,' Mrs Lambert remarked. 'Not pleasant at all.'

'How well did you know the family?' I asked Dr Lambert, ignoring his wife.

'Well, they moved to Devizes a long time ago, when I was still at school. My father was the doctor here then. I took over the surgery when he retired. My first patient at Marble Hall was Leylah Crace, when she was pregnant. She had a daughter, a lovely, healthy baby. After that, I got to know most of the family – though not socially. I think I probably treated every one of them for something or other over the years.'

Mrs Lambert peered at her husband over the top of the newspaper. 'I used to meet the children in the village. Roland and his brother, Eliot. Those two were never apart. And what was the name of the sister? She used to waddle along behind them.'

'That's a little unfair, dear.' Dr Lambert had the decency to look embarrassed. 'I examined Julia Crace on more than one occasion. She had a very low BMR.' He smiled at me. 'Basal metabolic rate. Her thyroid levels were abnormal and I recommended a change of diet . . . green vegetables, fruit, fatty fish. Not easy for a young girl, especially in those days.'

'Eliot told me that his grandmother was quite cruel to her,' I said.

'You only have Eliot's word for that and I can assure you I saw no evidence of it. I would have been very surprised if Miriam, a much-loved children's author, had been anything but sympathetic and kind to her granddaughter. She gave money to children's charities, you know, and she was the patron of an orphanage in Devizes.'

'Salisbury!' Mrs Lambert's disembodied voice corrected him. 'You should tell her about Eliot and your medicine bag.'

'What was that?' I asked.

'Oh, it was nothing, really. But it doesn't reflect well on Eliot.' I waited for him to continue. 'I was at the house attending to Kenneth Rivers. Now, he was a very nice man. Very quiet. He was a civil servant when he married Miriam, but he no longer had any need to work, not with all the money his wife was making.'

'He did taxidermy.'

'Yes. He started out buying specimens, some of them fifty or a hundred years old, and when that ceased to satisfy him, he started creating them himself. It was an unusual hobby – and that was why I was there. He'd come into contact with some quite unpleasant chemicals which had caused health problems. A darkening of the skin, warts, lesions. It could have been quite serious if I hadn't intervened. I put him on a course of dimercaprol and it cleared up in no time. Anyway,

Eliot happened to be in the room while I was treating his grandfather and when I turned round, you won't believe what I saw! He had his hand in my medicine bag. He was rummaging through the different medicines and before I could stop him, he'd snatched one of my bottles and run out of the room.'

'Little thief!' Mrs Lambert exclaimed.

'That's true, dear. But I checked what was missing and it was only a bottle of Liqufruta. A cough medicine. It wasn't poisonous or anything like that. Of course, I had to tell his parents and I must say, I was very disappointed by their response. One of the children had a birthday that week and they didn't want to make a big thing of it. I insisted that they talk to Eliot, though. You can't have children rummaging around in medicine bags.'

'And stealing!' Mrs Lambert added.

'In the end, his father gave him a good talking-to. Eliot said he'd done it as a dare and insisted that he'd thrown the bottle away, so no harm had been done. I would have given him a good hiding – but whatever Eliot may be saying about them now, his parents weren't like that and he got off scot-free.'

'When was this?'

'The twenty-fifth of June 2003.' Dr Lambert was pleased that he could remember the date. 'It was exactly two days later that Mrs Crace died.' He realised the implications of what he had just said and went on hurriedly. 'Before you make any false connections, let me assure you that she could have drunk a whole bottle of Liqufruta with no effect whatsoever. It was a herbal remedy. Nothing more.'

'Miriam Crace was suffering from heart disease,' I reminded him.

'Yes. She had mitral stenosis.'

'A narrowing of the mitral valve controlling the flow of blood to the heart.'

'That's correct.' He was impressed by my medical knowledge, but all I was doing was repeating what Eliot had written about Lady Chalfont. The two women had the same disease.

'Was that the reason she had to take six months off?' I asked. This was something I had read in Miriam's biography. 'She went to a clinic in Lausanne,' I added.

'Oh no. That was a long time ago, before she even bought Marble Hall. It was in the medical notes I inherited from my father – but it was nothing to do with her heart. She was worn out. Stress caused by overwork.'

'And you're certain it was the mitral stenosis that killed her.' It was time to get to the point. I felt myself closing in on the target I had set myself. 'You see, that's what worries me, Dr Lambert. Eliot is saying something very different.' I paused, as if afraid to put my thoughts into words. 'He's suggesting that his grandmother might not have died from natural causes.'

'He said that?' Dr Lambert was instantly outraged.

Next to him, the newspaper came down, folded into his wife's lap. She glared at me from the other side.

'Is he pretending he poisoned her with cough medicine?'

'He never mentioned the cough medicine. He hasn't told me what happened, but that's why I felt I ought to see you. I have warned Eliot against going into print with this sort of accusation—'

'If he's saying that, it's a downright lie! I was the first person to examine Mrs Crace. Mrs Rodwell – she was the housekeeper – called me up to Marble Hall at six o'clock in the morning. Miriam Crace died minutes before I arrived. I issued the MCCD – the medical certificate of the cause of death – and delivered it to the registrar. I also referred the death to the coroner. If there had been the slightest indication of there being anything suspicious or unnatural about her passing, I would have been obliged to report it under the Registration of Births and Deaths Regulations of 1987. Otherwise I would have been committing a criminal offence. But there was not. Miriam Crace's heart condition was well known to everyone who was close to her. Mitral stenosis is fatal in eighty per cent of cases, usually within ten years, and especially if there is secondary pulmonary hypertension – which in this instance was most certainly the case. And why would anyone want to harm her, anyway? She was loved all over the world.'

'You're positive it had nothing to do with the liquid that Eliot took from your medicine bag?'

'One hundred per cent. I'm sorry I even mentioned it now.'

'You didn't say anything at the time?'

'I told his uncle what had happened, as I recall, but otherwise there was no need to. No.'

'And I don't suppose you noticed, but was there an empty glass beside her bed? You may have known that Miriam drank a glass of lemon and ginger every morning when she woke up.'

'I did know that, but I can't say I noticed it at the time. As you can imagine, I had other things on my mind.' He shook his head. His patience had finally run out. 'I think you should leave,' he said.

'You've been very helpful,' I said. 'And believe me, all I want to do is to stop Eliot writing things that will cause harm to you or to the family. You've made it crystal clear that they don't make any sense.'

That calmed him down a little. His wife was still glaring at me, but he got up and showed me to the door. When he opened it, I glanced at the car, as if noticing it for the first time. 'It's beautiful,' I said. 'Is it yours?'

'Yes.' His pride got the better of him. 'It's a Suffolk Jaguar SS100. A beautiful car – a 4.2-litre twin-cam straight-six engine. It purrs along, and there's plenty of legroom too. I've got a Triumph Spitfire in the garage. I'm proud to have them and it's all thanks to Miriam Crace. She left me a generous bequest in her will. She was a wonderful woman. I still miss her.'

'We all do,' I said.

I turned and walked away, but he stood there, watching me, until I had gone.

The Miriam Crace Estate

I wasn't at all surprised when my mobile rang the following morning and an officious-sounding woman asked me to hold while she connected me with the CEO of the Miriam Crace Estate, Mr Jonathan Crace. I wondered who had been first to contact him after my adventures in Wiltshire: Frederick Turner or Dr John Lambert?

There was a brief silence and then a voice came on. 'Is that Susan Ryeland?'

'Yes.'

'I'm Jonathan Crace. I understand you're working with my nephew Eliot.' He had got straight to the point, though, to be fair, he sounded perfectly pleasant.

'That's right,' I said.

'I'm sure you're very busy, but I was wondering if we might have a chat about this book he's writing.'

'On the phone?'

'Actually, if you had time, I'd be grateful if you could look into the office.'

'And where is that?'

He gave me an address in Kingston Street, which, he said, was close to Trafalgar Square. 'Would eleven o'clock suit you?' he asked. 'Eliot's brother, Roland, works with me, so it'll be a chance for you to meet him too.'

'That would be fine.'

'Eleven o'clock, then.' He rang off.

I had a feeling that my reception wasn't going to be quite as amicable as the call had suggested, but I didn't hesitate. This was a chance to meet two more members of the family and perhaps to unpick whatever it was that was going on in Eliot's mind. Anyway, I was in no mood to tackle the Nordic noir manuscript Michael Flynn had sent me, and apart from that I had nothing else to do.

At five to eleven, I found myself outside the office where Frederick Turner had once worked. It was one of those solid Georgian buildings with white pillars and ornate railings from which the war might once have been planned and won. It was a perfect location for the Miriam Crace Estate: expensive but still anonymous, right in the middle of London, but in a long, quiet street, keeping its distance from restaurants and shops. Mr Banks, the banker in *Mary Poppins*, would have enjoyed working here. It would have suited his briefcase and bowler hat.

I rang the doorbell and heard its echoing clang. The door buzzed open and I went into a reception area that had Miriam Crace all over it: books, posters, photographs and awards that had spilled over from Marble Hall. I introduced myself and was given an ID sticker and directions to the third floor. A smartly dressed young woman, perhaps the one who had called me, was waiting when the lift door opened. She smiled pleasantly but said very little and I wondered if she had been warned not to give anything away. This was, after all, the land of the NDA. Perhaps I might be asked to sign one.

I was shown into a conference room with an oval table, eight pens, eight notepads, eight glasses and eight chairs. Sitting in one of them, the CEO of the Miriam Crace Estate was thumbing away at his mobile, writing what had to be a very important text but might have been timed for my arrival. He pressed send and stood up.

'Susan – thank you for coming in.'

'Jonathan – it's a pleasure to meet you.'

'Please, sit down. Would you like a coffee?'

'Thank you. White, no sugar.'

'Can you see to that, Olivia? And tell Roland that Susan is here.'

The assistant slipped out quietly and Jonathan Crace turned his attention to me. His ginger hair was the first thing I noticed, although it wasn't as wild or as fiery as that of his alter ego, Jeffrey Chalfont. It was cut straight across his forehead, drawing a parallel line with his rectangular spectacles, which sat like two television screens in front of eyes brimming not exactly with hostility but with a warning to keep your distance. He was wearing suit trousers but no jacket, as if to better display his monogrammed cuffs. A chunky gold ring (something else he shared with Jeffrey) weighed heavily on one hand.

'Good of you to come round at such short notice, Susan,' he barked, in a way that told me he'd expected nothing less. At the same time, he ushered me to a chair about halfway along the table. 'I understand you've been living in Crete.'

'Until recently,' I said.

'My wife and I were there last year. We stayed in Chania.'

'That's the other side of the island.'

'I understand you ran a hotel – following the collapse of your business.'

'It didn't collapse. It burned down.'

'And now you're working with Eliot.' His smile was brief and businesslike, informing me that the small talk was over. 'I knew your name, of course, because I worked with your boss, Charles Clover. He helped us with my mother's last books and he did a pretty good job.'

'I never thought of him as my boss. We were partners.'

'I was sorry to hear about what happened.' I waited for what was coming next and Jonathan didn't disappoint me. 'I find it quite hard to believe the accusations that were made against him.'

'They weren't accusations, Jonathan. Charles killed Alan Conway and tried to kill me. He left me unconscious in his office, which he then set on fire. I'm lucky to be alive.'

'Nothing like the man I knew! I'm lost for words.'

'I'm glad he helped with the books, though,' I said.

We were interrupted – at exactly the right time – by the return of Olivia with a tray and a porcelain cup of coffee. She had also brought a plate with two iced gingerbread figures that must have come from the same tin as the ones served at Marble Hall. These ones were both cut in the shape of Little Biscuits, the dog.

'So, how is Eliot?' Jonathan asked after the assistant had left. He already sounded wary, as if the very mention of Eliot's name was enough to spoil his day.

'When did you last see him?' I countered.

'I don't see him as often as I would like, although I'm hoping he'll be at the party next week. Tuesday the twenty-seventh.'

The date obviously meant something, but it was lost on me.

'It's the anniversary of my mother's death. We have a tradition. The whole family gets together – or as many of us as are in the country. We also invite business partners and friends. This anniversary is important because it's been exactly twenty years. I'll ask my assistant to send you an invitation.'

'Thank you.' I kicked myself for missing the significance.

'I'll be glad to catch up with Eliot,' he went on. 'As you can imagine, I have quite a full-time job here, keeping things afloat, and he never lifts a finger to help the family. I did of course know about this book he was writing. I feared the worst from the start.' He paused. 'Why did you lie to Frederick Turner?'

He had spoken in a way that was quite matter-of-fact, but he could hardly have been more provocative. An invitation one minute, this the next. It was the good-cop-bad-cop routine but played by the same person. I took a sip of my coffee. 'Was he the one who called you?' I asked.

'I've spoken to Frederick and to Dr Lambert. It seems that you deceived both of them. You said you were trying to protect Eliot when all you were doing was digging for dirt. As for Eliot, I've reached out to him, but he's not returning my messages. I'm sure it won't surprise you, Susan, that I take this matter extremely seriously. You come blundering into this family, repeating the most ludicrous – and unsubstantiated – accusations made by a young man with a history of mental illness and substance abuse. If you had any sense of propriety, you would have come straight to me so that we could discuss all this civilly, instead of which you go sneaking into Marble Hall—'

'Marble Hall is open to the public,' I reminded him. 'I had every right to go there.'

'To visit, yes. But not to go in undercover, like a spy. You tell Fred one thing and Lambert another, but the bottom line is that you seem to think there was something suspicious about my mother's death. And what's all this business about a stolen bottle of cough medicine? Are you seriously suggesting that Eliot was involved in some sort of conspiracy to commit murder? He was twelve years old, for heaven's sake!'

'It was Dr Lambert who told me about that,' I said. 'And as for Eliot, it was because he was twelve years old that your mother was able to terrify him.'

'I resent that interpretation.'

'It's irrelevant, anyway. Eliot is writing a whodunnit set in France in the 1950s. Have you heard of Atticus Pünd? It's a continuation novel that's got nothing to do with Marble Hall.'

'That's not what I've heard.' Jonathan examined me with something close to distaste. 'From what I understand, there are characters in this book that are clearly taken from real life . . .'

'Eliot has a right to draw inspiration from his childhood.'

'He can write whatever he wants, but if he – or you – is going to make trouble for the estate, I think I should warn you that I spend a fortune on lawyers and you could both be making a very expensive mistake.'

It was remarkable how he had managed to say all this with a straight face – which is to say, he had shown no emotion at all. He hadn't raised his voice. He seemed completely relaxed as he sat at the table, perfectly convinced of his superiority over me.

'Would you really sue your own nephew?' I asked. 'You talk about the estate, but isn't he a part of it? And to be honest, I don't think it would be a very good look for you to take him to court. You must be aware that he's had difficulties throughout his life—'

'Most of them inhaled up his nose, from what I understand.'

'I would say that's a rather cold-blooded point of view, Jonathan. I've spent some time with Eliot and I'd say most of his problems began at Marble Hall – but you were there, so you probably know that already.'

'There was nothing wrong with Marble Hall. It was a lovely place, a miniature paradise in some of the most beautiful countryside in England, and most children would have been happy to grow up there.'

He was about to go on, but just then the door opened and Roland Crace came in.

I knew at once it was him, and would have known even if Jonathan hadn't told me he was joining us. He was physically similar to Eliot but better-looking, more toned, more comfortable in his own skin. He dressed, moved and smiled like someone who took care of themselves and knew that their efforts had paid off. I was struck by his hair, which was darker than his brother's, thick and well groomed, by the whiteness of his teeth, by his skin, which positively glowed with good health. In his polished shoes and made-to-measure suit, he could have stepped out of the pages of an expensive fashion magazine. I wondered if I was going to like him. He was, after all, working for Jonathan Crace and if he was anything like his uncle, perhaps I should be making my excuses and heading for the door.

'This is Roland, Eliot's brother,' Jonathan exclaimed. 'We were just talking about Marble Hall, Roland. I'm afraid Susan has a rather dim view of the place.'

Roland ignored this. He strode over to my side of the table and we shook hands. 'It's a pleasure to meet you,' he said. 'Gillian told me she'd had dinner with you. I know Eliot's writing a book and I'm glad. He needs something to focus on.'

'That may be your view.' Jonathan was disconcerted. 'It certainly isn't mine.'

'He said he was writing a mystery story, Uncle Jon. And even if he's based some of it on Grandma and stuff that happened at Marble Hall, nobody else is going to know.' Roland pulled out a chair and sat next to me.

It struck me as interesting that he referred to the CEO of the Miriam Crace Estate as 'Uncle Jon' and that Miriam Crace was still 'Grandma'. After all, Roland Crace was in his late thirties and presumably senior within the organisation. It was as if, like Eliot, he hadn't quite escaped from the shadow of his childhood.

Jonathan glared at me. 'What exactly *were* you doing at Marble Hall?' he asked.

I thought for a moment before answering. 'I was trying to understand Eliot – and what he's writing.'

'By asking personal and intrusive questions? By deliberately misrepresenting your intentions? It seems to me that you have some sort of agenda against the family—'

'That's not true.'

'—and that Eliot's intention is to peddle a series of untruths about his childhood simply to promote a book which might otherwise pass unnoticed. I can see quite clearly that this would be in your interests too. Nothing sells quite like scandal.'

'You'll forgive me, Jonathan, but that's an utterly false characterisation of me, of Eliot and of the book. The Atticus Pünd novels have sold almost twenty million copies worldwide without any help from Miriam Crace, and there will certainly be huge interest in a tenth outing.'

'Why do you think Eliot was hired?'

'Because he's a good writer. Why else?'

Jonathan sneered. 'You really don't know anything, do you!'

I had no idea what he meant by that, but I forged on anyway. 'I went to Marble Hall because I was worried about Eliot.'

'Well, let me try and get something into your head, Susan. Nothing happened there. People may have different memories of my mother, but she was a brilliant writer and creator who died from a heart attack at the age of eighty-two. A perfectly natural death with not a whiff of suspicion. That's all there is to it. And if you or Eliot suggest otherwise – either in your book or in the publicity surrounding it – I can assure you that you will find yourselves in very serious legal hot water.'

He'd already made that threat once. Making it a second time only halved its effectiveness.

'Perhaps I can step in?' Roland suggested. He had addressed himself to his uncle, but now he turned to me. 'Eliot and I grew up together and I probably know him better than anyone in the world. Except Gillian, of course. I've said all along that I'm sure he wouldn't deliberately do anything to damage the estate.

'At the same time, though, this is a critical moment for us. If you've looked in the trade press, you'll know that we've been in discussions with Netflix and that we're about to sign a major deal that will bring Grandma's characters, the Little People, to a whole new generation. My job mainly concerns press and public relations – the family image. So I can't impress upon you enough how important it is right now that we don't do anything or say anything that could rock the boat.'

'A deal worth two hundred million dollars,' Jonathan growled. 'They're talking about a feature film followed by five seasons of a television series, just to kick off with. They're lining up some of the biggest names in Hollywood to perform the characters and I hardly need tell you that they will go to any lengths to protect their interests. We're not going to sit here and let Eliot put a spanner in the works. I'm not going to let that happen.'

'I'm sure that's not Eliot's intention.' Roland was doing everything he could to placate his uncle.

'Eliot needs to be kept under control.'

'Isn't that what Susan's doing? I think we should be working on this together, Uncle Jon. It's in all our interests to ensure that Eliot's book is a success. That's certainly my hope, anyway.'

Was he being completely sincere? I couldn't be sure, but at least Jonathan Crace seemed to have calmed down. 'That's why I wanted you here, Roland. I think, moving forward, you and Ms Ryeland should stay in close communication. Obviously, I wouldn't want to harm Eliot in any way. He may not have much time for us, but he's still family.'

I didn't believe a word of that. Nor, I think, did he.

'Eliot has been commissioned to write a book and maybe if we'd heard about that earlier, we could have done something about it – but it's too late now.' Jonathan's eyes in their rectangular frames settled on me. 'But now that you know the stakes, Susan, I'm sure we can rely on you to keep him in line.'

'I'll do what I can,' I promised him.

'Shall I show you out?' Roland said.

The two of them stood up. And just like that, the meeting was over.

Roland Crace

Neither Roland nor I said anything as we took the lift back down to the ground floor. We stood there rather stiffly, avoiding each other's eyes, and I was glad nobody held us up on the way. I felt like a prisoner being escorted to the main gate by a junior warder after serving a long sentence and I couldn't wait to be out.

But as we stepped into the reception area, Roland surprised me. 'Would you like a coffee before you go?' he asked. Maybe there was an attractive side to him after all.

'Thank you.'

'There's a room we can use. It has a coffee machine. Not a bad one.'

The room was on the other side of the reception desk, with windows but no view. There was a capsule coffee machine, a fridge, two sofas shaped like an L. Roland pressed the right buttons and made two cappuccinos.

'I wanted to say I'm sorry if Uncle Jon came over as a bit aggressive,' he began.

'Not a bit,' I said. 'Very.'

'If we're all going to work together – with Eliot – I think you should know that his bark is much worse than his bite. The thing is, he's been involved with *The Little People* ever since he was my age. He was pretty much running the estate while Grandma was still alive and he oversaw the opening of Marble Hall. He was the one who suggested the new characters. He was a producer on the musical and he worked on the ITV television series. It nearly killed him when Grandma told him she was planning to sell the IP to an outside company. He took it as a personal betrayal. Her creations mean everything to him and so he's always quite nervous when someone like you comes along. It's nothing personal, I assure you.'

'Why did she want to sell the IP rights?' I asked.

'I never asked her. I was seventeen when she died. From what Uncle Jon has always said, she just hated the idea of losing control. She didn't trust anyone and I suppose if she was going to say goodbye to Little Jack and Little Harry and all the rest of them, it was easier to pass them on to a complete stranger in return for pot loads of money.'

'Jonathan would still have been rich if the sale had gone through.'

'That wasn't enough. You've got to understand, he really does love those characters. He grew up with them. They're like little friends.' He smiled in a way that was both amused and mournful at the same time. 'You know he named his daughter after one of them.'

'Jasmine. Yes. She died in an accident.'

There was an implied question and Roland answered it for me. 'She fell under a train at Sloane Square tube station.

That was back in 2006. She was twenty-one years old at the time . . . one year older than me.'

In *Pünd's Last Case*, Elmer Waysmith's first wife had also died under a train, in her case a suicide at Grand Central Station. I was beginning to see that Eliot had taken the members of his family and shuffled them like playing cards. For example, he had expressly said that the character of Cedric Chalfont was based on himself, but in the manuscript, Cedric was an only child. So what did that make Roland? If he was connected to anyone in Eliot's book, it would have to be Robert Waysmith, Elmer's son. '*Slim and athletic*' with the '*waywardness of a poet*'. The description seemed to fit.

'Uncle Jon ended up running the estate,' Roland went on. 'Which is exactly what he wanted. My father was also left money, which he shared with the three of us, so we can't complain. There were no other bequests . . . apart from one to Uncle Frederick. He didn't get as much as the rest of us because he wasn't a blood relative, but at least he got something. You mustn't be angry that he snitched on you. He's another of the guardians at the gate. You've got to understand. Grandma wasn't just a children's writer. She was more like God issuing the Ten Commandments, with everyone in the family wanting to be Moses.'

'Including you?'

Roland laughed. 'I don't need to work, but I've got nothing else to do and when you have a surname like Crace it doesn't take anyone long to work out who you are. Uncle Jon offered me a job and I decided I might as well roll over and accept it. My parents weren't too pleased.'

'Why not?'

'Dad hated everything to do with *The Little People*. He wanted his own life. He wasn't comfortable growing up in Marble Hall and after Grandma died he moved to a house in Notting Hill Gate. That's where Eliot lives now.'

'Are you telling me you didn't dislike your grandmother too?' Before he could answer, I went on. 'That's what Eliot told me. He said that the three of you – you, your sister and him – hated her so much that you wanted to kill her. I know you were only children, but it still sounds as if life at Marble Hall was miserable for all of you.'

Roland thought for a minute. He glanced around, as if checking we were alone in the room. Finally he spoke: 'All right, Susan. I can see you're on Eliot's side and I'm glad about that. I hear things aren't good between him and Gillian right now. He's drinking again, and he needs all the help he can get. So I'll tell you what you want to know. But this is just between the two of us. Is that a deal?'

'Of course.'

'Grandma was not a good person or a kind person. In fact, she was vile.' He stopped, allowing the words to hang between us. Had this room, with its hand-finished wallpaper and soft Italian lighting, ever heard anything like them? 'Everything Eliot has told you about her is true. She was cruel. She was racist. We turned a blind eye to her failings and did what she wanted because she made it clear that if we complained she'd cut us off without a penny. Quite honestly, she wouldn't have cared if we starved. I often wonder how she managed to create these characters who are so sweet and kind and who have given pleasure to millions. I meet kids in cancer wards who have *The Little People* beside their bed.

You should see the letters we get sent – even in the age of emails. '*My parents are always arguing – can Grandma Little come and talk to them?*' '*I'm being bullied at school, please ask Harry Little to sort them out!*' '*My mum won't let me have a dog. Can Little Biscuits come and stay?*' My job is to lie to them. I spend every day of the week keeping alive the big lie that Miriam Crace was an angel when in fact she made all our lives a misery – and by that, I mean Grandpa, my parents, everyone who came close to her, with the single exception of my uncle Jonathan, who always had his eye on the main prize and blinded himself to the truth.'

'Wow!' I said. The word slipped out of my lips. I couldn't quite believe what I was hearing.

'You may want to know how I live with myself. Funnily enough, it's easy. There have been a lot of famous artists who have behaved badly. Look at how Charles Dickens treated his wife! Tolstoy, the same. If you look at children's writers, Roald Dahl had some pretty ripe things to say about the Jews, Enid Blyton had loads of affairs, and Lewis Carroll . . . well, let's not talk about him and little girls. The same could be said for a hundred musicians, artists, film-makers . . . You have to divorce their personal lives from their works or you're going to end up with nothing on TV, nothing on your walls, nothing on your shelves. I wouldn't put so much as a bunch of dandelions on my grandmother's grave, but that doesn't stop me making sure she's piled high in Waterstones.'

'Why do you say she was a racist?' I asked. 'She adopted Frederick Turner and when I spoke to him, he didn't make any complaints.'

'That's because he can't. He was left very little money in

the will – even if he was her adopted son. He depends one hundred per cent on the estate and Uncle Jonathan for his lifestyle, and after his car accident he wasn't exactly marketable.' He paused. 'I'm sorry. That sounds a bit heartless. All I'm saying is, he toes the line because he can't afford not to – but when he was at Marble Hall, he was always the underdog. Unlike the rest of us, he was sent to the local comprehensive and then he was pushed into accountancy school so that he could become an unpaid bookkeeper for the estate. He didn't even eat with the family half the time.'

As much as I hated hearing it, what Roland was saying chimed with what I already knew or suspected. I remembered Frederick talking about Miriam Crace. '*I never thought of her as a mother.*' Odd words to come from an adopted son.

'And there's more to it than that,' Roland continued. 'Grandma never got on with my aunt Leylah.'

'Jonathan's wife.'

'She's Egyptian. She and Jonathan met on a Nile cruise and Grandma was always making jokes about her being a belly dancer or a handmaiden or things like that. She got off more lightly than poor Freddy because she was whiter than him and because her family had money. But if you're talking about racism, there's something else you ought to know. It was the real reason why she fell out with Uncle Jonathan and almost sold the entire estate.'

'Because he married an Egyptian?'

'No. Because he was the one who persuaded her to add ethnically diverse characters to the Little People. Njinga and Karim in particular. She hated doing it, but he assured her that the books wouldn't survive in the twenty-first century if they didn't reflect modern times. She went along with it, but she never forgave him. It's the reason why, at the end of her life, she was thinking of selling the rights.'

I took a breath. 'Why are you telling me all this?' I asked.

'Because if you want to help Eliot, you need to know about my family.'

'Why have you and Eliot fallen out?'

'We haven't.'

'He told me he hadn't seen you for a while.'

'We've both been busy.' Roland sighed. 'All right. He never really forgave me for joining the estate. He thinks of it as treason. I've tried to explain that there was no harm in it, but he won't listen to me.'

I wasn't sure Roland was telling the whole story, but I let that go for the moment. 'Is it true that you wanted to kill your grandmother when you were children?' I asked.

'I'll tell you about that, Susan. But first you need to believe me when I say that there is absolutely no truth in the suggestion that Grandma died an unnatural death. Uncle Jonathan is right about that – and if that's what you're hearing from Eliot, it's rubbish. Yes. We talked about killing her. I've already told you – we hated her. But we were children! We were growing up with R. L. Stine and Agatha Christie on TV. It wasn't some sort of dark conspiracy. It was all in our heads, and for what it's worth, Eliot was the most imaginative of the three of us.

'Here's the thing. I've already told you how horrible Grandma was to Fred and to Aunt Leylah. But she was much, much worse to my sister, Julia. You've spoken to Dr Lambert. Did he tell you that she had a thyroid problem? She was large. For some reason, my grandmother took this as a personal insult – that someone in the family should have a shape that didn't conform. God knows how she managed to keep all these prejudices out of her books, but maybe that was down to her editors. At any event, she made snide remarks and teased Julia at every opportunity, and Eliot and I both hated her for it. That was why we talked about pushing her under a bus or poisoning her. I was seventeen when Grandma died. Julia was fifteen. Eliot was only twelve. Do you seriously think we had it in us to become murderers?'

'But Eliot did steal medicine from Dr Lambert's medicine bag.'

'Cough medicine, yes – but it wasn't poison. It was something called Liqufruta!' Roland gave a sniff of laughter. 'Eliot thought he could concoct something with it. Toothpaste, shoe polish, chilli sauce and cough medicine . . . You get the general idea. We were just kids! What did we know?'

Roland glanced at his watch. We had been in the room for ten minutes or more. He had to go back to work.

'Thank you,' I said. 'You've been very helpful. Would it be possible to speak to your sister Julia?'

He reached into his top pocket and took out his business card. 'She teaches geography at a school in Lincoln. If you text me your number, I'll ask her to call you. But she's coming to the party, so you might meet her there.'

'Is she married?'

'Sadly not.'

'What about you?'

He smiled. 'I'm still available too.' He stood up. 'I just want Eliot's book to be successful,' he said. 'If you can help make that happen, I'll be more than grateful. I'm not sure why, but I think he was the most damaged of the three of us by our life at Marble Hall. Maybe it was his arguments with Dad? I don't know. But if he became a big-shot writer like Grandma, it would be the making of him. I'd love to see that happen.'

'I'll do what I can,' I promised.

We moved to the door, but as we passed into the reception area, something he had told me right at the start of our conversation came to mind. 'You said that your grandmother left no bequests in her will outside the family, apart from a small sum paid to Frederick Turner.'

'That's right.'

'What about her charities?'

'She'd already set up trusts for them while she was alive.'

'So, no-one else?'

'That's what I always understood.'

We shook hands and I left the building. But as I stepped into the street, this is what I was thinking. Dr Lambert had boasted to me that his two expensive classic cars had been paid for by money left to him by Miriam Crace. Roland had just told me that wasn't true.

So how, then, had he afforded them?

Part Two

I thought I'd had enough of the Crace family for one day, but I was wrong. As I arrived back at my new home in Crouch End, I heard a car door slam shut and saw Eliot Crace on the other side of the road, getting out of a beaten-up BMW coupé. He was grubby, unshaven, his hair greasy, a moth-eaten scarf hanging around his neck. He was wearing a black shirt and skinny jeans. I waited for him to cross the road and come over to me.

'You're in a residents' parking zone,' I warned him.

'I can afford a ticket and you're worth it, Susan.'

There was something almost licentious in the way he said that, leering at me. He wasn't drunk, but the smell of alcohol and cigarette smoke from the night before still clung to him, as if he had crawled out of bed in the same clothes he'd been wearing when he got into it.

'You look terrible,' I said.

'I was at Boon's . . .'

'I'm sorry?'

'It's a club I go to in the Portobello Road. Don't tell

Gillian! It's my little bolt-hole. I met some friends and then I worked all night. I thought you'd be pleased.' He lifted a hand and I saw that he was holding an A4 manila envelope. 'I've got something for you. Can I come in?'

'Have you just got here? Or have you been waiting for me?' I didn't mean to be offensive, but there was something about Eliot that was a little disgusting. I knew he'd been damaged, that his childhood at Marble Hall had been disastrous. But this was Crouch End on a sunny afternoon and there was something pathetic about this rich kid who had an attractive wife, an expensive house in Notting Hill Gate, a publishing deal with Causton Books and much less to complain about than a hundred thousand other young people struggling to make ends meet in the grindstone that London could all too easily become.

'I just got here,' he said. He was surprised by my abruptness.

'How did you know where I live?' I asked.

'Michael Flynn told me. I thought you'd be pleased to see me.'

In fact, I was a little surprised that Michael would be handing out my address without asking me, but I relented. Eliot was still my author, my responsibility. 'I'm always pleased to see you,' I said. 'Come in. I'll make you some coffee.'

I was half tempted to take him through to the bathroom and throw him in the shower, just as Elaine had once done, but instead I led him into the kitchen, flicked on the kettle and searched for the strongest coffee I could find. Hugo, the cat, had heard us arrive and leapt onto the counter, arching his back, purring and generally going through his feline repertoire.

'I didn't think you were the sort to keep cats,' Eliot said.

'I'm not,' I assured him. 'My sister got him for me.'

'Have you been here long?'

'I used to live round the corner, so I know the area. But this place is new.'

'Do you mind if I smoke?'

'I'd prefer it if you didn't – but you can go out in the garden, if you like.'

Whenever I'd visited my sister, Katie, she'd also made me go out into the garden to keep the smell of cigarette smoke out of the house. It reminded me that she'd always thought of me as the wild one, racing around town in my red MG, married to my work, to launch parties, to drinking sessions that stretched into the small hours. What right did I have to make any judgement about Eliot? Here I was, well into my second half-century. What sort of person was I becoming?

I made the coffee and carried it over. He was sitting at the table with the envelope in front of him.

'Is this the next section of the novel?' I asked.

'Yes. I printed it out for you.'

'That's very thoughtful of you, Eliot. Do you have a new title yet?'

'I hate titles. Have you noticed? All murder mysteries are the same. It's *Death* . . . this or *Murder* . . . that. It's like there are only half a dozen words in the English language you can use.' He counted them off on his fingers. 'Blood, Kill, Murder, Death, Knife, Body . . . I'd like to call my book *The Man with White Hair* – but you wouldn't like that at all, would you?'

'Actually, I do quite like it,' I said. 'Although it might give too much away.'

'Why?'

'Well, it suggests that Elmer Waysmith is the killer.'

'He might not be.'

'Don't tell me. I don't want you to spoil the ending.'

He sipped his coffee and winced. 'Have you got any sugar?'

I went over to a cupboard and pulled out a bag of granulated, deliberately ignoring the little bowl with the teaspoon and the sugar cubes beside the fridge. 'So you must have been working very hard,' I said. 'When I met you at Causton Books, you said you'd only done another ten thousand words.'

'I've been working non-stop since then.' He smiled at me and I remembered the wild child I'd met all those years ago and always liked. 'You must have inspired me.'

'I'm glad to hear it.'

'I haven't made any changes to the first bit. Not yet. I just want to get to the end before I go back to the beginning.'

'I think that's sensible. And you're sure you want me to keep reading?'

'I've put my phone numbers on the envelope. I'll be interested to know what you think.'

'I'll call you.'

I took the envelope. Just from the weight, I knew that Part Two was quite a bit shorter than the section I'd already read . . . probably around twenty thousand words. There was an editor I once worked with who could tell the length of a manuscript to the nearest five hundred words just by holding it in her hand.

'By the way, I took your advice and went to Marble Hall,' I said.

'Oh.' He looked alarmed. 'What did you think?'

259

'I found it hard to imagine you living there when you were young. All those things you said at Elaine's. You obviously had a horrible time. But I thought it was a nice enough house and the grounds were beautiful. It's sad, really. Lots of children would have loved growing up there.'

'Not if they had a horrible old crone watching over them.'

'I bumped into the manager . . . Frederick Turner. You've been very naughty, Eliot. Turning him into a French detective.'

'You don't think he'll be amused?'

'He might be offended, going on about his injuries.' Eliot said nothing, so I asked: 'Is that how your character lost an eye? Careless driving?'

'Frédéric Voltaire got blown up in the war. You'll read about that in the new pages. And as for Uncle Fred, it wasn't careless driving.'

'So what was it really?'

'He was drunk or something . . . I don't know. I remember when it happened. Fred said he wasn't concentrating, but the police asked him a lot of questions. Leylah – my aunt – said he was breathalysed.'

'Did he lose his licence?'

'No. But he never talks about it. He was different after the accident. He was angry. He wasn't much fun to have around.'

That was hardly surprising. Frederick Turner had lost an eye and he was still in pain. 'Why did you put him in the book?' I asked.

Eliot shrugged. 'No reason. I was just having a bit of fun.'

In other words, he wasn't going to tell me. I was tempted to ask him about his father, how Edward Crace had become

Elmer Waysmith, but this wasn't the right time. I wanted Eliot to finish the book before we had our inevitable set-to. 'Frederick mentioned that you once set fire to the house,' I said.

Eliot smiled. 'That was in Notting Hill. It was no big deal. I fell asleep with a cigarette and it burned a hole in the carpet. It set off the smoke alarms, though. My dad hit the roof, but then everything I did seemed to annoy him.'

'Are you going to the party?' He looked blank. 'Next Tuesday. It's the twentieth anniversary of your grandmother's death.'

'Oh – that!' He shrugged. 'I might. What else did Fred tell you about me?'

'He didn't say anything bad about you, if that's what you're asking.' Once again, I was tiptoeing around the truth. I seemed to have done nothing else since I had been introduced to the Craces. 'He told me you were very imaginative and he hoped the book would be a success.'

I had already decided I wasn't going to say anything about my meeting with Dr Lambert. Nor did I tell him that I had just come back from the office in Kingston Street, where I'd met both his brother and his uncle. I didn't want Eliot to think that I was snooping around, asking questions about him behind his back. He looked worn out. I was keen to get him out of the house so that I could read the new pages, and perhaps he sensed this. He drank some more of the coffee, yawned and stood up.

'I'll leave you to get on with it,' he said. He looked around, as if noticing his surroundings for the first time. 'Nice place you've got.'

'Thank you.'

'You live here alone?'

'Yes.' I'm not sure he meant to offend me by asking me that, but I still found the question intrusive somehow. What business was it of his who I lived with or if I didn't live with anyone? He probably knew about Andreas and me. Elaine would have told him. Not for the first time, I got the sense that I was being drawn into something more than the editing of a continuation novel. But it was too late to walk out now. Michael Flynn might never forgive me and it would certainly be the end of my career at Causton Books.

We walked to the door.

'By the way,' he said. 'I've had an invitation to go on *Front Row*.'

'On the BBC?' *Front Row* was a magazine programme broadcast on Radio 4. It covered books, films, TV . . . everything to do with the arts. When I was working at Cloverleaf, I'd often tried to get my authors invited.

'Yes.'

'I'm not sure you should do it, Eliot,' I said. The news really troubled me. 'It would be much better to wait until next year when the book is published. Why talk about the book now when we haven't got any copies to sell?'

'They don't want me to talk about my book. They don't even know I'm writing it. You reminded me just now when you mentioned the anniversary. Twenty years since her death. They want me to talk about my grandmother.' He breathed out and once again I smelled cigarette smoke and the dregs of old white wine, now mixed with coffee. It was an unpleasant combination. 'I've got a few stories I could tell that might surprise them,' he added.

'I recommend you don't do that, Eliot.' It occurred to me that I was doing exactly what Jonathan wanted – but it wasn't the estate I was protecting. It was Eliot. 'If you say bad things about your grandmother, it won't help you. Quite the opposite. When we come to publicise your book, it'll really help that you're her grandson. Whatever you may think of her, she still sells millions and if only one per cent of her readers decide to give you a go, that'll push you into the bestseller lists.'

'You don't think the book is good enough on its own?'

'That's not what I'm saying. I told you. I love what you're writing and I can't wait to start on the next section. But it's too soon to go on *Front Row*. If people think you're being negative, that's simply going to turn them away from you. Please promise me you'll reconsider and that you won't do it.'

'I haven't given them an answer yet.'

'Would you like me to call them for you? I'll be happy to talk to them and we can ask them to have you later in the year. Please take my advice. I don't think a radio appearance right now will do you any good at all and that would be a shame after all your hard work.'

He stood there, clearly wondering whether to be annoyed. Then he relaxed. 'All right, Susan,' he said, with a lopsided grin. 'You don't need to worry. I'll call them. I didn't want to do it anyway.'

He reached towards me and I thought he was going to kiss me goodbye, but instead he patted me clumsily on the shoulder. Fishing out his car keys, he disappeared through the door, and with a sense of relief, I closed it.

Should I call Jonathan? Or Michael Flynn? When it comes to media appearances, you always have to be careful. What can look like a marvellous piece of publicity can all too easily turn into a trap. Twenty years ago, I'd published a book about a Sinhalese detective and I still remember sitting outside the studio, listening in horror as the discussion turned into a barrage of accusations about cultural appropriation, with the author completely out of her depth. It was a series that had extended to exactly one book. These days, publishers are much more in tune with what is and what is not acceptable, but we all know that a single step over a line that's so ill-defined as to be practically invisible can cause all sorts of problems, and that there are any number of ambitious young journalists out there keen to make headlines.

I picked up my mobile phone and my thumb hovered over the speed dial, but in the end I didn't make the call, and I'm afraid that was a mistake I would soon come to regret. Eliot would never have forgiven me if I'd shopped him to his uncle and I still thought there was a chance he would take my advice and ignore *Front Row* until there was a reason to go on it. I persuaded myself that I was acting in his best interests and put the phone down.

Instead, I opened the manuscript and began to read.

TWELVE

'We have found the *pharmacie*!'

Frédéric Voltaire was pleased with himself and didn't try to conceal it. He had been waiting in the reception area of the Grand-Hôtel when Pünd and Fraser came out from breakfast, sitting beside the main door, smoking a cigarette. From the way he told them the news, it was as if outsmarting the famous Atticus Pünd mattered to him more than making a breakthrough in the investigation.

'So, where is it?' Fraser asked.

'In Nice. The Rue Lafayette. We interviewed more than fifty pharmacists in the area. To begin with, this fellow was reluctant to admit that he had provided the poison which killed Lady Chalfont. And with good reason! He may lose his licence.'

'The Rue Lafayette.' Pünd might have ignored everything else the detective had said. 'That name is familiar to me.'

'It is a small street, only a short distance from the Galerie Werner-Waysmith.'

'That is certainly interesting. Have you spoken to the pharmacist?'

'I am leaving now. You may join me if you wish.'

Voltaire was back in control. He led the way out to the car and sat with his arms crossed and a half-smile on his face for the entire journey. They drove into Nice and, perhaps deliberately, crossed the Place Masséna, passing the gallery before entering a maze of backstreets and alleyways further away from the seafront. Finally, they arrived at a sunless street that might have been forgotten by the rest of the city, lacking anything that would attract a tourist or visitor. There was a uniformed gendarme standing outside the Pharmacie Lafayette, which had been closed for the day.

They went in.

Pünd could see at once why a killer might have chosen this place rather than any other. It was twenty years out of date, with bottles and boxes stretching out along wooden shelves that had warped with age, a pair of scales that was positively antique and an ugly-looking cash register that took up far too much space on the counter. The pharmacist himself was in his sixties, nervous and sullen, with bad eyesight. He had not yet spoken a word and seemed to have no intention of doing so, afraid that he would only get himself into more trouble.

Voltaire took charge of the interrogation, speaking in French. Fraser did his best to provide a translation, although part of him was still wondering if Pünd might not actually speak the language better than he did.

'You are Hector Brunelle,' Voltaire began.

'Yes, monsieur.'

'And you recall selling aconitine to a customer three days ago?'

It was the same day that Lady Chalfont had died.

'Yes, monsieur. He told me he was a doctor. I had already noticed that he had the smell of surgical spirit on his clothes. He showed me his licence.'

'And how carefully did you examine it?' Voltaire lifted a hand. 'How many fingers am I holding up?'

Brunelle squinted, but it was obvious he couldn't see that far. 'I need my spectacles,' he admitted.

'And were you wearing your spectacles when this customer came in?' Voltaire asked.

'I don't remember,' Brunelle replied miserably.

'Can you describe him for us?' Pünd asked in English, then waited for Fraser to translate. 'Was he French?'

'No, monsieur. He spoke in French but with an accent . . . English or maybe American.'

'What of his appearance?'

'It was not easy to see him. He was wearing sunglasses and a hat made of straw with a band. I noticed that he kept his head down, as if he was afraid of being recognised. When another customer came into the shop, he looked away. He was not young. He had white hair and an ebony walking stick. He told me that he had a patient who was suffering from the gout. Aconitine is a well-known antidote for this condition if used in small doses and I sold him only two grams.'

'What else was he wearing?' Voltaire asked.

'I cannot remember exactly, monsieur. I think it was a linen suit, either blue or grey. I seem to recall that it did not fit him well.'

'Do you have any idea what time he came into your establishment?'

'I can tell you that exactly. The other customer was a lady and she was in a hurry. She asked the time and he told her: twelve fifteen.'

'That was all?'

267

'"*Je suis un peu pressée. As-tu l'heure?*"'

'I'm in a bit of a hurry. What time is it?' Fraser translated.

'Those were her exact words?' Pünd asked.

'Yes, monsieur.'

'What did this lady purchase?' Voltaire demanded.

'She did not purchase anything. She asked for a certain shampoo, but we did not have it. She left.'

'And the man?'

'He took his purchase and he also went. I did not see in which direction.' Hector Brunelle was close to tears. 'I did nothing wrong,' he complained. 'The man told me he was a doctor. He had a licence.' A thought occurred to him. His eyes brightened. 'He signed his name in the register.'

'Let me see it!'

The pharmacist ducked down behind the counter and reappeared with a thick leather volume with deckle-edged pages. He found his glasses and put them on, then laboriously searched through the entries. At last, he found the date he was looking for. 'Here!' he said. But he sounded disappointed.

Pünd saw why. When the book was turned round, the signature was nothing more than a scribble of turquoise ink in which not a single letter was legible. The so-called doctor had not even pretended to add an address.

Brunelle knew immediately that he was at fault. He should have worn his glasses. He should have taken more care. 'I only provided him with two grams of the medicine,' he protested. 'It was not a fatal dose!'

But once the three men were back out in the street, Voltaire took a different view. 'The man is a fool,' he snapped.

'Two grams would have been more than enough to kill an elderly woman with a heart condition.'

'Will you prosecute him, Monsieur Voltaire?'

Voltaire considered. 'No. What good will it do? But this will be a warning for him to take more care in future.' He glanced at a café that was just a few steps away. 'I would like a coffee,' he said. Perhaps it was an invitation. Pünd and Fraser exchanged looks, then joined him at a table underneath the awning.

The café was not the most charming in the city, but there was something honest and authentic about the striped canopy and the tables spread out along the pavement that put all three of them at ease. For a moment, the murder and the friction between the investigators could be forgotten. A waiter with a long white apron appeared and they ordered three coffees. Voltaire lit another cigarette.

'You live in Paris?' Pünd asked.

'I have lived there for much of my life. I have a wife and a son in Montparnasse.'

'How old is your son?'

'His name is Lucien and he is seventeen.' Voltaire smoked contentedly. 'He was born two years before the war. During that time, he and his mother moved to the south, to Hyères, which is not so very far from here. They were safer staying with relatives.'

'And you?'

'I was a police officer but also an army reservist. I was conscripted and sent for training in a town called Bitche in the Moselle.' He glanced at Fraser. 'It is perhaps fortunate that your friend has no need to translate.' He paused. 'I found

269

myself serving in the Ardennes, part of the famous Maginot Line that was said to be indestructible until the moment it was destroyed. I was in one of the *petits ouvrages* – as we called them. A bunker connected to a network of tunnels. A German hand grenade ended my war on the twenty-eighth of May 1940. It left me as you see me now.'

'I am sorry,' Pünd said.

'Are you, Herr Pünd? It does not matter now, of course, but we were on opposite sides. I was in hospital for many weeks and spent the next five years as a prisoner of war. Some prisoners were exchanged under the *relève* system, but I was not considered to have any value and so remained in a stalag in Görlitz in the far east of Germany. At least I was spared forced labour. My injuries made that impossible. Instead, they tried to starve me to death.'

'You were fortunate to survive,' Pünd remarked. 'But if you will allow me, Monsieur Voltaire, I must say that you are wrong when you state that we were on opposite sides. I was born in Germany, but I come from a family of Greek Jews. I was, like you, a police officer in the thirties, but I made the mistake of speaking out against the Nazis. As a result, I spent the war in a prison camp.'

'Then our experiences were similar.'

'The camp where I was held may have had a different clientèle, but I would imagine the living conditions were equally unpleasant.'

'Then I apologise. I have perhaps allowed my experiences to have informed the way I have behaved towards you.'

'There is no need for an apology, Monsieur Voltaire. The war has cast a long shadow and its darkness reaches us even now.'

The coffee had taken a long time to arrive, but finally the waiter reappeared, balancing a silver tray with cups and saucers on the flat of his hand. Pünd waited until he had gone before he began again. 'What did you make of the story told by our friend *le pharmacien*?' he asked. 'The man with the white hair.'

'The only man with white hair who is known to me is Elmer Waysmith,' Voltaire replied.

'He also has an American accent,' Fraser chipped in.

'Indeed so. I have not, however, seen Monsieur Waysmith make use of a walking stick.'

'Well, perhaps he was trying to disguise himself,' Fraser said. 'The straw hat, the dark glasses, the way he tried to hide his face . . .'

'That is certainly one interpretation,' Pünd muttered. 'I would ask myself, though, why Mr Waysmith should have carried with him the scent of surgical spirit.'

'And then there is the question of timing,' Voltaire said. 'We know that he had lunch with his son on the same day that the aconitine was purchased. We are at least fifteen minutes from the Place Masséna, even at a brisk pace. It would be interesting to know at what time he arrived at the restaurant . . .'

'And what he was wearing,' Pünd added.

'It is interesting, do you not think, how the finger of suspicion points directly at just one man? Monsieur Waysmith alone had the motive to kill Lady Chalfont.'

'She had discovered something about him that might have persuaded her to change her will.'

'So it would appear. Why else would she have arranged to meet with Jean Lambert on the day of her death?'

271

'And it would seem almost certain that it was he who visited the pharmacy,' Pünd concluded. 'There is even the matter of the signature in the register.'

'Yes. I saw that too.'

'But there was no signature!' Fraser exclaimed. 'It was just a scribble.'

'You did not remark upon the colour of the ink?' Pünd asked.

'Turquoise.' Voltaire nodded in agreement.

'Exactly. The papers on the desk in Mr Waysmith's office were written in that same colour, James. I have no doubt that the same pen was used in both cases.'

'So it must have been him, then!'

'I do not know.' Voltaire finished his coffee and stubbed out his cigarette. 'There is something about this business that I find disturbing.'

'It is not as straightforward as it might appear,' Pünd agreed. 'I noticed a hotel at the end of this street. I would suggest that we look in and pay it a visit before we leave the area.'

'And why is that, Monsieur Pünd?' Voltaire asked.

'Because I saw its name when we were at the Chateau Belmar. There are some who would say that this is just a coincidence, but . . .'

'Mr Pünd doesn't believe in coincidences.' Fraser finished the sentence for him.

'Where did you see it?'

'Right here!' Pünd leaned forward and picked up the book of matches that Voltaire had used to light his cigarette. He turned it over and there, in red letters, were the two words:

HÔTEL LAFAYETTE. 'I hope you will not mind my asking where you found this, Monsieur Voltaire.'

Briefly, Voltaire's face clouded over, but then the moment passed. 'I believe I picked it up in the vestibule as we left the Chateau Belmar after the reading of the will,' he said. 'It was lying on a table and after the unpleasant scene we had witnessed, I had a desire to smoke a cigarette in the garden.' He glanced down the narrow street towards the hotel. 'I agree with you again, Monsieur Pünd. It cannot be a coincidence. Did Elmer Waysmith also visit the hotel?'

Pünd stood up. 'Let us find out,' he said.

THIRTEEN

'Yes. I do remember the gentleman of whom you speak. He was an elderly man who wore a panama hat and sunglasses. I never saw him without them, even when he was inside the building. He booked a room for two nights: Thursday and Friday, the second and third of this month. There is not very much more I can tell you about him. He arrived with a small suitcase, which he insisted on carrying himself, and paid in advance with cash. He was a man of few words. He used a walking stick.'

The speaker was an anxious-looking man with hollow cheeks and a moustache. He had introduced himself as Louis Baptiste and he was the owner of the Hôtel Lafayette as well as its manager, receptionist, barman and occasional chef. His wife and daughter were partners in the enterprise and they had another three employees who helped with the cleaning, the kitchen, security and general maintenance.

Pünd, Voltaire and Fraser were standing in the hotel's reception area, which consisted of a curved marble-topped counter with, behind it, fourteen wooden pigeonholes. To one side, the smallest lift Fraser had ever seen stood waiting, although if a family of four with luggage had decided to check in, the only way they would have been able to go up might have been one at a time.

'Did you ask him for his identity card?' Voltaire asked.

'He had already paid,' Baptiste replied. 'There was no need.'

'Did he enter his name into your visitors' book?'

'We ask every guest to register with us. I have it here.'

There was a black ledger in front of him and the hotel manager opened it at the correct page. Pünd and Voltaire leaned forward and immediately saw the name – JOHN FORD – written in capital letters and in the same turquoise ink they recognised from the pharmacy. There was a phone number but no address.

'John Ford . . .' Voltaire muttered.

'That's the name of an American film director,' Fraser said. 'He made *Rio Grande* with John Wayne. I thought it was rather good.'

'It is also the shortest possible name he could choose,' Voltaire added. 'He's written in capitals to disguise his handwriting, but we might still be able to compare it with some of the work written by Monsieur Waysmith. You see the way the crossbar in the letter H slopes down . . .'

'And what of the phone number?'

'It's a local number and I'll have it checked. But it is certain to be false.'

They seemed to have come to another impasse, but Pünd was not dispirited. Between them, the book of matches and the turquoise ink proved that *someone* from the Chateau Belmar had been here, even if they could not be completely sure that it was Elmer Waysmith. He turned to Louis Baptiste. 'How often did you see Mr Ford?' he asked.

'Only when he checked in on the Thursday evening. And once again on Friday.'

'When was that?'

'It was midmorning, sometime after twelve o'clock. Perhaps five past? I did not notice the exact time. The gentleman went directly to his room.'

'Which room was he in?'

Baptiste glanced at the register. 'Number thirteen. On the third floor.'

'Did he take the lift or the stairs?'

'He took the stairs, monsieur. He came in through those doors and proceeded straight upstairs.'

'Strange behaviour for a man with a walking stick,' Voltaire observed.

'I would agree, monsieur. Evidently, he was in a hurry. He did not acknowledge me.'

'He did not stop to ask for his key?'

'He must have taken it with him when he went out.'

Pünd glanced at Voltaire, who nodded. Fraser couldn't help noticing that a strange chemistry had arisen between them since they had driven into Nice. Each seemed to know what the other was thinking.

'We would like to see his room,' Voltaire said.

'Certainly, monsieur. It has, of course, been cleaned since Monsieur Ford departed, but it is empty now. My daughter will take you up.'

Baptiste reached out and slammed his palm down on a service bell that chimed out through the hotel. A few moments later, a door opened and a young girl appeared, holding a dustpan and brush. 'Yes, Papa?'

'Can you please take these gentlemen up to room thirteen, Marie. They are not guests. They are investigating a crime.'

'A crime at the hotel?' The girl's eyes widened.

'No, no, no. It has nothing to do with us.'

The girl put down the cleaning implements and removed a key from its pigeonhole, then started up the stairs. Pünd, Voltaire and Fraser followed in single file, their shoulders almost brushing against the walls on each side, the chintz wallpaper making the way seem even more narrow than it already was.

Room 13 was at the very top of the hotel, at the end of a corridor. Marie unlocked the door to allow them into a very basic, square room with a small window and a view only of the building next door. There was very little furniture: a bed, a bedside table, a half-sized armchair, a wardrobe, and a sink in the corner.

'The toilet and shower are down the corridor,' Marie said.

'Did you see the gentleman who occupied this room on the second and third of June?' Voltaire asked her, looking around him without much enthusiasm.

'I saw him very briefly on the Friday morning, monsieur. I think it was about half past eleven. He came out of the room while I was vacuuming the carpet.'

'Did you see his face?'

'He had a hat . . .'

'And sunglasses?'

'Yes, monsieur. I think, also, he had white hair. He seemed to be in a hurry. He walked past me, but he did not say a word.'

Pünd took over the questioning. 'He would surely have been observed each time he entered and left the hotel, mademoiselle. There must have been someone at the reception.'

Marie blinked. She had large eyes that amplified her every emotion. 'I'm afraid that is not always the case, monsieur. There is so much work in the hotel and in the morning and the night there are only the three of us – Mother, Father and myself. There is a bell if guests need us, but it is possible my father was in the kitchen . . .' She paused, trying to think of anything she could say that might help. Suddenly she remembered. 'I am not sure that the gentleman slept in the room on either night,' she said.

'Why do you say that, mademoiselle?' Voltaire asked.

'I cleaned the room that same Friday afternoon. Two o'clock is the time when guests are asked to check out. The covers were thrown back and the sheets were crumpled, but it felt . . . strange. The shower had been used, but when I stripped the bed, I had no sense that it had been occupied during the night.'

'Did you examine the wardrobe or the drawers?'

'No, monsieur.' Marie sounded offended, as if she had been accused of prying.

'But you cleaned the sink.'

'There was no need. The sink had not been touched.'

'So for what purpose do you think he had taken the room?'

'I cannot say, monsieur. Perhaps he had business meetings nearby and needed somewhere to rest?'

Neither Pünd nor Voltaire appeared to accept this explanation and, in truth, Marie did not sound convinced herself.

Pünd had noticed a waste-paper basket beside the bed. 'Did you also clear the rubbish from the room?' he asked.

'Perhaps the gentleman had letters or documents that he left behind? Or was there anything else he threw away?'

'There was a newspaper in the waste-paper basket,' Marie recalled. 'Oh, yes! And an empty bottle of shoe polish. I can even remember the manufacturer.' She screwed her eyes shut, concentrating. 'It was Esquire!' she exclaimed. 'I only recall the name because it has a similarity to the Rue Esquirol, where I once lived.'

'That's an American brand, isn't it?' Fraser muttered.

'I believe you are right,' said Pünd.

'There was another bottle also. The gentleman drank some Orangina. But he did not throw it away when it was empty. He left it on the table.'

Marie came to a breathless halt, pleased with herself.

'Thank you, mademoiselle.' Voltaire smiled at her. 'You have been most helpful.'

*

But had she?

Walking back out into the Rue Lafayette, Fraser tried to piece things together, but none of it seemed to make sense to him. 'If it was Elmer Waysmith who went into the *pharmacie*, why did he feel the need to take a room in the Hôtel Lafayette for two nights?' he said. 'He was carrying a small suitcase. We know that he didn't sleep in the bed . . .'

'It would seem, then, that his intention was to use the room only to change his appearance.' Voltaire took over. 'He was wearing an ill-fitting linen suit when he purchased the aconitine and, along with the hat and the sunglasses,

279

that could have been part of his disguise. If he was Elmer Waysmith, he could not have worn it when he met with his son, Robert, just fifteen minutes later. So he leaves the pharmacy, he goes into the hotel – we know from the testimony of the owner that he was in a hurry – and he enters room thirteen, where he has the clothes that he will wear for lunch with his son. He gets rid of the walking stick, the hat, the suit and maybe also the suitcase. Then he continues to the Place Masséna.'

'Everything you suggest makes sense,' Pünd agreed. 'But how, I wonder, does he dispose of the suitcase and the rest of it?'

Even as he spoke, he was looking around him and his eyes settled on a row of oversized dustbins resting against the wall on the other side of the street. There were three of them: metal boxes on castors with lids that slid open, designed for commercial rather than public use. Fraser crossed the road without waiting to be asked. He opened the first one and, after rolling up his shirtsleeves, rummaged around in the container, trying to avoid coming into contact with anything too unpleasant. The search revealed nothing and after a few minutes he moved across to the next one. This time, he was more successful. 'There's something here!' he exclaimed and drew out a length of wood, which he showed to Pünd and Voltaire.

Fraser was holding an ebony walking stick. Now he used it to stir the contents of the bin and managed to hook a second object, a suitcase, which he lifted to the surface. He laid it down in the road and opened it, revealing a straw hat and, beneath it, a very creased, pale blue linen suit. Voltaire

280

and Pünd had both crossed the road. They knew they were looking at the entire disguise of the man who had booked into the Hôtel Lafayette and who had also purchased the aconitine at the nearby chemist.

'You should not touch anything else, Monsieur Fraser,' Voltaire remarked, addressing him by name for the first time. 'I will take all this for forensic examination. The case is old. It may have been purchased at a local flea market. The walking stick also. Even so, the clothes have been worn by the man we are seeking and who knows what they may reveal?'

'It is curious,' Pünd said. 'Why did our friend discard all this in a container so close to the hotel? Would it not have been wiser to carry it with him – at least some distance?'

'He was in a hurry,' Fraser reminded him.

'That is true.' Pünd sighed. 'But even so, he has been most careless. First, the lid that he forgets to replace on the teapot containing the poison. Then the aconitine, which he purchases even though there are many dangerous plants that grow in the garden of the Chateau Belmar. The choice of the drug too. Why aconitine? The question of the timing. And now this!'

'There are many clever men who make clumsy murderers,' Voltaire remarked.

'Yes. But what we have here is a clever murderer who seems to have been almost deliberately clumsy.'

The two men stood silently for a moment. Neither of them needed to ask where they were going next. Voltaire took the case from Fraser and the three of them set off.

FOURTEEN

They walked towards the Galerie Werner-Waysmith, threading their way through a series of backstreets until they reached the Avenue Jean Médecin, a wide and empty thoroughfare that drew a straight line almost from one end of Nice to the other. Pünd was keen to examine the path that Elmer Waysmith might have followed – if it had been he who had rented a room at the Hôtel Lafayette – and to work out how long it would have taken him. It was hard to judge. Voltaire could only make slow progress and it was always possible that Waysmith had found a different route. He might even have flagged down a taxi.

The gallery was not immediately apparent, half concealed by the pillars that separated it from the main square. Even Voltaire, who had visited Nice many times, was unaware of its existence. They stopped in front of the door and glanced at the two paintings in the windows: views of the French countryside. They were beautiful but somehow unappealing, trapped behind thick glass in two tiny pools of light.

The door was locked. He rang the bell and a moment later an unsmiling woman appeared, dressed in black.

'I am a police officer,' Voltaire told her. 'I am here to see Monsieur Waysmith.'

She didn't show any surprise. Clearly, she had heard

of the death at the Chateau Belmar and the suspicious circumstances that surrounded it. 'If you are referring to Monsieur Waysmith senior, I am afraid he is not here,' she said, speaking in French. 'He left a short while ago.'

'You are?'

'My name is Estelle Dubois. I am the gallery director.'

'Is Monsieur Robert Waysmith here?' Pünd asked.

He had spoken in English and Madame Dubois changed language effortlessly. 'He is in his office, monsieur.'

'Then perhaps we can speak with him.'

'Of course.' She stepped aside to let them in.

They entered the sombre surroundings of the front office with its artworks hanging in frames, like so many prison windows offering glimpses of imagined worlds. Madame Dubois moved towards her desk, intending to call the office, but Voltaire stopped her.

'I wish to ask you a few questions relating to the death of Lady Chalfont, madame,' he said, also switching to English for Pünd's benefit.

'I hardly knew Lady Chalfont, monsieur. She did not visit often.'

'Nonetheless, can you tell me if you were here last Friday at around lunchtime?'

'I was here all day.'

'You were alone?'

'No. Monsieur Robert came early in the morning. He stayed for about an hour and then drove to see a client in Antibes. I did not see him again until his father arrived at twenty-five minutes past twelve and they left together shortly afterwards. I had reserved a table for them at Le Poisson d'Or at half past twelve. The senior Monsieur Waysmith is always very punctual.'

'Can you tell me what he was wearing?' Voltaire continued with the interrogation, but his questions were exactly those Pünd would have asked.

Madame Dubois had to think for a moment. 'He was in a white suit and waistcoat,' she said. 'He was wearing saddle shoes in two colours: white and beige.'

'Did he seem exercised? Had he walked or come here by car?'

'Why are you asking this?'

'Please answer the question, madame.'

'I do not know how he had come here. He usually parks his car in the square. He was not in any way exercised. He seemed completely relaxed.'

'And how is Mr Robert Waysmith today?' Pünd asked.

'It is a great tragedy, what has occurred.'

'But not such a tragedy that he has stayed away from work,' Voltaire muttered. He glanced at Pünd, who signalled that he had nothing more to add. 'We will see him now,' he said.

Madame Dubois picked up the telephone and pressed a button. 'There are three gentlemen to see you,' she said in a low voice.

The door to the inner office opened almost before she had put down the phone.

Robert Waysmith walked out with the confidence and poise of a man about to sell an expensive painting to a new client, a look that vanished when he saw Pünd and Voltaire. At once, he seemed to shrink back into himself, as if he had forgotten that his stepmother had been murdered just a few days ago and was hoping that the detectives had gone away.

'Mr Voltaire . . .' he said. 'If you've come to see my father, I'm afraid he's not here.'

'I told them that,' Madame Dubois intoned.

'We would have liked to have spoken to him,' Voltaire admitted. 'But in his absence, perhaps we could have a few words with you.'

'Me?' Robert was alarmed. 'There's not very much I can tell you . . .'

'Please do not concern yourself.' Pünd smiled, reassuring him. 'In a murder investigation, it is necessary to speak to everyone who is involved. Often it is the case that they will remember something even they did not realise they knew.'

'Well . . . of course. Come into the office.' Robert glanced briefly at the *directrice*, then led the way into the back room where he and his father worked. He chose not to sit in his chair. Instead, he remained half standing, perched on the corner of his desk while the three visitors sat around him.

'Have you made any progress?' Robert asked.

'We have made a great deal of progress,' Voltaire assured him. 'I would be grateful if you could inform us of your movements on the morning of last Friday, the day your stepmother died.'

'Starting from what time, Mr Voltaire? Do you want to know what I had for breakfast?'

There was something almost insolent in the way Robert Waysmith spoke. At the Chateau Belmar, in Elmer's study, he had seemed strangely vulnerable, younger than his thirty-two years and dependent on the father who had looked after him all his life. Later, just before the reading of the will, he had been apologetic, dismayed by Elmer's rudeness. But now he was on his own and, for the first time, Pünd felt that Robert had stepped out of the shadows and was prepared to stand up for himself. He had inherited more than his father's good looks. Smartly dressed in a suit and tie with a gold clip, he looked very much like the owner of a successful art gallery. This is my domain, he seemed to say. You can ask me questions, but I refuse to be intimidated.

'When did you arrive at the gallery?' Voltaire asked.

'I arrived a little before ten o'clock. I wasn't here very long. I had to deliver a canvas to a client in Antibes. I drove over and we chatted for about thirty minutes. His name is Lucas Dorfman and Madame Dubois will provide you with his address if you want to confirm this. It took me a while to get back because of the traffic, and I was a little nervous because I didn't want to be late. In fact, I was here by twelve fifteen.'

Pünd had noticed the second door. He nodded towards it. 'You came in that way?' he asked.

'Yes. There's an alleyway that leads round to the square. I always come in through the back to avoid meeting customers.'

'Is meeting customers not the point of your business?'

'I don't meet anyone I don't know, Mr Pünd. Do you really think I want to haggle over the price of one of the Henry Moret canvases you may have noticed in the window? I leave that to Madame Dubois.'

Robert stood there, his hands clasping the edge of the desk, poised for the next question. It came from Voltaire. 'How was Monsieur Waysmith that day?'

'I'm not sure what you mean.'

'His mood. His appearance.'

'Do you mean, did he look like someone who was planning to murder his wife? No! He didn't! And if he had somehow let slip that it was what he intended, do you think I'd tell you, Monsieur Voltaire? He's my father.'

'You would protect a killer?'

'I would protect my family.'

'If it was not your father who killed Lady Chalfont, who would you think might have done so?' Pünd asked.

'I haven't got the faintest idea. Jeffrey has lost money at the casino. Harry needs help with his hotel. Lola wants to go back on the stage and Judith wants to preserve a monument in the middle of Peru. Finally, there's my nephew, Cedric. He's a creepy little kid with an interest in poisons. I suppose any one of them might be a suspect, except for the fact that they all loved Margaret, and as it turns out, there would have been no point bumping her off because they hardly got anything from the will.'

'Where is your father now?'

'I imagine he's gone back to the chateau. He was in a bad mood this morning.' Robert went behind the desk and sat down. He produced an art catalogue showing a series of blue squares and turned it round for the others to see. 'These are by an artist called Yves Klein,' he explained. 'Pa was hoping to buy them. He'd been offered them at a very good price, but what with one thing and another, he was too slow putting in his offer and he missed out. He was very annoyed.'

'By "one thing and another", you mean the death of your stepmother.'

'Yes.'

287

'I am surprised he could think of anything else at a time like this.'

'Then you don't know him, Monsieur Voltaire.' Robert weighed his words carefully. 'Pa is incredibly single-minded. Buying and selling art is his life and it always has been. It's not just the money. It's the sense of being ahead, of knowing the game, of sniffing out the new talent. That doesn't make him cold-hearted. Quite the opposite. But it puts everything else into second place. Margaret, my mother, me! When Ma killed herself, he was in Geneva, meeting with his partner, Erich Werner. He told you he was too upset to travel back to New York, but that wasn't really true. He was in the middle of a sale and there was no way he would have got on a plane until the deal had gone through.'

'What are your feelings about your father?' Pünd asked.

'I think he's a great man – but that doesn't mean he's an easy one. He's not afraid to speak his mind. When I was young, all I wanted to be was an artist. It's hardly surprising. From the moment I opened my eyes, I was surrounded by great art. There was an Edgar Degas ballet dancer – a pastel – hanging in my nursery! All through my teens and into my twenties I was painting. It was all I ever wanted to do. I'd have been happy selling my work on the railings of Hyde Park – I didn't need to be rich or famous. But it was Pa who persuaded me to give it up. He said that I didn't have the talent for it and that I was wasting my time. He may have been right, but I'm not sure I wanted to hear it.

'On the other hand, look at me now! It's thanks to him that I'm working here and he's training me. I'm learning from the very best. One day, maybe, I'll be running this business and it won't matter what's happened in the past. So I've got plenty of feelings about my Pa, but the main one is gratitude.'

The telephone rang, diverting Robert's attention. 'That might be him now,' he said and picked up the receiver. There was a brief pause as Robert listened to Madame Dubois, who had called from her desk in the front room. 'Yes. Put him through.'

Another long silence. Then Robert spoke again. 'Can you wait one moment, Maître Lambert.' He cupped a hand over the mouthpiece and looked up at Voltaire. 'It's Jean Lambert, our solicitor,' he said. 'Perhaps you should speak to him. It seems that his assistant, Alice Carling, has disappeared.'

FIFTEEN

Voltaire had summoned a police driver to collect them from the Galerie Werner-Waysmith, but it was still the best part of an hour before they reached Saint-Paul-de-Vence and parked once again outside the main gate. Pünd had been deep in thought throughout the journey, but as he climbed out of the car, he looked anguished. 'I hope with all my heart that the young lady has returned and all is well,' he said. 'I should have prepared for this. I should have known what might happen. This is my fault.'

'What on earth makes you think that?' Fraser asked.

'Did you not see her face when we came here the first time and told her that Lady Chalfont had been murdered?'

'She was shocked.'

'To have been shocked would be normal, understandable. But no, James, she was afraid. More than that . . . she was terrified.'

'I saw that too,' Voltaire said. 'I guessed at once that she knew something she was keeping from us and I should have questioned her there and then. But fool that I was, I decided to interview her later. If anything has happened to her, I'm the one who is to blame.'

'Perhaps everything will be all right,' Fraser said. 'Maybe she'll be waiting for us in Monsieur Lambert's office.'

But they knew as soon as they entered the small office that Alice Carling had not come into work. The front room was unoccupied, the desk completely empty. The door to the communicating office was open and Jean Lambert came out as soon as he heard them arrive. As always, his wardrobe and appearance were half a century out of date, as if he were play-acting the role of the provincial *avocat*, but the concern in his face and in the way he spoke couldn't have been anything but genuine.

'Perhaps I have overreacted by calling you,' he began, before his guests had even sat down. 'But Mademoiselle Carling has worked with me for four years and she is the soul of punctuality. Never once has she been late and she knew that I was extremely busy today, so she would most certainly have called me if there was something wrong. In the end, I called her parents. They are as worried as I am!'

'Please begin at the beginning, Maître Lambert,' Voltaire said. 'What time does Mademoiselle Carling usually arrive?'

'She comes to the office every morning at nine o'clock sharp. I usually arrive thirty minutes later, by which time she has made the coffee, opened the post and generally arranged my affairs for the day. Mademoiselle Carling is extremely efficient and completely reliable.

'This morning, I arrived at half past nine to discover that the office was still locked. I was extremely puzzled and a little alarmed. She has not been herself the last few days.'

'In what way?'

'She has seemed nervous, unhappy. Only the other day, I returned to the office unexpectedly. I had forgotten my keys. I found her sitting at her desk and I was quite sure that she

291

had been in tears, although she assured me that it was a room of something . . .'

Fraser had been translating for Pünd.

'*Rhume des foins*,' Voltaire explained. 'Hay fever.'

'I blame this announcement of hers, that she was intending to be married. I think it is true to say that she has not been the same since then.'

'When did she tell you?' Pünd asked.

'Three weeks ago.'

'Was that before or after Lady Chalfont and her family arrived at Cap Ferrat?'

'It was a few days after. You don't think . . .?'

'Please continue, Maître Lambert. You say she had not arrived at half past nine. Did you not think that she might be ill?'

'It was indeed my first thought, Monsieur Pünd. That's why I rang her parents. I spoke to her mother, who told me that Alice had gone out the night before to meet a friend and had not returned home. She said that such behaviour was completely out of character and they had been most worried. They were waiting for her to telephone them and when they heard she had not come into the office either, they insisted that I should alert the police. I decided it would be more sensible to telephone you directly. I had already called the chateau before I called the gallery. If I had not found you there, I would have called the *commissariat de police* in Nice.'

'Have you spoken to Mademoiselle Carling's fiancé?' Voltaire asked. 'If she had worries and spent the night away from home, surely it would have been with him.'

Lambert sighed. 'I have no telephone number for him,' he

admitted. 'She had not even told me his name until Monsieur Fraser requested it, here in this office.'

'You did not know the identity of the man she intended to marry until that moment,' Pünd said. It was not a question. From the way he spoke, he might have known it from the start.

'That is correct.'

'She gave us a false name,' Pünd continued. 'The man she referred to as Charles Saint-Pierre does not exist.'

'How can you be so sure of that, Monsieur Pünd?' Voltaire asked.

'Have you searched for his number?'

'No. But I am sure we will find it in the directory.'

'I am less certain.' Pünd turned back to the solicitor. 'You announced that she had become engaged, but she did not introduce you to her fiancé or even tell you who he was. When James asked her for his name, she was clearly embarrassed and did not wish to meet his eye. I knew then that she did not wish to reveal it.'

'Then who is Charles Saint-Pierre?' Lambert asked.

'It was an invention. The poor girl had no idea you were going to mention her engagement. She was caught unawares and had to put something together immediately, by word association. As it happens, a few moments before, she had mentioned that her father played boules in the Place de Gaulle.'

'Charles de Gaulle,' Voltaire said.

'And Saint-Paul, where we are now, became Saint-Pierre.' Pünd turned to Voltaire. 'We should see her parents at once. They may be able to tell us more.'

'We will also begin a search,' Voltaire said. 'Let us just hope it is not already too late.'

*

La Gaude was one of those villages that seemed to have sprung up as if by accident, lying beneath a backdrop of mountains, half-asleep in the fierce Mediterranean heat. Like Saint-Paul-de-Vence, it was built into the hillside, with a maze of side streets, most of them too narrow for cars, along with ancient steps and walkways that led the unsuspecting visitor around corners to yet more steps and walkways on the other side. Nothing really led anywhere. There was a chateau that had fallen into disrepair, two churches, an unsanctified chapel that was used as a makeshift cinema, a pink-washed police station, a few shops, some cafés and the inevitable *bar tabac* close to a patch of gravel where the men played boules. The houses faced each other, providing welcome shadows for the residents as they went in and out, made of stone and wood, brick and plaster, all equally beaten down by the sun. Shrubs and flowers sprouted everywhere, climbing the walls, tumbling from window boxes, bursting out of terracotta pots that might have stood there for a hundred years.

Tom and Élise Carling owned a house at the end of a street, three storeys high but only one room deep. They had always lived vertically and had grown used to squeezing past each other on the narrow staircase that connected the floors. The front door opened into the hallway, kitchen, living room and workshop, which all occupied the same area, with a bathroom tacked on at the back. The room was cluttered but clean and tidy, with an enamel stove and provincial furniture that might have been reduced in size to fit the available space.

They were sitting opposite Pünd and Voltaire and perhaps it was the worries of the past twelve hours, but they also seemed diminutive, shrinking into themselves. Tom was thin and wiry, with silver hair and hollow eyes. His wife was rounder, softer, wearing an apron over her dress. After more than thirty years' marriage, she spoke fluent English, even if her husband's French had barely progressed beyond 'bonjour' and 'merci'.

'Alice hasn't been herself since the news of Lady Chalfont's death,' Élise was saying. 'The evening it happened, she came in and she went straight to her room. I could understand she was upset. She did a lot of work for the family, her and Maître Lambert. But when she finally came down for supper, I could tell she'd been crying.'

'We asked her what was wrong.' Tom sounded ashamed of himself, as if all this was somehow his fault. 'But she wouldn't talk to me. She hardly touched her food, then she went back to her room.'

'I did go up, but it was a long time before she would even let me in. Then I sat down with her on the bed and held her in my arms, just like when she was a child,' her mother continued. 'She was crying again. She said she'd done something terrible and that she was going to be in trouble. She wouldn't tell me what it was and the more I asked, the more upset she became. In the end, I decided that it had nothing to do with Lady Chalfont. After all, our Alice meets a lot of important people. Wealthy people. I decided she must have made a mistake at work. I couldn't think of another explanation.

'The next day was Saturday. She seemed happier in the morning and we did not speak of what had happened. After breakfast, we went to the market together, and then on Sunday we went to the Church of Saint Isidore, as we do every week. It was just before lunchtime that she received a call.' Élise pointed to a black telephone sitting on a pedestal in the corner. 'I knew it was bad news. It was as if a cloud had passed across the sun. After lunch, she told me that she was going out to see a friend. She did not say who it was, but I assumed she meant Adeline, who works at the bakery. The two of them have always been close.'

'It wasn't Adeline,' Tom muttered. 'I spoke to her after Mr Lambert telephoned us. She doesn't know anything about all this.'

'Alice went out at three o'clock. That was the last time we saw her. We went to bed early last night and we were busy this morning. Tom helps out at La Petite Ferme, outside the village. I had my housework. We were only aware that something was seriously wrong when Monsieur Lambert called to ask where she was.' She pulled a handkerchief out of her sleeve. Tears had appeared in her eyes. 'It was so stupid of me!' she whispered. 'I should never have let her leave the house.'

'It wasn't your fault, my dear.' Tom Carling rested his hand on her arm.

'It may be that your daughter is in the hands of a very dangerous man,' Voltaire said, speaking with his usual directness. 'But it is not too late. Help is on its way, madame. We have police officers coming from every town and village to help with the search.' He paused. 'What can you tell me of a man who may call himself Charles Saint-Pierre?'

'We've never heard that name,' Élise said.

'According to Maître Lambert, your daughter believed herself to be engaged to him.'

'Alice would never have found herself a young man without telling us,' Tom Carling exclaimed. Voltaire's comment had clearly angered him. 'He's talking nonsense.'

'He's mistaken.' Élise was more composed. 'He does not understand that although she is an adult, our Alice is still very much a provincial girl – by which I mean that she is respectful to her parents and she is a good Catholic. She is quiet. She works hard. She is in many ways very ordinary. But she is also a daydreamer. She visits expensive homes in Nice and Saint-Tropez and she sees the great wealth that is arriving in the area. Is it any wonder that she plays make-believe, that she dreams of a life which she may never have? She is young, despite her years, and it is quite possible that she has been led astray. But I will tell you this, monsieur. I am her mother and I am quite certain that there is no Charles Saint-Pierre. Never did she mention this name to me.'

'So where is she?' Tom Carling demanded, gazing at Voltaire. 'What do you think has happened to her?'

'We do not know,' Voltaire said. 'But have faith, monsieur. We will find her.'

*

Once he was outside the house, with Pünd and Fraser, Voltaire slumped against a wall and lit a cigarette. His face was grim. 'We will look for her,' he said. 'But it may already be too late.'

297

'If I may make a suggestion,' Pünd said.

'Anything . . .' Voltaire looked up.

'She must have telephoned from the house to arrange to meet the man to whom she believed she was engaged. Or it is possible that he called her. They will have spoken many times. Is it not possible that the local operator will have kept a record of the numbers that have been requested?'

'Of course. It is certainly something I will investigate.' Voltaire straightened up. 'My men will be arriving soon and I must also organise the search.'

'You have much to deal with, Monsieur Voltaire. We will return to the hotel. If there is anything we can do to assist you, that is where you will be able to find us.'

'Thank you, Monsieur Pünd.'

'And there is one other thing.'

'Yes?'

'Might it be a good idea to return to the Pharmacie Lafayette with a photograph of Mademoiselle Carling?'

Voltaire nodded slowly. 'I see there is nothing that passes before you that you do not notice. You are thinking of the young woman who came in and asked the time.' He almost smiled, and might have but for his fears concerning Alice Carling. 'She came in and asked the hour. "*As-tu l'heure?*" Those were exactly the words she used, according to the *pharmacien*. "Do you have the time?" But I did wonder why she used such an informal type of address. Any young woman addressing a stranger in a shop would ask: "*Avez-vous l'heure?*"'

'It would suggest that the meeting was deliberate,' Pünd said. 'She knew the person to whom she was speaking.'

'But what on earth was the point?' Fraser asked.

'To establish the time!' Pünd replied. 'The *pharmacien* is old. He has bad vision. But he has been told that it is twelve fifteen.'

'It could have been earlier,' Voltaire muttered.

'Exactly. If it was indeed Elmer Waysmith who was in the chemist's shop, and it was, let us say, just a few minutes after twelve, he would have given himself more time to enter the hotel, change out of his clothes and still be at the gallery at the agreed hour for lunch.'

In the distance, they heard the two-tone air horns of not one but several police cars approaching the edge of the village. 'I will keep you informed if there are any developments,' Voltaire said. He threw down the cigarette and ground it out. Suddenly, he looked exhausted. Fraser watched as, with shoulders hunched, he limped away to arrange the search for Alice Carling.

SIXTEEN

'To be honest with you, I'm confused,' James Fraser remarked to Atticus Pünd as they sat in the back of a taxi taking them from La Gaude to their hotel in Saint-Jean-Cap-Ferrat.

'And why is that, James?'

'Well, it seems quite likely to me that Elmer Waysmith killed his wife – so why haven't you and Mr Voltaire arrested him yet? As far as I can see, there are no other suspects. It's not like that business we had with Sir Magnus Pye where anyone could have done it. It had to be Waysmith who went into the Pharmacie Lafayette. He tried to disguise himself with the hat and the sunglasses. He bought himself an extra fifteen minutes by getting poor Alice Carling to come in and ask the time. Maybe he told her it was for a joke or something, but the point was, it allowed him to change his clothes at the hotel and arrive at the gallery by twelve thirty. Things only went wrong when Alice heard that Lady Chalfont had been murdered with aconitine. She put two and two together and realised the part she had played – so he had to kill her too.'

'There I disagree with you, my friend. If you accept that Alice Carling assisted Elmer Waysmith in the purchase of the poison, are you also suggesting that he was the mysterious

300

"Charles Saint-Pierre" whom Alice hoped to marry after the death of his wife? That seems to me most unlikely, given that he was so very much older than her – old enough, indeed, to be her father.'

'Well, she was a young country girl. She was out of her depth. She could have been foolish enough to believe it.' Fraser considered. 'And if it wasn't him at the pharmacy, who was it? His son?'

'Robert Waysmith was on his way back to Nice from Antibes. He could have arrived earlier than he told us.'

'But Robert had absolutely no reason to kill Lady Chalfont, Mr Pünd. He didn't inherit very much money from her, and he didn't need it anyway. That's the trouble. None of them did!'

Pünd and Fraser did not speak again until they reached the hotel. The taxi pulled in, Fraser paid and a moment later they were walking to the main entrance, a small crowd of porters fussing around them. At the same time, Pünd noticed a silver Peugeot parked to one side. A short, stocky man in a navy blue worsted suit got out and came towards them. It was clear that this was no guest returning to his room. The man had been waiting for Pünd to arrive and wasted no time cornering him.

'Excuse me, sir. Am I right in thinking that I'm speaking to Atticus Pünd, the famous detective?' He was American, with a round face, thinning hair and glasses. There was something about him that reminded Fraser of a schoolteacher or perhaps a small-town lawyer. He felt out of place in the glamour of the Côte d'Azur.

Pünd was flattered by the description. 'I am.'

'I hope you'll forgive me interrupting you, sir, but I

wonder if I could speak to you confidentially and on a matter of urgency.'

'I do not think we have met.'

'My name's Harlan Scott.' The man took a business card out of his top pocket and handed it to Fraser. 'I've seen you quite a few times in the last few days. You've been in and out of the Chateau Belmar, and this morning you were at the Werner-Waysmith Gallery in Nice.'

'You have been watching us?' Pünd asked. He sounded surprised rather than offended.

'Not you, sir. No. I recognised you the moment I saw you, and I can guess why you're here. I take it you're investigating the death of Lady Chalfont?'

'I am helping the police.' Pünd was non-committal.

'I'm hoping you can help me, too. In fact, maybe we can help each other. I'm also a detective of sorts – although my work is a world apart from yours. Even so, it may be that we're both investigating the same thing. Can we talk?'

'Of course, Mr Scott. It is a beautiful day. We can, if you like, have tea – or coffee, if you would prefer – on the terrace behind the hotel.' Pünd looked around him, at the porters and a group of departing guests. 'The tables are far apart and we are less likely to be overheard.'

'That would be great, Mr Pünd.'

Without speaking any further, they walked into the hotel and continued through the main lounge into the gardens, where there were several guests already enjoying afternoon tea. They had no trouble finding a table set apart from the others, and after Fraser had placed an order with a waiter, Pünd sat back and waited for Scott to begin.

'I described myself as a detective,' Scott said. 'But that's not quite accurate. In fact, I began life as an art historian. I studied at Yale and ended up at the Metropolitan Museum in New York, and I would be there now except that ten years ago I was asked to join the Monuments, Fine Arts and Archives programme, which was being run by the army. I was one of three hundred and forty-five volunteers who came to be known as "the Monuments Men", although there were plenty of women among us too. Our job was to help track down and return around five million artworks stolen by German forces during the war. These included paintings, sculptures, jewellery and rare books, the great majority of them seized from the Jewish families who were then wiped out.' He paused. 'Do you mind if I smoke?'

'Not at all.' Pünd was intrigued. He watched as the American took out not a cigarette but a small cigar, which he lit, sending clouds of smoke into the air.

'The MFAA was disbanded a few years after the war,' Scott went on. 'But you could say I got hooked on the work and I decided to stay on in a private capacity. There are still many thousands of artworks that have never been recovered and I'm now employed by some of the survivors of the families who still hope to get their property back. I'd like to give you a bit of background to what I do, Mr Pünd, if you'll allow me. I'm sure you're a busy man, but I believe it will prove relevant to you and, in particular, to the death of Lady Margaret Chalfont.'

'Please, continue.'

'Very well.' He drew on the cigar. 'As early as 1938, Hitler had his eye on the art collections of Europe and had

a determination to make them his own. His main reason
was ideological. Take a nation's art and you take its soul –
something Napoleon had already figured out. The Louvre is
full of German treasures the emperor snatched in his time,
and now it was Hitler's turn. He had plans for a gigantic
art gallery he was going to build in Linz, in Austria – the
Führermuseum. At the same time, he was going to destroy
all the art he considered degenerate – cubism, Dadaism
and pretty much anything that was too modern. He said it
was the duty of the state "to prevent a nation falling under
the influence of spiritual madness". He wrote that in *Mein
Kampf.*

'But there were other Nazi leaders who had less high-
minded reasons for getting their hands on all the loot they
could grab. Göring had a hunting lodge called Carinhall,
north of Berlin, and he filled it with works by Matisse,
Renoir, Dürer, Holbein, Cranach and so on. By the end
of the war, he had over a thousand pieces of art, worth
around two hundred million dollars. Goebbels had a taste for
German expressionism. Von Ribbentrop snapped up works
by Manet. And many other high-up Nazis were playing the
same game.

'There were no fewer than three government branches
involved in the confiscation of art. One was the *Kunstschutz,*
controlled by the Wehrmacht. Then there was the German
embassy in Paris, led by a guy called Otto Abetz, who
cheerfully went round the country plundering anything
he could get his hands on in the name of war reparations.
But the most active and the most avaricious organisation
was the ERR – or, to give it its full name, the *Einsatzstab*

Reichsleiter Rosenberg für die Besetzten Gebiete, which was secretly controlled by Göring. And once the Nazis had decreed that the Jews shouldn't be allowed to own anything with cultural significance, it was open house. A hundred thousand pieces of art were stolen in France alone.'

The coffee had arrived while he was talking. He stopped for a moment and added three sugar cubes to his cup, then stirred it as he continued.

'What I'm talking about here is a free-for-all,' Scott said. 'Everyone was at it. There were huge profits to be made from buying and selling art – even so-called degenerate art, which the Nazis were happy to turn into cash. Museums in Düsseldorf, Essen and other German cities seized the moment to enlarge their collections. Supposedly respectable French art buyers and dealers came rushing in like sharks. Remember, the Nazis had banned the exportation of paper money, and there was very little to buy in Europe anyway. It wasn't as if anyone was going shopping for new cars or clothes. Suddenly art was everything. Buy it, sell it, barter with it, hoard it, enjoy it. And when the war was over . . . if you had it, you were made.

'And then there was Switzerland . . .'

Scott's cigar glowed red, a single devil's eye. He exhaled and smoke wreathed itself around his head.

'Nazi art dealers loved the Swiss. The Swiss had more money than they knew what to do with. They were neutral, which gave them complete freedom of movement. And they were, to all intents and purposes, amoral. All their biggest galleries worked hand in hand with the Nazis. The Fischer Gallery in Lucerne, the Neupert Gallery in Zurich, the Dreyfus Gallery – they turned themselves into an open market for stolen works.

'And there was another, smaller gallery based in Geneva that had a very profitable relationship with Reichsmarschall Hermann Göring, no less, and it was run by a man called Erich Werner – and that name may be familiar to you.'

'Werner-Waysmith!' Fraser exclaimed.

'The very same,' Scott said. 'Werner went into partnership with an American dealer called Elmer Waysmith, and although he's now retired, Elmer is still active on his behalf with galleries here and in London selling one piece after another stolen during the war and kept quietly locked up ever since.'

He stopped and drank some of his coffee. A waiter was serving tiny sandwiches cut into triangles to a family at the next table. It was hard to reconcile the sun-filled terrace and the elegant façade of the hotel with the dark story being told.

'I only became aware of Werner-Waysmith very recently, when I received a tip-off from someone connected to the family,' Scott explained.

'And who was that?' Pünd asked.

'You'll have to forgive me, Mr Pünd, but I might get them into serious trouble if their name were to become known.'

'And you will have to forgive me, Mr Scott, but I am investigating what may turn out to be not one but two murders. If we are to help each other, I must know everything that you know, and you must trust me to keep this information to myself.'

'What about Voltaire?'

'Monsieur Voltaire and I are equal partners and I will have

to inform him of anything that is relevant, but I can assure
you he is entirely discreet.'

Scott scowled briefly, then came to a decision. 'Very well,
Mr Pünd. I will tell you the name, but I would ask you – all of
you – to protect my source.'

He drew a breath.

'The lady I'm talking about, Béatrice Laurent, was working
for a Jewish family in Paris at the start of the war and was
present on the day their house was raided. The family was
arrested and their extensive art collection seized. One
painting in particular she remembered clearly. It showed a
vase of tulips on a table. She didn't know the artist's name
or the title of his work, but she recognised it instantly when
she saw it again, thirteen years later, on the wall of the *grand
salon* in the home of Elmer Waysmith, where she is now
employed as the *femme de ménage*. As you can imagine, the sight
of it filled her with horror. She felt powerless. What should
she do? To go to the police was unthinkable. She didn't even
know if a crime had been committed, and anyway, she liked
Lady Chalfont and didn't want to hurt her. Elmer Waysmith
is a wealthy, respectable art dealer. There were all sorts of
different ways to explain how the painting could have landed
in his hands.

'This all happened a few weeks ago, just after the family
arrived at the chateau for the summer season. As it turned
out, Béatrice knew somebody who had worked as a secretary
for the MFAA and she had the good sense to tell her friend
what had happened. The MFAA has been disbanded, like I
said, but the friend had my telephone number and put her
in touch with me. It took me very little time to work out the

connection with Erich Werner and to identify the painting: a masterpiece by Paul Cézanne painted in 1890 and titled *Spring Flowers*.

'So, a couple of weeks ago, I visited the Werner-Waysmith Gallery and managed to talk my way past the old dragon who guards the place. Elmer Waysmith wasn't in that day, but I spoke to his son, Robert, who runs the place with him. I was in a tricky position. There are still hundreds of thousands of stolen objects scattered across Europe and, by and large, the galleries, museums and dealers don't want to talk. They'll pretend they don't know where the pictures came from or they'll say they bought them in good faith. And I'm not a policeman. I'm not a detective. I don't have any authorisation to go blundering around the place, making accusations that I may not be able to prove. At the end of the day, I just have to get people to cooperate. If a man like Elmer Waysmith is found to have been in cahoots with the Nazis, it's not going to look good on his résumé. The original owners of *Spring Flowers*, Mr and Mrs Steiner, were gassed to death. That's not something you want on a painting's provenance.

'Anyway, I spoke to Robert Waysmith, who was completely shocked by what I had to say. Either that or he's a first-class actor, but I'd like to think I've conducted enough interviews to know when someone is pulling my chain. He told me that he had no dealings personally with Erich Werner, but that his father would never have gotten his hands dirty with stuff like that. He invited me to meet Elmer Waysmith at the Chateau Belmar, where the Cézanne was temporarily on display. He was sure it was all a misunderstanding and that it could be sorted out.'

'He invited you to his home?' Pünd was surprised.

'It's like I said, Mr Pünd – he seemed a decent sort. I was a bit surprised myself, but it's not every day someone walks into your gallery and accuses your dad of being a crook. We made an appointment for the very next day and I turned up at eleven in the morning, as agreed.

'The meeting did not go well. Elmer Waysmith was nothing like his son. He was polite for approximately five minutes, defensive for another five and then outright aggressive. We met in their grand saloon and sure enough, the picture was on the wall. If I'd been him, I might have tried to hide it. But he was shameless. He accused me of being a crook, trying to blackmail him, threatening to damage his reputation if he didn't pay up, that sort of thing. He was shouting at me and Robert had to calm him down . . . It wasn't easy.

'In the end, it was Elmer who threatened me. I had no right to be in his house, asking him these questions, and if I didn't back off, he'd have his lawyers onto me before I could blink. He said that it was Werner who had bought the painting and that he had no reason to doubt his partner's word. Then he started quoting Swiss law. After five years, if a dealer has bought a painting in good faith, the painting is his – and if the family wants it back, they have to pay for it. Not easy when the whole lot of them are dead! He had never been so insulted in all his life and all the rest of it. And with that, he threw me out.'

'And that was the end of it?' Pünd asked.

'I don't give up that easily, Mr Pünd. Since then, I've been keeping a close eye on the Werner-Waysmith Gallery,

309

at the same time looking at some of the major sales they've made in both London and Nice in the last few years. The art world is a closed circle. There are good dealers and bad dealers, but it helps me that most of them know each other. I've already found two other paintings that definitely have Nazi connections, and only last week, Waysmith delivered a landscape by Alfred Sisley to a collector in Antibes. I followed him there and I got to see the canvas. I recognised it straight away. Fortunately, there are photographic records and it was stolen from the collection of Paul Rosenberg, a prominent Jewish dealer in Paris who managed to flee the country after the invasion. Göring was very fond of Sisley.'

'Did you follow Robert Waysmith when he left Antibes?'

'No. It would be too easy for him to spot my car. Anyway, I was more interested in the painting. I managed to get Lucas Dorfman – the collector – to show me the work and I've already contacted the Rosenbergs in New York. I'm waiting to hear back from them.'

Pünd thought for a moment. 'You said that we might be pursuing the same investigation, Mr Scott. Are you suggesting that the art thefts – if that is how they can be described – and the death of Lady Chalfont may be connected?'

'Art thefts are definitely what they are, Mr Pünd, and you could add that Elmer Waysmith and his partner in Switzerland are complicit in war crimes. As to Lady Chalfont, when I heard that the police had begun a murder investigation, of course it occurred to me that there must be something in the timing. I also wondered if it was something connected to art that had brought you to the South of France.'

'There I must disappoint you,' Pünd replied. 'I knew nothing of the Cézanne before I arrived in Saint-Jean-Cap-Ferrat, but from what you have told me, it is almost certain that Lady Chalfont heard the conversation between you and her husband and it was for this reason that she turned to me.'

'Her balcony is just above the room where Mr Scott met Elmer Waysmith!' Fraser exclaimed.

'That is correct. And you will recall, when we were in her bedroom, we were able to overhear the child, Cedric Chalfont, arguing with his father,' Pünd reminded him.

'So Margaret Chalfont heard them . . .'

'And that is why she wrote to me: "*I overheard something that shocked me to my core.*" She was accusing her second husband of being at the very least a collaborator in an act of great wickedness.'

'Did he kill her?' Harlan Scott asked.

'Everything would suggest so, Mr Scott.'

'It was the reason she was going to change her will,' Fraser said. 'She'd been married to him for six years without realising he was a crook.'

'Yes . . .' But Pünd sounded unsure. 'Where can we find you, if we need to speak further, Mr Scott?'

'I've written a phone number on the back of my card. I have a small apartment on the edge of Nice and the concierge takes messages for me.'

'Are you planning to make any further move against Elmer Waysmith or his son?'

'I have no interest in Robert, and there's very little chance that I can take any action against his dad. All I can hope for is the return of the paintings to their rightful owners. It's

311

a strange sort of crime, Mr Pünd, where the criminals are immune and the victims are powerless. But even so, I believe that in my own way I'm fighting for justice, and I suppose that puts us on the same page.'

He stubbed out his cigar. 'Thanks for the coffee,' he said. 'Let me know if there's any news.'

There was to be news soon enough. But it wasn't anything that either of them would have wanted to hear.

SEVENTEEN

By the end of the day, the police search for Alice Carling had yielded nothing.

It had seemed an impossible task from the very start. The village of La Gaude sat in the foothills of the Alps, the Préalpes d'Azur rising steeply behind it. The countryside, rich and unfathomable, stretched in every direction, all the way to Marseille and beyond, virgin territory with space enough for a million hiding places . . . or graves. There were valleys to the north and south where nobody walked and where Alice might even now be lying, fed on by insects and birds. There were rivers – the Cagne and the Lubiane, with its four and a half miles of rushing water – where she might have drowned. She could have been hidden in a cave, an abandoned windmill, a dry ditch, a meadow, a shepherd's hut or the ruins of a Roman mausoleum.

And then there were the woods: mile after twisted mile of pine and olive trees, cork oaks and chestnuts, the floor a sprawl of wild mimosa, nettles, thickets and ferns. Agriculture and construction both added their challenges to the search. Alice could have been locked away in one of a hundred barns, stables, grain houses, caravans or cowsheds. Half-built houses, temporary offices and taverns provided yet more hiding places.

The weather also made success less likely. With the sun beating down and the air thickened by the heat, everything seemed to be happening in slow motion. Almost nothing was moving. The birds were silent. Only the bees were droning lazily, barely completing their journeys around the tree trunks.

Voltaire had forty men at his disposal, but, given the enormity and complexity of the landscape, he might as well be searching for a single leaf in a forest. He had worked out that he had to start in La Gaude itself. There was a chance that someone might have spotted Alice before she left or while she was leaving. But the moment she'd found herself in the world outside, to all intents and purposes she would be lost to them.

What *did* he know?

It seemed almost certain that Alice had gone off with the man she believed to be her fiancé. Voltaire had spoken to Adeline, Alice's friend from the bakery. She confirmed that she had never heard of any Charles Saint-Pierre. Alice had kept the relationship a secret, which suggested that the man would not have risked driving into La Gaude to meet her. But then things had changed. Alice had become scared. Perhaps she had been about to go to the police and had threatened the man she believed she was going to marry. The man who called himself her fiancé had acted quickly. He must have picked her up in a car.

So, around three o'clock on Sunday, there had been a vehicle that did not belong to anyone in the village either outside the house or somewhere nearby. A single road ran the full length of La Gaude and this was a community where everyone knew everyone. It was more than likely that someone would have seen Alice leave.

Voltaire deployed half his men on a door-to-door inquiry throughout La Gaude and the neighbouring village of Saint-Jeannet. Had anyone seen Alice in the company of a stranger that day, or indeed at any time in the past few weeks? Had anyone glimpsed her as she drove past? In addition, he focused on the *bar tabac* and the square where boules was played. They would be the centre of gossip and rumour-mongering. If anyone knew of an illicit affair, it would come to the surface here.

At the same time, it occurred to him that the mysterious man would have taken Alice somewhere they could talk. She believed he was complicit in Lady Chalfont's death. He would want to calm her, to persuade her otherwise. Where might that be? The Baou des Blancs, a dramatic rockface that provided superb views over the surrounding countryside, was a favourite beauty spot for young people, with meandering pathways, trees and flowers. It was a few miles to the north-west. And then there was the Gairaut waterfall above Nice. Voltaire imagined Alice getting into the car, angry and suspicious. He would want to take her somewhere beautiful.

But not public. If he couldn't persuade her that he was innocent of any crime, if he needed to silence her, it would have to be somewhere with no witnesses. The woods. The rivers.

He sent the rest of his men into the surrounding countryside. A dog handler had arrived with a Belgian Malinois, but they were looking as miserable as each other, faced with the enormity of the task ahead of them. Still, he sent them on their way. He had to look as if they were trying.

In the end, it was a fisherman who found her. Alice

Carling had taken her last breath less than a mile from the place where she had been born.

Julien Lotte was seventy years old, bearded and sunburnt. He was in a good mood. There were two trout and a barbel weighing well over a kilogram in the oilskin bag he was taking home, following the River Var, heading south. When he noticed something lying on the shingle bank next to the water, his first thought was that somebody had abandoned a bundle of clothes. It was only when he was closer that he realised someone was still in them.

Lotte had served in the army as a young man and had seen action in French Equatorial Africa. He knew a dead body when he saw one. This was a young girl, not so pretty in life and less so in death, her eyes empty, any expression wiped from her face. There was nothing Lotte could do for her. He hurried back to his home on the outskirts of La Gaude and because he had no private telephone, he sent his wife out to the public phone box to call the police.

*

'She was strangled,' Voltaire said. 'We are speaking to everyone who was walking in the area, but no witnesses have come forward so far, and the fisherman who found her saw nothing. The riverbank is a short distance from the main road, so it would seem that the killer parked his car there and the two of them walked the short distance to the shingle beach. Perhaps they talked. I am sure that he tried to persuade her that he had done nothing wrong. But when that failed . . .'

Voltaire was sitting in the main lounge of the Grand-Hôtel, cupping a balloon glass of cognac. The sun had set by now and the waiters were serving dinner in the room next door. Pünd and Fraser were with him.

'I blame myself,' Voltaire went on. 'When we first went to the office of Maître Lambert and informed them that Lady Chalfont had been murdered, she was afraid. It should have been obvious to me that she was in some way connected with what had occurred.'

'I, too, saw that she was nervous,' Pünd concurred. 'But like you, Monsieur Voltaire, I said nothing. There are some young people for whom the very idea of murder is frightening. It was not necessarily the case that she was involved in the crime.'

'And then there was that business with the false name.' Voltaire was still angry. 'You saw that, Monsieur Pünd. I did not. Had I questioned her more . . .'

'It would have made no difference, my friend. She would have denied that she had lied to you. Poor Mademoiselle Carling could not believe how fortunate she was to have found a man who loved her, who was perhaps wealthy and well connected. Doubtless, he had told her to keep his identity secret.' Pünd had ordered a small sherry for himself. He took a sip. 'She took that secret to the grave.'

'But who was Charles Saint-Pierre?' Fraser asked. 'He couldn't have been Elmer Waysmith, could he?'

'No. He wasn't Elmer Waysmith.' Voltaire rested his glass in the palm of his hand, contemplating the dark, golden liquid. 'But whoever the fiancé was, his luck has finally deserted him. He has made two mistakes.'

Pünd and Fraser waited for him to explain.

'First of all, we spoke to the local telephone operator, as you suggested, Monsieur Pünd, and we have learned that the call Mademoiselle Carling received on the morning of her death came from the Chateau Belmar. In fact, she had received several calls from that number.'

'Anyone in the house could have made those calls,' Fraser said doubtfully.

'Maybe, Monsieur Fraser. However, Mademoiselle Carling had her handbag with her when she was attacked next to the river, and that was the second mistake. Her killer should have taken it with him, or at the very least examined the contents.' Voltaire emptied his glass. 'He must have been in a hurry to leave. He was careless.'

'What did you find in the bag?' Pünd asked.

Voltaire removed a black-and-white photograph, about three inches square, and placed it on the table. It showed a young man with circular wire-framed glasses, wearing a pale blazer and a straw hat. There were faded red lipstick marks on one corner of the image, and with a sinking feeling in his stomach, Fraser realised that Alice must have kissed it. At the same time, he recognised the man in the picture.

'It's Harry Lyttleton,' he exclaimed.

'That is exactly right,' Voltaire agreed. 'Harry Lyttleton who is married to Judith Lyttleton, the daughter of Lady Chalfont, and who visited the office of Maître Lambert many times. He would have known Alice well.' He picked up the photograph with a look of obvious disgust. 'Knew her, took advantage and killed her. Or so it would seem.

'Tomorrow, we will discover the truth.'

EIGHTEEN

'I don't know what you're talking about,' Harry Lyttleton said. He was sitting at the head of the polished rosewood table in the *petit salon*, the place usually taken by Elmer Waysmith. His wife, Judith, was next to him. It was early morning, but the breakfast things had already been cleared, the surface wiped down and the last crumbs swept away by an anxious Béatrice. Harry, wearing a short-sleeved shirt, his hair perfectly groomed, looked to all intents and purposes as if the Chateau Belmar belonged to him and he had invited Pünd and Voltaire to join him for coffee.

The two detectives were next to each other a little further down the table, with James Fraser at the far end, as ever taking notes.

It was strange how the Chateau Belmar had changed. The fountain still played, the sun still shone, but there was an emptiness about the place, as if the death of Lady Chalfont had been the first symptom of a much larger death and everything – the rooms, the furniture, the decorations, the very bricks – was fading away. The house no longer belonged to the people who lived there and it was letting them know it.

Pünd and Voltaire had been shown into the room by Béatrice, who had managed to avoid meeting their eyes. Voltaire had sent a message ahead of them and Harry

319

Lyttleton had been waiting for them with Judith. Everything
was very quiet. It was quite possible that the other members
of the family were in their rooms, but it was revealing that
not one of them had shown up to support the man who had
become Voltaire's principal suspect.

'It's quite simple,' Voltaire said, responding to Harry
Lyttleton. 'How well did you know Alice Carling?'

'I had several meetings with Jean Lambert, who was
supposed to be helping me with a hotel I'm constructing
down here in Cap Ferrat, not that he was very much use,
if you want the truth. She was always there, fussing around
him, doing the paperwork and that sort of thing. When I
telephoned Lambert, she usually answered. That was about
the extent of it. Why are you even asking me?'

Voltaire caught Pünd's eye and he took over. 'I'm sorry
to have to tell you that Miss Carling was found dead last
night.'

Sitting in the chair next to her husband, Judith Lyttleton
started. 'Oh my goodness!' she gasped. 'Are you saying . . . ?'

'She was murdered.' As always, Voltaire went straight to
the point.

'But why . . . ? Who . . . ?' All sorts of different thoughts
seemed to be fighting for a place in Judith's head, but finally
she arrived at the very worst. 'You can't think my husband has
anything to do with it!'

Voltaire ignored her. 'You would not describe yourself as
her friend?'

'No!' Harry Lyttleton protested.

'Or did you have a relationship that was even closer?'

'I don't know what you're talking about,' Harry Lyttleton

snapped. 'You're disgusting. I'm a very happily married man and my relationship with Miss Carling was entirely professional.'

'Then perhaps you can explain this, Mr Lyttleton . . .'

Voltaire had taken out the photograph, which he laid on the table. He had deliberately positioned it so that both the husband and the wife could see it. If Judith had been shocked by the news of Alice's death, the picture completely horrified her. 'Where did you get this?' she demanded.

'Miss Carling had it with her when she died,' Voltaire told her.

'But . . .' She tore her eyes away from the image and turned to her husband, demanding an explanation.

'I don't know where she got this,' Harry protested. 'I can't even remember when it was taken.'

'Perhaps it would be more helpful, Mr Lyttleton, to explain to us why Miss Carling would have been carrying it with her and why she should have chosen, it would seem, to have marked it with an impression of her lips.'

'You'd have to ask her that.' Harry ran a hand through his hair, sweeping it out of his eyes. 'Of course, you can't. That was stupid of me.' He took a moment to compose himself. 'I barely spoke to Miss Carling. If you're suggesting, because of this photograph, that she had certain feelings for me, all I can say is that I wasn't remotely aware of them.'

'And yet Miss Carling had informed us that she was engaged to be married.' Pünd had taken over the interrogation. 'Does the name Charles Saint-Pierre mean anything to you?'

'I've never heard it before. And how could I possibly have

been engaged to her? Judith and I have been together for seventeen years.'

'Eighteen years,' Judith said.

'It may well be that the young woman was a fantasist. But it is undoubtedly the case that she believed herself to be in a relationship with a man whose identity she attempted to conceal. She had informed Monsieur Lambert that she was soon to leave his employment. It seems very likely that her supposed fiancé picked her up in his car on the last day of her life and drove her to the place where she was later found dead.'

'Do you have a car?' Voltaire asked.

'I drive a Renault 4CV.'

'What colour?'

'Blue.'

'We will also need the registration number.'

'Wait a minute,' Judith cut in. 'You're saying that my husband picked this woman up in her village. What time was it?'

'We believe that it was some time after three o'clock on Sunday afternoon.'

'Well, that's impossible.' Judith's face was flushed with a mixture of relief and indignation. 'Harry was here with me.'

'We have only your word for that, Madame Lyttleton.'

'Are you calling me a liar, Mr Voltaire? We had lunch with Jeffrey and Lola and then we sat and read in the garden. You could talk to Cedric, although he may not have much idea of the time. He was swimming and then he lay on the grass with his comic. I even spoke to him briefly.'

'How long were you there?' Pünd asked.

'Judith was giving a talk at the Church of Saint-Jean-Baptiste just down the road,' Harry Lyttleton explained. 'She spoke for ninety minutes about the Quechua and Aymara cultures . . .'

'In French?'

'I do speak fluent French, Monsieur Voltaire, as well as Peruvian Spanish and ancient Greek. But the audience was entirely English and American.'

'The talk started at five o'clock,' Harry Lyttleton continued. 'Afterwards, we had supper at the Royal Riviera. We got home at about nine.'

'I'm sure a great many people saw us,' Judith added. There was acid in her voice. 'In fact, now I think of it, the Frobishers were there. Lance and Lettie. We spoke to them as we arrived.'

'Can you also tell us about your movements on the day Lady Chalfont died?' Voltaire weighed in. If he was disappointed by the fortuitous appearance of Lance and Lettie Frobisher, he was careful not to show it. 'I would like to know in particular where you were at midday.'

'I was in Nice,' Harry replied.

'For what purpose?'

'Is it really any of your business?'

Now Voltaire was angry. 'This is a police investigation into not one but two murders, Monsieur Lyttleton. You should know that we have been taking an interest in you for some time. You are involved with several people who might call themselves businessmen but whose businesses encompass only fraud, money-laundering and embezzlement. It is remarkable that you have not been arrested yet, but I would advise you that if you do not give me straight answers to my questions, this is something that could rapidly change.'

Harry Lyttleton blinked rapidly. 'It's my wife's birthday in two weeks' time. I went into Nice to buy her a present.'

'And did you?'

'No. It was more of a window-shopping expedition.'

'You did not by any chance visit a *pharmacie* in the Rue Lafayette?'

'Why would I have wanted to do that, Mr Voltaire?' Harry snapped. 'I'm not sure I even know where the Rue Lafayette is, and I didn't go into any pharmacy.'

'Did you meet anyone?'

'No – and I'm not sure anyone will have seen me, although I did spot Elmer in the Place Masséna. I don't think he saw me though. He was in a tearing hurry, making for the gallery.'

'What time was that?'

'A little bit before half past twelve.'

Judith got to her feet. 'We've had enough of this!' she announced. 'You come into our house making unfounded allegations. You have no evidence apart from a photograph that you say was in Miss Carling's possession. What's that got to do with Harry? She could have been carrying a photograph of the pope and would you have added him to the list of suspects? If she was infatuated, that's her problem. Harry is a very good-looking man. But I don't see why we should stay here a minute more.'

Pünd was unperturbed. 'I have one more question, if I may,' he said.

Harry glanced at his wife, who had moved to stand at his shoulder. He had clearly enjoyed her brief tirade and seemed more relaxed than he had when the interview began. 'Please go ahead, Mr Pünd,' he said.

'It is not a question for you, but for your wife, Mr Lyttleton.' He paused briefly. 'How well did you know Alice Carling?' he asked.

Judith looked puzzled, as if the question was irrelevant to everything that had gone before. 'I hardly knew her at all.'

'And yet you had met her how many times?'

'I can't say. She was there when the will was read – and I can't for the life of me understand what my mother was thinking of when she made that arrangement. I may have seen her once or twice last year. But I hardly ever spoke to her.'

'That is exactly what I would have thought.' Pünd looked pained, as if he was unwilling to continue. 'But as we were speaking just a few moments ago, you asked a question. You wanted to know at what time Miss Carling was picked up from her village. You made the point that it could not possibly have been your husband driving the car.'

'That's right. It's a ludicrous suggestion. So what's your point, Mr Pünd?'

'Only that I wonder how you knew that Miss Carling lived in a village.' Pünd smiled. 'She could have lived in Nice or in Saint-Paul-de-Vence, which is much more than a village and would, I think, be described as a town. She could have lived in a farm in the middle of the countryside. If you and your husband knew nothing of her personal life, how did you come to that conclusion?'

325

There was a stunned silence. Judith looked by turns shocked, angry and physically sick, steadying herself by gripping the back of her husband's chair.

Harry took over. She had defended him and now he did the same for her. 'I think you're reading too much into it, Mr Pünd,' he remarked languidly. 'I doubt if Miss Carling was earning very much money. If she didn't have a car, she'd have to live somewhere near her office and Saint-Paul-de-Vence is surrounded by villages.'

'It still struck me as more than a random observation, Mr Lyttleton.'

'I didn't mean anything by it,' Judith insisted. 'I have no idea where the silly girl lived. It could have been a pigsty for all I care. And we're not answering any more of your questions, so you might as well leave.'

*

'She is lying,' Pünd said.

He and Voltaire had left through the back of the house and were walking in the garden. In front of them, they could see the gazebo where Lady Chalfont had died. A gardener was crossing the lawn with a wheelbarrow, but otherwise there was nobody around.

'She also lied to us when we first arrived at the chateau,' Pünd continued. 'She was present in London when her mother asked for my help, but she claimed she had told no-one: "*I didn't think it was important.*" And yet Lady Chalfont had impressed upon me the urgency of her request. Later, Judith Lyttleton claimed that her mother often kept secrets and that she had forgotten all about it. This makes no sense. And there is something else.'

'What's that?' Fraser asked.

'At the clinic in London, it struck me that she was nervous. It was almost as if she knew what was going to happen.'

'It's just annoying that the two of them seem to have a secure alibi for both the time Alice Carling was picked up and the time she was murdered,' Voltaire said. 'I'm going to check out the Royal Riviera and I'll talk to those people they claimed they met. I'll also visit the church where Dr Lyttleton gave her talk. I'll let you know what I find – but I have a feeling they have an alibi that is as solid as rock.'

'It's almost as if they arranged it that way.'

'Yes. You could say that.'

Voltaire walked back into the house, leaving Pünd and Fraser alone.

'It is sad,' Pünd muttered, almost to himself.

'You mean the death of Lady Chalfont.'

'More than that.' Pünd waved a hand at the gazebo. 'All of this is beautiful, is it not? It could have come out of one of the paintings that Mr Waysmith and his son sell in their gallery. A Fragonard, perhaps, or a Watteau. But what will people remember it for, a hundred, two hundred years from now?'

'Murder.'

'Exactly, James. Buildings, like people, can be scarred with the mark of Cain and it will never leave them. We remember the houses where people became ill and died and the memory brings sadness and a sense of loss. But with murder it is something different. We do not wish to enter such a place. It carries with it a sense of fear and even revulsion.'

'Do you think Harry Lyttleton murdered Alice Carling?'

'I think he knows more than he is telling us. Judith Lyttleton too.'

'Maybe they were the ones who cut open the letter that Lady Chalfont sent you, inviting you here.'

'It is possible, James. And it was not the only communication that was intercepted. You will recall the letter that she wrote to me, summoning me to the Chateau Belmar. That, too, had been read.'

'How do you know?'

'There were two creases in the centre of the page. It had been folded, then taken out of the envelope and folded a second time. It suggested to me from the very start that somebody had been keeping a close watch on Lady Chalfont, the same person who took my reply and opened it using a knife with a serrated edge.'

'That could only have been her husband.' Fraser gave a start. 'I say, Mr Pünd. I've just thought of something! Harry Lyttleton told us that he saw Elmer in the Place Masséna and that he was in a tearing hurry. That was when he was on his way to have lunch with his son. But the woman in the gallery – Madame Dubois or whatever her name was – said that he usually parked his car in the square and he was completely relaxed when he arrived.'

'There is indeed a contradiction here.'

Before Pünd could continue, they were interrupted by two sharp explosions. Fraser twisted round to see a gun pointing at them from the side of the pagoda. He frowned. 'Are you really sure this is the right time to go around the place shooting people?' he asked.

Cedric Chalfont stepped into sight, carrying the cap pistol he had just fired at them. The eight-year-old was wearing a cowboy hat and had a sheriff's star pinned to his shirt. In his imagination, he was far away from the South of France, searching for outlaws. He wasn't put off by Fraser's criticism. 'You're both dead!' he exclaimed.

'I think you missed,' Fraser remarked. 'Anyway, Mr Pünd here is a very famous detective. You'd be in a lot of trouble if you shot him.'

Cedric lowered the gun. He knew who Pünd was and he was glad to meet him. 'Am I a suspect?' he asked.

'You tell me,' Pünd replied. 'Should you be?'

'Yes!' Cedric nodded vigorously. 'I didn't like Grandma. She made us come out to the chateau every year and I don't enjoy it here. I'm on my own the whole time. Nobody ever plays with me. I'm bored.' Another thought occurred to him. 'I know lots about poisons. I can help you, if you like.'

'We most certainly need help,' Pünd replied. 'I understand that there are a great many poisons growing in this garden.'

'Do you want to see?'

'If you can show us, I would be most grateful.'

Cedric tucked his gun away. He was now imagining himself as a detective's assistant, which was much more fun. 'Follow me!' he said.

They set off, moving further away from the house and into the wilder stretches of the grounds.

'There are lots of varieties,' Cedric said. 'Sometimes Bruno shows them to me. He's the head gardener and he doesn't like it here either because he says they don't pay him enough. He gave me some deadly nightshade once. *Atropa belladonna*.' He enunciated the syllables carefully. 'I brought it in for dinner, but Grandma took it off me and made me wash my hands. There's white lilies over there. They're poisonous to dogs.' He pointed to an orchard. 'And there's something called "a shiverful of eyes" that Bruno told me about, although I haven't found any yet.'

'A shiverful of eyes?' Fraser asked.

'It is possible that Cedric means *chèvrefeuille des haies*,' Pünd explained. 'It is a toxic plant which I came across when I was writing *The Landscape of Criminal Investigation*. There is a chapter on poisons, although it appears only in the glossary.'

'I'm not sure which sounds worse,' Fraser muttered.

Cedric was hurrying ahead and finally reached a fruit and vegetable garden with nets stretched out over ripening clumps of raspberries. He stopped just outside the entrance and pulled a handful of leaves out of a piece of rough ground. 'Here you are!' he announced proudly. 'This is monkshood.'

He was holding an entire plant with spiky dark green leaves and mauve flowers shaped like hoods – obviously the reason for the name. He was holding it out for Pünd to take. But the detective stepped away. 'I would suggest you drop that immediately,' he said. 'You are certainly well informed about the toxic plants that grow in this garden, but even to touch this one can do you harm. Please leave it and clean your hands immediately on the grass.'

'I've handled it lots of times,' Cedric replied, but he did as Pünd had told him, first wiping his hands on damp grass, and then drying them on the sides of his shorts.

'You would make an excellent detective,' Pünd told him.

'But I would also like to test your powers of observation. Did you happen to be out in the garden on Sunday afternoon?'

Cedric nodded. 'I was out here all afternoon. I went swimming and then I read my *Archie* comic.'

'Can you tell me who you saw?'

Cedric fell silent as he gathered his thoughts.

'Mummy and Daddy had lunch with Uncle Harry and Aunt Judith,' he said, at length. 'Uncle Robert was with them. He's not really my uncle, but that's what I call him. He's always nice to me and everyone likes him, except for his father, who's always shouting at him. They had cold salmon and boiled potatoes, but they didn't enjoy it very much. They were cross because Grandma gave all her money to Elmer. No-one likes Elmer any more because he wants to control them, and if they ever want any of the money, they're going to have to ask him! Grandma left me lots of money in her will, but I'm not allowed to have it until I'm twenty-one.

'Uncle Harry stayed in the garden after lunch, but only for a bit. Then he went out in his car. Uncle Robert came for a swim and he asked me what I was reading, but then he went inside too.'

'Do you know what time that was?' Pünd asked.

Cedric shook his head. 'I didn't have my watch because if it gets wet, it won't work any more. Everybody else went inside. They always drink too much wine and then they go to sleep after lunch. I didn't see anyone else except Bruno and he was too busy to speak to me.'

Pünd nodded. 'You have done very well, Cedric, and you have been very helpful. But perhaps it would be best if you did not mention that we talked.'

'I'd like to be a detective when I'm grown-up. Or a murderer. I think they both sound fun.'

'I would recommend the former.'

Cedric ran off. Once again, Pünd and Fraser were alone.

'So, Harry Lyttleton wasn't here all afternoon,' Fraser said.

'He said he drove his wife to a lecture that began at five o'clock – which seems to leave little time to meet with Alice Carling in La Gaude, drive her to a beach and strangle her.' Pünd walked a few steps in silence. 'It is interesting that the child should have known exactly where to find monkshood. You know that it has another name, James.'

'Don't they call it wolfsbane?'

'You have a good memory!' Pünd beamed. It was Fraser, of course, who had typed the chapter on poisons in his book. 'It is also called leopard's bane and devil's helmet, but chemists will know it as aconite.'

'Is it related to aconitine?'

'They are very much the same.'

'So if Elmer Waysmith wanted to poison his wife, he didn't need to go to a chemist at all.' Fraser remembered the conversation he had been having with Pünd before Cedric interrupted them. 'If it was Elmer Waysmith in the Rue Lafayette,' he added.

Pünd stopped and sighed. 'It had to be Elmer Waysmith. It should have been Elmer Waysmith. Who else but Elmer Waysmith had a motive to kill Lady Margaret Chalfont and perhaps also Alice Carling, if he had tricked her into helping him with his crime? And yet, James, there is one thing that persuades me that there is more to all this than we are seeing.

We are up against a mind of great cunning and ingenuity and the killer has so far made just one mistake.'

'And what was that?'

'The empty bottle of shoe polish that was left in the bedroom of the Hôtel Lafayette. It tells us almost everything we need to know and soon, very soon, the puzzle will be solved.'

Pünd walked off. Fraser, as baffled as ever, followed.

The Second Anagram

I had to hand it to Eliot, he liked his cliffhangers. It was almost as if he was deliberately teasing me, reaching a point in the manuscript that made absolutely no sense at all and then jumping into his car to deliver it to me. What relevance could there possibly be in a bottle of shoe polish? Once again, it pointed to Elmer Waysmith as the killer. He had been on his way to the gallery and a smart lunch with his son and would have wanted to look his best. But why, then, would Pünd have made such a big deal about it? '*It tells us almost everything we need to know.*' My biggest worry was that Eliot was an unknown quantity and he might not be quite as clever as I'd thought. I mean, the book was well written. I was enjoying it. But what if it turned out that Elmer Waysmith really had killed both Lady Chalfont and Alice Carling and that before leaving the Hôtel Lafayette he'd simply polished his shoes?

It's what makes a murder mystery unique in the world of popular fiction. It may seem brilliant, but an awful lot depends on the last chapter. Only when you get there do you find out if the book was worth reading to begin with.

To give Eliot his due, I thought he'd come a long way since the ill-fated Dr Gee mysteries. I was still unsure about some of the Second World War references. The book was set ten years after VE Day, but Eliot had already referenced millions of deaths and concentration camps, and now we had Voltaire being blown up by a German hand grenade on the Maginot Line and a lengthy subplot about stolen art. I liked both these things – and in particular Voltaire's growing friendship with Pünd – but I had to ask myself if fans of the first nine books would enjoy these extraneous details. Maybe that's the difference between the editor and the author. The author lives inside the work. The editor has to keep half an eye outside it.

And then there was the setting. Were the South of France, Cap Ferrat and Saint-Paul-de-Vence helping the plot? I kept on stumbling over irrelevant details. Would you have been able to drink Orangina in Nice in 1955? Would they really have had commercial dustbins sitting on pavements like we see in cities now? The answers to both questions might well be yes, but even asking them somehow made it harder to lose myself in the reality of what was being described. I wondered about La Gaude too. Would it have been quite as populated as Eliot suggested, with a police station and a commercial cinema? Had he visited the place or was he still relying on Google Earth and Wikipedia?

It was early evening by now and I was beginning to think about what I was going to do for the next five hours. This was the part of the day I found hardest, when I was most aware of living on my own. I heard Hugo purring and looked down. He was curled up next to my feet and it bothered me that I was beginning to like him. A gin and tonic? No. Too early. An early-evening quiz on TV? I'd rather shoot myself.

I decided to call Eliot.

It seemed the right thing to do. Eliot had been keen for me to read his work and I'd promised to get back to him quickly; he'd even written his address and phone numbers (two of them) on the envelope. I wouldn't let him draw me into any further criticism of what he'd done, but I would make the right noises and urge him to finish it. At the same time, I wanted to ask him about *Front Row*. He'd said he wasn't going to do it, but what if he'd changed his mind? I could see all sorts of dangers in an appearance on BBC radio, not the least of which was that he might be drunk when he turned up at the studio. I really didn't want him to do it.

I called the first number, Eliot's mobile, which went straight to voicemail. Not wanting to leave a message, I tried the second, a landline. It rang four or five times before it was answered, but it wasn't Eliot whose voice I heard at the other end. It was his wife, Gillian.

'This is Susan Ryeland,' I said. 'I was wondering if Eliot was there.'

'No. No, he isn't. I don't know where he is.'

I could tell at once that something bad had happened. Gillian had been crying. I could hear it in her voice. She sounded desperate. 'Gillian, are you OK?' I asked.

'No. I'm not.'

'What's happened?'

'It's Eliot. He was so angry with me. I've never seen him like that before.'

'You've had an argument . . .'

'Yes.'

'Has he hurt you?'

A pause. Then: 'He hit me.'

I felt a sickness in my stomach. 'Is there anyone there with you?'

She started crying again and for a few seconds all I could hear was racking sobs, which sounded all the worse for being transmitted across the ether. 'I'm on my own,' she said eventually.

'I'm coming round.'

'No. There's nothing you can do.'

'I'll be with you as soon as I can. I'm on my way.'

*

I was weaving in and out of the rush-hour traffic and knew I'd be lucky not to set off every speed camera between Crouch End and Notting Hill Gate. As I drove across London, part of me was screaming that none of this was my business. After all, barely a week ago, Eliot Crace had been little more than a memory and I hadn't even heard of his wife. But what else could I do? I felt terrible about Gillian, who had seemed so vulnerable when I met her at Elaine's. Although there was no good reason for it, I felt responsible for what had happened to her. I was supposed to be looking after Eliot and that meant looking after her too.

At the same time, I couldn't ignore the more cynical voice whispering in my ear. If it got out that Eliot had behaved violently towards his wife, there would be no book. Nobody would want to go near him, and quite right too. I wasn't sure

I wanted to continue working with him myself and as I made my way down towards King's Cross Station and the turning onto the Euston Road, the thought was growing in me that it could all be over: the book, our relationship – and my career.

By the time I reached Madame Tussauds and the traffic snarled up, as always, around the Baker Street traffic lights, I'd had second thoughts. I couldn't do this on my own. Elaine Clover had started all this when she had introduced me to Eliot and Gillian. She was much closer to them than me. She should be the one to sort out this mess. Surrounded by cars and buses going nowhere, I eased my mobile out of my bag and speed-dialled her number. I was relieved when she answered at once.

Quickly, I explained what had happened. I had put the phone on speaker and was balancing it on my knee. The traffic still wasn't moving. 'I feel terrible for Gillian,' I told her. 'My first instinct was to go to the house, but now I'm not so sure.'

'Where are you?'

'I'm stuck in traffic at Baker Street.'

'I'm only five minutes from the house. I can meet you there.'

'Are you sure, Elaine? It might be better if—'

She interrupted me. 'It'll be a lot easier if there are two of us. And I'd like you there if Eliot shows up.'

I couldn't argue with her. 'All right,' I said. 'But you'll probably get there ahead of me. I'll arrive as soon as I can.'

'Don't worry. We'll sort this out.'

That was the Elaine I remembered. No fussing around, just making a decision and getting on with it.

I felt less anxious after that, although it took me another thirty minutes to reach the house. Roland had told me that Eliot was living in his parents' home in Notting Hill and my first sight of it provided striking evidence of the Crace Estate's wealth. It was a gorgeous, white-fronted jewel of a house standing on the corner of a street that didn't feel like London at all. Everything about it was ordered and symmetrical, a complete contrast to Eliot himself. Only the front garden, with its unloved hedges and patchy lawn, along with a rusting bicycle lying on its side, hinted that it wasn't owned by a banker or a lawyer or, indeed, by anyone who was proud to be living here.

I parked in a residents' bay and walked up to the front door, which opened as I approached. Elaine had seen me arrive. She was as smartly presented as ever in a cashmere jersey and jeans, but I saw from her face that things were as bad as I'd feared.

She got straight to the point. 'Gillian's inside. I should warn you, Susan, she's not looking pretty. He hit her in the face and she's badly bruised. And there's something else you need to know before you go in. She's pregnant.'

'Oh my God!' I thought about what she'd just said. 'Does Eliot know?'

Elaine looked at me reproachfully. 'I haven't asked her and she hasn't told me. One step at a time!'

The house was beautiful, but the moment I walked in, it told me another sad chapter in the history of the Crace family's life. It was untidy and unloved. The parents had gone, leaving the children home alone. The first thing I noticed was a large wine stain on the hall carpet. There was a smell of cigarette smoke and cooking oil in the air. A table opposite the entrance had a huge scratch running across the surface and there was clutter everywhere. A bag of rubbish was waiting to be carried out to the bin. This was where Edward and Amy Crace had lived immediately after Miriam Crace's death and I guessed it was Miriam's money that had originally purchased it. But now Edward and Amy were in America, Roland presumably had a bachelor pad somewhere in town, and Julia was working at a private school in Lincoln. That just left Eliot and Gillian, not so much living here as squatting. This wasn't their house or even their life. It was the temporary home of two people who had nowhere else to go.

'I'm so glad you've come,' Elaine said in a low voice. 'Gillian's in the kitchen.'

'How long have you been here?' I asked.

'I got here twenty minutes ago. I was in Kensington when you called me. You did the right thing, Susan. I had no idea how bad things were.'

We went into a kitchen that needed cleaning . . . or replacing. The surfaces were cluttered with old bottles and glasses, and the white goods had turned a faint yellow. A door was hanging diagonally off one of the cupboards and the oven had been defeated by grease and neglect. The far end of the room had a seating area with doors leading into the garden, and this was where I saw Gillian, sitting on a sofa with her legs curled up, her feet bare, cradling a hot drink that Elaine must have made for her. She was wearing her NHS nursing uniform. At first sight, she seemed unharmed, as pretty as I remembered her, but hearing me arrive, she turned her head and I saw that her cheek was bruised and swollen, her eye half-closed.

'Hello, Susan,' she said. 'Thank you for coming. But you really didn't have to . . .'

I turned to Elaine. 'Have you called a doctor?' I asked.

'I don't want to see anyone,' Gillian said. 'It's not as bad as it looks.'

I went over to her and sat on the arm of the sofa, keeping a distance between us. I was still wondering if I had been right to come. I was Eliot's editor, not a member of the family, and it was a great relief to have Elaine here with me. 'When did this happen?' I asked.

'An hour before you rang.' She glanced at Elaine. 'Have you told her?'

Elaine nodded. It was obvious what she meant.

'How many weeks?' I asked.

'Two months. I'm expecting it in January.' Perhaps it helped that Gillian worked as a nurse. She had to deal with difficult personal issues every day of the week and it had taught her to keep her emotions in check.

Despite Elaine's reticence, I had to ask her. 'Have you told him?'

'Yes. I told him. That was when he did this.'

That shocked me. He had hit her knowing she was pregnant.

Elaine had taken a seat opposite us. She looked grim.

'I'm grateful to you for coming over here, Susan. Both of you. But I want you to understand that it's not Eliot's fault.' There was a dull quality to Gillian's voice, as if she was describing events that had happened to somebody else. 'I met

342

Eliot when he came into the hospital and of course I knew he was trouble. I mean, he'd just taken a drug overdose. It wasn't as if he'd been hit by a car while helping an old lady cross the road or something like that. He almost died that first night and it was twenty-four hours before we knew he was going to make it. I think by that time I'd fallen in love with him. It was as if we were made for each other. I mean, I was a nurse and he was in so much pain. He was almost like a child. I could tell he was hurting and I wanted to help him.

'It's hard to imagine what it was like for him growing up in Marble Hall. Miriam controlled every inch of his life. She'd started with her own children – Eliot's father and his uncle – and then it continued with the grandchildren. They all suffered and in the end it killed Jasmine, Eliot's cousin. She was only twenty-one when she died.'

'Eliot told me it was an accident,' I said. 'She fell under a train.'

'That's what they all say. That was the official story when it happened. She fell under a tube train at Sloane Square station. But it's not true. They all know it, even if they pretend they don't, but Eliot told me the truth when he was drunk. She didn't fall. She jumped. She wrote them a long letter, telling them that she wanted to get away from the Little People, that they'd been following her all her life. She'd said the same thing to her therapist, but he couldn't help her. The next day, she was dead. Maybe that gives you an idea of what Eliot had to live with. Even the suicide of his cousin had to be covered up so that it wouldn't do any damage to the lovely image and the wonderful stories of Miriam Crace.'

It was another secret hidden in Eliot's book. He had

described the death of his cousin, Jasmine, but he had given it to Marion Waysmith, Elmer's first wife.

'If you don't believe me, you should talk to Julia. I don't see her very often because she lives so far away and she doesn't like visiting us. It brings back too many memories. But she knows how it was at Marble Hall. She couldn't wait for Miriam Crace to die. She and Eliot used to talk about it all the time . . .'

'And Roland,' I said.

She flinched. 'The way Eliot sees it, Roland betrayed him. When they were young, it was the three of them against the world. It hurt Eliot so much when Roland went to work for Jonathan Crace. Can you believe that man? Uncle Jonathan? He lost his own daughter to those books and he still wants to promote them and keep selling them.' She sighed. 'But I suppose we're just as bad. We wouldn't have this house if it wasn't for Miriam Crace. The Little People still support us, like they do the rest of the family. Eliot once said to me that taking her money was like taking drugs. You know it's going to kill you eventually, but you can't stop yourself.'

'But Eliot has stopped taking drugs,' Elaine said.

Gillian looked up scornfully. 'He's never stopped. He drinks too much, he smokes and he still takes whatever he can get his hands on. I've given up trying to boss him around. Drugs were the start of all his problems and it didn't take me long to realise that if I went on at him, I'd only lose him.'

She took a sip of whatever was in the mug, still cupping it in both hands.

'Eliot and I have been together for six years. I was the one who encouraged him to start writing again because I knew he'd be good at it. I don't know why he decided on murder stories. I wanted him to write romance or something big like *The Lord of the Rings*. He's got such an imagination. There are whole worlds exploding in his head. He was so disappointed when the Dr Gee books didn't do well.'

'Charles did everything he could,' Elaine said.

'I know, Elaine. I'm not blaming him. You were both so kind to Eliot – and he needed you. He needed someone a little bit older and more sensible in his life.'

'What about his parents?' I asked. 'I know they're in America, but do you ever speak to them?'

'Not really. I've seen them exactly three times since our wedding. They call us when they come to London and I've told them they can stay here. It is their house, after all. But they don't understand Eliot. The drug thing, when he overdosed, really horrified them. It was so completely outside their experience. And there's still the shadow of Miriam Crace hanging over them. Edward said it would be better for all of us if we kept apart.

'I know you both feel sorry for me and you probably think Eliot is horrible to have hit me when I'm pregnant, but I don't want you saying anything to him because it's not fair and I'm partly to blame.'

She put the mug down and clasped her hands between her knees.

'I love Eliot and I've done everything I can to make him happy. I knew what I was letting myself in for when I met him and I was just grateful for the good days we had together, when we were the same as any normal couple. But there were lots of bad times too, when he went off on one of his binges

345

and I didn't see him for a week. Whenever that happened, I'd be worried sick about him and when he finally turned up, or when he was dropped off by one of his cronies or in a police car or an ambulance, I'd be furious with him for putting me through it, because he knew I still cared about him.

'The trouble was, there were more bad days than good ones. I felt so lonely. It was like he didn't need me any more and I began to wonder what I was doing, staying with him. Staying in this house. It was almost like he'd turned me into a prisoner, just like he'd been at Marble Hall.'

She sighed. 'I suppose what happened was inevitable. I was feeling low and I was stressed out at work and Eliot was away from home.' She took a breath. 'And I met some-one. I had an affair. I knew it was wrong. I knew it would kill Eliot if he found out – but I couldn't stop myself. I just wanted a little happiness and when it was offered to me, I took it.'

She fell silent. But I'd seen it in her eyes. I knew what she was about to say.

'The baby isn't his,' I volunteered.

'Eliot has a hormonal imbalance, and the drugs haven't helped.' Once again it was the pragmatic nurse who was speaking. 'He's infertile. We've both had to accept that we can't have children together.'

There was a long silence as we took this in.

'Are you going to tell us who the father is?' Elaine asked and I noticed a certain iciness in her voice. She had been Eliot's friend when he was just a boy. Perhaps she had come to the conclusion that this was, after all, Gillian's fault.

'No!' For the first time, Gillian looked alarmed, afraid

even. 'Eliot began to suspect that I was seeing someone about three months ago . . .'

That was about the time he started writing the book, I thought.

'. . . and then he saw a text on my phone. How could I have been as stupid as that? He saw a message and he worked it out and he was furious with me. Worse than that. He stormed off and I didn't see him for three weeks, and when he finally got back, he was different. He was moody, tearful, bitter, silent. I swore to him that it was over, that it had all been a terrible mistake and that it wouldn't happen again – and I meant it! I thought it might be a sort of warning signal and it would help get us back together.'

'And then you found you were pregnant,' Elaine said.

'I saw the doctor this morning. I told Eliot when I got back from my shift. That was just a few hours ago and he went crazy.' She pointed to her face. 'He didn't know what he was doing. I've never seen him so angry, so out of control!'

Eliot had gone home after seeing me. All this drama had been playing out while I was reading his new pages.

'Do you know where he is?' Elaine asked. She appeared to be more concerned about Eliot than Gillian.

'No. He didn't say. He just stormed out.'

Gillian was beginning to crumple again. We both saw it. The tears returned to her eyes. She looked exhausted.

'I think you should see a doctor,' I said. 'If not for you, then for the baby. It's not just the physical side. This whole thing has been very traumatic. Do you have a local GP?'

Gillian was too exhausted to argue. 'I could see someone at St Mary's.'

'I'll go with her,' Elaine said.

I would have offered, but I was glad Elaine had got there first.

I reached out and held Gillian in a clumsy embrace. It was awkward, the two of us next to each other on the sofa, but I wanted her to know I was on her side. 'This will all work itself out,' I told her. 'You're going to have a baby. That's a wonderful thing . . .'

'Eliot wants me to get rid of it.'

'It's not his choice, Gillian. You know that.'

'I don't know anything any more.'

I got up. Suddenly I wanted to be out of here. Why was it that whenever Atticus Pünd came into my life, I inevitably found myself somewhere I didn't want to be?

'I'll call you,' Elaine said.

'Thank you. I'll see myself out.'

I went back into the hallway and as I was leaving, I noticed a table beside the front door with a scattering of letters, all of them too uninteresting to have been opened. One of them was a fashion catalogue or something, addressed to GIL-LIAN CRACE, and without even thinking about it, I saw it at once. A second anagram. It was extraordinary, really, after everything I had just heard, but maybe that's the way anagrams work. You either see them or you don't – but this one I most definitely had.

*

There was a parking ticket attached to my window when I got back to the car, but I ignored it. I knew that I had stumbled onto a clue that might help me unravel the secrets of Eliot's book or, indeed, his life.

Gillian Crace was Alice Carling.

I might have spotted it earlier. After all, Alice Carling was an unusual name for a young woman living in a small French village. But that said, I had never thought of Gillian as Gillian Crace. For all I knew, she could have kept her maiden name. So half the letters in the anagram had been missing, making it impossible to see.

What exactly did it mean, though? Well, first of all, in the book, Alice Carling was having an affair with the so-called Charles Saint-Pierre and as a result she had been murdered. Could there be a clearer insight into Eliot's mind? I wondered how much of the book he had written when he found out about the affair. It was always possible that he had changed the name of Monsieur Lambert's assistant after he'd started writing. It also confirmed what I had feared all along. *Pünd's Last Case* — or whatever he was going to call it — wasn't just a cheerful murder mystery bringing back a much-loved character. It was a bubbling cauldron in which Eliot's unhappy childhood, the death of his grandmother, the suicide of his cousin, the issues with his father and now his wife's infidelity had all been stirred together. And they were giving off noxious fumes.

I think that was when I had my first presentiment that this was all going to end very badly, that Eliot might be putting not just himself in danger but quite possibly me as well. I'd been here before, don't forget. I'd almost died in a burning office. My eyesight had been permanently damaged. I'd lost my job, my reputation and most of my friends. When was I ever going to learn?

It was time to take control of the situation and I suddenly knew where Eliot might be. When he had come to my house, he had mentioned a club he belonged to, a place called Boon's in the Portobello Road. He'd specifically said that it was his bolt-hole, where he went when he needed to be on his own.

It took me one minute to find it on Google and that was where I went next.

Boon's

Boon's was at the bottom end of the Portobello Road, past the Electric Cinema and well away from the pastel-coloured houses and smart antique shops that attracted the crowds at weekends. Bizarrely, it was named after a television series that had been filmed in the eighties, the story of two out-of-work firemen – later I learned that it had been set up by one of the actors who had appeared in it. There was a framed picture in the tiny reception area showing Michael Elphick, who played the title role, and some quite uninteresting props in glass cases going up the stairs. The club had just three rooms, one on top of another, two of them bars. The walls had light bulbs coated with the yellow tinge of cigarette smoke, even though smoking was no longer allowed, and the carpets were sticky and threadbare.

I thought I'd have to argue my way past the tattooed, shaven-headed receptionist who guarded the entrance, but I only had to ask for Eliot by name and she waved me upstairs. I found him on the top floor, slumped in a chair as if all the air had been sucked out of him, full of self-pity . . . and drink. There were another eight or nine people in the room, all of them in various stages of self-destruction, grouped together at tables or on sofas, a couple of them staring at a chessboard without moving any pieces, another pair leaning into each other, deep in conversation. They were all men and it occurred to me that Boon's was a cut-price Garrick Club where an exclusively male clientele came to hide from their girlfriends, their wives, their mothers or all the women who had made the world such a difficult place. The master of ceremonies – the barman – stood behind a wooden counter, slowly wiping a glass in a way that suggested that although he had been doing the same thing for hours, it still wasn't dry.

He was the only one who noticed me as I walked in and sat down opposite Eliot. I was already wondering how we were going to talk to each other with so many people in earshot, but just then some jazz music started playing – the system must have been between tracks – and I was grateful for the cover it provided. Eliot didn't appear to be happy to see me. His expression didn't change, but everything about him was a little more alert – like a drunk driver who had spotted a police car in his rear-view mirror.

'What are you doing here?' he asked.

'I'm looking for you, Eliot.'

'Who let you in?'

'A very charming lady downstairs told me you were here. Can I buy you a drink or is it members only?'

'They'll take money from anyone.' He straightened himself in his chair and waved at the barman. 'Bruce! I'll have another V and T. A double.' He glanced at me. 'What would you like?'

'No alcohol for me, thanks.' I twisted round. 'Do you have Diet Coke?'

'We've got Pepsi.' Bruce scowled. 'And it's not diet.'

'I'll have a tonic water, then.'

I laid a twenty-pound note on the table to cover the two drinks and turned back to Eliot.

'Are you all right?' I asked. I didn't know where to start. I could have just laid into him, but that would have been counterproductive. Instead, I tried safer ground. 'I've just finished the second part of your book,' I said. 'I called you, but you're not picking up, so I drove all the way over here to tell you I think it's very good.'

'Really?' He perked up at that.

'Absolutely. I loved that shoe polish clue at the end. I haven't got the faintest idea what it means, but it's exactly the sort of thing that Alan would have written. And I thought the scene with Cedric was very entertaining. All those poisons! Did you really base him on yourself?' I was having to think on my feet. The one thing I didn't want to discuss was the murder of Alice Carling, even though it was covered in about half of the new pages. 'The stolen art material was very good too. The whole thing is shaping up very well. So, congratulations.'

He was pleased, but that didn't stop him taking a dig at me. 'So what are your notes this time, Susan?' he drawled.

'I don't have any notes. You don't need them. Actually, I do have one and it's simply that you shouldn't be sitting here, wasting your time. You should be at home, working. The deadline isn't that far away and anyway, I can't wait to find out what happens. Do you have any more murders planned?'

'In the book or in real life?'

I half laughed as if I thought he was joking. 'As long as you don't murder me,' I said, keeping it light, keeping it friendly.

'And why would I want to do that, Susan?'

I'd always known that Eliot had a Jekyll and Hyde personality. Even when I'd met him at Cloverleaf, all those years ago, he'd managed to be charming but offensive, vulnerable but slightly dangerous, and I think I'd always been uneasy in his company. It was what I was seeing now. The difference was that I'd just come from his home – I'd seen the state Gillian was in and I was less willing to make allowances. To learn that she was expecting another man's child must have been awful for him, all the worse given his medical condition – but there could be no forgiving what he'd done and I wasn't even sure I wanted to work with him any more. I forced myself to stay calm. I needed time to work out what I was going to do.

Bruce arrived with the drinks. He put two glasses down and whisked away the twenty-pound note in a way that told me not to expect any change.

'So, did you call *Front Row*?' I asked, trying to sound casual.

'What do you mean?' He had already drunk half of the vodka I had bought him.

'We talked about it – don't you remember? When you came to my house, you said you were going to tell them you weren't going to do it.'

'I had second thoughts. Why not? It's good practice for when the book comes out and I've got plenty to say. I'm in the studio the day after tomorrow.'

'Oh, Eliot! I thought we'd agreed—'

'I don't think it's got anything to do with you, Susan. I asked Elaine and she thought it was a good idea.'

I was annoyed, but there was clearly no point arguing. 'You must do what you think best, Eliot,' I said. Then, as an afterthought: 'I could come with you, if you like.'

'I don't need you to hold my hand.'

'That's not what I'm suggesting. I just have more experience of working with the media than you and you might find it helpful to have me there as moral support.'

'No, Susan. I'm going alone.'

It was his laziness, his insolence that finally did it for me. I'd had enough. 'We need to talk,' I said.

'What about?'

'You know what about, Eliot. I've just come from your house.'

A twitch of irritation passed across his face. 'Why?' It was as if that was all he could manage.

'I was trying to reach you, to congratulate you on the work. Gillian answered the phone. She sounded upset, so I went in to see her.' I didn't tell him that I'd driven across London. 'I can't believe what you did to her, Eliot. What were you thinking of? It makes me feel I don't know you.'

He said nothing, sitting there with his drink, almost daring me to continue. I knew that I had already crossed a bridge, that things between us would never be the same. I was tempted to get up and walk out – permanently. But still I lingered a few moments, wondering what he would say, hoping for contrition. It didn't come.

Eliot took another sip of the drink I had bought him and

looked at me with unforgiving eyes. 'You went to Marble Hall,' he said. His voice was soft, venomous.

Why was he mentioning that now? Hadn't we already talked about all this? 'Yes,' I said. 'You may remember you suggested it.'

'You met Frederick Turner.'

'He happened to be in the house when I was there and he invited me for a coffee.' Eliot had put me on the defensive, even though there was absolutely no reason for me to feel that way.

'And Dr Lambert just happened to be at home when you called in on him?' he continued.

'I don't see what your problem is, Eliot. You've turned all these people into characters in your book. You're obviously writing about Marble Hall and your grandmother, and you're doing exactly what I warned you against: mixing fiction and real life to settle a score. That's what got Alan Conway killed, and what nearly did for me too. So why should you be surprised that I spoke to the people involved with your family? I'd say I was protecting you from yourself, although given what you did to Gillian, I'm not sure why I should bother.'

It was as if he hadn't heard me. 'My uncle Jonathan rang me. You saw him, too, and you met my brother. I can't believe you talked about me with my *brother*!' He sounded disgusted. 'I thought I could trust you, but you've been creeping around behind my back, digging into things that are none of your business.'

'The book is my business.'

'Exactly, Susan. The book. Not me, not my family and not my sodding private life. You know what? I'm not so sure

I need your help with my book either. So far, everything you've said about it has been completely unconstructive. You didn't like the title. You didn't like the opening. You didn't like the setting.'

'I wouldn't have said anything about your great masterpiece if you hadn't shoved it into my hands, Eliot. You also insisted I give you my thoughts. But as I told you at the time, my comments were suggestions, not criticisms. If I'd known you had such a thin skin, I wouldn't have said anything.'

'What you did was you undermined my self-confidence and . . .' he jabbed a finger against the side of his head '. . . you screwed up my thinking. All I wanted was encouragement. You gave me the exact opposite.'

I knew exactly what he was doing. He'd steered the conversation away from himself and what he had done to Gillian. Instead, he was turning the tables, as if I was the one throwing the punches and he was the victim. Looking at him lolling in his worn-out armchair in this shabby excuse for a club, I was disgusted.

I stood up.

'There's no point talking to you when you're like this, Eliot, and I'm not sure I want to work on your book, if you really want the truth. You should go home and look after your wife.'

'My wife has got nothing to do with you.'

'And if she's got any sense, she'll have nothing to do with you either.'

'Go to hell, Susan.'

'Drop dead, Eliot.'

I walked out, angry with myself for losing my temper but

still glad that it was over. I didn't want to work with him. I had been right from the start. He was trouble and so was his book. I should never have got involved.

As I left, I noticed that the other club members hadn't moved. The chess players were still not playing chess. Bruce, the barman, had started wiping another glass. It was as if none of them had heard the conversation between Eliot and me.

But they had.

Front Row

Transcript of the interview between Samira Ahmed and Eliot Crace, broadcast on *Front Row*, 21 June 2023.

SA: This year marks the twentieth anniversary of the death of one of the UK's best-loved children's authors. Miriam Crace was the creator of the Little People series of books about a miniature family who are devoted to helping 'the bigguns' – which is how they describe the rest of humanity. She wrote sixty-three adventures during her lifetime and Netflix have announced a deal reputedly worth two hundred million dollars to bring the characters to the screen. Eliot Crace is her grandson and a published writer himself. He has just been named as the author of three continuation novels that will feature the detective Atticus Pünd, created by Alan Conway. Eliot is with me in the studio now.

        Eliot, we'll come to Atticus Pünd in a minute, but first I'd like to ask you about your grandmother. You grew up in Marble Hall, near Devizes, which was the house where she lived and worked. I imagine you must have had quite an unusual childhood?

EC: Well, that's one word for it, Samira. I was born in Marble Hall – well, in a hospital near Marble Hall – and I was there until my grandmother died and my parents moved to a place in London. To be honest, we couldn't wait to get out of there. By 'we', I mean my brother and sister and me – and everyone else, really.

SA: Miriam was born in 1920 and was home-schooled by her father, who was a deacon in the town of Ilminster, Somerset. For several years, she was the church organist. Apparently, she got the idea for the Little People from an image in a stained-glass window, and many of her books have connections with the church calendar. She was married to Kenneth Rivers, a junior civil servant in the Department of Agriculture – although due to the success of her books, she preferred to keep her maiden name. He was, of course, your grandfather. Do you have any memories of him, Eliot?

EC: We never saw very much of Grandpa. He sort of kept himself to himself. He was interested in taxidermy and he used to spend hours in a room in one of the towers, fiddling about with stuffed animals. I remember one in particular – a kingfisher. He hadn't actually stuffed that one himself. He'd bought it in a shop in Islington. It was Victorian and you always think of kingfishers as being such beautiful birds, but this one was evil. It sat in its own glass case, which was kept locked. It used to scare the hell out of me when I was a kid. I was frightened it was going to escape.

Anyway, Grandpa stayed in the house after Grandma died, but he didn't last long without her. My last memories of him are ... he was an old man in his eighties, but he seemed older, living on his own in an enormous house, although he had a nurse to look after him. My grandfather was always complaining about her. He didn't like her. I think she reminded him of my grandmother ... My grandparents had separate rooms and I never saw them together.

SA: Still, it must have been exciting for you, growing up in Marble Hall. Your grandmother was one of the most famous writers in the world. The Little People brought happiness to millions and you were right at the heart of it all.

EC: I was at school. I used to get bullied because I was her grandson. My cousin, Jasmine, hated the Little People. She was named after one of them and ... I mean, can you imagine? There was no escape for her ... not until she died. But Grandma didn't care. She was out there, travelling all over the place, meeting famous people, going to parties and film premieres and cruises and fancy hotels, and we were all stuck at home, waiting for her to come back. None of us wanted to be at Marble Hall and she didn't want us there either. Not really. She just wanted to control us.

SA: Did you tell her you wanted to be a writer?

EC: Yeah. I once showed her a story I'd written. It was about a boy who travelled into outer space, which was something I'd always dreamed about doing. It was as far away from Marble Hall as I could go. So he builds himself a space rocket using stuff that he's found at school and

361

around the house – like dustbins and sticky tape and iron filings and all these chemicals that he's nicked from the chemist in the village. The book was called 'Space Boy' and I showed it to her. She said it was no good at all. She laughed at me. She said I had no imagination and no idea how to tell a story. I was ten years old.

SA: I have to say, I'm quite surprised. It sounds like you're painting a very dark picture of her, Eliot.

EC: I'm sorry if I'm disappointing you, Samira, but I'm telling you the truth. Just because she wrote these great books, it doesn't mean she was an easy person to live with.

SA: So she didn't inspire you to write murder mysteries?

EC: That's the funny thing. She did. I was at home when she died and everyone said that it was natural causes because she'd been ill for a while, but I don't think there was anything natural about it. In fact, I've never said this before and I'm probably going to get into trouble, but when I was twelve years old, I saw someone creep out of her room in the middle of the night. I saw it with my own eyes – and the next day she was dead. I can even tell you how they did it, if you're interested.

SA: Go on.

EC: They poisoned her.

SA: That's quite an accusation, Eliot. And I wouldn't want to question your recollections, but, as you just said, you were only twelve years old when Miriam Crace died and it was well known that she had a heart condition. Isn't it possible that you had more of an imagination than she gave you credit for?

EC: I know what I saw, Samira.

SA: Did you ever go to the police?

EC: I couldn't. There was no way I could have done that. And I didn't want to ... not then. But things are different now, so that's what I'm writing about. My new Atticus Pünd novel is set in the South of France in 1955, but it's inspired by what I saw at Marble Hall and if you read it carefully, I've put in a secret message. That's what Alan Conway used to do. Did you know that? He hid things in his books and because this is a continuation novel, I'm playing the same game. I know that my grandmother was murdered. That's a scoop for your radio programme. If you can work out the puzzle, you'll know the truth about what really happened. Right now, there should be some pretty nervous people out there, but that doesn't bother me. I've decided it's time.

SA: Does your new book have a title?

EC: I'm thinking of calling it *The Man with White Hair*.

SA: And do your publishers know the secret?

EC: Nobody knows except me. And the person I saw.

SA: I'm sure we'll all look forward to reading it. But in the meantime, would you like to tell us which is your favourite Little People book?

EC: *Little and Often.*

SA: Why that one?

EC: Because it was the last.

SA: Thank you. That was Eliot Crace, giving a very personal view of his grandmother, Miriam Crace, who died exactly twenty years ago next Tuesday.

*

Story in the *Daily Mail*, 22 June 2023.

HOW WOULD MIRIAM CRACE FEEL TO BE TRASHED BY HER TALENTLESS GRANDSON?

By Kate Greene

Do you remember the Little People books? I read them as a child and, like so many of my friends, they always seemed to bring the smile back to my face when I was down in the dumps.

There was Grandpa Little with his stopwatch that had stopped permanently at teatime. Jack Little, who dreamed of sailing round the world in a teacup. Mr and Mrs Little, who didn't have first names, but who loved each other so much that they celebrated their wedding anniversary every day.

Later on they were joined by Karim and Njinga Little, who were colour-blind (like their creator in real life) and who genuinely believed that everyone in the world looked the same. I remember reading *Little League* – where Njinga sneaks into the United Nations and gets everyone to join in a song. It made me laugh out loud.

But it also brought tears to my eyes. If only the world could be more like the way the Little People saw it. That was the genius of their creator, Miriam Crace. She never had an unkind word to say about anyone. Her books had none of the spite or vulgarity you find in so many modern offerings. She saw the best in everything.

So what are we to make of Eliot Crace, who appeared on the BBC Radio 4 arts programme *Front Row* – with some very questionable opinions about his grandmother?

Let's ignore for a moment the fact that young Eliot seemed to have felt the need to fortify himself before he went on air. His voice was slurred. Some of his pronouncements were incoherent.

According to him, she was mean and uncaring. She was a control freak. Although she paid for her family to live in the gorgeous surroundings of Marble Hall, deep in the heart of the Wiltshire countryside – and her generosity also extended to Eliot's private education, by the way – he says all he wanted was to get away from her.

I'm not saying that Miriam Crace was perfect. Nobody is. I remember interviewing her long ago, when she was seventy, and she couldn't wait to get out of the room. She wouldn't even talk to me until I had given her £20! But then, a week later, she sent me a charming note and a receipt from the St Ambrose Children's Home.

But what exactly is the point in laying into her on the twentieth anniversary of her death? What good does he think it will do?

And then there's his extraordinary claim that someone in the family might have murdered her! 'Piffle and poppycock', as Grandma Little might have said. (And often did!) She had terminal heart disease. Her private doctor examined her after she had peacefully passed away.

Funny, isn't it, that nobody has ever had a bad word to say about Miriam before. Just little Eliot – who was only twelve years old himself when his grandmother died.

So here's the question. Is it a coincidence that Eliot Crace is promoting his own book, a new Atticus Pünd murder mystery that he has – mysteriously – been commissioned to write?

And here's the answer. Probably not!

Eliot Crace has published two crime novels. Their titles were *Gee for Graveyard* and *Gee for Gunfire*, about a detective with the unlikely name of Dr Gee.

I've never read them myself, but let's just say that they didn't exactly set the world on fire. According to the critic of this newspaper at the time, they were 'poorly written and confused'. It makes you wonder why Causton Books have decided he's the right man for the job.

Unless, of course, they're buying into the famous name that it just so happens he's attempting to drag down.

I quite enjoyed the Atticus Pünd novels, but I'll tell you this. If you're thinking of buying me *The Man with White Hair* for Christmas, please don't bother. I'm sure it will be Gee for garbage.

The Party

It had been more than a week since my last encounter with Eliot Crace and I hadn't heard a word from him. Michael Flynn hadn't been in touch either. I didn't know if I was still employed by Causton Books, if Eliot had fired me as his editor or if I'd resigned. The last of these seemed the most likely. After all, I'd walked out on him and told him to drop dead, which could hardly be called a celebration of our working relationship.

I didn't care. The *Front Row* interview had been the last

straw as far as I was concerned. In a drunken flurry, Eliot had announced to the whole world that Miriam had been murdered and that he knew who had done it. What exactly was going on in his head? Did he think it would be good for sales? Had he learned nothing from what had happened to Alan Conway?

There had been quite a furore following the broadcast. A lot of newspapers had carried stories similar to the one in the *Daily Mail*, there had been an item on the six o'clock news and one journalist had even managed to track down my mobile phone number to call and ask me for a comment. I declined. There had barely been a mention of Eliot's new book in any of the reports. That's what he should have realised before he opened his mouth. Miriam Crace was the story and she didn't need the publicity.

Jonathan Crace had telephoned me too. I didn't answer the phone when I saw his name come up on the screen, but he left me a voicemail message that was as aggressive as I'd expected.

'*Susan — this is Jonathan Crace here. I'm calling you about this absurd interview that Eliot has done on the BBC. You told me he wasn't writing about his time at Marble Hall and now he comes out with a series of outrageous accusations at the worst possible time as far as the estate is concerned — particularly in light of our dealings with Netflix. You also promised me you would keep him under control, but I very much wonder if this so-called interview wasn't your idea in the first place. I'd be very grateful if you could call me back as soon as possible — and if you see Eliot, you can tell him from me that he has done himself and his book nothing but damage. I can assure you both that the estate will be pursuing this matter further.*'

The one thing he hadn't done was to uninvite me from the celebration of his mother's life. Perhaps he'd forgotten that he'd asked me to come in the first place, but there it was on my kitchen table, a thick piece of card with Copperplate lettering inside a gold border and my name on the dotted line. It didn't take me very long to make up my mind. Everyone would be there: Jonathan, Roland, maybe Eliot and Gillian. I doubted that we would come to blows over champagne and canapés and I was keen to find out whether the book was still going ahead.

Which explains why, at six o'clock in the evening of the following Tuesday, I found myself standing in front of a full-length mirror with a gin and tonic in one hand and a sequinned silk clutch bag in the other. I had chosen a figure-hugging black dress I'd bought in one of the few boutiques in Agios Nikolaos that sold clothes I could imagine myself wearing. It would have worked equally well at a party as at a funeral and since this was the anniversary of Miriam's death, it seemed appropriate. I wasn't going to drive. The tube would take me directly from Highgate station and although that meant sacrificing stiletto heels, at least I could have a drink.

The party was being held at the address in Kingston Street where I had met Jonathan Crace. It was a balmy evening when I arrived and the entire street had been taken over by attendants in grey shirts and waistcoats, helping the guests park on both sides, from one end to the other. I wondered how the Crace Estate had managed to arrange this with their neighbours, but then it occurred to me that they were so rich it was possible they owned all the properties. Flaming torches had been arranged outside the front door, and given that the building was Georgian and everyone arriving was elegantly dressed, I felt as if I was walking onto a giant film set.

There were two young women with clipboards in the reception area, checking off the guests as they entered, and I did have a moment of doubt as I presented my invitation. Was I about to experience the humiliation of being turned away? But either Roland had been looking out for me or Jonathan had forgotten to press the delete button and I was shown in with no problem.

'There's a cloakroom just over there and you can take the lift or the stairs to the reception room on the fourth floor. Have a lovely evening.'

I was wearing a light coat over my dress and I handed it to an attendant and received a numbered tag in return. I slipped it into my bag and had just joined a small crowd of people waiting for the lift when I saw her. 'Elaine!'

Elaine Clover was standing in front of me, looking down at her mobile phone. She was wearing an off-the-shoulder opal-pink evening dress and a pretty necklace with multi-coloured stones. As she turned round and smiled at me, I felt seriously underdressed, but I was still delighted to see her. A friend in the enemy camp.

'Susan! I was hoping you'd be here tonight.' She slid the phone into her bag, a fluffy thing with pink feathers.

We stepped to one side, allowing other guests to go past us and enter the lift.

'Who invited you?' I asked.

'Eliot arranged it for me.'

'Is he coming?'

'Yes. At least, he said he was. I was just looking to see if he'd texted me.' She sighed. 'It was awful what happened, Susan, but we must try to forgive him. He didn't know what he was doing and he felt terrible.'

'You've spoken to him?'

'I stayed with Gillian after you left. She didn't go to the hospital in the end and I didn't like to leave her alone. He came in about an hour later, very much the worse for wear. She wouldn't speak to him, but I sat with him in the kitchen and managed to force some black coffee into him. I must tell you, he broke down. He genuinely loves her and he's terrified of losing her. She's the only thing that's been keeping him sane these last few years.'

'But she's expecting someone else's child.'

'Well, it's too soon to say what's going to happen. But the way he is now, I think he'd even forgive her for that. He doesn't know what to do with himself – and that radio thing. What was that all about?'

'Does he know who the father is?' I asked.

'No. She hasn't told him. She hasn't told me either. I'm not sure it really matters, does it? The whole thing is a mess.'

The lift had come back down again. 'Let's join the party,' Elaine said.

She was right. It was too exhausting trying to keep up with Eliot and Gillian and the world they had created for themselves. It reminded me of a book I'd once edited, written by a woman who'd spent ten years working on a television soap opera. It had been a litany of affairs, betrayals, surprise revelations, confrontations and fist fights until I'd almost dreaded

371

turning the next page. I'd been put in my place when sales reached five figures.

We shared the lift with half a dozen other people so it was impossible to have any further talk. After what felt like far too long a time, we were released into a vestibule with a set of double doors folded back to reveal a party in full swing on the other side. There were about two hundred people gathered there, most of the men in suits, the women in designer dresses and expensive jewellery.

The fourth storey of the building consisted of a single space with a polished ballroom floor, windows on two sides, tall tables covered with pristine white cloths, a scattering of gold chairs, waiters circulating with champagne flutes and glasses, bottles wrapped in serviettes, trays of canapés. Gilt mirrors reflected the light from chandeliers spaced out in two long lines. A classical quartet was playing Vivaldi in one corner.

And at the far end, a huge black-and-white photograph of Miriam Crace covered almost the entire wall, looking at the guests who had gathered in her honour with eyes that, to me, seemed unimpressed, as if she was peeved they were all enjoying themselves at her expense while she was only present as a ghost.

'If you need me, shout,' Elaine said and moved further into the room. I saw Jonathan Crace ahead of her, but she swerved to one side as if deliberately avoiding him and disappeared from sight.

I plucked a glass of champagne as soon as I could, not just because I wanted a drink but because it gave me a sense of legitimacy. I'd been invited and the glass in my hand was proof that I was allowed to be here. I took a sip and noted that it was indeed champagne and not unchilled Prosecco, the curse of so many publishing parties.

Across the room, I noticed Frederick Turner, his black eyepatch making him easy to spot in a crowd. He was holding a champagne flute in his left hand, his right hand deep inside the pocket of his velvet jacket. He was talking to a young woman who had her back to me. I made my way towards them. I would be interested to see how Frederick greeted me. He had been pleasant enough when we met, but he had called Jonathan Crace the moment I left. I really couldn't work him out. Eliot had suggested that he had been badly treated, sidelined by the family. But here he was at its very epicentre, celebrating the life of the woman who had adopted him.

'Good evening, Susan,' he said when he saw me.

'Hello, Frederick.'

The woman he had been talking to turned round to examine me and I guessed who she was. When he had created the character of Judith Chalfont, Eliot had described her as 'substantial', by which he meant overweight. But what struck me more about Julia Crace was her energy, her smile, her beautiful skin and her air of resilience. Everyone I had met in the Crace family – and that included Eliot – had somehow been trapped: by their blood, their shared history, their relationship with Miriam. She alone seemed to have found her independence. She had escaped from Marble Hall and all its associations and I wondered what had brought her here tonight.

'This is Susan Ryeland,' Frederick told her. 'This is Julia Crace,' he added. 'Eliot's sister.'

She looked at me with coolly inquisitive eyes. 'I've heard everything about you,' she said. 'You're working with Eliot on his book.'

'That's right. I'm very pleased to meet you.'

'So you can ask me more questions about Grandma and the family?'

She was putting me in my place, but for some reason I didn't feel offended. I already liked her. 'I had no interest at all in your family until I met Eliot,' I said. 'Since then, I feel that I've been drawn in.'

'Like a groupie?'

'More like a fish in a net.' I turned to Frederick. 'I'm sorry if you thought I was being intrusive,' I said. 'You may not believe it, but I have no interest in digging up dirt on Miriam Crace or anyone else. All I've been trying to do is help Eliot.'

'I appreciate that, Susan. And perhaps I was a bit hard on you when we met at Marble Hall. But whatever you may think about me or Miriam Crace, or the entire family, for that matter, you must admit that she was a force for good and that's what this is all about.' He looked around the room, taking in the huge photograph at the far end. 'How many people devote their whole lives to making the world a happier place? Isn't that what we're celebrating tonight? It's what I told you when we first met. I'm sure you can find all sorts of bad things to say about Mrs Crace, but it's not relevant. It's her brilliant creations that matter, the joy that they bring.' He smiled. 'I'm sorry. We don't need to have this conversation right now, so I'll leave the two of you together. Have a nice evening.'

He walked away.

'Do you really think that Grandma was murdered?' Julia asked me the moment he was gone.

I was taken aback. I hadn't expected her to be so blunt.

'I'd have imagined you'd know better than me,' I retorted. 'Have you spoken to Eliot since he went on the radio?'

'No. He emailed me a couple of weeks ago. He had nice things to say about you.'

That was then, I thought. 'So what can you tell me about Marble Hall?' I asked.

'Susan, I'll tell you something straight away. You're not going to upset the apple cart. The Miriam Crace Estate is too big. We learned that when we were kids. I'm sure Eliot's told you . . . we hated Marble Hall. We hated everything about it. But there was nothing we could do – not until we grew up and got the hell out.

'But you have to remember – it's not as if the Crace Estate is selling oil or weapons or health insurance. Everyone loves the Little People. Do you know, at St Hugh's – the prep school where I teach – they have every single one of Miriam's books? They draw pictures of the characters in art class. On Book Day, half the kids still come as Littles. If they found out I was part of the family, I think they'd die of shock.'

'You changed your name?'

'I changed it the day I left. The kids know me as Miss Wilson and that suits me fine. I don't want anything to do with my family – and that's why I didn't get in touch with you when Roland contacted me. I hope you're not offended.'

'I completely understand, Julia. It was never my intention to take on the Crace Estate, and for what it's worth, I'm not even sure that I'm working with Eliot any more. I advised him not to do the radio broadcast, but he didn't listen to me. There is one thing I'd like to ask you, though.'

'Go ahead.'

'If you hate your family so much, what are you doing here?'

She smiled. 'I don't hate the family, Susan. Well, my uncle Jonathan is a bit of a shit and Freddy is sad, but the main reason I come to these anniversaries is to remind myself of what I left behind. It's a chance to see Roland and Eliot. You have no idea how close we were, growing up. I'm staying in London until the weekend and we'll have dinner together – if Eliot decides to show his face. The one thing we're not allowed to do, ever, is to go public about life with Grandma. I was left money in her will, but I had to sign a privacy clause before I got it.'

'You too?'

'It's the only time I can ever talk about it,' Julia went on. 'At family gatherings like this one. And sometimes I need to get my feelings out there. We're survivors, you see. Roland, me and Eliot, we stuck together and that made us strong. You heard about Jasmine?'

'She killed herself.'

'The official story is that she slipped and fell. I feel bad about her, although we were never that close. She lived in a separate house with Jonathan and his wife, Leylah, and so she wasn't part of our group.'

'Tell me about the three of you,' I said. 'You, Roland and Eliot. What exactly was your "group"?'

'We had a sort of secret society. We called ourselves the Rogue Troopers, which came out of one of Eliot's comics.

We asked Jasmine if she wanted to join, but she wasn't interested. At the end of the day, when we were meant to be doing our homework, we'd slip away and meet up in an empty cottage in the grounds. It was a horrible place – most of the rooms were damp and full of spiders – but we had a table and chairs and we stole bottles of lemonade. We could be alone together and could say anything we wanted there. Roland used to smoke cigarettes, even though they made him feel sick.'

'Is that where you plotted to kill your grandmother?' I asked.

Julia laughed. 'We were children, Susan. We talked about lots of things. We plotted to run away, to join a circus, to set fire to the house, to stow away on a ship sailing to Argentina – but do you really think we would have done any of those things?' She looked at me disdainfully. 'Roland would never have let us do anything stupid. And he was the one who saved my life. I mean that quite literally. He was my knight in shining armour at a time when I really needed one. He looked after Eliot, too. He was older than both of us and he wasn't afraid.'

She had been looking across the room as she spoke and, following her eyes, I saw Roland in animated conversation with another guest. He was wearing a Savile Row suit and I had to admit that he looked remarkably handsome. It wasn't just his dark, wavy hair and film star looks. It was the way he carried himself. I've met one or two famous actors in my time and it's something I've often noticed. They can introduce themselves and draw you in with their body language long before they open their mouth.

The man he was talking to turned his head briefly and I started. Surely it couldn't be possible. Roland was talking to Michael Flynn, my boss at Causton Books. But there was no reason he would have been invited here. On the contrary, he had commissioned Eliot's book. He was, theoretically, the enemy. What possible connection could he have with Miriam Crace?

I wanted to go over to him, but Julia was still talking.

'I did want to kill her,' Julia said, talking about her grandmother. 'Miriam Crace died a few days after my birthday. I'll never forget – it was almost the last time I saw her. My mother took me out so I could buy a dress for the party. There weren't going to be many of us there – just the family and a few friends from school. Miriam asked me to put it on to show her and I should have known better, but Mummy persuaded me. So I dressed up and came down after lunch.'

She stopped and for a moment the anger and humiliation of twenty years ago welled up in her.

'I walked into the living room wearing this pink and white thing, and maybe it was a bit tight-fitting. I don't know. Anyway, Miriam laughed at me. She laughed and she laughed and she laughed. She said I looked like Miss Piggy in that television show *The Muppets*. She made a joke. She said that if I had too much birthday cake it would explode . . . something like that. The whole family was there and I was standing in front of her, just wanting to cry and forcing myself not to. In the end, I ran out of the room and when the day of the party came I just wore jeans.'

'How could she do that?' I exclaimed. 'I mean, nobody

in their right mind behaves like that. Especially not to a child.'

'Do you know what, Susan? I don't think it really matters.' Julia became reflective and it was as if the party that was happening all around us had somehow faded away, as if we had been removed from it. 'I often ask myself what was wrong with Miriam Crace, but that's a big step forward. You see, because of what happened to me in my childhood, I spent half my life wondering what was wrong with *me*. I'm not sure I'd have got through it without Roland. He was the barrier between Miriam and me. Without him, maybe I would have killed her. Or myself . . . like poor Jasmine.

'I'm a survivor. I know that sounds dramatic, but it's true. I've been in therapy for a long time now, but finally I understand. None of it was my fault. Every child expects their mother to love them. It's human nature. But the mother – or grandmother, in my case – who deliberately withdraws that love is doing it for the sense of power it gives her. Maybe Miriam had been abused herself as a child. She had money. She had success. But at the end of the day, she was trapped in some sort of misery of her own making and she took it out on us as some sort of revenge.'

The black-and-white photograph was right in front of us. It was as if Miriam Crace was listening to every word. The matriarch. The monster.

'Couldn't your parents have protected you from her?'

'They didn't dare. They'd grown up with her all their lives and they were too scared of her.'

'And I suppose there was the money.'

'That was part of it. But you don't know what it's like being part of a literary estate. How can you hate someone who is loved by every single person on the planet? How can you have any life of your own when your very name is defined by her genius and everything you do will be compared to it? That was what killed Jasmine, her realisation that she would spend her whole life unable to escape from its shadow. It nearly killed me too. Eliot hid himself in his books and his stories, but Roland was the only one who wasn't afraid to fight back. When Grandma was going on about my size and my weight, or when she was telling Eliot that he was stupid and he'd never have any success as a writer, Roland was the one who stood up to her. He wasn't afraid of her. If anything, I think she was a little bit afraid of him!'

'You must have been surprised when he chose to work for the estate.'

'If you want the truth, I was bloody angry and upset. But I've got used to it. We're grown up now and we've all gone our separate ways. Roland needed something to do. But he's not like Uncle Jonathan. He's dealing with the books and the business and the legacy. It's just a job for him. He's not a high priest in the Church of Saint Miriam.'

'Thank you for talking to me, Julia. I still can't get my head around how horrible it must have been for all of you.'

'Take care of Eliot, Susan. I sometimes think he's the only one who hasn't managed to put it behind him and I do worry about him.'

'I will. I promise.'

I said that, but after everything that had happened, I wasn't certain it was a promise I could keep. I turned back to look for Michael Flynn, but he had moved away and Roland was talking to someone else. I was about to search for him when there was a stir in the room and I saw the other guests around me turning towards the double doors. Coincidentally, the quartet had just reached the end of a piece and their sudden silence only made the change in atmosphere more noticeable. Eliot had arrived. He was standing in the doorway, trying to keep his balance, wearing a thigh-length velvet jacket, black trousers and a crumpled white shirt open at the neck and exposing much of his chest. His fair hair was even more tangled than usual, falling in knots down his neck. He could almost have stepped out of an opera. All that was missing was the sword.

He looked around the crowd, then stumbled forward, knocking into people, pushing them out of his way. Crossing one foot over the other, he diverted briefly towards a waiter, snatched a flute of champagne and threw back the contents without seeming to know what he was drinking. I'd never seen him as bad as this. I'd never dreamed this was how bad he could be. I wondered how he had got to the building. Public transport would have been impossible and it was unlikely a taxi driver would have considered slowing down to pick him up.

Jonathan Crace appeared, blocking his way, and suddenly Roland was there too. They closed in on him just as the quartet started up again: more Vivaldi.

'That's what you call making an entrance,' Julia said cheerfully. 'Shall we go and say hello?'

She was already moving towards her brothers and I followed. The three people I most wanted to meet were all together in one place and whatever they were going to say to each other, I wanted to hear it.

'What do you think you're doing, Eliot?' That was Jonathan Crace. '*Front Row*. Have you gone mad?'

'I didn't do any harm,' Eliot protested.

'I suppose you think this sort of publicity is going to help us, just when we're trying to get the Netflix deal over the line! You talk to him, Roland.'

Roland glanced uncertainly at his uncle. 'It wasn't great timing, Eliot,' he muttered, none too convincingly.

'Go to Hell, Roland.'

Listening to Eliot speak, I realised I had underestimated the hatred that had developed between him and his brother. And what a tableau they all made! Eliot beyond redemption, Jonathan as coldly unlikeable as he had been when we first met, Roland helpless, no longer the leader of the Rogue Troopers, and Julia watching from the sideline, not saying anything.

And then a second woman swept in, taking control of the situation. 'Eliot, darling! You should have told us you were coming. Have you been drinking? You look ghastly! Where's Gillian? Hasn't she come?'

'Leylah . . .' Jonathan Crace reached out for his wife's arm. 'I'm handling this. There's no need to get involved.'

'I am involved, Jonathan.' She shook herself free.

Leylah Crace. If I hadn't heard her name, I'd have known at once it was her. Her skin colour, her jet-black hair and both the shape and the colour of her eyes signalled her North African origins. She was wearing a gorgeous caftan dress, a blaze of colours sweeping down to the floor, and long gold earrings. She spoke with the faintest trace of a foreign accent, like a character in a classic movie. But there was also an inexpressible sadness about her that reminded me of the loss of her daughter and made me wonder how anyone in this family had managed to survive their own lives.

'Hello, Leylah.' Just for a moment, Eliot was crestfallen, apologetic. It occurred to me that when he was talking about his family, he had never said anything bad about her.

She put her arm around him. 'Why don't you go downstairs and lie down, Eliot, darling? You don't want to be here. It isn't going to do you any good.'

Julia stepped forward, moving in on the other side. 'Leylah's right. Why don't we go somewhere a bit quieter and have a chat?'

Eliot turned towards his sister and everything might have been well, but that was when he saw me. He looked straight past her. 'What are *you* doing here?' he demanded.

'I was invited, Eliot.'

Jonathan Crace had also noticed me. Those hard eyes of his in their rectangular frames zeroed in on me. 'I'm afraid that was a mistake, Susan. You're not welcome here.'

'Hold on—' Roland began, coming to my defence.

But Eliot had broken free. He lunged towards me, out of control. 'You're not working on the book any more!' Even with the Vivaldi still playing, his voice could be heard around the room. 'You're nothing to do with me, Susan. I shouldn't have trusted you. You lied to me. You're not on my side. Nobody is!'

Eliot spun round. The alcohol on his breath was days old and repellent. The music had finally stuttered to a halt.

'I'm sorry, everyone,' he shouted. 'This is Susan Ryeland, my completely useless editor.' He pointed towards the photograph. 'And that's my grandmother, Miriam Crace, who was murdered by one of the people who hated her. Actually, everyone who knew her hated her! But I saw one of them tiptoe into her room the night she died and one day, quite soon, I'm going to tell the whole world who it was.' He grinned madly. 'They're in this room right now! So you all go on enjoying yourselves. Celebrate her life and then, when you buy my book, you can read about her death.'

Jonathan signalled and two security guards hurried towards us. I assumed that they had come for Eliot and was shocked when they stopped on either side of me.

'This is your fault,' Jonathan exclaimed. 'You started this. Now get out of here and don't come back.'

The guards placed a hand on each of my arms. They were careful not to hurt me, but there was no room for argument. With everyone in the room watching me, I found myself being led out. It was one of the most mortifying experiences of my life. As we reached the double doors, I saw Elaine in front of me, watching what was happening with a look of complete horror. I was afraid she was going to intercede and shook my head to warn her to stay away. I just wanted this to be over.

It took a whole minute for the lift to arrive and we stood in the outer hallway in an awkward silence. Two burly security men and a guest they were forcibly ejecting. What were we going to talk about? The weather? I was still trying to make sense of the situation when I heard the swish of fabric accompanied by the scent of a strong floral perfume. Leylah Crace had followed us out.

'Susan,' she began. She wasn't allowed near me. The guards

were forming a barrier between us. 'I need to talk to you. Can we meet?'

'Where? When?'

I heard the lift doors slide open.

'Tomorrow evening. Seven o'clock. The Savoy.'

'All right. I'll be there.' I just had time to say the words before I was bundled into the lift. Leylah was cut off by the closing doors.

When we reached the ground floor, one of the attendants was already waiting for me with my coat. It was pushed into my hands, the front door was opened and all at once I was outside in the street. I walked away, dazed by what had happened. I didn't look back.

The Morning After

I woke up at seven o'clock with a headache and an unpleasant taste in my mouth, a hangover not from the party (I'd only managed one glass of champagne) but from the two hefty measures of whisky I'd drunk once I got home. The first thing I heard was a purring sound and I looked down at the end of the bed. Hugo was on the duvet, lying on his back with his front legs and paws stretched out as if in a gesture of surrender. This was not good. Cats on the bed was one intimacy too far and I gently pushed him onto the carpet with the flat of my foot. As he padded off, I looked around the room and saw my black dress on the chair where I'd thrown it, along with my shoes, tights and bag. The dismembered corpse of my evening out.

I was angry with myself. I knew now that I should never have gone to the party in the first place. What had I been expecting? Hugs and kisses all round and a souvenir edition of *Little Wonder*, Miriam's first book? I had allowed myself to be humiliated in front of two hundred complete strangers, and although I'd enjoyed meeting Julia Crace — at least she seemed to have got some of her life back together – she'd hardly told me anything that I didn't already know. And what was I going to do with myself now? I had the entire day ahead of me and nothing to fill it with. Just for a minute, I wished I was back at the Polydorus. There might be a crisis in the kitchen, a chef who hadn't shown up, the early risers shouting for their breakfast . . . but at least I'd have a reason to get out of bed. With Eliot Crace and Atticus Pünd both out of my life, I suddenly felt very alone. Was this the horrible truth about my life? That if you took away work, there would be nothing left?

The doorbell rang.

I looked at my watch, double-checking the time, making sure that it really was seven o'clock, too early even for Amazon. I hauled myself out of bed, put on a tracksuit and slippers, went to the door and glanced through the peephole. A balloon-shaped face, distorted by the lens, looked back at me. It was a middle-aged man, wearing a tie. He looked harmless. I opened the door.

He could have come from the local council. He could have been a local politician asking me which way I intended to vote. At a pinch, he might even have been a Jehovah's Witness. There was a sort of solemnity about him, something that separated him from everyday life. As well as the tie, he was wearing a suit, which felt weird on a sunny morning in Crouch End. He was in his early fifties, but he'd kept himself in shape. He was clean-shaven with neatly combed hair and intelligent brown eyes. It was strange how someone who looked so ordinary should make such an immediate impression on me. I knew straight away that he was a danger to me.

He was not alone. The peephole had failed to reveal the woman who was standing a few steps away from him. She was considerably less attractive. Twenty years younger than him and about ten inches shorter, she seemed to have got out of bed in too much of a hurry even to look in a mirror. Her carrot-coloured hair was unpleasantly tangled, her lipstick had barely touched her lips, her eyes watched me with sullen indifference. I don't think I'd ever met anyone so small and hostile.

'Ms Ryeland?' the man asked, with a look of enquiry.

'Yes,' I said. I braced myself for bad news.

'I'm Detective Inspector Blakeney.' He opened a leather holder to show a warrant card with his name, photograph, and the legend METROPOLITAN POLICE in blue. His first name was Ian. 'And this is Detective Constable Wardlaw. Can we come in?'

'What's this about?' I asked, although I think I already knew.

'It would be better to talk inside, if you don't mind.'

I didn't want to invite them in. I was in a tracksuit. I hadn't showered or brushed my hair. I tried to visualise the state of the flat. I didn't think I'd left any unwashed plates by the sink or crumpled clothes in the corridor. 'I suppose that's all right,' I said, but as the detective constable stepped forward, I stopped her. 'You didn't show me your ID,' I said.

She stared at me. 'I'm with him.'

'Even so . . .'

I could see that I'd annoyed her, which was exactly what I wanted. If she was going to come knocking on my door before breakfast, she could at least smile. She took out a warrant card and thrust it at me like an offensive weapon. EMMA

388

WARDLAW. She hadn't photographed well, which didn't surprise me.

I closed the door behind them and showed them over to the kitchen table, feeling grateful that the cat was out of sight. I'd had dealings with the police before, of course. Detective Superintendent Richard Locke had entered my life on two occasions and neither of them had been a positive experience. I was expecting rather more from DI Blakeney. He was looking round the flat approvingly. 'Nice place,' he said.

'Thank you.'

'Been here long?'

'Just a few months. Would you like a coffee?'

'Do you have decaffeinated?'

'I think so.'

'If you're making one, that would be good. Black, please. No sugar.'

'Not for me,' Emma Wardlaw said.

I made the coffee, watched by the two police officers, who sat silently at the table. It took a couple of minutes and I needed them. I was making the most of the last vestiges of normality.

'I'm afraid I have bad news for you,' Blakeney said as I sat down. 'You're a friend of Eliot Crace?'

'I'm working with him. Yes.'

'I'm sorry to have to tell you, he was killed last night.'

It shouldn't have come as a surprise. There was something about Eliot that had always told me he was doomed. But still the news shocked me, as death always does.

'He was struck by a car in Kingston Street, just as he was leaving a party at which you'd been present.' It was as if

Wardlaw had insisted that she should be the one who told me. She had volunteered the information with a certain eagerness and I was sure I detected an element of malice in her voice. Or perhaps it was just her Scottish accent. I almost smiled at the way she twisted the words to suit her occupation: '. . . *at which you'd been present.*' Who but a police officer would speak like that?

'Have you found the driver?' I asked. It was the first question that came to mind.

'Not yet,' Blakeney replied. 'It was a hit and run.'

'Someone must have seen something. What about cameras?'

'There are nine hundred and forty thousand cameras in London,' Blakeney agreed. 'The average person is photographed seventy times a day.' It was odd how he reeled off those figures as if they were common knowledge. Sitting next to him, Wardlaw was unimpressed. 'But there are also a lot of cars and it may take a while to match the two hundred guests at the party with the driver, even with ANPR.'

'ANPR?' I asked.

'Automatic number-plate recognition.'

'Oh, yes. Of course.'

'The car could have been borrowed or rented. The number plate may have been concealed. We're looking into it, but in the meantime, we're interviewing some of the people who were there.'

The implications of what he was saying finally dawned on me – but then I had only just woken up. 'Are you suggesting that the driver of the car was someone at the party?' I asked.

'Mr Crace was struck down in the same street, fifty yards from the entrance . . .'

'And they didn't stop? You think it was deliberate?'

'What do you think, Ms Ryeland?'

I knew exactly what I thought, but I wasn't sure I should say it. *'My grandmother, Miriam Crace . . . was murdered by one of the people who hated her . . . and one day, quite soon, I'm going to tell the whole world who it was. They're in this room right now!'* I still heard Eliot's voice echoing across the ballroom. He'd been the centre of attention, just as he'd wanted. And he'd done exactly what I'd warned him against.

'How can I possibly answer that?' I replied. 'Eliot arrived at the party late and he'd obviously been drinking. He was on his own. I'm afraid he'd been going through a rough time with his wife and I suppose that didn't help.' I paused, trying to find the right words. 'When did he leave?' I asked.

'About five minutes after you,' Wardlaw said, nastily.

'Why did you leave so suddenly?' Blakeney asked.

He knew the answer, obviously. It was still early, but he must have spoken to a few people before he had come round to see me. 'Eliot was quite offensive,' I explained. 'I'd been helping him write a book. I was his editor. He decided he wasn't happy with the relationship and he asked me to leave, although it was his uncle, Jonathan Crace, who told me to go.' I cradled my coffee cup, needing its warmth. 'They didn't give me any choice. They would have preferred not to have invited me in the first place.'

'What was the book Eliot was writing?'

'It was a continuation novel. Have you heard of a character called Atticus Pünd?'

DI Blakeney surprised me. 'Oh yes. I've read all the Alan

Conway novels. I very much enjoyed them. You worked on them?'

'Yes. I was Alan's editor.'

'Atticus Pünd was a good character, although I have to say that I was a little disappointed by the last one. *Magpie Murders.*'

'Why was that?'

'He was killed off. I never think it's fair – when you've been following a character for eight or nine books and the author kills him off. It seems unnecessary.'

'Agatha Christie killed Hercule Poirot.'

'But the book wasn't published until the very end of her life.' I got the feeling that Blakeney could have talked all morning, but then he remembered why he was here. 'You commissioned Eliot Crace to write a new story,' he said.

'Actually, that was Michael Flynn at Causton Books. He brought me in to help Eliot with the writing.' It was only then that I realised the implications of what had happened. It was as if the universe was playing some huge practical joke on me. History was repeating itself. 'He'd written about fifty thousand words,' I said. 'But he hadn't finished it.'

I desperately wanted a cigarette. The pang had hit me before I knew it, even though I hadn't smoked for three years.

'He hid something in the book,' I went on. 'It may sound crazy, but he believed that somebody had murdered his grandmother, Miriam Crace, twenty years ago and that he'd seen them going into her room. Last night he announced in front of everyone that he was going to reveal who it was in his new book. I'd told him this was a bad idea. He didn't listen to me.'

DC Wardlaw sneered at me, not hiding her contempt. Blakeney was a little more reasonable. 'So what you're saying is that you think the person who murdered Miriam Crace may have taken action to prevent Eliot Crace finishing his book.'

'That's exactly what I'm saying. Yes.'

'Do you know how unlikely that sounds?' Wardlaw sounded almost pitying.

'No more unlikely than the accusation that I ran him over because he had insulted me in public – which is where the two of you seem to be heading. You've obviously spoken to people about what happened last night. That's why you're here. But for what it's worth, I didn't drive to the party, I took the tube.' I drew a breath. 'And since you ask, this has happened before. You should check out the murder of a man called Frank Parris at Branlow Hall in Suffolk. Alan Conway went there and recognised the killer as someone he knew, but instead of calling the police, he strung a whole lot of clues through the novel he was writing at the time.'

'*Atticus Pünd Takes the Case*,' Blakeney said.

'Yes. He liked playing games with his readers. His books were full of secrets and none of them were ever very pleasant ones. Eliot was writing a continuation novel and the first time I met him, he told me he was planning to do the same thing. His book was set in 1955 in the South of France – at a place called the Chateau Belmar.'

Blakeney thought for a moment. 'That's an anagram of marble.'

'Got it in one, Detective Inspector.' Despite everything, I was impressed. 'His whole family was in there, disguised as characters. He was doing it quite deliberately because that was what Alan Conway did, even though, in the end, that was what got him killed.'

'That's all very interesting,' Wardlaw cut in. 'But there are a few problems with this version of events. The first one is that Miriam Crace died twenty years ago from natural causes, and even if Eliot had thought he'd seen something, he was only twelve years old at the time, so what would he know?'

I was impressed. The two police officers must have been working non-stop through the night. They had visited the crime scene, talked to some of the witnesses, done background research and, without even stopping for a bacon sandwich, had called in on me. And yet looking at them now, they both seemed wide awake.

'Eliot made the threat,' I insisted. 'He knew that the killer was listening. "*They're in this room right now*." Those were his exact words. And from what you say, less than half an hour later, he was dead.'

'That's one interpretation,' Wardlaw said. 'But here's another. He humiliated you in public. He said you were completely useless and he sent you packing. That can't have been very pleasant for you.'

'So I sat outside in my MG – even though it was parked in Crouch End – and waited for him to come out?'

'I wonder if we could take a look at your car, Ms Ryeland?'

'Of course you can, Detective Inspector. And there's no need to keep calling me Ms Ryeland. My name's Susan. If you'll just wait a moment, I'll get the keys.'

I went to the bowl on the kitchen counter where I usually kept the keys, but they weren't there. I looked on the windowsill, but they weren't there either. Annoyed with myself, I stood where I was, trying to think what I'd done with them. I noticed the coat I'd worn the night before, lying on a sofa. I picked it up and felt the pockets. The keys were inside.

'It's just round the corner,' I said.

'One moment.' I'd made an enemy of Detective Constable Wardlaw and now she was taking her revenge. 'Were you wearing that coat last night?' she asked.

'Yes.' There was no point denying it.

'Well, if you took the tube, how come the car keys were in your pocket?'

There was no easy answer to that. 'I don't know,' I said. 'I did some tidying up before I went to bed and I remember picking up the keys. If I don't put them away, the cat steals them. I must have put them in my pocket and forgotten them. I often do things like that.'

Wardlaw looked doubtful.

'Let's see the car,' Blakeney said.

We trooped out of the house together. I had left the MG round the corner, next to a fence. The streets were reserved for residents' parking, but I'd already discovered that with so many extended families living in the area, half of them with more than one car, I often had to fight for space. I don't know why, but I had a horrible thought that the MG wouldn't be there when we turned into the next road and I was relieved to see it sitting where I had left it, bright red and reliable.

'Can I have the keys?' Blakeney asked.

'Sure.' I handed them to him. 'But this is completely unnecessary.'

He opened the car while Wardlaw examined the exterior. For once, there was nothing inside. I often left books, manuscripts, notepads and newspapers strewn over the back seat, but with only one novel – the Nordic noir – on my desk right now, my life was less chaotic than usual. Blakeney leaned in but there was nothing for him to see.

'Sir . . .?'

Wardlaw was at the front of the vehicle. She had disappeared from sight. Blakeney walked round and I followed. The DC was squatting on the road, her hand splayed out on the bonnet of the car, her face close to the grille. She looked up sharply. 'There's some damage to the radiator grille,' she said.

It's extraordinary, but right then I was more concerned about the car than anything else. I peered over her shoulder and saw that she was right. There was a visible dent in the metalwork.

'And there's something caught inside.'

She was wearing blue latex gloves. She must have put them on as she walked along the pavement. I watched with a certain fascination as she carefully removed something from one of the air channels above the number plate and held it up for Blakeney to see. It was a tiny piece of cloth. I had no idea how it had got there, but right then I heard the screech of wheels, the thud of my car hitting Eliot as he staggered across the road, his jacket getting torn, some of the fabric – bloodstained, obviously – getting caught in the radiator grille. Except that it hadn't happened. The MG had never been anywhere near the party. I hadn't taken it the night before.

'Are you quite certain you didn't drive this car last night, Susan?' Blakeney asked. At least he had used my first name.

'Of course I am.'

'After a few drinks, you might have forgotten how you got home.'

'Even after half a bottle of wine, I can tell the difference between a car and a tube train,' I said.

'So you admit you consumed a lot of alcohol,' Wardlaw remarked spitefully.

I felt a spurt of annoyance. 'That's not what I meant. I had one glass of champagne. That's all. Then I was asked to leave.'

'You weren't asked, exactly. You were trashed in front of a whole crowd of people and then escorted out by security. You must have been very angry.'

There was no point discussing it with her. I watched as she pulled an evidence bag out of her pocket and carefully placed the little piece of material inside. It was about the size of a fingernail. I could see a red stain in one corner. The fabric was a dark shade of green. Now that I thought about it, I remembered that Eliot had been wearing a velvet jacket that was the same colour. Could someone have stolen my car and driven it? No. That was impossible. I had two sets of keys. One had been in the back of my kitchen drawer, well out of sight.

The other had been in my coat pocket.

I didn't want the ground to open up beneath my feet and swallow me. But it felt as if that was exactly what it was doing.

'We are impounding the vehicle under the Road Traffic Regulation Act 1988,' Blakeney said. At least he had the decency to sound regretful.

'We're going to need both sets of keys,' Wardlaw added.

I ignored her. 'How long do you intend to keep it for?' I asked Blakeney. I felt a strange pang, thinking of my red MG

397

being towed away and dumped in some police pound. It was like losing a friend.

'It could be up to six months,' Blakeney told me. 'We'll be keeping it while you're under investigation.'

'Is that what I am? Under investigation?'

'I'm afraid so.'

'I didn't kill Eliot Crace,' I said. 'There'll be CCTV cameras showing me getting on the tube at Highgate and presumably more CCTV cameras at Leicester Square.'

'Nobody is accusing you of anything, Susan,' Blakeney assured me. 'We'll take away this sample and have it analysed and I'm sure that will clear up the matter very quickly.' He smiled reassuringly, then added, 'You're not planning any foreign travel in the next few days?'

'Are you asking me to surrender my passport?'

'No. But we'll be keeping an eye on you.'

We walked back to the house together, none of us saying anything. I gave them the keys from the kitchen drawer. Wardlaw gave me a receipt and they left.

As soon as they had gone, I went out.

Causton Books

I was sad that Eliot Crace was dead – and for a lot of reasons. He was young. He was talented. He had hurt his wife, but his whole life had been a series of hurts, starting with his childhood at Marble Hall and continuing with the failure of his first novels, the separation from his parents, his diagnosis of infertility and the betrayal of perhaps the only woman he had ever loved. Now there was going to be a baby that couldn't have been his, a twist of the knife. I had promised I would look after him. If only he had spoken to me at the party instead of turning his back on me. We might have had a drink together, come to some sort of understanding. Elaine could have helped patch things up between us. Instead, I'd always be haunted by the thought that I could have saved him.

First, I needed to save myself. I knew from my experiences in Suffolk – Alan Conway and Branlow Hall – that in real life, murder investigations move at a frightening speed. I somehow couldn't imagine Detective Inspector Blakeney sitting in an armchair, mulling things over with a pipe and bedroom slippers, and as for Detective Constable Wardlaw, she'd been drooling so much over the evidence she'd plucked out of the grille of my MG, she'd risked contaminating it. They'd be back, the two of them, and soon. And the next time it wouldn't be for a cosy decaffeinated coffee in my kitchen.

It was just possible that my MG had been vandalised at the same time I'd been at the party – one of those coincidences that Atticus Pünd so deplored – but I didn't think so. That little scrap of cloth looked too similar in colour to the jacket Eliot had been wearing and I had to face up to the strong possibility that someone was trying to frame me. They'd kicked in the grille and added the cloth. But who . . . and why? Could it have been the same person who had killed Eliot? I had no answers to those questions, but sitting at home turning them over in my head wasn't going to do me any good. I had to do something – whatever that might be.

I decided to start with Michael Flynn at Causton Books. What had he been doing at the party and why had he never mentioned his connection with the Crace Estate? It might seem the least important part of my worries, but any fly caught by a spider will need to examine every strand of the web, so that was where I was heading now. Thinking back to our meeting when Michael had told me about the new book, I remembered a few things that hadn't felt right. How had he connected with Eliot in the first place? Why had he smiled so much, as if he knew something I didn't? And there was something he'd said that had puzzled me at the time. '*The book is important to us for a great many reasons.*' What reason could there be apart from the sales success of the book itself?

I took the tube to Victoria (feeling a pang for my missing MG), made my way past a row of featureless office blocks and hurried through the glass doors of Causton Books as if they might have been programmed to lock when they saw me coming. I had a feeling that I wasn't going to be welcome and even Jeanette, the kindly receptionist, looked a little startled to see me.

'Susan! I didn't know you were coming in!'

'I just wanted to see Michael Flynn for a few minutes.'

She looked at her computer, then picked up the phone. 'I'll tell him you're here.'

I moved away and pretended to examine the digital book display to allow her a little privacy. She was the guardian of the gate and I hated the thought that she might be asked to keep it closed against me. However, when she put down the phone, she was smiling. 'He's sending someone.'

It was still a good ten minutes before a nervous-looking assistant arrived to collect me. I could tell from the silence in the lift that this meeting would not go well. Michael was waiting for me in the same conference room where we'd met before, but this time without the coffee. He was sitting in his shirtsleeves, glasses on his nose, the cord hanging down on either side.

'I'm afraid I can't give you a lot of time, Susan,' he said. He hadn't stood up as I came in and the smiles he had turned on and off the last time I was here were conspicuously absent. 'I've got a sod of a day. You should have rung first.'

'I thought it would be more sensible to meet face-to-face.'

'You're probably right. It's devastating news about Eliot Crace. I was shocked to hear it.'

He had got straight to the point and I did the same. 'What are you going to do about *Pünd's Last Case*?' I asked. I'd used its original title because that was the only one he knew, but it felt strange saying it. It reminded me of the conversations I'd had with Eliot.

'We haven't had time to discuss it yet. How much more had Eliot written?'

'He'd got up to about fifty thousand words.'

'Have you read it all?'

'Yes. My gut feeling is that the book was going to come in at around seventy thousand words – a little shorter than I'd have liked.'

'You told me you thought it was good.'

'It is.' I waited for him to continue, but he was either lost in his own thoughts or unwilling to express them. 'I don't think it'll be too difficult to finish it,' I went on. 'Eliot must have left notes. And I'm sure there are plenty of clues in the pages I've read so far. It's just a question of finding them.'

'Do you know the ending?'

'No. I've never been any use at working these things out. But another writer – someone who works in crime fiction – would be able to do it. The book doesn't feel too complicated. The characters are all there. And it might be quite fun for someone else to bring all the different strands together.'

Michael considered what I had said, then shook his head. 'I'm not sure. Alan Conway is already dead. Now Eliot Crace. To have a third writer coming along feels a bit . . . indecent.'

'It seems a shame to stop now. I think it's going to be a good book, Michael. And do you really want to throw away the advance?'

'Well, the advance wasn't too much to worry about.' I'd been in the business for most of my life and I'd never heard a publisher so blasé about losing money. 'I'm afraid my instinct is to let it drop, Susan.' He shook his head, as if this wasn't something he'd decided long before I came into the building. 'I wish there was something else we could offer you, but right now there isn't anything.'

'There's that other mystery you sent me from Norway.'

'We're having second thoughts about that too.'

I saw the way this was going. 'You're ending my contract,' I said.

'Actually, we don't have a formal contract.'

'But you're still letting me go.'

'You could put it that way. But let's think of this as a temporary measure. There's every possibility something will come up in the future and if it does, we'll get in touch.'

He was lying to me. We both knew it.

'You were at the party,' I said. 'I saw you.'

'Yes.' He looked uncomfortable. 'I noticed you there too. I wasn't expecting to see you. They told me you weren't coming.'

'I think they forgot to cancel my invitation.'

'Under the circumstances, you might have done better to stay away.'

'And what circumstances are those, Michael?'

Finally he lost his temper. He hadn't wanted to speak to me today. He obviously didn't care if he never spoke to me again. 'For God's sake, Susan. I don't know what's got into you. It must be that business with Alan Conway and what happened with the Trehernes. Yes. I heard about that too.

You seem to think that the entire world is a conspiracy theory and that it's your job to sort it all out.'

'I don't think that at all,' I protested.

'Then why did you go to Marble Hall, asking questions about a murder that never happened? Why did you allow Eliot to go on that blasted radio programme, making absurd accusations about his grandmother and damaging her reputation at the worst possible time? Your job was simply to edit a book, not to make trouble for the Crace Estate.'

'You're working with them, aren't you,' I said. 'You and Jonathan Crace. That's why you were at the party.'

He looked embarrassed. 'As it happens, yes.' I waited for him to continue. I wasn't going anywhere until he had told me the truth. 'I may not have been completely straight with you, Susan,' he said at last. 'When I first proposed the book to you, perhaps I should have mentioned that we were also dealing with the estate. It won't be announced until the Netflix deal has been fully agreed, but at the start of this year, we won an auction for three more adventures with the Little People. The first one – *A Little More* – is coming out at Christmas.'

'Another continuation novel!' I was amazed. 'Who's writing it?'

'Michael Morpurgo. We're absolutely thrilled he's agreed. I mean, he's one of our greatest children's authors. His books are classics.'

'So how did Eliot fit into all this?'

'He didn't.' Michael shuffled in his seat. 'Someone suggested Eliot for Atticus Pünd because he'd written crime novels. I'll be completely honest with you and say that I agreed because I thought it would cement our relationship with the family and support our bid in the auction.'

'You mean, you only gave him the job to score brownie points.'

'I think that's putting it a little crudely. There was a tactical element to the decision, though, I'll admit. And anyway, it backfired. We weren't to know it, but the family was far from happy that we were working with him. They thought of him as a liability. It was very lucky for us that we'd signed the deal with them before they found out that he was involved.'

'But they didn't want him to write it.'

'He'd already started writing and it would have been very difficult to get rid of him. But I persuaded them that we'd manage the situation.'

'That's why you brought me in!' I stared at him. If there had been a coffee cup or an ink bottle at hand, I might have thrown it at him. 'You didn't really want me to edit the book. You wanted me to keep him under control.'

It should have been obvious all along. Even Frederick Turner in far-off Marble Hall had known Eliot was writing a book. Jonathan Crace had admitted it too. '*I feared the worst from the start.*' At the end of our meeting, he'd gone on to taunt me: '*You really don't know anything, do you!*' I'd wondered what he meant at the time, but I could see it now. I'd been brought into all this like some kind of sacrificial lamb.

'You lied to me,' I said. 'Or at least, you didn't tell me the complete truth. And it's worse than that. It may be thanks to you that Eliot was killed.'

'What are you talking about?' Michael's eyes widened. 'It was a drunk driver. A hit and run.'

'The police are treating it as murder.' I didn't mention the fact that right now I was their main suspect. 'You heard what he said. You were there. He believed that his grandmother was killed deliberately and he was going to name the person who did it in his book.'

'That was all nonsense. I've already spoken to Jonathan Crace—'

'I'm sure you have. You all think that Miriam Crace died of a heart attack and Eliot was making it all up to promote himself.'

'You think he wasn't?'

'Somebody thought he wasn't. That's why he's dead.'

Michael got to his feet. 'The trouble with you, Susan, is that you've been involved in one real-life murder too many and you've lost all sense of proportion. You know, it makes me wonder if Charles Clover really did kill Alan Conway or whether you imagined that too. I knew him for ten years – he was a good friend of mine – and I never thought he had it in him to commit a crime like that. I don't deny that he attacked you, but maybe he was defending himself against exactly the sort of accusations that I'm hearing now. I really don't think we've got anything more to say to each other.'

I stood up too. 'Of course, Michael. Charles was a charming man and I'm sure the two of you got on splendidly when he wasn't pushing people off roofs, something he confessed to, incidentally, and which even his wife has admitted he did. But I agree with you about one thing. When you say we've got nothing more to say to each other, you're absolutely right.'

I walked out of his office, out of a job and – I was beginning to think – fast out of options.

As I made my way towards the station, I thought about what I'd just heard. I'd assumed that it was a secret hidden inside the book that had led to Eliot's death. That was what I had told Blakeney and Wardlaw and it was what I still believed. But it now occurred to me that the identity of Miriam Crace's killer might not matter – assuming they even existed. From the very start, Eliot had been an embarrassment. To his uncle Jonathan, to Frederick Turner at Marble Hall, to everyone involved in a deal that was worth hundreds of millions of pounds. In other words, it might not have been what was inside the book that got him killed. Eliot might have been a target before he had even written a word.

The Man with White Hair

My next stop was Eliot's home in Notting Hill Gate.

Gillian Crace hadn't been at the party and I needed to see her. She was one of the only members of the family who was on my side and I was worried about her. I think she still loved Eliot, despite everything that had happened, and I wondered who had told her about his death and who would be with her now. I hoped it would be Elaine. There were questions I wanted to ask her about what had happened after I'd left the night before. How long had she stayed? Had she managed to talk to Eliot? How soon after me had he left and had she seen anyone following him?

But there was a more pressing reason why I'd come to the house. Eliot had spent months working on the structure of his book and he must have left notes, outlines, diagrams . . . whatever. I wanted them. They might tell me who had poisoned Margaret Chalfont. That same person might have killed Miriam Crace, run over Eliot and gone on to frame me. I knew I was being coldly opportunistic, but what choice did I have? If I was going to persuade the police of my innocence, it would help to know who had actually committed the crimes.

I rang the bell and, after a long pause, the door was opened – but not by Gillian or Elaine. The man who was standing in front of me was someone I had never met, but I recognised him at once. He was in his sixties, bearded, examining me with tired eyes that sat beneath a crop of prematurely white hair – at odds with his charcoal grey eyebrows. These were the exact attributes that Eliot had given Elmer Waysmith, the stepfather in his book. He was casually dressed in jeans, a jersey and trainers – all of which looked American. From the way he stood there, leaning against the doorway, he made it clear that he was the true owner of the house.

Edward Crace.

'Yes?' He was a man who had just learned of the loss of his younger son. They might not have been close, but the news had still drained the life out of him.

'Mr Crace?'

'I don't think we've met, have we?'

'No. But I was working with your son. My name is Susan Ryeland.' I paused for a moment, wondering if he knew who I was. Fortunately, my name didn't seem to register with him. 'I am so very sorry for your loss.'

'Thank you.' He didn't move. He didn't want to invite me in. 'Working with him in what way?' he asked.

'I'm a freelance editor. I was helping him with his book.'

He looked puzzled, as if he had a faint recollection of Eliot working on something but couldn't remember what it was. 'Oh, yes. Gillian told me. He was writing a mystery story.'

'That's right. I only met Eliot a short time ago, but he was very talented and I couldn't believe it when I heard about the . . .' I couldn't complete the sentence. What was the missing word? The accident? The murder? '. . . about what happened,' I concluded lamely. 'I had dinner with him and I met Gillian for the first time just a few days ago. How is she?'

'She's taken it very badly. Right now, she's resting . . . upstairs.'

'Can I come in? If only for a few minutes. I'd love to see her.'

He would have preferred to send me away, but he didn't have the strength. 'Of course. I'm not thinking straight. I'm afraid the news hasn't really sunk in yet. Please . . .' He stood aside and I went in.

He led me into the kitchen, where I had met Gillian and Elaine the last time I was there. I remembered my first sight of Gillian on the sofa by the window, her legs bent and her knees together, her face bruised. Edward Crace gestured and I sat at the table.

'Can I make you a coffee?' he asked.

'I can do it, if you like.'

'No, no. It helps to keep busy.' He set about loading a capsule into a machine, filling the reservoir with water, taking two mugs out of the cupboard. He knew where everything was kept.

'Have you come all the way from America?' I asked. I'd been wondering how he'd arrived so quickly. Surely, he wouldn't have had time to fly overnight from Miami.

'I was already here.' He pressed the button that set a little light blinking, indicating that the water was heating up. 'I was meeting a number of artists and writers. It's my job.'

'You run a gallery in Miami?'

'It's more of a foundation . . . a private club for art col-
lectors and enthusiasts. Every now and then they send me on
a fishing expedition to get people to speak. I've found that a
personal approach works better than emails. I was in London
when I heard the news.'

'Staying here?'

'No. A hotel in Covent Garden.' He took a breath. 'I don't
really feel comfortable coming here. This is my house, but I
handed it over to Eliot and Gillian and I don't like to intrude.'
I wondered if Gillian had told him she was pregnant, but
there was no way I could ask him that, not with everything
else that was going on. 'I come to London quite often,' he
continued. 'I don't usually see Eliot. I'm sorry I didn't contact him this time – but how was I to know what was about
to happen?'

'You weren't at the party,' I said.

'No.'

'You weren't invited?'

'I have no idea. It's possible they tried to get in touch
with me, but there's nothing in this world that would have
dragged me to an event celebrating the legacy of my mother.'
He was suddenly cold. 'I didn't even want to come to the UK
this week because I knew the dates coincided, but I had no
choice. I imagine Eliot will have talked to you about Marble
Hall.'

'I know he wasn't happy there.'

'None of us were. I should have left years ago, when he
was still young. If I had, he might have grown up in a normal
environment and made something of his life. He might still

411

be alive. My wife, Amy, and I hated it there and she was always urging me to break away. But my mother pulled all the strings. The puppet strings. The purse strings. At the end of the day, we wouldn't have had this house if I'd disobeyed her and gone my own way. But I'd still have my son.'

He broke down, covering his face with his hands. I wasn't sure what to do, but I couldn't just leave him there, standing against the counter. I went over to him and put a hand on his arm. 'Please, Edward, sit down. I'll make the coffee.'

He let me lead him to a chair and he sat there, sobbing, while I made two cups of coffee and carried them over. More than ever, I wished that I hadn't taken on the book, that I hadn't allowed myself to get involved in all this.

'Forgive me,' he said eventually. 'I'm sure Eliot will have told you that we weren't close. I'm sure he blamed me for keeping him at Marble Hall as much as I blame myself. I was weak. I was so weak. And yet, sometimes . . .' There was a box of tissues on the table. He took one and wiped his eyes. 'Sometimes I think we were like the royals . . . the royal family. All that wealth and comfort. My mother was famous the world over and her books were our crown jewels. *The Little People*. We'd all been born into it. Jonathan and me . . . even Freddy. None of it was our own choice. And even if we had walked out, those books would have followed us wherever we went. Jasmine tried and it didn't do her any good.'

He drank some of the coffee, took a deep breath.

'Would you mind leaving, Susan?' he said. 'I don't think Gillian is going to come down and if she does, she won't want to talk to anyone. Did you know that she's expecting Eliot's child?'

He was deluding himself even now. Or perhaps Gillian had lied to him. I might have done the same in her position. She had told me the truth when she was angry, just after Eliot had hit her. But now that he was dead and she was alone, everything had changed. She had decided to bring up the baby as his, keeping herself inside the family and ensuring their financial support. Edward was right about one thing. I was the last person she would want to see when she came down.

But I wasn't ready to leave yet.

'There's something I need, Edward. Can you help me? I told you I was working with Eliot, helping him with his book. I've come here because I need his notes, his work in progress. They're terribly important to me.'

'Why?'

'It's difficult to explain.' I decided to tell him the truth. 'In his Atticus Pünd novel, Eliot was writing about his time at Marble Hall. He believed that your mother's death might not have been natural. That someone might have poisoned her. Did he ever talk to you about that?'

'Eliot was twelve years old when my mother died and thirteen when we left Marble Hall. He was always a fantasist and if he had said anything like that, I would have dismissed it. But he never did – not to me.'

Not to me. There was something about the way he spoke, a wistful look in his eyes, that alerted me to another possibility. 'Could there have been someone else?' I asked.

He hesitated. 'There was a man who used to come down from London. He was working with my mother, overseeing the last two books she wrote. Eliot latched on to him because he was already thinking of becoming a writer and the two of them were close.'

'Are you talking about Charles Clover?'

'That was his name. Yes.' He paused. 'I should tell you that even before we left Marble Hall, Eliot and I had fallen out. He was such a wilful child, always looking for someone to blame. And it only got worse after Miriam died. I don't know why. I thought that once we were free, we would come together as a family, but the complete opposite happened. Anyway, Charles Clover stepped in and to be fair to him, he was very kind to Eliot. The two of them spent a lot of time together and if Eliot had any secrets – imagined or otherwise – he wanted to share with anyone, I suppose it could well have been with him. But before you ask, you won't be able to meet him. At least, it won't be easy. He's in prison.'

That was the moment when the fog cleared and Edward Crace finally realised who I was. 'Wait a minute,' he said. 'Susan Ryeland! You were responsible . . .!'

'Charles Clover tried to kill me—' I began.

'You burned down the office! You destroyed his life.'

'It wasn't quite like that.'

'I can't believe you've come here like this. Lying to me and pretending you were trying to help Eliot. If it wasn't for you, he would never have started this bloody book.'

'I didn't ask him to write it. I tried to protect him.'

'You seem to bring death and misery wherever you go. Please will you leave?'

There was no point arguing. I felt hollowed out by the way the conversation had turned and close to tears myself. I got up. 'I just need the notes,' I said.

'What?'

'Eliot's pages. The work we were doing together. Somebody killed him, Edward. They may have the answer.'

He might have let me look for them. Or he might have grabbed me and dragged me out into the street. I never found out because just then, I heard someone unlock the front door and, a moment later, Roland Crace came into the room. He didn't notice me to begin with. I had my back to him and his eyes were fixed on his father.

'Dad! What are you doing here?'

'Roland . . .'

'I need to see Gillian. Where is she?'

Edward Crace was staring at me, exasperated that I was still there, and that was when Roland saw me. 'Susan!'

'I came to see Gillian too,' I explained hastily.

'Why?'

'I was worried about her.'

'She wants Eliot's notes.' Edward had been in tears just moments ago. Now he was utterly cold. 'That's why she came here.'

Roland frowned. 'Is that true?'

'I want to know who killed Eliot.'

'Eliot was knocked down by a hit-and-run driver. The police are looking for them now.' He came to a decision. 'You shouldn't be here.'

'I was just going anyway.' The whole thing had been a disaster. They weren't going to give me anything Eliot had written.

Roland came with me to the door. As he opened it, he was apologetic. 'Susan . . . I'm sorry about what's happened.

415

It's all been horrible. I really wish I didn't have to say this, but I've spoken to my uncle Jon and he'd much prefer it if you stayed away from now on. The Atticus Pünd book isn't going to happen. You ought to know that. I'm sorry you've wasted your time.'

I took a breath. 'It was you, wasn't it,' I said. 'You're the father of Gillian's child.'

He stared at me and the colour drained out of his face. That's not hyperbole, a line written for effect. It really did.

How did I know? Well, his arrival at the house should have told me: the desperation in his voice, the fact that he had a key to the front door. But there had been other clues. Roland had been the hero of Marble Hall and the best man at his brother's wedding, but then something had happened and the two of them hadn't just fallen out, they were no longer speaking. Even so, when I'd first met him, Roland had known all about Eliot's state of mind – he'd mentioned that Gillian had texted him. That should have told me they were close. More than that, she had been afraid, terrified even, to tell Elaine and me the name of her lover. She knew how we'd react. And finally, there was her behaviour now, pretending that Eliot was the true father. She was confident that the baby would have a family resemblance.

Roland didn't deny it. He must have known it was too late. 'Just go . . .' he said, and for all his good looks there was an extraordinary ugliness in his face.

'Roland—'

'You should never have got involved with my family. Just piss off out of here.' He pushed me out, slamming the door behind me. Quite honestly, I was glad to leave.

New Evidence

'Elaine? It's Susan . . .'

'Susan? Oh my God! Where are you? Are you OK?'

'I'm at home . . .'

'I can't believe what's happening. I can't believe any of it. Eliot's dead! And the family . . . they're all blaming you.'

'They're horrible, Elaine. All of them. When they're not at each other's throats, they'll bring down anyone who gets in their way.'

'But it's not just them. The police were here. They were asking me questions about you.'

'What questions?'

'They wanted to know about you and Eliot. They know all about the party, of course. But they're also saying that the two of you had an argument at that club of his. Boon's. They asked me about the dinner you had here.'

'What did you tell them?'

'I didn't want to tell them anything, but of course I couldn't deny that we were all here together. I said you and Eliot were getting on fine, that you were helping him with his book and couldn't have been more supportive.'

'Thanks for that. You heard Eliot fire me at the party?'

'He was drunk. He didn't know what he was saying. But they think that may be the reason why . . .'

'I killed him?'

'It's ridiculous, Susan. I told them that. I've never heard anything so stupid.'

'I told them – I wasn't even driving that night. Did you see Detective Inspector Blakeney?'

'There were two of them. He had a nasty, smirking girl with him.'

'DC Wardlaw.'

'I'd watch out for her. She's really got it in for you.'

'Elaine – did you talk to Eliot at the party? Were you there when he left?'

'I spoke to him very briefly. I asked him about Gillian.'

'You know who it is she's been seeing. The father of her child . . .'

'I think I do know. Yes.'

'Roland.'

'That's what I thought.'

'Why didn't you tell me?'

'Because I didn't know for sure, Susan. I only suspected. I'm sorry – but I couldn't come out with an accusation like that when I only had my feelings to go on. There was no proof.'

'Elaine, I've got a favour to ask you.'

'I'll do anything I can to help.'

'Do you think Charles would agree to see me?'

'Charles? Why?'

'I know it's asking a lot and he's got no reason to want to help me, but this isn't just about me. It all goes back to Marble Hall. Eliot told me his grandmother was murdered. He saw something and he put it in his book. It turns out that Charles knew Eliot better than anyone. It's just possible that Eliot may have said something to him.'

'Charles never mentioned anything to me.'

'Could you at least ask him? Charles befriended Eliot when he was ten years old. I met Edward Crace and he said that Charles was almost a second father to him. I think this whole thing begins with Eliot, Roland and Julia, but the family won't talk to me. There's no-one else I can ask.'

'Well, I can talk to him. But I've got to warn you, Susan, you're not his favourite person.'

'I can understand that.'

'I'll do what I can. I have a call booked with him this afternoon.'

'Thanks, Elaine.'

'Take care of yourself, Susan. Stay strong.'

*

I had barely put the phone down before DI Blakeney and DC Wardlaw arrived. I saw the car pull in and, as if sensing trouble, Hugo jumped off the sofa and ran into the back bedroom. It was twelve thirty and I wasn't looking my best after a rushed morning and a bad night's sleep. On the other hand, I didn't think they had come here to invite me out to lunch. I opened the door before they had time to ring the bell and immediately regretted it.

'Were you expecting us, Susan?' Blakeney asked.

'No. I was on the phone. I saw you arrive.'

We sat in the kitchen. I didn't offer them coffee.

'We have a lot to talk about,' Blakeney began. 'And none of it is good news.'

'It's not good at all,' Wardlaw added, portentously. What was wrong with that woman?

'I might as well tell you straight away that the piece of fabric which we recovered from the grille of your car has been positively identified as coming from the jacket Eliot Crace was wearing last night. We have also found obvious bloodstains, both on your car and on the cloth, which have provided a one hundred per cent match.'

'Well, that sounds pretty conclusive, Detective Inspector. Are you arresting me?'

'You're in a very serious situation, Susan. I won't lie to you. But we'd like to speak to you first.'

'Well . . .' I spread my hands, a gesture of surrender. 'I'll help you any way I can. But I already told you. I didn't drive to the party. I took the tube.'

'You're sure you wish to stick to that statement?'

'Why would I want to change it?'

'Because you could be perverting the course of justice,' Wardlaw suggested.

I pretended I hadn't heard that. I was doing my best to look relaxed, but they weren't making it easy.

Blakeney was more reasonable. 'We have new evidence, Susan. A witness has come forward with a sighting of a red MG speeding away from Trafalgar Square a minute after Eliot Crace was struck down,' he explained. 'The caller was only able to get two digits of the number plate, but they're the same as yours.'

'Did the caller give you their name?'

'They did not. But that's not unusual. You'd be surprised how many civic-minded people want to help the police but are nervous of getting involved.'

'So they were anonymous.'

'Yes.'

'Were they male or female?'

'I'm sorry. I can't give you that information.'

'Well, they're lying to you. The car was parked outside this house all night. It would be there now if you hadn't taken it.'

'So how do you explain the damage to the grille and the forensic evidence?' Wardlaw asked.

'There can only be one explanation,' I replied. 'Someone is trying to incriminate me.'

'You mean, someone came across the body in Kingston Street, recognised who it was and knew about his connection with you. They snipped a piece of bloody cloth off his jacket, then came out to Crouch End, found your car, kicked in the grille and planted the evidence. Is that what you're saying?' DC Wardlaw had done her best to make the proposition sound absurd and, to be honest, it hadn't been difficult.

'Exactly,' I said.

Wardlaw sniffed.

'Who do you think would want to do that?' Blakeney asked.

'It could be the killer Eliot named in his book, but it could also be anyone working for the Crace Estate. I've been think-ing about it. This isn't just about an unpleasant family with

421

secrets they want to bury. It's about a television and publishing deal worth literally hundreds of millions of pounds. When the stakes are that high, you'll agree that people will go to extraordinary lengths.' I glanced at Wardlaw. 'And what may seem unlikely may be worth the risk.'

'The last time we came here, you spun us a story about Eliot Crace revealing a murder in his book,' she reminded me.

'Concealing it, not revealing it. Yes, that could also be the reason someone killed him. But I didn't have any reason at all. I liked him.'

'He had just humiliated you in front of two hundred guests,' Wardlaw reminded me.

'I could live with that.'

'And there was also that altercation at Boon's,' she continued. I had to admit, the two of them were fast movers. 'Another argument – in which you accused him of assaulting his wife.'

'It was true. He had.'

'According to the people who were in the room, it turned into a shouting match. I don't suppose you remember the last two words you spoke?'

'I'm sure you're going to tell me.'

'You told him to drop dead.'

'He said much worse to me.'

'You're still alive.'

There was no answer to that. 'All right,' I said. 'I admit it doesn't look good. But we talked about CCTV cameras. I went into Highgate tube station at around eight o'clock and arrived at Leicester Square about forty minutes later. You must have picked up an image of me somewhere.'

Blakeney shook his head. 'We're still looking, but you might as well know that one of the cameras at Highgate station was broken. If anyone had gone down the central stairs instead of taking the escalator and then stood at the right end of the platform, they'd have been invisible.'

'What about the ANPR?' That was one acronym I wasn't going to forget.

'Nothing there either, but I already explained, there are ways to get around it. We've had suspects fiddle with their number plates. You can turn an E into an F with black tape. Or an eight into a three. It's not that difficult. If we find your MG was on the road somewhere between here and Kingston Street, then we will arrest you.'

'You should admit what you've done,' Wardlaw said. 'You'll make it much easier on yourself.'

'That's enough.' Blakeney turned to his assistant. 'You go and wait in the car. I'd like a quiet word with Ms Ryeland.'

Wardlaw looked annoyed, but she didn't argue. 'I need a cigarette,' she announced, as if that was the only reason she was leaving. She sloped out, banging the door behind her.

Blakeney sat in silence for a few moments after she'd gone. When he looked up at me, he was almost apologetic. 'Wardlaw is a good police officer,' he said. 'She may seem aggressive, but she's got nothing against you.'

'Except that she thinks I'm a liar and a killer,' I said.

'You must admit that the evidence is definitely weighing up against you, Susan.'

'Then why haven't you arrested me?'

Blakeney took his time before replying. I still hadn't quite worked him out. He was certainly less aggressive than my old friend DS Locke. I got the sense that he might well be a decent man and that if we had met in other circumstances, we might have got on. I remembered that he had read all the Atticus Pünd novels and that certainly recommended him to me. I thought there was a slight melancholy about him. On the two occasions we'd met, I'd never seen him smile – not that I'd given him much reason to.

He ignored my question. 'I want you to tell me something,' he said. 'If you didn't kill Eliot Crace, who do you think did?'

'That's a very good question, Detective Inspector.' I fell silent for a moment, not because I didn't have an answer but because I wondered if it was something I ought to share. 'Has Gillian Crace told you she's pregnant?' I asked.

'Yes. I know all about that.'

'You know she was having an affair.'

'With her brother-in-law. Yes.'

I wished I could have been a fly on the wall when Blakeney and Wardlaw had conducted that interrogation. How had they managed to prise the information out of her? 'I'd put Eliot's brother, Roland Crace, high on my list,' I said. 'I think he's a creep, but it's more than that. Eliot was about to tell the world who killed Miriam Crace. He could have ruined the Netflix deal. And he was married to Gillian. That's three reasons to kill Eliot, and Roland Crace is connected to all of them. You might also like to consider the fact that Roland will do anything his uncle Jonathan tells him, and that might have included planting evidence to get me out of the way.'

'Interesting.' I had thought Blakeney was being dismissive, but he was giving serious consideration to what I said.

'Can I give you a word of advice, Detective Inspector?'

'Go ahead.'

'I've been here before. I know what I'm talking about.' Was that the best way to start? I moved on quickly. 'The two deaths are inextricably linked: Miriam Crace's twenty years ago and Eliot Crace's now. I still believe that the killer's name was concealed in the book that Eliot was writing. He told me that himself and he said the same thing at the party. You need to read it.'

'I understand it's not finished.'

'I was coming to that. Eliot had only written about half the book – but he must have made notes. I'm sure he wrote down a structure which will have a beginning, a middle . . . and an end. It could be on his laptop or maybe he used pen and paper. You've got access to his home. You can go in there and take it. You said you'd read all of Alan's books.'

'Yes.'

'Did you ever solve them?'

'I guessed about half of them. *Gin & Cyanide* was easy. I knew it had to be the wife.'

'Then put the two together – the manuscript and the notes – and you should have no trouble. If you want, I'll help you. I'm not brilliant at solving murder mysteries, but I knew Alan and I worked with Eliot and I have a good idea about the way they both thought. It's not just about clues. Half the characters in the book are based on people he knew. It's very likely he was doing that to tell us something. And you have to look out for anagrams and word games – all that sort of stuff. The Chateau Belmar – Marble Hall. Alice Carling – Gillian Crace.'

'He put his wife in the book?'

425

'I'm afraid so. Eliot Crace wasn't just writing a novel. I can see now that he was writing a suicide note. I couldn't save him, but maybe you can help save me.'

'You think you need saving?'

'I might.'

He reached into his pocket and took out a business card. It had his name, rank and contact details printed on one side, but as I watched, he scribbled something on the back. 'Well, if you want me to come to your rescue, you can reach me on this number. And if anything comes to mind that you've forgotten to tell me, you should use it too. My DS is going to ask me why I haven't taken you into custody and right now I don't have an entirely credible explanation except that I like you and I don't think you have it in you to kill anyone.'

He handed me the card. I turned it over. He'd put his private number on the back.

Leylah Crace

Everything was quiet at the Savoy Hotel when I arrived a few minutes before seven o'clock on a warm evening, leaving the Strand and some of my troubles behind me. The revolving doors spun me into another world that began with the entrance hall and its black-and-white tiled floor, the black-and-white columns and the brilliant flower displays on black marble tables. I asked for Leylah Crace at the concierge desk and was directed to the American Bar. I'd only met her for a minute and a half, but somehow all this suited her. I could imagine her in a feathered hat with a cigarette in an absurdly long holder and could easily see why Eliot had turned her into the actress Lola Chalfont in his book.

She was waiting for me at a table near the bar, dressed in a mauve two-piece suit with an oversized black silk flower on one lapel and a floppy black hat. She got up as I came in and embraced me.

'Susan, I'm embarrassed about what happened at the party. You were treated badly. I'm so glad you've come.'

I hadn't been sure she would turn up. When she had

427

followed me out to the lift following Eliot's outburst, she had sounded desperate, but his death that same evening might have given her second thoughts, particularly if she thought I was involved. I was glad to see that she had decided to give me the benefit of the doubt.

We sat next to each other. Leylah had arrived early. She already had a flute of pink champagne. She handed me the cocktail list and I ordered a Jabberwock Sour because it was gin-based and I liked the name. There was a pianist in black tie playing Broadway favourites, the music occasionally overwhelmed by the rattle of ice in a cocktail mixer behind the bar. The room was huge, divided by fat columns, the waiters swerving round them in black trousers and nifty white jackets. Those two colours seemed to be the theme of the hotel.

'I'm broken-hearted about Eliot,' Leylah said. 'He wasn't just my nephew. I knew him from the day he was born. He was such a sweet, strange little boy and from the very start I was always afraid that he'd come to a bad end. He was unhappy at Marble Hall, of course, and I hoped that his talent and his good nature would be the saving of him, especially after Miriam died. But everything just got worse and worse. I don't know how Edward and Amy could have taken off like that, leaving him behind. How could they have done that to their own son? They should have recognised that he needed their support, and it's no surprise that as soon as they were gone he fell into the wrong company. I heard about the drinking and the parties and the drugs, but what could I do? He didn't want to speak to me. When he met Gillian, we all hoped he would turn a corner. I only met her a couple of times – we weren't invited to the wedding – but I thought she was a lovely girl. And now I hear that's all gone wrong too. You know she met him in hospital. She was his nurse, but that didn't last long, did it.

'And now this! The police are saying he was killed deliberately, that it wasn't just a drunk driver or something like that. And according to my husband, Jonathan, you're the one they suspect. Of course, I don't believe that for a minute, my dear. That's not the reason I wanted to see you. But tell me – how did you get to the party? Did you drive?'

'No. I came by tube.'

'Of course you did. So maybe this whole business will go away and the police will leave you alone. Jonathan said you were going to be arrested. I didn't tell him I was seeing you, by the way, and I hope you won't tell him either. I expect you're wishing you'd never heard of the Crace family. You won't be the only one, I can tell you. They're cursed. They always have been. If I'd known what I was getting myself into when Jonathan proposed to me, I think I'd have thrown myself overboard into the Nile and hoped that a crocodile would gobble me up. I'd have been better off for it.'

Leylah had a strange way of talking. She didn't seem to stop, not even for breath, but at the same time her speech was unhurried, her faint Egyptian accent like oil, lubricating the chain of words. I got the sense that she felt liberated being here. She had chosen the venue and it suited her. She could say anything she wanted without being overheard. She had already been indiscreet. I was sure there was more to come.

The waiter arrived with my cocktail. By now, I needed it. Leylah drained her glass and signalled for another. I took a sip of mine. The Jabberwock Sour was ice-cold, very dry, golden-coloured, with a twist of lemon.

'I don't love Jonathan, you know. I'm sure I don't need to tell you that. You've met him. You've seen for yourself what sort of man he is. I know he's been unfaithful to me many times – he and Roland are just the same – but I don't care. I don't have any feelings for him. I've thought about leaving him, but I ask myself, what's the point? I'm sixty years old. It's far too late to think I'll find happiness on my own. And there are advantages to being part of the Crace family, as long as I don't lose my temper one day and murder him. Have you ever been married?'

'I was in a relationship for a while, but it's over.'

'Men are just so ghastly. That's why we girls have to stick together. How's the cocktail?'

'It's very good, thank you.'

'They do a wonderful martini. I come here all the time. I'm telling you, darling, I'm halfway to becoming an alcoholic. That's why I stick to champagne. It's the only drink you can have any time of the day and people won't think you're a lush.'

'You were telling me about Jonathan . . .'

'Oh, yes. It's been a long time since there were any feelings between us. He has such a high opinion of himself. You wouldn't believe it! Just because his mother wrote those books and made all that money, he thinks he's the one everyone should look up to. You should hear him when he's meeting people . . . Netflix, the publishers, anyone who has anything to do with *The Little Bastards*. That's my name for the books – my private joke. They all get on their knees when

Jonathan comes into the room. He's the big businessman, the brilliant negotiator, when really he's just his mother's son and they're all laughing at him behind his back.

'We had a daughter. I'm sure you know that. He was so desperate to ingratiate himself with Miriam, he named her after one of his mother's characters.'

'Jasmine,' I said.

Leylah flinched. 'I never called her that. I used to call her Jazz, just to annoy him. And I tried to protect her from him, from all of it. She and I were a team when we were at Marble Hall. We looked after each other.'

The waiter arrived with the second (or maybe third) flute of champagne and she had swept it up and drunk half of it before it had even settled on the table.

'You know, to this day, Jonathan insists that her death at Sloane Square tube station was an accident, that she slipped and fell. How do you slip on a perfectly dry, half-empty platform and just when the tube is racing in? But he has to keep telling himself that to avoid taking responsibility. It was all too much for her. That was the truth of it. Jazz was a beautiful girl, but of course she had issues. She partied. She drank. She took drugs. Eliot used to get them for her, and can I say something very wicked, Susan? I'm glad someone ran him over. If I met them, I would give them a medal. He was Jazz's supplier and not for one single minute did he think of her welfare or the consequences of what he did.

'Jazz couldn't cope with life. The paparazzi were always after her. And the headlines! "Little Girl Lost . . . Little Woman Arrested . . . Jasmine's Little Drug Problem . . ." She couldn't bear to hear that word when she was alive and

431

ANTHONY HOROWITZ

she'd have hated seeing it all over the newspapers after she'd gone. But Jonathan wouldn't hear a word of it. He never accepted his part in it, taking away the one thing in my life that mattered to me.'

Huge tears welled up in her eyes but refused to fall, as if she had spent half her life keeping them in.

I was both appalled and fascinated by Leylah Crace. I don't think I'd ever met anyone so broken and Eliot had set the bar pretty high. She was as beautiful as her daughter might have been and here she was in a deluxe hotel, expensively dressed, swigging champagne at twenty pounds a glass, but I'd met trauma victims who were stronger and more stable than her.

'Tell me about Miriam Crace,' I said, moving the conversation forward. 'Did you get on with her?' I already knew the answer to my question. Roland had told me that Miriam had never approved of her son marrying an Egyptian woman. But I wanted to hear it from her.

This time she surprised me. 'I never had any problems with Miriam,' she said. 'Perhaps it helped that we weren't living in the main house. You know we had a place in the grounds? We still had dinner with her two or three times a week and she could be quite difficult, complaining about the food or the conversation or the weather. It's funny. For someone who had done so well in life, she was a miserable old bag. She was sixty when I met her, but the way she behaved, she could have been much older. I felt quite sorry for her, really. But she never did any harm to me.'

'I heard she was racist.'

'Who told you that?'

432

'Eliot.' In fact, it had been Roland, but I didn't tell her that because I didn't want to be dragged into any further confrontations with the Crace family. One wrong word and I might have Jonathan and his posse of lawyers coming after me.

'Well, darling, it's not true. Or maybe it is, but it's more complicated than that. She made jokes about me being from the land of the pharaohs and belly dancing and things like that, but she thought she was being funny. I didn't find her at all amusing, but I never got the sense that she was picking on me for my heritage or any other reason.'

'But – forgive me, Leylah – I thought she fell out with Jonathan because he made her put two ethnically diverse characters in her books.'

'Njinga and Karim. Yes. But it wasn't their colour that bothered her. She just didn't like being bullied and told what to do. You know what, Susan? I think when that happened, she saw Jonathan for the complete bastard that he was. She realised he was already planning to take control of the estate and that was why she threatened to sell everything to one of the big American publishers – just to spite him. And she might well have gone ahead if she hadn't had a heart attack and died. But racist? I don't think so. She was a patron of the St Ambrose Orphanage, which looked after kids of every creed and colour, and as you know, she adopted Freddy. Have you spoken to him?'

'Yes.'

'And . . .?'

I remembered that Frederick Turner had referred to Miriam Crace as the woman who saved his life. 'He didn't make any complaints,' I admitted.

'Think about it. A racist with a mixed-race child? Seriously? She had a Black chauffeur too. Bruno – she adored him. He'd gone years before I arrived, but there was a photograph of the two of them on the piano standing in front of her Bentley. And there was a Nepalese gardener.'

'But why would Eliot lie to me?'

'Because they are all liars, Susan. Every one of them. Jonathan lied about his own daughter and how she died. Gillian lied to Eliot. That girl! Looks like butter wouldn't melt in her mouth, but she was having an affair with his brother, and of course Roland was lying too. The baby's his and he knows it.'

'Did she tell you?' I was amazed to hear this coming from her.

'She didn't need to, my dear! I've seen the two of them together, the way they try to avoid each other's eye. I'm not a fool. And then there's Freddy.' Once Leilah had started, nothing would stop her. 'He lied about his car accident – you should ask Julia what really happened. She was in the car! Kenneth lied about his marriage to Miriam. He pretended he loved her, but they'd been sleeping in separate rooms for years before I came to Marble Hall and that hobby of his – all those grisly stuffed animals – was just his way of escaping from her.

'And all of us were lying about Miriam – every one of us. She may not have been a racist but she was a dreadful woman and we had to make sure that the public never found out. Every public event, every time anyone asked us anything about her, we had to say anything except the truth.'

Roland had said the same thing when he'd described his work. '*My job is to lie to them. I spend every day of the week keeping alive the big lie.'* What Leylah was telling me fitted in with what I already knew.

'Can I give you a word of advice, Susan?' Leylah had finished her third glass of champagne but there was no sense of celebration or pleasure about her.

'What's that, Leylah?' I asked.

'The police aren't going to arrest you for the death of Eliot. I mean, that's ridiculous. How stupid can they be?'

'Who do you think killed him?'

'I think it was an accident. He was drunk. He didn't know where he was going. But this is my advice. Stay away from the Crace family. Just forget about them. They *are* the Little People! But they don't save the world – they do the exact opposite. They hurt everything they touch. They took my daughter from me. Really, they took my whole life. I'd walk away from them while you still can, keep going and don't look back. It's too late for me now. But you seem like a good person. Don't let them do the same to you.'

Hellmarsh

I didn't recognise Charles Clover until he sat down opposite me a few days later and even then, I had to look twice to make sure it was him. It wasn't that he was fatter or older or more dishevelled, wearing an ugly, shapeless tracksuit – although he was all these things. It was more that prison had sucked something out of him. The Buddhists call it 'vīrya' and it means energy, vitality, positivity . . . the ability to overcome whatever life throws at you. The moment Charles took his seat – or sat in it, rather, as it was screwed to the floor – I saw that Belmarsh had defeated him. He was a horrible, marsh-mallow version of his former self.

To my surprise, Elaine had come through and arranged the visit for me, although it meant giving up her own appointment. Charles was only allowed personal visits once every two weeks. I'd been confident she would do her best, but I didn't think she'd be able to persuade him to see me. He was in prison because of me and he had been sentenced to life with a minimum of twenty-three years. I had to wonder how the judge had arrived at that figure. Twenty years for killing Alan and three more for trying to kill me? Either way, he would be in his eighties by the time he came out and I couldn't think of any reason why he would want to help me now.

Just the sight of HMP Belmarsh, next to the Western Way in Thamesmead, south-east London, had given me a queasy reminder of my own part in what had happened. When I'd visited Elaine at her house, I'd had the same thought, but looking at the fences and the razor wire, the solid grey walls, the gates and the barriers, the sprawling car park and the sheer size of the place brought home the reality of what I had achieved by first investigating the murder of Alan Conway and then confronting Charles. He had been my friend and now he was somewhere inside all this. Approaching the front entrance, I was overwhelmed by the amount of bricks that had been used in the prison's construction: thousands and thousands of them, virtually unbroken by any windows. Belmarsh is a Category A prison and home to around six hundred prisoners who have been found guilty of murder, manslaughter, rape or terrorism: the very worst of the worst. Alsatian dogs patrol the grounds and sniff out visitors as they come in. Surely Charles wasn't as bad as all that? He had been sixty-three years old when he was arrested. Like me, he had spent his whole life in books.

It took me almost an hour to get from the front entrance to the gymnasium-style room where I had been given a seat number (C11) and was instructed to wait for him to arrive. I had shown my passport to one officer who had looked at me as if I was mad to be coming here, and surrendered my phone and handbag to another who had slammed them into a locker. My photograph had been taken and I'd been patted down by a third officer who might well have held a grudge against the entire world. No friendly welcome here. Once I'd been given the all-clear, there had been a bewildering number of doors sliding and swinging, opening and closing, accompanied by the buzzing of electronic locks and the jangle of old-fashioned keys. Nobody who has entered a prison can ever forget the experience and any politician who has ever called for more prisons to be built should come and visit one. It's an exercise in hopelessness.

There were five rows of tables, with all the prisoners on one side and the visitors on the other. I'd bought chocolate bars and crisps from the little canteen that supplied the wives, parents and friends who had all come to take part in this ghastly masquerade. And suddenly Charles was there, though not at all the Charles I remembered, wearing clothes he would never have worn, not in a million years, sitting opposite with dead eyes, a bad haircut, no colour at all.

'Hello, Susan,' he said.

'Hello, Charles.'

I was back in the office in Bloomsbury. I was lying on the floor with a terrible pain in the back of my head and blood pooling around my neck. I could barely see. It wasn't just the smoke and the flames, which were all around me. It was as if a splinter had cut into my optic nerve. I could only make out Charles Clover in silhouette, moving like some sort of demon through the flames.

And then, as abruptly as it had come, the vision disappeared and it was just this broken man in his ill-fitting tracksuit.

'I was never expecting to see you again. Certainly not this way. You know, they run a Restorative Justice programme here in Belmarsh. Prisoners get to meet their victims. You should have come in on that.'

'Would you have seen me if I'd tried?'

'I don't want to see you now! Elaine persuaded me. She told me that the two of you have become quite good chums.'

'Charles, I am so sorry about what happened.' I had promised myself that no matter what happened, I wasn't going to apologise to him. After what he had done, he deserved to be here and none of it was my fault. Yet here I was, barely past the 'hellos', already doing exactly that. 'I didn't want it to be you who killed Alan,' I went on. 'I just wanted to find the missing chapter. I never dreamed it would end up like this.'

'How are you, Susan?' It was as if he hadn't heard anything I'd just said. 'Tell me about yourself. I hear that you're back in England. Crete didn't work out?'

'I loved Crete,' I said. 'But I couldn't live there.'

'So you broke up with Andreas.'

'Yes.'

He didn't sound particularly sympathetic and I got the sense that he was toying with me – that I had become Clarice Starling to his Hannibal Lecter. I had no choice but to play along with him. I needed information from him and although he had very little choice about anything any more, not in this world, he could choose whether to give it to me or not. At the same time, I was aware of the minutes ticking by. A clock on the wall showed ten minutes past three and visiting time finished at four. I hadn't come here for a chat.

'It's a shame,' he said. 'I always liked Andreas.'

'We're still friends,' I assured him, although I hadn't heard from Andreas since I'd left.

'Are you back in publishing?'

'I'm doing some freelance work.'

'It must be very frustrating for you. I've been told that nobody wants to employ you any more. I'd happily give you a reference, Susan, although it might not be worth very much nowadays. I don't think I've ever met anyone who was so dedicated to books – even at the expense of their own life. You always were a bit introverted. I could have told you that Crete wouldn't work out for you. How many bookshops were there in . . . Agios Nikolaos? That was where you went, wasn't it?'

'Yes. And there were three.'

'You have absolutely no idea how horrible it is here,' Charles continued, speaking as if this was the natural riposte to what I had just said. 'When I came here, I thought I was going to die. It was the smell and the noise in the first week that I remember most. People shouting all through the night, arguing, screaming at the moon. Doors slamming all the time. All the time! And it seemed to me that everyone I met was either dead in the head or psychopathic. One extreme or the other.

'They put me in the medical wing to begin with and I thought that might be more comfortable but in fact it was vile. Then I went to Beirut.' He half smiled to himself, a queer little smile that hovered over his lips. 'You won't know what that is. It's what they call Block Three for new arrivals and remand prisoners. Now I'm in Block One. I'm not sure why they're keeping me here . . . I mean, in this prison. It's one of the worst in the whole system, or so I'm told. They call it Hellmarsh. I'd have thought they would have moved me on

440

by now, given my age and my lack of previous convictions. But the first thing you learn about the prison system is never to question anything because nothing ever makes sense. Even the prison officers don't know what they're doing – or they may do, but they don't know why.

'Hellmarsh is the right name for it. I shared a cell for the first year. I had three different cellmates and they were all as bad as each other. Sometimes we were stuck together for twenty-three hours at a stretch. And the stench of it, Susan. Three men, one toilet, no privacy. I say they were as bad as each other, but Jez was the worst. He'd killed his girlfriend for cheating on him. He tied her up and he tortured her. They say you should never tell anyone what you've done to be in here, but he boasted about it. You'd have been quite right to send him here. Even if he was your closest friend. He was an animal and they put me in a cage with him for two months until someone stuck a shank in him in the shower and he was taken away.'

'Charles, you can't blame me for what happened . . .'

'Things have got a little better for me, though. They say that men who have been to private school always fit in more easily here and that includes me, but what it tells me is that human beings will get used to anything. You learn how to cope with it. Even the food. You should see what they serve here. To start with, I couldn't touch any of it, but now I put it in my mouth and swallow it even when I have no idea what it is. It's probably best if you don't.'

He half smiled.

'But you see, the thing is, you learn how to play the system. Somehow, you need to get the doors to open. That won't mean anything to you, not in Crete, not in Crouch End – but a door that opens, even if it's only letting you into the corridor or out for forty-five minutes' exercise in the yard, is a little taste of freedom. That's why I started going to church. Not because I believe in God – because I don't. Or maybe I do. The vicar gave me a Bible and do you know, I've read it cover to cover. She also put me forward to become a Listener, and as well as that, I help with the literacy programmes. Did you know that half the people who come here can't read? It's a funny place for a publisher to find himself, although it might interest you to know that one of the writers you discovered – Craig Andrews – is very popular. We've got lots of his books in the prison library and I volunteer there too.

'In return, they've given me my own cell. That's a big deal. I won't be here much longer. They've got to move me. Maybe to somewhere in the country. It would be nice if I could see birds. When I was in Block Three, I could see planes taking off from City Airport and it always gave me a sense of comfort. I could imagine being on them, maybe heading off to the Frankfurt Book Fair with you. No birds ever fly over here. At least, I haven't seen any. Not one.'

I'd had enough of all this. I hadn't come here to listen to his endless whining.

'I want to talk to you about Eliot,' I said.

'Eliot Crace.'

'Yes.'

'Elaine told me you were working with him. It seems to me that writers don't have a lot of luck working with you. First Alan, now Eliot.'

'You knew him when he was a child.'

'That's right.'

'Was that why you agreed to publish his books?' It was completely irrelevant but I couldn't help asking.

'No. I liked them. I thought they'd do well.'

'We lost thousands of pounds, Charles,' I reminded him. I swallowed my anger. 'Eliot believed that someone killed his grandmother, Miriam Crace. He said he saw it happen. Did he ever say anything about it to you?'

Charles contemplated me and I saw that he was enjoying himself. He had no control over his life in Belmarsh, but right now he had a measure of control over me. 'Give me one good reason why I should help you, Susan.'

'Eliot was your friend. He looked up to you. Don't you owe it to him?'

'It won't make any difference to him. Not now. And Elaine told me that the police know who ran him over.' For a moment his eyes lit up in the same way they had once done when he stumbled across a great manuscript or persuaded a successful writer to sign up with us. 'Maybe you'll end up in Bronzefield Prison,' he said. 'That's where they send the worst female offenders.'

'I didn't drive that night, Charles, and the CCTV cameras will prove it . . . eventually.'

'I wonder.' He picked up one of the chocolate bars and took a bite, chewing it slowly, daring me to interrupt him. I waited. 'Who do you think killed her?' he asked eventually.

I'd been prepared for this. 'I think it had to be one of the three children,' I said. 'Roland, Julia or Eliot. They talked about it. They planned it. They even concocted some sort of poison out of various household chemicals. It couldn't have been Eliot. So that leaves Roland and Julia.'

'You know, when Miriam Crace died, I was quite sure that it was Kenneth who had killed her.'

'Her husband?'

'Kenneth Rivers. He was a strange man. I met him a few times. He was in his eighties by then and he was like the original eccentric professor. You know the type . . . stuck up in the attic with his stuffed animals and nobody to talk to. He'd been a paper-pusher in some government department when he met her, and when he married her, she was nothing. She played the organ in her local church and she would probably have ended up as a piano teacher except she wrote *The Little People* and became staggeringly rich.'

'So why would he kill her?'

'Because he genuinely loved her. I met him a few times and felt sorry for him. He was a decent man – perhaps the only decent person in the entire family. But she'd treated him abominably.'

'How?'

'Well, when she was young, she cheated on him. Over and over again. The big secret about Miriam Crace was that, as well as being the most popular children's author in the world, she was incredibly promiscuous. Anyone in trousers was a target for her and there were even rumours that she had it away with one of the nannies.' He leered at me, as if it was something that amused him. 'Do you know about that famous breakdown of hers? When she had to go to a retreat for six months?'

'She went to Lausanne.'

'I don't know where she went, but the only breakdown she had was her marriage. Kenneth finally lost his patience with all her affairs and threatened to walk out on her. Worse still, he threatened to talk to the press. It would have been the end of her reputation.'

'Wouldn't it have been easier to divorce her?'

'They were both Roman Catholic. Miriam had no faith, but she was the daughter of a deacon and divorce was out of the question. They agreed to a trial separation and she took off for six months to see if they could manage without each other. In the end, they decided it was more convenient to stay together. Better the devil you know and all that. Miriam came back to Marble Hall, which was their new home. This was a few years before the birth of their first child, Jonathan. It was a marriage of convenience. He made her respectable. She made him rich. But they were never happy.'

'He told you all this?'

'He didn't need to. There was a biography of Miriam Crace written by an author called Sam Rees-Williams. A nice enough chap and he put his heart into it, but it was never published. When I was asked to work on the last books, I managed to get a look at the manuscript. It's all in there. The infidelities, the rows, the casual racism, a dysfunctional family. No wonder the estate got it scrapped.'

There was something about this version of events that didn't ring true, but my mind was on other things. 'So how do you know he didn't kill her?' I asked.

'Because Eliot told me who did.'

'So who was it?'

Charles had already said he had no reason to help me.

445

Now he hesitated, wondering what to do. Finally, a sly look came into his eyes and that was when I realised there was almost nothing left of the man I had once known. The warm, witty, cultured bon viveur I'd worked with for eleven years had been wiped away, replaced by this empty husk. What had done this to him? Was it the act of murder itself, the killing of Alan Conway on the tower of Abbey Grange, and the viciousness of his attack on me a few weeks later? Or was it his incarceration here in Belmarsh, the daily stripping away of his personality until the last shred had gone? It had never occurred to me before but crime and punishment go hand in hand. They are equally dehumanising, but in different ways.

'You were right,' he said eventually. He looked around him as if afraid of being overheard. When he spoke next, he lowered his voice. 'It started with the three of them – Roland, Julia and Eliot. Eliot told me about it years later. He was drunk. He was always drunk, but this time we got talking and I'll tell you what he told me.' He paused. 'When they were kids, they called themselves the Rogue Troopers. They were the resistance. And they often talked about killing their grandmother. It was a game. A fantasy. Not like the people in here. I've never met a single person who's talked about killing someone. They've just gone out and done it.

'What changed everything for those three children was Julia's fifteenth birthday. Her mother helped her buy a dress...'

Julia had already told me about this. 'She was ridiculed by her grandmother,' I said.

'It was more than that. Miriam tore into her in front of the whole family. She made her feel fat and ugly ... it was nothing less than child abuse! Julia was devastated – and the Rogue Troopers decided enough was enough. They were going to do it! They were going to get rid of the monster who had caused them so much misery throughout their lives.'

'They decided to poison her.'

'Let me tell the story, Susan. You always did have a habit of jumping in whenever we had meetings. Yes. Eliot stole medicine from the family doctor. But Roland and Julia were older and they knew better. There were plants growing in the gardens at Marble Hall – deadly nightshade, wolfsbane. They'd often been warned not to touch them, so that's what they used. They were very careful. They wore gloves. They used a pestle and mortar to crush the berries and they created a liquid which they really did believe might kill the old lady. She wasn't well anyway. It wouldn't be difficult. Julia put it in an old perfume bottle and took it to her room. She was the injured party. She was the one who was going to do it.

'Isn't it exciting? It's just like something Alan Conway would have written. But there's a twist. The three children had rooms next to each other and in the early hours of the twenty-seventh of June, three days after Julia's birthday, Eliot was woken up by the sound of a door opening. He got out of bed and opened his own door just in time to see Roland coming out of Julia's bedroom with the perfume bottle in his hand. He'd stolen it! Eliot saw him head down the corridor towards his grandmother's room and he knew exactly what he was doing. You see, Roland had always been their protector. He would never have let his little sister get into trouble. He was going to do it for her.

'And the next morning, Miriam Crace was dead. They said

it was a heart attack, but nobody looked too closely. Eliot told me that the doctor was paid to keep his mouth shut. None of the family cared who murdered her — they just wanted to avoid the scandal that might damage the sales of her books. It was always about the books. And that was that. Apart from that one time he spoke to me, Eliot kept quiet about it for twenty years.'

Eliot had protected Roland. He had worshipped his older brother. But then Roland had betrayed him by having an affair with his wife and that had changed everything. I hated the way Charles had told the story, relishing it, but I had no doubt that it was true.

'Thank you,' I said.

'There's no need to thank me, Susan. It's not going to help you.'

I met his eyes.

'First of all, nobody knows this story except for you and me, and if anyone asks me, I'm going to deny all of it.'

'Why . . .?'

'Why do you think I agreed to meet you?'

'I thought you wanted to help.'

'Then you're even more stupid than I thought.' He took another bite of the chocolate bar. There was something animal about the way he ate it, his face showing no pleasure at all as he masticated. 'Let me tell you something,' he said.

'I was wrong to kill Alan Conway. I know that. But it wasn't as if I planned it. It wasn't premeditated or anything like that. I mean, you weren't there, Susan. You didn't hear him tell me how he was going to rip the heart out of Atticus Pünd and make sure we never sold another copy of his bloody books. He was going to destroy the business. You know as well as I do that Cloverleaf couldn't have continued without Atticus Pünd. Eleven years down the drain! He didn't give a damn about me – or about you. And to listen to him, sneering at me in that way of his . . . well, if it had been you, who knows? You might have done the same. I didn't think about it. I didn't know what I was doing, really, until I'd done it. A simple push – that's all it took. Children in the playground have done worse.'

'You weren't in the playground, Charles. You were on a tower.'

'What difference did it make, anyway? The doctors had given him six months to live. I told you, Susan. I did it for both of us. And for everyone who worked at Cloverleaf. And for anyone who ever enjoyed the books. Alan was a pig. He was ungrateful, entitled, utterly negative – and I don't think there's a single person in the world who wouldn't have had some sort of sympathy for me.'

He paused.

'Except you.

'You worked out the truth. I'll give you that. But let me ask you this. What possible benefit was there, shopping me to the police like you threatened to do? I was sixty-three years old. What good did you think it would do, putting me in here? It wasn't as if I was a mass murderer or something. I killed Alan Conway – yes. I did it to save everything I had and everything I'd planned for and if you'd left me alone, I'd have retired and spent the rest of my life going to the theatre and opera, playing with my grandchildren, and quite possibly doing good works. I wasn't going to kill anyone else. You know that! You

449

couldn't have thought society needed to be protected from me. Did I give the impression that I'd enjoyed killing Alan? I can assure you that I didn't. I felt guilty about it. I wished it hadn't happened. Maybe you believe in the Bible, although I never saw you as the religious type. "Thou shalt not kill." Was that what motivated you?

'When we were in my office together, you could have tried to be more understanding. You could have put yourself in my position. It might even have occurred to you that you would have benefited from Alan's death if you'd only left well alone. You were going to be the CEO of the company. Look at what's happened to you since then! You've gained absolutely nothing. You've lost your job, your reputation, your boyfriend, everything that ever mattered to you. What are you now but a freelance editor that no serious publisher wants to hire unless it's to work on a book that nobody else can be bothered to read? Don't you sometimes wish you'd been a little bit less high-minded, Susan?'

His voice had changed. He was still trying to sound reasonable but all I could hear was the venom bubbling beneath the surface.

'Maybe you feel justified, seeing me like this. Do you know, I haven't even seen my new grandson? I won't let him come in here. I won't let him breathe the air I have to breathe. Every day I wake up here, I want to die. They put me on suicide watch for the first month. My whole life ruined for a single reflex action. My retirement taken from me. My company gone. All thanks to you.

'Well, I'm glad you've come here today. Elaine didn't think I'd want to see you. She was quite tearful on the phone.

But do you know why I agreed? It was because I wanted you to get a glimpse of what could be coming your way. There's absolutely zero proof that Roland killed his grandmother, and if he was the one who ran over Eliot, I'm pretty sure he's going to have worked out a way to make sure no-one ever finds out. Anyway, he's not the main suspect. You are!

'Elaine told me everything. And maybe, just maybe, you'll get a taste of your own medicine. That will give me something to smile about.'

I knew there was an answer to everything he'd said. I could have tried to argue with him or find a good put-down. But what was the point? I got up and left.

I could. He couldn't. That was enough.

Killer

I tried not to be upset by my meeting with Charles Clover, but, standing on the platform at Woolwich Arsenal with a seven-minute wait for the next train, I couldn't put it out of my mind. His accusations didn't bother me too much. I mean, you hardly need a degree in moral philosophy to reach the conclusion that, all in all, it's the right thing to report someone to the police for murder, particularly when they've also tried to kill you. But I did find it hard to get my head around his description of the murder of Alan Conway as a 'reflex action', something a child might have done. Was it as easy as that? All those thousands of books published every year about detectives, police investigations, suspects, clues, conspiracies . . . did they really hinge on something so banal? And what about that other remark of his? '*You might have done the same.*' I couldn't help wondering if it might not be true. Given the right circumstances, are we all potential killers? Was that the ultimate appeal of murder stories, that they reveal not just the facts of a particular crime but the truth about all of humanity, that civilisation and decency are only skin-deep and just beneath the surface we are all potentially monsters?

That was what had made Belmarsh so morbidly fascinating. There had been a whole crowd of prisoners in the room where I'd met Charles and all of them had been stripped of that outer layer, revealed for what they were. Sitting among them had been a disquieting experience. I thought of Charles at one of his dinner parties, standing there with a glass of Gavi – his favourite Italian wine – expounding on literary awards. Compare Ian McEwan's *Amsterdam* (lightweight, it won the Booker Prize) to *Atonement* (a masterpiece, short-listed, it didn't). The Booker vs the Costa. The virtues of the Women's Prize for Fiction. And then the Charles Clover I had just met, sullen, angry, biting into his Double Decker. It was almost impossible to accept that the two men were the same. What had separated them? Was it what they had done? Or was it being found out?

My mobile rang. I looked at the screen and saw that it was Elaine. I didn't want to speak to her. I didn't feel I was ready. But it would be unfair to ignore her and I still had five minutes until the train arrived. I answered.

'Susan? Where are you?' She knew I had come out of the prison. Otherwise, I wouldn't have been able to answer the phone.

'I'm at the station,' I told her.

'Did you see him? How was he?'

I searched for the right words. 'It wasn't easy, Elaine. To be honest, I don't know why he agreed to see me. He hates me. I suppose I can't blame him. He thinks I was wrong to turn him in, that I should have covered up for him.'

'That's understandable.'

'You don't think that, though?'

'I think it must have been a very difficult decision for you. But you had to do what you thought was right.'

It hadn't been a difficult decision at all – but I couldn't tell her that.

'I did warn you,' she went on. 'He gets very depressed. More than that. Sometimes he thinks he'll never get out of there, and it is such a dreadful place.'

'He wants the police to arrest me.'

'That's not going to happen.' Elaine almost scolded me, as if what I'd just said was ridiculous. 'Charles wasn't happy when I asked him to see you, but I persuaded him to help you because we all owe it to Eliot. I'm sorry, Susan. Didn't he tell you anything?'

'There was some new information he gave me. The trouble is, I'm not sure how it's going to help.'

Four minutes until my train arrived. I just wanted to be on my way.

I heard a doorbell ring at the other end of the line. 'There's someone here,' Elaine said, lowering her voice. 'I have to go.'

'Yes. My train's just pulling in.'

'Let me know if there's anything else I can do. Call me any time.'

The line went dead.

*

The journey back to Crouch End felt endless, crossing the whole of London and changing trains twice. Then there was the walk down the hill from Highgate station with the after-noon sun and no hint of a breeze. I got to the house just after five o'clock. I let myself in through the front door. There was an Amazon package lying on the mat – a book, I guessed from the shape. Why did I notice it? Why did I even think about it when, in the same glance, I saw what had happened while I had been away?

Someone had broken in. The flat had been trashed.

It took me several seconds to work out what I was seeing and for the images to make any sort of sense in my head. It took me longer to persuade myself to step forward and cross the threshold. My first thought was that I had been burgled, that I had become just another London statistic to be ignored by the police. Then I realised that it was something much worse.

Everything that was of any value to me had been deliberately smashed, ripped apart, soiled, cut to pieces. The kitchen and the living room were unrecognisable. Someone had blocked the sink and turned the taps on full so that the water had over-flowed all over the floor and there were white polyurethane clouds floating on the surface. The same person had taken a kitchen knife to my cushions and sofas, giving the impression of a devastated miniature landscape. I saw pages ripped out of my books, sodden and hopeless, and these hurt me most. Insur-ance would pay for the damage, but whoever had done this had known how to make it personal. They had taken special care with my photographs. The frames were mangled, the glass in pieces, the images torn up. Katie and the kids, Andreas, Crete, dinners, holidays . . . anything connected to my life had been mutilated beyond recognition. There was no way I would ever be able to wipe away the violence of what had been done.

In a daze, I drifted from room to room. The French windows were open, but I didn't dare go into the garden, not yet. Part of me wondered if the intruder might still be outside. I was numb with sadness and shock. My drinks cupboard was empty, the wood kicked in, the contents of every bottle emptied. I continued to the rear of the flat, following a trail of what looked like dark red ink that had been splattered onto the carpet. The bathroom door was open. Looking in, the first thing I noticed was that the mirror above the sink had been smashed. Then I saw the weapon that had been used. It was the one award that I'd hung on to, which had travelled to Crete and back: British Book Awards, Editor of the Year. It was a heavy thing and it had been used as a hammer against the glass and then thrown into the toilet, cracking the porcelain.

I went into my bedroom. I barely noticed the bed linen in rags, the duvet cut open, the curtains pulled down, my make-up smeared, poured or thrown everywhere. My attention was drawn to the single word scrawled with a tube of my own lipstick on the (Little Greene Loft White) wall opposite me.

KILLER

Somebody thought I had killed Eliot Crace and they had taken revenge on his behalf. I couldn't think of any other reason for this. How had they got in? Nobody had keys except for me. Then I remembered the rickety back door leading into the garden from the street and the French windows open downstairs. I'd meant to buy a surveillance system when I moved in. I could have bought a camera off the net for fifty quid. But this was Crouch End. It hadn't felt like a priority. Well, I was paying for it now.

The red marks I had noticed on the carpet continued under the bed and suddenly, as if I'd been electrocuted, I knew what they were.

Blood.

Hugo hadn't been waiting for me when I came in and I knew with absolute certainty that he had been stabbed in the living room or the kitchen and that he had made his way back here to die. I burst into tears. I'd managed to persuade myself that I didn't like the cat very much, that he somehow represented a style of life I wanted to avoid, but there's something about animals: cats and dogs. They've learned how to make themselves indispensable and the thought that he'd been here on his own when someone broke in and that he had become another object of their fury was too much to bear. I knew he was under the bed but I couldn't bring myself to look. I just stood there and cried.

And then I heard a whimper, so faint as to be almost inaudible. I dropped to my knees and saw him curled up in a ball, lying on a carpet stained red by his own blood. But still alive. He saw me and yowled pitifully, as if blaming me for not being there when this had happened. His eyes were bright with pain. Very slowly, I reached out and pulled him towards me, cupping him in my hands, trying not to hurt him any more than he had been hurt already. He didn't try to resist. He cleared the edge of the bed and I swept him up in my arms, certain that he could not live much longer. His fur concealed most of the stab wound in his side, but from the amount of blood lost, I could tell that it was deep and had happened a while ago.

Right then, everything else was forgotten. I was determined to save him. Holding him against my chest, I half ran, half stumbled into the kitchen and laid him down on the counter. He didn't move. He was barely breathing. I opened the fridge. All the food – eggs, milk, yoghurt, vegetables – had been scooped out and thrown on the floor but there was still ice in the freezer. I grabbed a tea towel, filled it with ice cubes and wrapped it round the cat. I looked for my car keys, remembered I no longer had a car, then picked up Hugo and ran out of the house.

There were several vets in Crouch End, but the nearest one was half a mile away – fortunately, downhill. I ran the whole way, Hugo now moaning as he reacted to the stress of the journey. It was a choice between moving fast or moving carefully and I was certain the poor creature would stop breathing at any moment. With every step, I was cursing the police for impounding my MG – irrational, but my grief and fury needed a target. I reached the Clock Tower in the middle of the village. Twenty past five. I would never be able to see the clockface in the same way again. There were still a few shoppers around and they looked at me in horror as I ran into the road, swerving through the traffic. A madwoman with a half-dead cat. Out of the corner of my eye, I saw a bus bearing down on me and I thought it might even be a welcome end to this whole experience if I was run down and killed.

But I reached the other side of the road and continued past a row of shops until I came to a veterinary surgeon I'd walked past a hundred times but had never thought I'd need. I barged in. There were three people sitting on plastic chairs surrounded by sacks of dog food and brightly coloured toys.

I ignored them, running straight to the receptionist, a young woman talking on the phone.

'Please, you've got to help me,' I gasped. 'My cat has been stabbed.'

To her credit, she reacted instantly, putting down the phone mid-sentence and rushing to a door at the back of the surgery. I heard her call someone and, seconds later, she came back with a man dressed in blue scrubs. He was young, bearded, immediately professional. He took the cat from me. 'When did this happen?'

'I don't know. I just got home.'

'Do you have any idea who did this?'

'No . . .'

He had already given the wound a cursory examination. 'This is bad. But maybe not as bad as it looks. Please, take a seat . . .' He took the cat and disappeared the way he had come.

The other pet owners were looking at me in alarm. I'd jumped the queue but nobody complained. The receptionist asked me if I wanted some tea and I nodded. I was feeling very cold and I was shaking. I kept trying to tell myself that it was just a cat and that I didn't even want it, but that wasn't how I felt. About fifteen minutes later, the vet reappeared.

'He's going to be OK,' he said. 'It's a serious abdominal wound, but you did the right thing putting an icepack on him and getting him here quickly. He was lucky. He's been stabbed, but the blade missed the neck and the thorax and it didn't hit any major blood vessels.'

'He's lost a lot of blood,' I said.

'Yes. We're giving him a blood transfusion, but if he was

going to die, it would have been hypovolemic shock that killed him. And that would already have happened. My colleague is with him now and we'll stitch the wound. He may have to stay in a couple of nights – we'll keep an eye on him. Are you registered here?'

'No. I haven't had him very long.'

'Is he insured?'

'I don't know . . .' I suddenly couldn't remember if I'd insured him or not. I knew I'd meant to.

'Well, I should warn you that you could be looking at several hundred pounds . . .'

'The cost doesn't matter.'

'OK. Give Jocelyn your details and we'll call you later this evening and tell you how he's progressing. But I honestly don't think you need to worry.'

I handed over my name, phone number, email and home address to the receptionist and left.

Walking back to my flat, I felt completely exhausted, and it didn't help that this time it was uphill. I didn't want to go back inside but I had no choice. I hadn't even locked the door. I walked into the horrible mess that someone had made of my lovely flat and wondered what I should do. It seemed obvious that I should report this to the police, although, for obvious reasons, they were the last people I wanted to see. Also, I wasn't sure what number to use. It wasn't an emergency. What could I expect them to do?

And then I remembered. I found the card that Detective Inspector Blakeney had given me. He had written his private number on the back.

I called it.

DI Blakeney

I did almost nothing until Blakeney arrived. I sat in a chair in the middle of the wreckage, trying not to look at it, vaguely wondering who had done this to me. Someone thought I had killed Eliot Crace and had decided to punish me – that had to be the motive. But who could have loved Eliot so much that they felt themselves driven to this course of action? Gillian, perhaps. Or Roland. He could have allowed the guilt of what he had done to his younger brother, along with the fact that I had found out about it, to propel him into this madness. I wasn't thinking straight and I was utterly miserable and drained. It was only the fact that Hugo had managed to survive and was, miraculously, going to be all right that was holding me together. I'd never been, by nature, an animal lover. I suppose I'd become one now.

The entire flat reeked of wine and spirits, which was ironic as my visitor hadn't left me a drop to drink. Not that I wanted anything. I'd always associated alcohol with friendship and celebration. I wasn't going to pour it into myself like medicine. I reached down and picked up the Amazon parcel that had been delivered sometime that afternoon. All in all, I didn't think I would be able to stay here. I wished I had never come back. Bloody Alan Conway! When was I going to learn to stay away from him?

The doorbell rang. I went over and opened the door.

Blakeney came in, casually dressed this time, no suit or tie. He looked around the flat and I saw the expression on his face, the disbelief. 'Are you all right?' he asked.

'Not really.'

'I'm not surprised. This is horrible. When did you get in?'

'About five o'clock.' It was now well after seven. 'I had to take the cat to the vet. Whoever did this also stuck a knife in him.'

'How is he?'

'Amazingly, he's going to be OK.'

'And how long had you been out?' I was surprised how quickly he had set about interrogating me. There was no small talk, no coffee or tea. But I didn't mind. This time it felt as though he was on my side.

'I left around one o'clock. I've been out all day.'

'Where?'

'HMP Belmarsh.'

That stopped him in his tracks. He examined me briefly, as if I was deliberately lying to him, realised I was serious and came to a decision. 'This is what we're going to do,' he said. 'First of all, I'm going to look around and check that the place is secure and that whoever did this hasn't left any other unpleasant surprises. You don't have CCTV installed?'

'No.'

'No alarms?'

'No. I only moved in a few months ago.'

'Yes. You told me. Does anyone else have a key?'

'No. Just me. I think they got in through the garden. The door into the street doesn't close properly.'

'I'll take a look. You wait for me here.'

He left the room. Despite everything, I was impressed. He was very different to the man who had threatened to arrest me just a short while ago. He was milder, more softly spoken and, like the vet, immediately professional. I waited a couple of minutes before he came back. 'There's no-one here,' he said. 'And you're right. They came through the garden and forced the French windows. It wouldn't have been difficult. The lock is flimsy.' He paused. 'I saw the message left for you in the bedroom.'

'Killer.'

'Yes. And the blood on the carpet.'

'That was the cat.'

'I'm sorry.' He took a breath. 'Do you have anywhere you can go? A friend or a relation who can put you up?'

'I have a sister in Suffolk, but I don't really fancy traipsing up there.'

'All right. I've made a few calls. This is a crime scene now and I've got a team coming in. They'll take photographs, look for fingerprints . . . any other evidence. I also know a company who can clear up some of this mess. But you'll need to book into a hotel or somewhere for a few days. I wouldn't advise you to stay here.'

'I have friends in Muswell Hill. They may be able to put me up.'

'Have you had anything to eat?'

'No.'

'Then you'd better come out and have some dinner. I'm sure it's the last thing you want right now, but you've had a terrible shock and something warm and a glass of wine will do you good. There must be somewhere in Crouch End. I'll come with you.' I was about to protest but he stopped me. 'We need to talk about this, Susan. We can't do it here and I don't think you'll find it very pleasant in a police station. Especially after a day in Belmarsh.'

'Who will look after all this?' I asked.

'Emma Wardlaw is on her way.'

'I'd prefer not to see her, if you don't mind.'

'Then why don't you go and get changed. Try not to move anything, but you can use the sink in the bathroom to wash your hands.' I looked puzzled. 'You've got bloodstains all over you.' There was the faintest twinkle in his eye as he added: 'When I arrived, my first thought was that you'd murdered someone else. You go and get yourself ready. I'll wait here.'

*

We went to an Italian restaurant near the Clock Tower and I ordered soup and spaghetti: comfort food. We shared a carafe of red wine. Blakeney didn't say anything about drinking on duty and we hadn't discussed who was going to pay. We had a banquette in a quiet corner and the restaurant was only half-full, which made it easier to talk. While I waited for the food to arrive, I tried to get used to the idea that I was having dinner with the senior detective who was investigating me; at the same time, I examined him in this new, more sympathetic light.

Fifty years old and unmarried, I thought. No sensible woman would have allowed him to set that brown Marks & Spencer jersey against blue slacks. Divorced or single? He was surely too good-looking to have always been on his own, and at close quarters I thought there was also a slight melancholy about him that suggested the former. Definitely not gay. He just looked and acted like a nice man – once you'd got him away from the murders, the forensic evidence, his detective constable and all the other trappings of his job.

'Can we be straight with each other?' he asked me as the first courses arrived.

'Why don't you go first?' I suggested. 'What exactly are we doing here? Do you always go out to dinner with your murder suspects?'

'I wouldn't characterise this as "going out for dinner" – not in the social sense, anyway. Normally, I wouldn't be here. But you were understandably upset about what happened to your cat and all the damage to your property and I felt you might appreciate the company. But if it's making you uncomfortable having me here, I'll happily leave you to your own devices.'

'No. That's not what I meant. I'm grateful to you, Detective Inspector. But if you really want me to feel comfortable, would you mind if I used your first name, just until we leave the restaurant? It'll make it easier to talk to you.'

'Of course. It's Ian.'

'I know. I saw it on your warrant card. And can I ask you to answer one question? Do you really think I killed Eliot Crace?'

ANTHONY HOROWITZ

I saw him think about how to answer that. He had poured himself about an inch of red wine, but I noticed he hadn't drunk any of it yet. He had ordered a prawn cocktail, which somehow suited him: retro and blokeish. 'The jury's out on that one,' he said, at length. 'Let me ask you a few questions first, starting with what you were doing at Belmarsh today.'

'I went to see Charles Clover.'

'He was your former partner at Cloverleaf Books.'

He'd done his homework. He probably knew everything about me. It made me wonder how much information he could summon up with the click of a mouse, sitting at his police computer. 'Yes,' I said. 'He also knew Eliot when he was twelve years old. He visited Marble Hall several times.'

'So you thought he might be able to tell you something about the death of Miriam Crace?'

'That's right.'

'And did he?'

'He'll deny it, but, yes, he did. He wasn't at all pleased to see me and if you repeat what I'm going to tell you now, he'll say I'm making it up. But he told me that the three children at Marble Hall – Roland, Julia and Eliot – often talked about killing their grandmother. It was all a fantasy to start with, but then they turned it into reality . . .' I repeated everything Charles had told me. 'Roland had the poison and Eliot saw him heading for his grandmother's room.'

'He might not have used it.'

'Why don't you ask him?'

'Because you're talking about something that happened twenty years ago and there's no evidence to support this version of events.'

466

'Except Miriam died very suddenly early that morning. Wouldn't you say that's quite a coincidence? And I think the family doctor, a man called John Lambert, covered up the true cause of death.'

'You need to be careful, bandying about accusations like that.'

'Dr Lambert collects classic cars. He told me that Miriam Crace left him money in her will, but that was a lie. Can't you get the body exhumed? That will tell you how she died.'

'I'm sorry, Susan. I'm not sure I could get that authorised. Apart from you, nobody is suggesting that there was anything suspicious about Mrs Crace's death. It also won't help that she is a much-revered public figure. Digging her up would upset a lot of fans.'

'Did you read *The Little People*?' I asked him.

'No. I read the books to my children, but they never really liked them. All the characters were too good to be true.'

Children.

At least he had given me one clue about his own background.

We finished the first courses and I drank some of my wine. He still didn't touch his. I liked the silence between us. It allowed me to pretend that this was an ordinary evening out.

'Did you tell anyone you were going to Belmarsh?' he asked, suddenly.

'No. Why do you ask?'

'Somebody must have spent at least twenty minutes in your flat, to do all that damage. They would have had to know you were going out.'

'I didn't tell anyone.'

'That suggests they were waiting for you to leave. You didn't notice anyone lingering in the street?'

I shook my head. 'I'm afraid not.'

'We'll ask your neighbours. It's always possible that one of them may have seen them coming in or out. We'll also get in touch with Amazon.'

'I'm sorry?'

'You were holding an Amazon package when I arrived.'

'Oh, yes. It had been posted through the letter box.'

'If a courier came to the door, he or she might have heard or seen something. It's probably worth following up.'

The waiter came and took our plates away. 'How many children do you have?' I asked.

'A girl and a boy. Tom's at university. Lucy's studying to be a lawyer.'

'Criminal law?'

'No. She's more interested in human rights. Tell me about Alan Conway.'

I could tell that Blakeney didn't want to talk about himself. We were bouncing the conversation about like a ping pong ball, but he was in complete control. And he still hadn't said if he believed I was a dangerous criminal. 'What do you want to know?'

'What sort of man was he? He's been dead for quite a long time, but he still seems to be having a malign influence on your life. And from what you've already told me, Eliot Crace may have been as much Alan Conway's victim as anyone else's.'

'That's true.'

'You believe the answer to everything that's happened can

be found in the book Eliot was writing. More than that, if we can work out the identity of the killer in the book, we'll know who killed Eliot in real life. Is that how it works?'

'I'm afraid so.'

'Then take me into Alan Conway's mind. Give me an idea of what I'm supposed to be looking for.'

The main courses arrived and, as I fiddled with my spaghetti, I spent the next twenty minutes doing exactly that. I was glad to be able to focus my mind on something other than the thought of DC Wardlaw rifling through my flat or poor Hugo lying in the vet's surgery on a drip, and it helped that DI Blakeney had read the books. It made it easier to explain how they mirrored real life, how Alan had distorted people he knew, turning them into often unsympathetic caricatures that he forced into the narrative. Even as I spoke, I had to wonder if any modern writer had done so much harm with what was meant to be an entertainment.

'So what you're effectively saying is that the killer in *Pünd's Last Case* is the same person who killed Miriam Crace.'

'That's exactly what I told you when you first came to my house, Ian. It will also tell you who ransacked my flat.'

'Assuming it was the same perpetrator.'

'Perpetrator. Now that's a word you don't hear very often.'

He smiled for the first time. 'Perhaps I've spent too long with the police.'

Somehow, we had managed to get through the main courses while I had been speaking and we waited while the waitress cleared away the plates. Neither of us wanted desserts. I ordered a coffee. He asked for a builder's tea with milk.

'So, how long have you been with the police force?' I asked.

He didn't need to work out the answer. 'Thirty-two years.'

'Man and boy . . .'

'That's right.'

'Was that what you always wanted to do?' I was asking him partly because he interested me and I wanted to know more about him. But I was also afraid that he was going to dismiss everything I had said and I was putting off the moment for as long as I could. I felt safe in the restaurant with its warm lighting, white tablecloths and views of Crouch End through the plate-glass windows. Once I left, I would be re-entering the maelstrom that my life had become.

'Yes. I knew I wanted to go into the police when I was at secondary school, although the other kids laughed at me.'

'Where was that?'

'Brighton.' I didn't say anything, waiting for more, and eventually he obliged, speaking slowly and in a matter-of-fact way. 'I can't really explain it to you, Susan, but it was just something I wanted to do. My father was an accountant. My mother was the manager of a private-car company . . . minicabs, limos, couriers. They're both retired now, living in Eastbourne. I was their youngest child. I have a brother and a sister. But the thing was, I just thought there was a lot wrong with the world. There was plenty enough crime in Brighton – drugs, vandalism, disorderly conduct and worse. But even when I was very young, I had this sense that all over the country there was a failing of morality and I wanted to do something about it. So when I was eighteen, I decided to skip university and applied to become a PC.'

'Was that also in Brighton?'

'No. I became a police cadet in Hendon, north London. I loved it. I was there for two years and I had a fantastic time . . . a great bunch of people. A lot of them are my friends to this day. The discipline was tough and they made us work hard. Basic policing, law, citizens' rights, street operations. And I was only being paid twenty-five quid a week, but I felt I'd arrived. I won't say I breezed through my exams, but I passed and the next thing I knew, I was a police constable in Hackney and Stoke Newington.

'I always wanted to be a detective, though. There's a lot of rivalry between uniform and CID – I'm sure you know that. I wanted to get onto the other side of the fence because I thought that was where the real work would be done. That's where you get thrown in at the deep end and you must think for yourself. And I was lucky. I was still in my twenties when I got assigned to a specialist football unit. It meant going undercover with West Ham fans, getting in with the trouble-makers and working out where and when the next hot spot was going to be. That went well and afterwards I took my sergeant exams and worked my way up to where I am now.'

'Detective inspector.'

'The higher up you go, the further away you are from the action and the more aggravation you get. I was a detective superintendent in Tower Hamlets for a time and I had a thousand cops working for me. And all the paperwork! In the old days there was too little of it. Now there's too much. Anyway, I prefer to be out on the street. This business of yours, for example. Eliot Crace. I've never come across anything quite like it and I've been around, I can tell you. But

471

don't think of me as an Atticus Pünd. I'm not like that. I'm not that clever – although, more often than not, I get results.'

'How come you've read all the books?' I asked. My coffee had arrived and was getting cold on the table in front of me.

'I like crime fiction. I always have.'

'Any favourites?'

'American writers mainly. Everything from Chandler to Michael Connelly, Harlan Coben, Robert Crais. Shari Lapena – she's Canadian. I read Golden Age stuff too.' He tore open a sugar sachet and stirred the contents into his tea. 'I shouldn't really say this to you, but I've always thought about writing a crime novel. I've done a few short stories to try my hand, but . . . I don't know. It was something my wife always said I should do.'

The unasked question hung between us.

'She died three years ago. Breast cancer.'

'I'm sorry.'

'Life's difficult without her, I'll admit it. But you take what life throws at you and I'm lucky. I still have my kids. A brother and a sister, both married. And my parents.'

I picked up my coffee; a tiny measure of espresso in a por-celain cup. 'There's one thing you haven't told me,' I said. 'And it was almost the first thing I asked you. Do you think I killed Eliot Crace?'

He had been about to drink his tea, but he put it down.

'I would have thought the answer to that would be obvi-ous, Susan. If I thought you were a killer, I wouldn't be sitting here with you and I certainly wouldn't have told you anything about myself. All that stays between us, anyway. I hope you understand that.'

'Of course.'

'I won't lie to you. You're a person of interest and we're still searching for any sighting of your car in central London on the night Eliot Crace was killed.'

'You won't find it. It never left Crouch End.'

'But unless it was planted, there's strong forensic evidence that puts your MG at the scene of the crime, including dust samples in the tyre treads that definitely came from Kingston Street, although you'll probably say that they could have been planted too. But let's not forget that we have a witness statement that has you driving away from Trafalgar Square.'

'An anonymous witness statement.'

'That makes no difference. They were still able to give us part of your registration number – and if it's not true, it does make you wonder how many people there are in this city with a grudge against you.'

'It sometimes feels like it's half the population,' I agreed.

'But on the plus side, I know everything about what happened with you and the death of Alan Conway. I've spoken to Detective Superintendent Locke – who doesn't send you his regards and didn't have a lot of nice things to say about you. But even he thought it unlikely that you had it in you to kill anyone.'

'That's very nice of him.'

'I've come to the same conclusion. Eliot Crace humiliated you in front of a large group of people. Thanks to him, you've lost your job. The motive's there, but I'd be very surprised if you had the temperament. You strike me as a very sensible person and the fact that you spent half the day at Belmarsh Prison is proof that you believe in your own story, even if it's one of the most unlikely things I've ever heard. All of which leaves me in a bit of a quandary. Where do we go from here?'

'The answer's in the book.'

'*Pünd's Last Case*. Yes.' He raised a hand, calling for the bill. 'Just so you know, Susan, I've been round to Eliot's home in Notting Hill Gate. I've read his book, or as much of it as he'd written, and I've also got hold of his notes.'

My heart leapt. 'Can I see them?'

'I'm afraid I can't give them to you. They're evidence. But we can look at them together, if you fancy doing that. You've been here before, so you probably have a good idea what might be hidden inside the text. You talked about anagrams and you've already found two of them. It's always possible that Eliot came up with a third, although I haven't managed to locate it just yet. Maybe we'll have more luck if we combine our efforts.'

'You're allowed to do that?'

'I can do whatever I think is right if I think it's going to solve the case. And you haven't been arrested. Yet.'

'I wish you'd left off the "yet", Ian,' I said.

The bill had arrived and we split it fifty-fifty. Then he drove me home.

The Watch

Ian Blakeney and I didn't meet until the weekend. I picked up a few clothes from my flat and moved in with a gay couple I'd known since university. Rob and Steve provided exactly the right amount of kindness and sympathy without digging too deeply into the various catastrophes that had brought me to them. They were well off, with a three-bedroom house on the edge of Muswell Hill and a second home in Yorkshire, and after a couple of days, they announced that they were heading off for two weeks, but they were fine about leaving me on my own. They gave me the keys to the house, instructions to eat or drink anything I found, and then disappeared in their electric Jeep Avenger with their two dogs and a pile of luggage.

With the dogs out of the way, Hugo could move in. The vet's bill was going to be astronomical, of course, but I was glad to see that he seemed to have completely recovered from his experience and there were few side effects, apart from a missing patch of fur and a scar where his wound had been stitched together. I think we were closer than we had been before. He was certainly puzzled by his new surroundings. Every time I looked down, he would be close to my feet, and at night he slept under the bed.

Meanwhile, I'd contacted the same builders who'd done up the flat when I moved in. Blakeney's team had removed a lot of the debris and tidied up the place, but it still needed repairs and redecorating. I'd decided by now that I had no intention of moving. I wasn't going to let the Crace Estate, the ghost of Alan Conway or anyone else drive me out of the life I had chosen, even if that life was feeling a little fragile. Once Rob and Steve had left for Yorkshire, I was on my own – and I didn't much like it. I had no job. I had nobody to see, though I wasn't in the mood for dinner or the theatre anyway. I'd brought the first two parts of Eliot's manuscript with me and read them again, no longer with any interest in their literary merits. I was more interested in finding any clues that might have led to his death. I made a few notes, but it wasn't enough to fill the long stretch of hours that I now realised made up each day. I knew perfectly well there was nothing wrong with being an unemployed single woman in my fifties, but even so, I couldn't shake off the feeling that, somehow, this wasn't me.

So I was glad when my phone rang and Ian Blakeney asked if he could come round the same day. I gave him the address and then went out and bought a few snacks and drinks. I put fresh flowers in the kitchen too. They gave the illusion of home.

He arrived in the middle of the afternoon, suited and carrying a leather briefcase. He asked how I was and how the cat was doing, but otherwise he was aloof and business-like, which made me wonder if, along with the dust in the tyres, there had been another development in the murder investigation, one he didn't want to share with me. He said nothing about that, but sat down at the kitchen table and removed from the briefcase a sheaf of pages I recognised as a printout of Eliot's novel and an A5 notebook with a Japanese cover – white birds flying over bamboo. That had to be Eliot's too. I made us both tea and finally we sat down together.

'There are three things we have to discuss,' he said. 'The first is the death of Lady Margaret Chalfont in the book. The second is the death of Miriam Crace twenty years ago. And the third is Eliot Crace and your relationship with him, as well as anything that might connect the first with the second.'

'Do you have any news?' I asked. I was concerned about his lack of warmth.

'There's nothing I can discuss with you, Susan. But it's irrelevant anyway. I think we should start with something you said to me the second time we met. Eliot Crace used people he knew as characters. Find the killer in the book and we find the killer in real life. Is that how it works?'

'I know it sounds unlikely . . . but yes.'

'OK. So where do you want to start?'

'This might help.' I had a notepad and opened it, showing him a list of names I'd drawn up.

Miriam Crace	Lady Margaret Chalfont
Jonathan Crace	Jeffrey Chalfont
Leylah Crace	Lola Chalfont
Edward Crace	Elmer Waysmith
Roland Crace	Robert Waysmith
Julia Crace	Judith Lyttleton

Eliot Crace	Cedric Chalfont
Frederick Turner	Frédéric Voltaire
Gillian Crace	Alice Carling
Dr John Lambert	Maître Jean Lambert

'I've put the Crace Estate and their associates on the left. The characters that they inspired are on the right.

'Let's start from the top.'

'Fine.'

I moved the sheet of paper between us.

'Miriam Crace is obviously Margaret Chalfont. They have the same initials, they were both matriarchs who had been married twice and they were both ill with heart disease. If Eliot's accusations are true, then they were also both poisoned. It's interesting that Margaret is a much nicer character than Miriam. Almost everyone in the family had a motive to kill Miriam – I'll come to that as we go along – but there was no reason at all to kill Margaret. Elmer makes exactly that point. So does Jeffrey and so does Lola. It seems to me that the whole plot of Eliot's book depends on it – and at the end of the first section, Atticus Pünd says something very strange. James Fraser asks the same question again. "*Why murder a woman who is already dying?*" And Pünd replies: "*Because, my friend, it does not matter.*" It's a neat chapter end, but what does it mean? *Who* doesn't it matter to? And *why* doesn't it matter?'

'Yes. I wondered about that,' Blakeney said. 'It's strange because Lady Chalfont was about to change her will and the whole family needed her money. So you'd have thought that killing her to stop her doing that would be very important indeed.'

'Unless the will had nothing to do with it.'

'I'm pretty sure the will had everything to do with it. But go on.'

'Jeffrey Chalfont seems to be modelled on Jonathan Crace, if only because of the ginger hair. They're also both elder sons. Jeffrey inherited the Norfolk estate and Jonathan got the management of the Crace Estate: the books, the TV series and all the rest of it. It's worth remembering that Miriam Crace was thinking of selling the Little People to an outside interest. Jonathan Crace would have done anything to stop that happening.'

'Including killing her?'

'He's not a very attractive man.'

'That doesn't necessarily make him a killer.' Blakeney glanced at the list. 'I take it Jonathan's wife, Leylah, becomes Lola.'

'Apart from the fact that she wanted two thousand pounds to support her return to the theatre, Lola Chalfont doesn't seem to have any reason to kill her mother-in-law in the book. It's difficult to be sure, because there are at least twenty thousand words missing.'

'How do you know that?'

'Because Eliot couldn't have delivered a manuscript under seventy thousand words, and anyway, it's my job. I always have a feel for this sort of thing. Atticus Pünd hasn't done nearly enough investigating. I think there may be a whole plot segment that Eliot never got around to writing.' I checked the last pages of the batch that Blakeney had brought. There were just the eighteen chapters. 'You didn't find any more pages?'

'No. Eliot has a notebook and we'll talk about that in a

minute, but otherwise he seems to have worked directly on his laptop.'

'Like most writers.' I sighed. 'I'm the only person I know who still likes paper.'

'I've noticed. Anyway, I had my tech department look through his files, but there was nothing else there.'

'The denouement would have run to five or ten thousand words. All the suspects lined up in the library or whatever. But that still leaves a big hole.' I was annoyed that I had never asked Eliot for details of what was coming next. With *Magpie Murders*, there had only been one chapter missing. It was much more difficult this time.

'What about Leylah Crace?' Blakeney asked.

'I met her at the Savoy and she didn't have anything bad to say about Miriam Crace. "*She never did any harm to me.*" Those were her exact words. Of course, she could have been lying,' I went on. 'Her mother-in-law used to make racist jokes about her. And it's always possible that Leylah might have blamed Miriam for the death of her daughter, Jasmine. She killed herself under a train. But if there is anyone in the family Leylah really hates, it's her husband, Jonathan.'

'No love lost,' Blakeney muttered. 'I noticed that too.'

I went back to the list. 'In the world of the book, Elmer Waysmith is the main suspect,' I said. 'Margaret found out he was involved in the sale of art stolen by the Nazis and she called the solicitor to talk about her will. James Fraser set it all out at the start of Chapter Sixteen, and although the sidekick is nearly always wrong, all the clues seem to be pointing to him. He was the man in the pharmacy . . .'

'Are you sure about that?'

'White hair. American accent. And Harry Lyttleton said he saw him in the Place Masséna at half past twelve. He was in a hurry. It was as if he'd just got changed at the hotel and he didn't want to be late for the meeting with his son.'

'I suppose that's one way of looking at it.'

I glanced at him. 'You sound like Atticus Pünd,' I said. He didn't smile and once again I knew that something had happened since I'd last seen him and he was keeping it from me. 'Elmer Waysmith and Edward Crace both have white hair, and the way Eliot saw it, they were both difficult fathers,' I went on. 'There was no love lost between Eliot and Edward either, but even if Edward had decided to kill his mother, it's hard to believe that he would have it in him to come back to England and run over his own son.'

'I agree.'

'So now we come to Roland, Julia and Eliot himself, and this is where it gets a bit tricky. Julia is obviously Judith Lyttleton. They're physically the same and Julia's a geography teacher in real life. Eliot's turned her into an ethnologist with a thing about Peru.'

'What about her husband, Harry Lyttleton?'

'I wondered about him too. He isn't anyone I've met. But I've worked out where he came from. Julia is single, but in the book, Eliot has married her to one of the Little People. Harry Little has become Harry Lyttleton. I suppose it's a private joke.'

'Not a very funny one.'

'I agree. Eliot also told me that he had based the little boy, Cedric, on himself, so that's easy. I'm not sure about Robert Waysmith, though. I'm guessing that he's a version of Roland. He's not part of the family. He's Elmer's son from his first marriage. But he's described as good-looking, like a poet or an adventurer, and in Chapter Eighteen, Cedric says that everyone in the family likes him. All of this is true of Roland – or at least it was until he broke the faith by having an affair with Gillian.

'The big question is – did Robert Waysmith kill Lady Chalfont? And if so, does that mean that Eliot is identifying Roland as the killer of Miriam Crace?'

I got up and poured myself a glass of cold water. This was all getting far too complicated.

'Roland, Julia and Eliot were all children when they were living in Marble Hall,' I went on. 'Roland admitted to me that they often talked about killing their grandmother. They even put together some sort of potion. It was an idea they got from a Roald Dahl book – *George's Marvellous Medicine*. Charles Clover knew all about this. He said that Julia had put the poison they concocted in one of her perfume bottles, which she kept in her room, but Roland stole it from her the night Miriam died. He had the room next to hers. It makes complete sense. Roland was the oldest of the children and he was their protector. If anyone was going to slip something into the old lady's lemon and ginger pick-me-up, it would have been him. Lady Chalfont also drank lemon and ginger tea, so it follows that if it was Robert Waysmith who poisoned his stepmother in the book, then it must have been Roland who killed Miriam Crace in real life.

'There's just one problem. Motive. In real life, I suppose it's quite possible that Roland might have killed Miriam Crace when he was seventeen. Miriam had been vile to his sister. He was her protector. By poisoning Miriam, he would have been getting his own back on her and preventing Julia from doing it herself. But I still can't see him killing his own brother, especially when you consider his relationship with Gillian.'

'You should also know that Roland Crace can't drive,' Blakeney said. 'He never got a licence. He was driven to the party in a private car — like most of the guests. We've put together a list of everyone who drove themselves that night.'

'Am I on it?'

'There's still a question mark on that one, Susan.'

'Well, if Roland can't drive, he can't have killed Eliot. And if Robert Waysmith is his alter ego in the book, I'm not sure that works either because Robert has no reason to kill Lady Chalfont. He inherited ten thousand pounds in her will, but he didn't particularly need it and he certainly wouldn't have killed her for it. If there was anyone he might have wanted to murder, it was his father. I'm sure Eliot would have written more about Marion's suicide in the missing pages, but it's already clear that Robert Waysmith partly blamed his father for her death. Elmer Waysmith didn't even break off his business trip to come home.'

'What about the others?' Blakeney asked. He seemed keen to move on.

'We can deal with the last three pretty quickly. Frédéric Voltaire is my favourite character in the book and I really like his relationship with Pünd. He's obviously based on Frederick Turner, who was adopted by Miriam Crace, and I did challenge Eliot as to why he did that. Turner gets smashed up in a road accident and Eliot turns him into a casualty of war. The same injuries. Incidentally, Leylah Crace told me that Turner lied about the cause of the accident . . .'

'Had he been drinking?'

'Maybe you can find out. If he was breathalysed, would they have kept the records?'

Blakeney nodded. 'I'll check.' He took out his smartphone and tapped in a few words.

'Julia Crace was also in the car, so maybe she'll be able to help,' I said. 'What's strange about Frederick Turner is this whole racism thing. Was Miriam a racist or wasn't she? She seems to have treated Frederick as a second-class citizen, but he wouldn't say a word against her. It was the same with Leylah. But neither of them had any reason to kill anyone. And that just leaves Gillian Crace and John Lambert.'

'I'm going to let Emma Wardlaw loose on Dr Lambert,' Blakeney said. 'If you're right and the family paid him to keep quiet about the cause of Miriam Crace's death, she'll force it out of him.'

'I'd like to see that.'

'As for the character of Alice Carling, you'll be interested to know that she doesn't appear in Eliot's original notes,' Blakeney said. He pushed over the notebook with the Japanese design on the cover. 'This is Eliot's notebook, the one I mentioned, all written in his own hand. He changed a lot of the names. Monsieur Lambert's assistant was originally called Gabrielle Mazin – who also happens to be the head of Netflix in France.'

'Eliot found out about the affair around the same time he started writing the books – so he put his wife in and killed her. I always thought that Alice Carling was an odd name for a young woman living in a French village.'

'She was also Celia Carling, Clair La Cinge and Clarice

Laing.' Blakeney showed me a page full of names with letters crossed out and rearranged. 'He seems to have spent as much time planning his anagrams as he did plotting the book.'

'May I see that?' I asked.

He handed it to me. 'Of course.'

Eliot had filled about half the book with notes and diagrams using four different colours: red, blue, green and black. He had tucked in photographs of paintings by Sisley and Cézanne and there was also a clipping from a magazine that showed the Villa Ephrussi de Rothschild, which he had obviously used as his inspiration for the Chateau Belmar.

It was like a snapshot of his brain. He'd started with point-by-point analyses of all nine Atticus Pünd novels before he'd sat down to create his own. He'd drawn a family tree for the Chalfonts, circling the names and connecting them, adding their dates of birth and how old they were when Lady Chalfont died. There were timelines showing, for example, where everyone had been – and when – on the day of the murder. These were mixed in with pages of research and ideas for storylines, not all of which he'd used in the end. Everything was so jumbled together that if I hadn't read the book, it would have made no sense at all, and even with the story very much in my head, it was hard to work out what fitted where. What I was mainly looking for was anything that indicated which way the book might go.

The Primogeniture System. Entail follows the title (see Julian Fellowes – Downton Abbey).

The Einsatzstab Reichsleiter Rosenberg (ERR) and The Monuments Men.

No chemical test to identify ACONITINE in the blood.
Death immediate. Monkshood, wolfsbane possible ingredient in 'George's Marvellous Medicine'.
'PLOT IDEA – we'll release you from concentration
camp in return for art. DOUBLE CROSS!'
Mitral stenosis – a valvular disorder of the heart. Narrow-
ness of the mitral valve which controls the flow of blood.
KENNETH RIVERS involved in taxidermy. Treated for
arsenic poisoning. (Symptoms – warts and lesions, sore
throat, darkening skin.)
Housewife syndrome = oppression/cruelty. Elmer Waysmith coercive. Doesn't return from business trip. 'He
can be a monster at times.'
ESQUIRE SHOE CLEANER 3/9d. Manufactured
in USA.

And then there were riddles. Eliot didn't just think about
what he was going to write. He put it all down on the page,
interrogating himself. There were dozens of questions but
unfortunately no answers. Once he'd worked out what he
was going to do, there had been no need to make a note of it.

How do we find out that ~~Gabrielle~~ Alice revealed the will?
How does Lady Chalfont overhear the conversation?
Why did they buy poison from French chemist so close to
using it?
Why talk about the tea as if it was poisoned? (Jeffrey and
Harry could have lied.)
How did Judith know that ~~Gabrielle~~ Alice lived in a village?
Why did Bruno leave?

Perhaps most perplexing of all was a page simply entitled: CLUES. Eliot had used a process known as seeding whereby a seemingly innocent detail in an early chapter will have a pay-off when the reader gets to the end. In *Magpie Murders*, for example, Alan had mentioned a dog collar left in a drawer in an old house. It had been a perfect piece of deception: seemingly irrelevant but pointing directly at both the identity of the killer and the motive for the murder. But did these clues make any sense? I could feel Blakeney examining me as I searched through the notebook, trying to look as if I was getting somewhere.

CLUES

Judith shocked to see Pünd.

Double crease in letter to Pünd.

Ginger and lemon tea for Margaret.

Why talk about the tea as if it's poisoned? Why not lie?

Someone goes down servants' stairs at 4 pm.

Frédéric Voltaire mentions guillotine.

Lola performs as Mata Hari.

Matches.

Tutoyer in pharmacie scene. Surgical spirit.

I would have liked to have examined every single page, but Blakeney looked anxious to leave. I was disappointed. When he'd suggested an alliance, combining our efforts, I'd felt a distinct Tommy and Tuppence vibe and I'd thought it would be fun. But he'd been stiff and formal from the moment he'd arrived at the house. I was wondering if I should call him 'Detective Inspector' again.

I handed him back Eliot's notes. 'Did you find any of this useful?' I asked.

'It gave me some ideas.'

It was the vagueness of his reply, his refusal to share anything of value, that finally did it for me. 'What's wrong?' I snapped. 'You were kind to me after someone broke into my flat and I thought we'd come to some sort of understanding. You're still wondering if my car was used to kill Eliot Crace, but you must have twigged by now that I'm hardly Jack the Ripper. Has there been some sort of development in the case that you're not telling me? Because you're nothing like the man I met the other night.'

Blakeney looked at me in surprise — not because I was wrong but because I had been able to see through his thin veneer of amicability. We might have been talking about the book, but the last half hour had passed with all the formality of a police interview under caution.

He took a few moments to consider what I had said. Then he nodded. 'You're right, Susan. I haven't played fair with you and I'm sorry. I did wonder whether I should come here at all, but, to be honest, I needed your insights. In return, I've treated you badly.'

'So what's happened?'

'I'm sure you're aware that in a police investigation there are often pieces of information that we hold back from the public. I must ask you to promise me that you won't share this with anyone else.'

'If I'm the cold-blooded criminal that you seem to think I am, I wouldn't have thought my promises would mean anything. But yes. You have my word.'

'Did you know that Eliot Crace had an expensive watch?'

'I think I did notice a watch when we first met. It was a Rolex.'

'That's very well observed. It was a vintage Rolex Explorer, to be precise, released in 1953. Stainless steel with a leather strap. A very nice piece, worth about fifteen thousand pounds. It belonged to Kenneth Rivers and he left it to Eliot in his will.'

'Why is the watch relevant?' I asked.

'Eliot was wearing it at the party,' Blakeney replied. 'We have several guests who are quite certain they saw it on his wrist – and according to Gillian, he never took it off. But here's the thing. When his body was discovered, the watch was gone.'

'That's awful,' I said. 'Someone saw him lying there and they took it.'

'That was our immediate assumption. A random pedestrian passes a man who has just been knocked down, notices his expensive watch and nicks it. It's sick, but it's not such a strange thing to happen in the middle of London. But we were wrong. Because we found the watch.'

He reached into his jacket pocket and took out a clear plastic evidence bag, sealed at the top. He held it up and I could see the watch quite clearly, coiled up like a snake. I recognised it at once. He'd been wearing it when we met Elaine at Causton Books.

'So where did you find it?'

His deep brown eyes settled on me. 'It was in your flat.'

Alexandra Palace

'Who found it?' I asked.

'I'm not sure that's relevant,' Blakeney replied.

'Well, where was it?'

'In the drawer beside your bed.'

'Is that why you offered to clean up my flat? So you could search it? Is that even legal?'

We were no longer in the house. Blakeney's declaration had shocked me so much that I'd felt a physical need to get out. I would have preferred to go on my own, but I had to know more and when he'd suggested coming with me, I hadn't complained. I'd turned into Alice down the rabbit hole, but instead of white rabbits and playing cards, I'd been sucked into a nightmare landscape – more Hieronymus Bosch than Lewis Carroll. It was impossible for Eliot's watch to have been found in my bedroom. It was impossible for a scrap of his bloodstained jacket to have wedged itself into the dented grille of my MG. Both of these things had happened.

And here I was, walking round the grounds of Alexandra Palace with a police officer who had been friendly enough the last time we'd met but who now seemed determined to put me in jail. I had no-one to turn to. My sister couldn't help. Should I be calling a lawyer? I needed fresh air and sunshine to clear my head.

Alexandra Palace. Ally Pally to anyone who lived nearby. It had been built on a hilltop overlooking London and opened to the public in 1873 – 'The Palace of the People'. It had burned down sixteen days later. It was rebuilt, burned down a second time in 1980 and was now something of a white elephant, although a handsome one with a theatre and an ice rink. In a way, it reminded me of my career. That had repeatedly burned down too.

We were walking through the grounds. The sky was clear and I could see all the way to south London, almost as if I was in a plane. The park was still busy. We passed a group of teenagers, about a dozen of them, playing football with piled-up clothes used as goalposts. A couple came the other way, pushing a pram. A man threw a ball for his dog. Here and there, people sat on the grass, enjoying the late-afternoon warmth. I was surrounded by the normal world but completely separated from it.

'If that's what you think, I'm disappointed, Susan.' Blakeney had taken his time to reply to my last point. 'If I'd wanted to search your flat, I'd have got a warrant. I was just trying to help you. But if you really are going to suggest I acted illegally, then I'll have to remind you that you had been informed of the reason we entered the premises and if you look at Section Nineteen of the 1984 Police and Criminal Evidence Act, you'll find – and I quote – that "the constable may seize anything which is on the premises if he has reasonable grounds for believing that it is evidence in relation to an offence which he is investigating".'

'Why only *he*?' I growled.

'Good point. But this was 1984.'

I wanted to be angry with him but couldn't. 'Just tell me,' I said. 'If you believed I ran Eliot over because he insulted me and then stole his watch and hid it in my bedroom, you'd already have arrested me. What do you think is going on?'

We walked on in silence. I glanced at a father flying a kite with his children and not for the first time, I thought of Mary Poppins. I could see Blakeney struggling with himself, deciding how much to tell me. The sun was dipping and suddenly I felt a strange sense of peace. I trusted him. He was like one of those Edwardian heroes created by Erskine Childers or John Buchan, dragged into an adventure without quite wanting to be there.

'I'm not sure what I believe,' he began at last. 'For what it's worth, my DS thinks I must have a soft spot for you or something, and I won't even start with DC Wardlaw. We have motive, timing, opportunity and solid evidence, and there is absolutely no way that you and I should be walking in a park together. It may not mean very much to you, especially after what you just said, but I'm putting my neck on the line for you and if it does turn out that you ran over Eliot Crace, I'll be saying goodbye to my career.'

I didn't know how to respond. It had never occurred to me that he'd been defending me, even putting his own prospects at risk. He was a decent man and I was beginning to wish I'd handled this conversation differently.

'So let me tell you why I'm sticking up for you.

'First of all, this sort of crime is vanishingly rare. There was a kids' writer who got drugged and suffocated by her partner – it was a nasty story – a while ago, and there's always Christopher Marlowe, I suppose, but, by and large, famous authors don't get murdered. Can you name another? We're none of us used to handling this sort of situation.

'And then you need look at what modern police officers have to deal with—'

I was about to interrupt, but he stopped me.

'Let me explain this my own way. All right?

'I joined the police thirty-two years ago and nothing is the same. The cutbacks have been a big part of the problem. You know the old complaint. We're not on the streets any more. Hardly a surprise when six hundred police stations in the UK have been shut down since 2010 – and there were only nine hundred to begin with. We've had our own self-inflicted wounds too. Scandals involving racism and sexism and all the rest of it. The result is that people no longer have much confidence in us. Trust and respect . . . all that's gone.

'At the same time, the whole landscape of crime has changed. *The Landscape of Criminal Investigation*! That was the book Atticus Pünd was writing – but what would he do if he walked into a crime scene nowadays? Think about it. The victim's wearing a smartwatch. She's got a smart TV, a laptop, a tablet, a smartphone, an Oyster card. Even the thermostat is controlled by Wi-Fi. And every one of these is a line of inquiry. Ninety per cent of reported crime now has a digital element, and don't get me started on cybercrime! Social engineering, credit card fraud, old ladies being done out of their life savings.

'The point that I'm trying to make is that what you're involved in is an anomaly and it's hardly surprising that some of my colleagues want to deal with it as fast as they can. Basically, my DS is right. I should have arrested you the moment that Rolex turned up. Be honest with yourself, Susan. Do you think there's a jury in the country that wouldn't convict you?'

'Then why haven't you?' I asked. 'Arrested me?'

'Two reasons. I know you – a little. I don't believe you killed Eliot Crace. And you were right, just a moment ago. Even if you had killed him, there's no way you'd have stolen his watch. That's rubbish. You might like to know that we found some of your DNA on the strap – but no fingerprints. What does that tell you?'

'I'm sorry. I don't have the faintest idea.'

'Well, I'll help you a little. We also found traces of sodium lauryl sulphate and calcium carbonate.'

I shook my head. 'Maybe I'm being slow today, but I'm none the wiser.'

'They're ingredients used in the manufacture of toothpaste. What it means is that you never touched the watch – not unless you were wearing gloves when you ran Eliot over. But whoever planted it in your bedroom must have rubbed your toothbrush against the strap. They hoped to transfer some of your DNA—'

'—but they also transferred elements of the toothpaste.'

'That's what I think.'

'And do you have any idea who this mysterious person might be?'

'That's why I came to see you today, Susan. I think you're better placed to find the answer than us. It would seem that

494

somebody very close to Eliot Crace believes you were responsible for his death. They wrote the word "KILLER" on your bedroom wall. Who might that be? Eliot had a wife and a sister. Gillian Crace might have been angry with him, but she didn't necessarily want him dead. He had a brother who had shared the whole experience of growing up in Marble Hall. His father, Edward Crace, wasn't at the party, but he's been unable to provide us with an alibi for seven o'clock that evening until the following day. The list goes on.'

'So how do you think I can help you?'

'You've spent the last few weeks rummaging around in the Crace Estate. You've been rubbing a lot of people up the wrong way. Has anyone threatened you? Has anyone said anything that might lead you to think they would want to hurt you? And here are a few questions. Somebody reported seeing your car in Trafalgar Square. They identified part of your registration number. So if it wasn't a random member of the public, ask yourself this. Who knew you drove a red MG and might have got close enough to see the number plate? You drove to Marble Hall. You visited Dr Lambert. Was there anybody else?

'Also, they must have found out you were going to be away for much of the day before they broke in. You've already said that you didn't tell anyone you were going to HMP Belmarsh, but was there any unusual activity around your house that day? Could someone have been waiting until you left? And that broken garden door of yours. Had you mentioned that to anyone? Had you said you were fond of the cat?

'Finally, I don't want to scare you, but I think you should look out for yourself. I'm afraid I'm not in a position to offer you police protection, so I'd recommend you stay in your friends' house, if that's possible. Don't give anyone the address. If you do decide to go home, keep the front door locked at all times, even when you're in the flat. Especially when you're in the flat. I've had the garden door fixed, but don't go in or out until you're sure you're safe.'

'You think they might try again?'

'Not at once. They're waiting for us to arrest you. But when we don't take any action, they may get impatient and come back. They've got it in for you, Susan, and they could decide to make another move.'

We walked on in silence. Somehow, we had curved round so that we were now heading back to the house. The father with the children had pulled in the kite. There were fewer people around us. The day was drawing to a close.

'I'm sorry I doubted you,' I said. 'And it was wrong of me to accuse you of doing something illegal.'

'Look, I can imagine how upsetting this must be for you.' He paused. 'But I have got one thing that may cheer you up.'

'What's that?'

'That discussion we had about Eliot's book. You said something very interesting about the stepfather, Elmer Waysmith.'

'And . . .?'

'I'm still not sure how much it will help me with my investigation, but I'm fairly certain I've worked out who killed Margaret Chalfont and why. Don't ask me now! I need a day or two to think about it – but as soon as I've got it sorted in my mind, I'll let you know.'

Special Delivery

Two days later, just as I was getting dressed, a car I recognised pulled up outside the house. I still hadn't moved back into my flat while the decorators continued their work. I had given them my phone number and my new address in case any packages arrived for me, but it would be another few days before the place was habitable. I saw the car stop, quickly pulled on a dress and examined myself in the mirror. I hadn't slept well. I was living out of a suitcase and it showed. I didn't look my best – but there was no time to do anything about it. The doorbell rang. I went down.

Detective Constable Emma Wardlaw was standing on the pavement, looking at me in the sullen, ever-so-slightly hostile way she had made into her trademark. It worried me a little that she had come alone, but I smiled as if I was delighted to see her, knowing that nothing would annoy her more.

'Good morning, Detective Constable. How can I help you? I'd invite you in, but I'm afraid this isn't my house.'

'I don't want to come in, thank you very much. DI

Blakeney asked me to give you this.' She lifted her hand and for the first time I saw that she was carrying a white A4 envelope.

'Where is DI Blakeney?' I asked.

'He's busy. I was passing so I said I'd do it for him.'

She delivered the package, pushing it towards me as if it were an offensive weapon. With her attitude, she wouldn't have lasted a week as an Amazon driver.

'Thank you,' I said.

That should have been it. She should have just walked away and left me to get on with whatever was in the envelope – but she had taken such a strong dislike to me that she couldn't help herself. I saw her take two steps and then turn and come back again.

'You know, we are going to get you, Ms Ryeland,' she said.

'I prefer to be called Susan.'

'You may think you're very clever and that you've got Detective Inspector Blakeney twisted round your little finger, but you don't know anything. He's lying to you!' She couldn't keep the malice out of her voice as she spoke those last four words. 'He knows you killed that boy. We all know it. But what he has to do is, he has to make the case watertight – and that's why he's getting close to you, pretending to be your friend. When he's back in the office, mind, you might be surprised what he says about you.'

'Why are you telling me this?' I asked.

'We both have to do it,' she went on, not answering me. 'It's normal procedure. You cosy up to a suspect, gain their trust and wait for them to make a mistake.'

'I can't imagine you being cosy with anyone, Detective Constable.'

'You can laugh all you like now, Ms Ryeland, but your time's running out and while you're standing there smiling at me in that snooty way of yours, you might as well know it.'

She had said her piece. She left.

And I'd thought Detective Superintendent Locke was bad!

I closed the door and carried the envelope into the kitchen, but I didn't open it straight away. I couldn't stop thinking about what Wardlaw had said – and I wasn't sure what to make of it. Although it was true that I had antagonised her – deliberately – when we first met, there had to be another reason for her almost psychotic dislike of me. After all, she should never have spoken to me like that. If what she said was true, then she had just revealed the secret methodology of a police operation. I didn't think Blakeney would be pleased.

Was it true? I didn't want to believe her. I suddenly realised that after our meal in the Italian restaurant and our walk around Alexandra Palace, I'd begun to take a liking to Ian Blakeney. At the very least, I'd thought we could work together. If it turned out that it had all been a charade, that he'd been playing me from the start, I'd be more than disappointed. I'd be furious – with him and with myself.

I didn't know if I even wanted to look inside the envelope, but I grabbed a kitchen knife and cut it open, leaving the same serrated edge that Pünd had noticed on the envelope delivered to Lady Chalfont in the book. I pulled out around thirty pages of text, stapled together. There was a handwritten note attached.

Dear Susan,

I thought I might try this out on you.

I mentioned to you that I fancied my hand at being a crime writer and that Fiona — my wife — always encouraged me. So I found myself wondering what the final chapter of Eliot's book might have looked like and here it is. The writing style may be rubbish, but I'm pretty confident it's the right ending. I suppose I've read enough of these sorts of books to know.

By the way, I didn't get there on my own. You remember what you said when we were sitting in the kitchen of that house you're now in? We were talking about Robert Waysmith and your exact words were: 'If there was anyone he might have wanted to murder, it was his father.' You were exactly right — so you get half the credit.

Anyway, I've enjoyed writing my own version of Atticus Pünd and I hope it will help us both sort out the rest of this strange business.

Sincerely,
Ian Blakeney

PS I've also worked out the third anagram. We can talk about that when we next meet.

Intrigued, I unstapled the pages and reached for a pen. The first thing I noticed was that Blakeney had used the same font as Eliot Crace. I've always had a fondness for Garamond, a very neat and classical typeface designed by a Frenchman, Claude Garamond, back in the sixteenth century. Glancing over the first two sentences, I saw at once that

Blakeney could write, but as he'd said in his note, it wasn't his style that mattered.

It was the last thing I would have expected, but I was about to read the end.

THE LAST CHAPTER

Atticus Pünd had requested them all to assemble in the *grand salon*, the same room where the will had been read, only this time it was Pünd and Voltaire who had taken their places behind the card table. The entire family was present with the single exception of an angry Cedric, who had been told that children had no place here and had been banished to his room.

'But I want to be a suspect,' he had complained.

'No, dear,' his mother had cajoled him. 'That's the last thing you want to be, and anyway, you're much too young.'

'But I didn't like Grandma. I didn't like having to come here all summer. And I knew lots about poisonous plants.'

'Just go to your room, Cedric. And if you talk about killing anyone ever again, you won't have ice cream for tea.'

Jeffrey and Lola Chalfont had taken their places as soon as their son had left the room. They were joined by Harry and Judith Lyttleton, the two couples mirroring each other on opposite sofas. As always, Elmer Waysmith was on his own, dressed as if he was about to leave for a picnic in a blue blazer and white summer trousers. Robert Waysmith, who had chosen to distance himself from his father, was on the other side of the room. Three other witnesses who were not part of the family had been invited. James Fraser was never far away from Pünd, although he had tucked himself into a corner, trying not to be noticed, his notepad resting on his knee. Jean Lambert, the family solicitor, was next to him, diminished somehow, not just missing Alice Carling but blaming himself for her death. The last arrival had taken everyone by surprise. Pünd had invited Harlan Scott to the house. The art-historian-turned-detective was sitting, legs crossed, in an armchair that almost devoured him, smoking a cigar, his eyes fixed on the new painting that now hung above the fireplace. It was a very ordinary piece of work, but it was as if he were looking through it, still seeing the Cézanne it had replaced. Neither Robert nor Elmer had spoken to him and, like the rest of the family, they clearly resented having him there.

'I hope you're not going to keep us too long.' Jeffrey Chalfont had looked impatient from the moment he had entered the room. 'I have a lunch appointment at one o'clock.'

'You have no interest in the identity of the person who killed you mother?' Pünd asked.

'I know I didn't kill her, and nor did my wife. That's all that matters to me. If you just tell us who it was, we can all get on with our lives.'

'You will remain here and listen to what Monsieur Pünd has to say,' Voltaire said, pinning Jeffrey down with his one good eye. 'Your lunch is of no interest to me and you will leave only when I say you can.'

'I want to know the truth,' Robert Waysmith said. 'This whole business has been horrible. Let's get it over with.'

Pünd glanced at Voltaire, who nodded. It was his invitation to begin.

504

'It was Lady Chalfont who invited me here,' Pünd said. 'She wrote to me a letter in which she stressed the urgency of her situation and hoped that I would arrive before it was too late. Unfortunately, due to my health and the strain of the journey, I disappointed her. By the time I was able to come to the Chateau Belmar, accompanied by my friend Monsieur Voltaire, she had been deliberately poisoned with aconitine and it was too late. I had met Lady Margaret before and thought her a generous and intelligent woman. It will always be to my regret that I was unable to help her in her hour of need.

'For reasons that I do not need to share with you, this will be my last case and it is some consolation that it has provided such an unexpected challenge. Although on the face of it, the crime is a most straightforward one, the solution is nothing of the sort. The deaths of Margaret Chalfont and, indeed, of Alice Carling will provide a valuable appendage to *The Landscape of Criminal Investigation*, a work I have spent many years constructing.

'Let us look first at the facts as they presented themselves. Lady Margaret Chalfont knew that she had little time left to live. She had also made an extraordinary will in which she had left the control of her estate not to her family but to her second husband. You all know the reason for this. It was because she did not believe her children had the wisdom or the judgement to manage a considerable sum of money without guidance.'

'Only because that was what Elmer told her,' Harry Lyttleton muttered.

'No, no, Mr Lyttleton. She was aware, for example, of the

505

construction of your hotel, the losses that you have sustained, and perhaps she also knew that you were consorting with businessmen of a dubious nature. Her son, Jeffrey, was gambling. She had a daughter-in-law wishing to put money into the theatre, a sure way to lose it. At the same time, she believed she could trust Elmer Waysmith, who was already wealthy as a result of his art business and had no need of the money himself.'

'My father inherited plenty of money from his first marriage,' Robert said. 'He had no need of yours.'

'Exactly.' Pünd nodded in agreement. 'But in the weeks before the death of Lady Chalfont, an event of great significance occurred – and one which must surely have influenced everything that followed. In her letter, she wrote to me how she had overheard a conversation that had shattered her faith in her husband. Later, we learned this conversation concerned a painting that once hung in this very room and which was entitled *Spring Flowers*, by the artist Paul Cézanne. May I ask where it is now, Mr Waysmith?'

It was Robert Waysmith to whom Pünd had addressed the question and he replied: 'It's at the gallery. We're looking for a buyer.'

'Well, it is the reason why I have invited Mr Harlan Scott to this meeting. He met Elmer Waysmith and his son in this very room.'

'I want to get one thing straight,' Elmer cut in. 'I do not accept any of the accusations you make regarding that painting, its provenance or its past history. It was purchased by my partner and no owners have ever come forward to suggest otherwise.'

'That's because the owners are dead,' Harlan Scott growled. He was not a powerful man. With his thinning hair and glasses, he was more like a teacher than a detective. But his anger was palpable, cutting through the room. 'Their whole family was wiped out in the war. You and your business partner know that and it's disgusting that you should have uttered those words.'

'I'm not arguing with you, Mr Scott,' Elmer retorted. 'I know a lot of bad things happened in the war. All I'm saying is that I was unaware the painting had been stolen and, as I told you at the time we met, if you could prove otherwise, I would have been happy to talk to the true owners.'

'Talk to them or give it back to them?'

Elmer fell silent.

'It was a hot day. The windows were open. And Lady Chalfont heard what was said. Because she was travelling to London the next day, she immediately telephoned the family solicitor, Monsieur Lambert, and told him that she wished to speak to him about her will.' He turned to Lambert. 'That is correct?'

'*Oui, monsieur.* She did not say that she wished to change it, but she asked me to bring a copy. There is no doubt in my mind that she was having second thoughts.'

'When a very wealthy person decides to alter her will, it is often a motive for murder,' Pünd continued. 'And it cannot be a coincidence that Lady Chalfont was killed before the meeting could occur. She had maybe only weeks left to live on account of her illness, but that was not soon enough for the person who wished her dead. He had to strike immediately and that is what he did.'

507

'*He?*' Lola asked. 'You're saying it was a man?'

'There is only one man in this room who had everything to lose if he did not take action and, as I have already explained, that man was Elmer Waysmith.'

'Now you look here.' Elmer sprang out of his chair, his face deep red. 'I'm not going to sit here and listen to any more of this—'

'You will sit down and be silent, monsieur, unless you wish to spend the rest of the morning in a prison cell,' Voltaire exclaimed. 'Nobody is to leave this room until I give them permission.'

'Sit down, Pa,' Robert said. 'I know you didn't do it. Mr Pünd is just playing games.'

'It is not a game, the investigation of murder.' Pünd waited until Elmer had retaken his place. 'Not only did Elmer Waysmith have the most obvious motive, every single piece of evidence points to his guilt.

'His wife believed he was a criminal. She was quite possibly intending to cut him out of her will. And although it pains me to say it, Margaret Chalfont would not have been the first woman who married him and died unnaturally.'

'Leave Marion out of this!' Elmer snarled.

Pünd had already moved on. 'We must discuss what happened at the *pharmacie* in the Rue Lafayette,' he said. 'On the very same day that Lady Chalfont died, a man wearing sunglasses and a straw hat and using an ebony walking stick purchased two grams of aconitine, the same poison that the police would discover in Lady Chalfont's tea. We are led to believe that this occurred at a quarter past twelve. He spoke in French but with an accent – quite possibly American. He did everything he could not to show his face.'

'I've never been anywhere near any pharmacy,' Elmer insisted.

'The same man had taken a room at a neighbouring hotel. The chambermaid was able to give us a description of the person she had seen very briefly . . . the hat, the sunglasses, the walking stick. She also added one important detail, however. He had white hair. There are two other indications that he may have been American. It is almost certain that he used a false name when he checked into the hotel and he chose an American film director, John Ford, as his alias. Also, he left behind a bottle of shoe polish produced by an American manufacturer, Esquire.

'Was this man Elmer Waysmith? There are two further clues that suggest it was. He signed the hotel register using turquoise ink. I saw exactly that same colour when I was in his office. He had been producing, I believe, a catalogue – and there were several pages written in turquoise. Also, I noticed a book on the shelf behind his desk. It was *Erskine's Toxicology*, a study of poisons.'

'I told you. It was relevant to my work.'

'But it was jutting out, Mr Waysmith. You had clearly used it quite recently. Again, it cannot have been a coincidence.'

Waysmith gazed at Voltaire. 'Mr Voltaire! You are an officer with the Sûreté. Are you going to sit there and allow an amateur with no credentials to spout this nonsense?'

'On the contrary, Monsieur Waysmith.' Voltaire was impassive. 'Monsieur Pünd is one of the most celebrated detectives in the world. He was invited here specifically by

509

your late wife. I intend to sit here and listen to every word he has to say.'

Pünd nodded his gratitude, then continued. 'Finally, we can piece together the movements of Mr Waysmith on the day of the murder. Let us return, once again, to the *pharmacie.*'

'You said I was there at twelve fifteen.' Hope flared in Elmer's eyes. 'Where is the Rue Lafayette?'

'It is to the north of the Voie Pierre Mathis.'

'That's at least twenty minutes from my gallery in the Place Masséna. But I met my son at half past twelve, so I couldn't possibly have got from one to the other in time.'

'But it was not twelve fifteen, Mr Waysmith. Monsieur Brunelle, who runs the pharmacy, has poor eyesight, but even so he was able to confirm from a photograph that it was Alice Carling who came in at the same time as the man who was buying aconitine and the two of them engaged in a little performance to establish a false time. It was, in fact, closer to twelve o'clock and you would have had plenty of time to change your appearance at the hotel and then dispense with the walking stick and the clothes you had been wearing in a nearby dustbin. If you walked quickly enough, you would be able to reach the gallery at half past twelve, which is when you arrived.

'And, indeed, you were seen running across the square just before that time. This was mentioned by Harry Lyttleton. He hoped you might be able to supply him with an alibi.'

'Well, he's wrong. I didn't cross the square. I used the back door to enter the gallery.'

'I wasn't trying to get you into trouble, Elmer,' Harry muttered miserably. 'But I did think it was you. You had on that same white suit and bow tie you'd worn at the breakfast table. You were some distance away, though. I suppose I could have been wrong.'

'Of course you were wrong. I've just told you. It wasn't me.'

'We also know that you returned to the Chateau Belmar at exactly three o'clock. On this occasion it was Jeffrey Chalfont who heard the clock strike in the *petit salon* and saw your car at the same time. Do you deny this?'

'I only spent an hour with my son. I don't know what time I got home, but I was in my study for the whole afternoon.'

'And your study is very close to the service stairs that connect with the kitchen.'

'Yes.'

'Approximately an hour after you returned to the house, Lola Chalfont heard somebody go down to the kitchen, using that staircase. It was at this time that the aconitine was placed in the teapot intended for Lady Chalfont.'

'Well, it wasn't me.' Elmer glared at Lola as if she had deliberately accused him. 'I have never used the service stairs in my life and I certainly didn't go anywhere near the kitchen that afternoon.'

'But who else could it have been?' Pünd asked. 'Only yourself, Lola Chalfont and Judith Lyttleton were in the house.'

'I was reading,' Judith said. 'I was very involved in my work. I didn't hear anything.'

Pünd waved a hand. 'We have established your motive, your method and your movements,' he concluded. 'Nobody else in this room had the slightest desire to harm Lady Margaret Chalfont. Why do you not admit your guilt?'

'Because I didn't do it!' Elmer Waysmith exclaimed.

There was a long silence, broken by Robert Waysmith. 'My pa would never hurt anyone, Mr Pünd,' he said. 'You must have made a mistake.'

'I said at the very start that this was a straightforward crime,' Pünd said.

'But you also said that the solution wasn't,' Voltaire reminded him.

'That is indeed the case, Monsieur Voltaire. I have outlined a sequence of events that is unarguable. Unfortunately, it also leaves many questions unanswered.'

'What questions?' Harry demanded. 'Elmer did it! You've made that crystal clear. Who else could it have been?'

'You yourself have questions to answer, Mr Lyttleton,' Pünd replied. 'It is certain that Alice Carling was killed to keep her silent. She had been persuaded to take part in a charade that went against her better nature and she knew the identity of the man who purchased the aconitine in the Pharmacie Lafayette. She believed herself to be engaged to this man and it was your photograph that we found in her handbag.'

'We've already gone into this, Mr Pünd. She may have had fantasies about me, but I knew nothing about it.'

'I find it beyond belief, though, that she would consider marriage to Elmer Waysmith, a man who was the same age as her father. You, on the other hand, have good looks and charm . . .'

'And I'm happily married. I had no interest in Alice Carling whatsoever.'

'But there are other peculiarities, things that I do not

understand.' Pünd turned to Voltaire. 'Would you say that Elmer Waysmith is a stupid man?' he asked.

'I would say he's anything but,' Voltaire replied.

'So why did he make so many foolish mistakes? We have already mentioned the copy of *Erskine's Toxicology* that protruded from his shelf and the turquoise ink with which he signed the pharmacy's ledger. Even using the name of an American film director in the hotel's register pointed to his nationality. Then there was the American bottle of shoe polish he left in his hotel room. And why dispose of the walking stick and the blue linen suit in a dustbin close by in the street? My colleague, James Fraser, recovered them in less than a minute and I remarked upon this at the time. Also, why leave a book of matches with the name Hôtel Lafayette printed on the cover at the Chateau Belmar? That is the work of an imbecile and seems even more remarkable when you consider that Mr Waysmith does not smoke.

'But the most foolish mistake of all takes place at the time of the murder. Elmer Waysmith has returned home. He makes his way down the service stairs, ignoring the fact that they will creak and alert the entire house that they are being used. He enters the kitchen and slips the aconitine into the pot containing the lemon and ginger tea. *And he fails to replace the lid.* Of course this was noticed by the housekeeper, Mademoiselle Béatrice. Think for a moment. An elderly lady with a heart condition dies on a hot day in the garden. Nobody for one minute will suspect there is anything amiss. But Mr Waysmith has almost deliberately signalled that he has added something to the tea. He has invited the police to suspect foul play.'

'I suggested to you that the killer did not have time to replace the lid,' Voltaire said.

'I did not wish to argue with you, Monsieur Voltaire. But it struck me that this was unlikely. It was the work of two seconds to replace the lid, but to leave it off would be a catastrophe.'

'You're right, Monsieur Pünd. I can't disagree.'

'Mistake after mistake after mistake,' Pünd went on. 'But there are other aspects of this case that make no sense – and this I have said all along. Let us return to Lady Chalfont. She has overheard a conversation with her husband that suggests he is a criminal. She telephones her solicitor to change her will. And then she meets me in London and asks me to investigate what she has heard. Why does she not then cancel her meeting with Monsieur Lambert? Either her husband is guilty or he is not. If he is, she does not need me. If he is innocent, she does not need Monsieur Lambert.

'And there is something else that I have always found strange. Why was Dr Lyttleton so unhappy to see me?' Pünd turned his eyes to Judith. 'You did everything you could to move Lady Chalfont quickly out of the room.'

'We had a plane to catch, Mr Pünd.'

'You were not concerned that your mother had consulted a detective?'

'Of course I was. I had no idea what was going on in her head.'

'But still you did not mention the encounter to anyone else in the family.'

'I've already told you this. My mind was on other things and I forgot.'

'I do not believe you, I'm afraid, Dr Lyttleton.'

Judith's face went red. 'It's true. I came back to France, to the sunshine, and I forgot all about it.'

Pünd turned his attention back to the rest of the people in the room. 'The most important question still remains,' he said. 'It has been asked many times, but I will mention it once more. Why kill a woman who has only weeks to live? Why risk prison or the guillotine when the outcome is already assured?' Pünd looked across the room at James Fraser. 'You will recall that we had exactly this discussion after the reading of the will. And what did I say?'

'I did wonder about that,' James remarked. 'I asked you why anyone would murder a woman who was already dying and you answered, "Because it does not matter." I have to say, I had absolutely no idea what you meant.'

'And now I will tell you, my friend. Now I will describe what really occurred.'

There was another silence, finally broken by Robert Waysmith. 'Are you saying that my father didn't kill Lady Chalfont?' he asked.

'That is exactly what I am saying,' Pünd replied.

'Thank God for that. I told you. He wouldn't kill anyone.'

'Of course I didn't kill her,' Elmer rasped. 'I loved her.'

'But if he didn't, who did?' Voltaire exclaimed.

'To answer that question, we must consider the character of Lady Margaret Chalfont, a woman who was kind and generous, who had no enemies and who was in the last weeks of her life. Never has there been a victim of a murder who deserved to die less. It seemed to me from the moment I arrived in France and heard what had happened that she could not have been the true target.'

'You mean . . . the poison was intended for someone else?' Robert asked.

'No. That is not what I mean. When I said to James that her death did not matter, I meant that since she was going to die anyway, she could be killed with a clear conscience, even by someone who loved her – if her death could be used to benefit them in a certain way! Do you understand what I am saying? The murder of Lady Chalfont was not an end in itself. It was simply a means to an end.'

'And what was that?'

'Her wealth. Not the small amounts that she left in her will, but her entire fortune. Above all, it was about control.'

Pünd looked around the room, taking in the entire family.

'This was ingeniously planned,' he continued. 'Even before Lady Chalfont came to England, it had all been decided. It was only the fact that she happened to meet me in a doctor's waiting room in Harley Street that changed things. Ah, yes! That meant the plan had to be modified, to be accelerated. The poison had to be purchased on the very same day it was to be used. But otherwise it all went ahead as had been agreed.'

He turned to Judith. 'You lied to me, Dr Lyttleton – and you insult my intelligence if you ask me to believe that you kept the accident of our meeting to yourself. You told your husband. You told everyone. When Lady Chalfont wrote to me, the letter was opened and read. Likewise, the telegram that I sent to her. And it was decided that I would be folded into the plan. A murder needs not just a victim. It needs also a detective, and that was the part I was to play.

'Every single member of this family has been an actor, a

516

participant in what followed. All of you worked together to convict Elmer Waysmith of a crime he had not committed.'

'Wait a minute—' Jeffrey Chalfont exploded.

'You will not speak, Monsieur Chalfont!' Voltaire slammed his fist down on the card table in front of him. 'If anyone interrupts before Monsieur Pünd has finished, I will have them arrested!'

Silence returned to the room.

'All the mistakes that I have described – the lid of the teapot, the book on the shelf, the matches from the Hôtel Lafayette, the turquoise ink – were placed deliberately for me to find. And then there is the little pantomime played by Jeffrey Chalfont and Harry Lyttleton at the moment Lady Chalfont dies. "No, no, no!" they say. "We never thought she had been poisoned." So why, then, do they call the police? Why do they describe her death throes in such detail and even mention that she complained her tea had a strange taste? If anyone had wished to kill her, they could simply have remained silent and the whole world would have believed that she had succumbed to her heart disease. But there must be a clear signpost. This is not a natural death – it is a murder. They are demanding the police investigate.

'And every time anyone speaks to me, they incriminate Elmer Waysmith. Harry Lyttleton supposedly sees him running across the Place Masséna. It is Jeffrey Chalfont who provides the exact time of Elmer's return to the Chateau Belmar because he hears a clock strike at the same moment as he sees the car – even though, as I demonstrated to James, it would be impossible to see out onto the driveway if you were standing by the *petit salon*, where the grandfather clock is located. And when I interrogate Judith Lyttleton and Lola Chalfont for the first time, they work hard. The picture they paint of Elmer Waysmith is not a pleasant one. He is a gold-digger. His first wife would have been happier dead than living with him. His second wife had changed since she married him. And for good measure, it is Lola who hears the creaking of the stairs as the unknown assailant – who can only be Elmer Waysmith – makes his way to the kitchen.'

'But if it wasn't Elmer Waysmith at the Pharmacie Lafayette, who was it?' Voltaire asked. He had broken his own rule, interrupting Pünd.

Pünd didn't mind. 'All along, it has been suggested that it was Elmer Waysmith who was buying the aconitine and who attempted to conceal his identity with the hat and the sunglasses,' he said. 'But what if it was another person, *pretending* to be him, even speaking with an American accent? Now, finally, we have the reason for the bottle of liquid shoe polish that was found in the room used by the killer and which was, I believe, the only real mistake that was made. It was thrown into the dustbin, where it was later discovered by the maid – and even I failed to ask the one question that was most important. What colour was the shoe polish? It was a natural assumption that the liquid in the bottle was either black or brown. But what if it was white?'

'Someone used it to change the colour of their hair!' Voltaire exclaimed.

'That is exactly the case, Monsieur Voltaire, and it explains why the pharmacist thought he smelled surgical spirit, which confirmed his belief that the man was a doctor. But it was, of course, white spirit that he smelled. This *is* the principal ingredient of liquid shoe polish.

'It all becomes clear. Our mystery man has taken a room at the Hôtel Lafayette. He changes into different clothes, disguises himself with the hat and the glasses, colours his hair and then visits the *pharmacie*. While he is there, he has arranged for Alice Carling to walk in and ask the time. The *pharmacien* is easily deluded into thinking that it is a quarter past twelve when in fact it is ten or fifteen minutes earlier. This extra time allows our man to return to the hotel, use the sink to remove the shoe polish, change his clothes and then disappear into Nice. At half past twelve exactly, Elmer Waysmith will arrive at the gallery for lunch with his son and it is assumed that the great detective Atticus Pünd will put two and two together and come to entirely the wrong conclusion.'

'You're saying they were all in on it!' This time it was James Fraser who had spoken. 'They were framing Elmer Waysmith. But why?'

'For the simplest reason, James. It is child's play – and indeed it was young Cedric who gave us the answer when we met him in the garden. "*They were cross because Grandma gave all her money to Elmer.*" That is what he said. Jeffrey and Lola Chalfont and Harry and Judith Lyttleton all loved Margaret Chalfont in their own ways and they would never have dreamed of harming her had she not been dying anyway. But they did not see hastening her end by a matter of weeks as being the same as murdering her. They were *using* her death to rid themselves of Elmer Waysmith. Monsieur Voltaire explained it to us. Had Elmer been found guilty of the crime . . .'

'. . . he would have faced the guillotine.' Voltaire completed the sentence.

'And under French law, he would have inherited nothing. It was not just about the money. It was the control of the money and so, by extension, their lives. And that was Elmer Waysmith's greatest crime. He was a man who always had to be in control.'

'So they all came together to get rid of the stepfather!' Voltaire exclaimed. He was staring at the family in disgust. 'But which one of them killed Alice Carling?'

'That, of course, was Harry Lyttleton.'

Sitting next to his wife, Harry jerked upright as if he had been electrocuted. 'No . . .' he gasped.

'There can be no doubt of it,' Pünd said. 'You pretended to be in love with her. It was from her that you learned the details of Margaret Chalfont's will and, as a result, this entire scheme was born.'

'It's not true!'

'She had your photograph. She believed everything you told her. It was you who played the part of Elmer Waysmith in the *pharmacie* and it is you who likes to wear white tennis shoes. You are wearing them even now. Unfortunately, when poor Miss Carling heard that Lady Chalfont had been poisoned with aconitine, she understood her part in what had occurred and threatened to go to the police. That was why she had to die.'

'You're wrong.'

'I am never wrong, Mr Lyttleton. And it is certain that you will face a terrible death, your head removed from your shoulders by the deadly fall of the guillotine.'

Harry Lyttleton had gone deathly pale. His wife was on the edge of tears. 'It wasn't Harry! He has an alibi. He was with me when I gave my talk at the Church of Saint-Jean-Baptiste!'

'You gave the talk. He was not present.'

'No!' Harry Lyttleton had got to his feet. 'It was him! He was the one who killed her. I had nothing to do with it. He was the one behind it! It was all his idea!'

He was pointing at Robert Waysmith.

Pünd smiled. 'And so, at last, the truth comes out.' He turned to Voltaire. 'You will forgive me, but I had to put the fear of death into him to force him to tell me what I already knew to be the case.'

'Robert Waysmith . . .'

'Yes. Robert Waysmith. He is the evil genius who concocted this entire plan.'

Harry Lyttleton sank back into his chair. Judith was crying now, clinging on to her husband's hand. Jeffrey Chalfont was scowling. His wife was in shock. Elmer Waysmith was staring at his son in disbelief. But Robert Waysmith had only contempt on his face. 'You bloody fool,' he muttered, addressing Harry. 'Why couldn't you keep your mouth shut? Don't you see? You've landed us all in it.'

'You're the devil,' Harry gasped, struggling for breath. 'You should never have come here—'

'That's enough!' Voltaire snapped. He nodded at Pünd. 'Please continue, Monsieur Pünd.'

Pünd began again. 'It was you, Robert, who impersonated your father at the *pharmacie* and purchased the aconitine before you joined him for lunch.'

'You're wrong, Mr Pünd. I told you. Before I met my father, I was with a client, Lucas Dorfman, in Antibes.'

'That may be true. But you also suggested that it took you a great deal of time to return to Nice because of the traffic and that was most certainly a lie.'

'How can you possibly know?'

'Because you were followed to the house by Mr Harlan Scott. He told me that he was unable to follow you back as it would be too easy for you to see his car. This suggests to me that the road must have been empty.'

The investigator leaned forward. 'You're right, goddammit,' he growled. 'There wasn't a single other car in sight. I had no choice but to let him go back on his own.'

'You stayed briefly with your client and raced back to Nice. This gave you more than enough time to enter the Hôtel Lafayette, change into your disguise, purchase the aconitine and then change back again, getting rid of the suitcase and walking stick before meeting your father at half past twelve as agreed.'

'You're suggesting I deliberately framed my father. Why would I want to do that?'

'On every occasion I have met you, you have defended your father and spoken up for him while at the same time making clear your hatred of him. It is evident that the way he has controlled you has considerably harmed your life. You wished to be an artist. That was your dream. But he refused to acknowledge your talent and forced you first into a career in law and then, when that did not succeed, into his own business, as a junior partner. You were terrified of him when you were a child. You told us this before the reading of the will. "*He's not quite the monster you think.*" That was what you said. But you were telling us that he was a monster nonetheless.'

'Robert . . .' Elmer couldn't believe what he was hearing. 'I always cared for you. I never did anything to hurt you.'

Robert said nothing.

'You son blames you for the death of the mother he loved,' Pünd said. 'She took her own life and he believes this was because of you. You told us that she suffered from a condition known as "housewife syndrome". I have read of this. The symptoms are said to be fatigue and unhappiness, but there are psychiatrists who are now suggesting that this may tell only half the story. A great many men see their wife as their property, someone who can do nothing without their approval. These women are shown no respect. Their self-confidence is destroyed. Is that how your mother was, Robert?'

'Yes!' When Robert looked up, there was something almost childlike about him; the child he had once been. 'She did everything for him. She lived for him . . . but only because she wasn't allowed any life without him. And in the end, it became too much for her. She killed herself because of him.'

'That's not true!' Elmer rasped.

'You didn't even come home when you heard the news, Pa! You were too busy in Geneva selling the paintings that you got cut-price from the Nazis!'

'That's a lie!'

'You know it's true.' Robert pointed at Harlan Scott. 'He knows everything!'

Pünd turned once again to the art historian. 'You spoke to Robert Waysmith at the gallery,' he said. 'He then invited you to the Chateau Belmar to meet his father. Were you surprised?'

'I was very surprised, Mr Pünd. I never thought he'd invite me into the house. But he insisted on his father's innocence and wanted me to see the Cézanne for myself, to show that they had nothing to hide.' He glanced at Elmer. 'I must say, his father was much less pleased to have me here.'

'You met in the *grand salon*. Can you recall if the windows were open?'

'They were closed when I arrived. Robert opened them to allow me to smoke.'

Pünd smiled. 'He opened the windows for the same reason that he invited you to the house. Always the manipulator! He knew that his father would argue with you. He knew that Lady Chalfont, on the terrace above, would hear everything that was said. He was creating a motive – a reason for his father to murder her.'

'And that was why she changed her will!' Jean Lambert had been listening to all this in horrified silence, but he couldn't wait any longer.

Pünd sighed. 'When we first spoke, you told me that Lady Chalfont was under a great deal of strain when she made that call. You said she did not sound well.'

'That's right. She had a chill, I think. A sore throat . . .'

'I do not believe it was Lady Chalfont at all. We have an actress amongst us. It was when she was playing Mata Hari that Lola Chalfont met her husband-to-be. Jeffrey Chalfont told us that she captured both the look and the voice of the famous spy. I am sure it would be a matter of no difficulty for her to impersonate Lady Chalfont, particularly if she feigned a sore throat.'

'I did what I was told!' Lola hadn't even tried to deny it. 'I never wanted any part in it! I didn't . . .' She buried her face in her hands.

'You must tell me about Mademoiselle Alice,' Lambert said. 'Did she really tell him what Lady Chalfont had written in her will?'

'I am afraid so. Poor Alice was an innocent, a country girl who dreamed of perhaps one day living in London or Paris. But she was also a Catholic who went every week to the church of Saint Isidore. There is, I am sure, no way she would have considered marrying a man who was divorced and it was not Harry Lyttleton who had beguiled her.'

'It was Robert.' Jean Lambert stared at him with something close to hatred.

'Handsome, ambitious, wealthy . . . and single! It could be no-one else. It was he, of course, who impersonated his father in the pharmacy. He had, after all, his father's looks. I do not know how he persuaded Miss Carling to help him. Perhaps he told her that he was playing a joke. But once she realised what she had done, she was finished.'

'But what about the photograph?' Lambert asked. 'You said she was carrying a picture of Harry Lyttleton!'

'Why do you not answer, Monsieur Lyttleton? You know it is all over. You have nothing more to lose.'

Harry had been sitting like a dead man. His face was grey, his eyes empty. He gestured at Robert. 'He made me give him a photograph of myself – and he pressed it against her lips to make it look like I was the one she had been seeing. He said we didn't have any choice.'

'It is an irony, is it not, that Robert hated his father because of his controlling nature – but he was exactly the same. He controlled all of you and talked you into this wicked scheme. It was a diversion! Harry Lyttleton was indeed at a lecture and then at a dinner where he would have been seen by many people at the time when Alice was killed. Robert committed the murder. But Harry had the alibi. They exchanged places.'

'I'm so sorry . . .' Harry was holding his wife's hand as if for the last time.

'What will happen now?' Jeffrey asked.

Frédéric Voltaire took over. 'Robert Waysmith – you will be charged with the murders of Lady Margaret Chalfont and Alice Carling . . . murders with premeditation. Jeffrey Chalfont, Lola Chalfont, Harry Lyttleton and Judith Lyttleton, you will be charged as accessories to murder and quite possibly for the attempted murder of Elmer Waysmith. As it turns out, Mr Waysmith himself is the only innocent man in the room – at least in so far as these deaths are concerned. But the Sûreté will be working with Monsieur Scott to discover the truth behind your repulsive trade in stolen art.'

Robert Waysmith looked up, suddenly defiant. 'Oh . . . I can give you lots of evidence, Mr Voltaire. I'm going to make sure Pa gets what's coming to him. At least I'll die with a smile.'

Voltaire shook his head slowly. He was disgusted.

'There are cars waiting for you outside. You will not take anything with you. You are all of you to leave with me . . . at once.'

Two days later, Pünd and Voltaire met for the last time.

James Fraser was overseeing the departure from the Grand-Hôtel, checking the porters had brought down all the cases and settling the account. He would have been happy to stay another week, but Pünd wanted to be on his way. The death of Lady Chalfont had affected him more than he had expected because it had been so arbitrary. It wasn't even as if she had been the real target. She had never harmed or offended anybody and hadn't deserved her life ending this way, even if he could console himself that it was already over and it was perhaps only a few weeks that had been taken from her. Pünd was feeling a chill wind in the Riviera sunshine and knew that he had to go home. This time, he and Fraser were taking the plane.

He had not expected the Frenchman to come to the hotel. Voltaire himself was on his way back to Paris, travelling on his own. There is nothing a police officer finds more disagreeable than paperwork, but there was a mountain of it for him to process as a result of the five arrests he had made. More than anything, he longed to be back with his wife and son in their *appartement* in Montparnasse. He looked worn out. From the way he walked, clutching his injured arm and holding it closely to his side, it was clear that the wounds he had suffered fifteen years ago were still plaguing him.

He was waiting in the reception area when Pünd came out of the lift.

'Monsieur Pünd!'

'Monsieur Voltaire. I hoped I would see you again.'

'You are leaving.'

'We have a flight in two hours.'

527

'Then perhaps you will allow me a few minutes? There is something I wish to say.'

'Of course. Perhaps a last drink on the terrace?'

'That would be excellent.'

They found a table close to where Pünd had met with the art expert, Harlan Scott. Voltaire ordered *un grand crème*. Pünd chose mineral water.

'I will be brief,' Voltaire began. 'I wish, first of all, to apologise for the antagonism that I displayed when we first met. I will be honest and say I was irritated to be advised by my superiors that a crime committed on French soil was to be investigated by a detective from England. But for reasons that will be obvious to you, I also considered us to be enemies. It was foolish of me and I regret my error.'

Pünd held up a hand. 'Please do not concern yourself, Frédéric. I may call you that? My work would have been a great deal more difficult without you and I fully understand your perspective. I might have felt the same had our positions been reversed.'

'I also want to say that I was astounded by your perspicacity. All the evidence was there before me. I was present at almost every single one of the interviews you conducted. I met every suspect. And yet I saw nothing. It was only through the brilliance of your mind that the true circumstances of this terrible crime came to light. Everything they say about you is true, Atticus. You are a remarkable man.'

Pünd smiled – but modestly. 'You are too kind.'

Voltaire's eyes clouded. 'It seems strange to me that an entire family should be so tainted. Robert Waysmith is evidently a psychopath, but his father is little better. And as

528

for Jeffrey and Lola Chalfont and Harry and Judith Lyttleton, they allowed themselves to be led down a very dangerous path, to risk their liberty, their wealth and even their lives simply to rid themselves of a man who might not have been as much of a threat to them as they believed.'

'You will arrest Elmer Waysmith?'

'I think it is quite possible that he will escape justice. But he will have lost his wife, his son and his reputation. He will spend the rest of his life waiting for the knock on the door that will tell him his crimes have caught up with him. Are you a religious man, Atticus?'

'My belief in God was taken from me by my experiences in the war.'

'That is a shame. I have a belief in, if not God, then the possibility of divine retribution and it is this that has been delivered to Elmer Waysmith as surely as human justice will lay claim to his son.' He paused. 'You are not well, Atticus.'

'You can see it?'

'I do not need to. You told us all that this was your last case. You also said that you had met Lady Chalfont in a doctor's waiting room. It is serious?'

'My time is limited.'

'The world will be a poorer place without you.'

'Do not be sorry for me.' Pünd smiled. 'I must tell you, Frédéric, that I am at peace with my life and the leaving of it. *Je suis fatigué.* I have been tired for a long time. It is strange, do you not think, the life of the detective. We are not like other people. We make our living from evil and from inhumanity. Lady Chalfont is poisoned. The poor girl, Alice Carling, is strangled, just like the actress Melissa James. Sir Magnus Pye

529

is decapitated. His housekeeper is pushed down the stairs. On and on it goes. We arrive, we ask questions, we find the killers and they themselves are arrested and perhaps executed. But what have we really achieved? For every Robert Waysmith there is another malefactor waiting in the wings, preparing for his entry onto the stage.

'And it is inevitable that they will bring us down to their level. We will walk through the streets and we will see this person and that person and we will wonder what they are thinking, what they are planning, who they hate, how far they are prepared to go to achieve their ends. Every day, we see only the worst of humanity until we come to believe that every person on the planet may be tempted to do evil. Murder, blackmail, larceny, revenge . . . they become what you would call our raison d'être. That is our life. The detective has no escape. Without evil, there is no reason for him to exist.

'I will not miss it. I am looking forward to the great tranquillity that must come to all of us. You speak to me of divine retribution and I find in that some consolation. I do not know where I am going, but when I think of the time we have spent together and the work we have done, I take great comfort in what I leave behind.'

'I understand exactly what you say. I have a wife and a son. Were it not for them, I might feel the same.'

The drinks had arrived while they were talking. Pünd lifted his water and looked at the bubbles dancing to the surface, each and every one of them reflecting the sunlight. '*Au revoir, mon ami*,' he said.

'*Adieu*,' Voltaire replied.

The Third Anagram

After I had finished reading Blakeney's manuscript, I sat in silence for a long time.

My immediate reaction was that he had written the pages incredibly quickly, but then again, Conan Doyle famously created Sherlock Holmes and wrote the whole of *A Study in Scarlet* in three weeks, so twenty-eight pages in two days was hardly a world record. The main thing was that it didn't show. From the moment I had re-entered the world of Atticus Pünd, I had been impressed by Blakeney's writing ability. There were one or two moments when the language of a life-long police officer had intruded into the text, but otherwise it seemed to me that he had almost perfectly captured the voice of Alan Conway – or perhaps the voice of Eliot Crace imitating Alan Conway. The first continuation continuation novel? If the book ever did see the light of day, that wouldn't look great on the cover. More importantly, he had his own perspective. There was a sensitivity in his writing, particularly in that last farewell, that had taken me by surprise.

As to the solution itself, there was a part of me that was

annoyed. He had managed to see so many things that I hadn't. It should have been obvious to me that Elmer Waysmith had never been anywhere near that blasted pharmacy or that all those clues – the teapot lid, the book of matches, etc. – had been planted on purpose. Why hadn't I seen it? Perhaps I hadn't trusted Eliot enough. I mean, it had occurred to me that the matches with the name of the hotel printed on the cover had been placed there all too conveniently. But I had attributed it to his authorship without seeing it for what it really was: another piece of trickery by Robert Waysmith.

The most important thing was that I was quite sure Blakeney had got it right, which wasn't surprising, given both his experience and his liking for crime fiction. I read the pages a second time, searching for any flaws in his narrative, but could find none. Robert Waysmith had killed Lady Chalfont to take revenge on his father. He had persuaded the family to help him and they had agreed because they wanted control of the money. It was as simple as that.

I was tempted to telephone Blakeney to thank him and to congratulate him, but I couldn't do it. I was thinking of what Emma Wardlaw had said when she handed over the manuscript. Should I believe her? She'd had it in for me from the beginning. Did she have a personal reason for breaking any connection between Ian Blakeney and me? Perhaps. But what she had told me sounded horribly plausible. *He's getting close to you . . . pretending to be your friend.* Blakeney had come to the house and we'd spent more than an hour talking about Eliot's book before he'd mentioned that he had new evidence against me: the Rolex watch. Everything he had done had been carefully calculated. He'd said straight out that he didn't believe I had killed anyone, but at the same time he had made it clear that I was still under investigation. He hadn't returned my MG! Nothing about him was straightforward.

He had also said – in his letter – that he had found the third anagram that Eliot had concealed in the book, along with Belmar and Alice Carling. I was determined to find it for myself rather than hear it from him. It was all well and good to have solved Eliot's mystery novel, but the whole point was that it had to unlock the truth about who had killed Miriam Crace – and, perhaps, Eliot himself. That was what I needed to know.

All along, I had suspected Elmer Waysmith and in idle moments I had fiddled around with his name. Surely any character with Elmer as a Christian name would have to be an anagram! But I hadn't found it. If his middle initial had been H, he could have made HEALTHY SWIMMER, which would have been fun, if irrelevant. Otherwise, he yielded nothing and I was glad to turn to his son, Robert Waysmith. I remembered what Eliot had said on the radio. '*I've put in a secret message.*' So I wasn't looking for a name. It had to be an announcement.

ROBERT WAYSMITH.

It took me ten minutes to find it and I had to kick myself because I should have got it in seconds. But then I've never liked anagrams, which I've always found (like golf, bridge and home baking) to be a complete waste of time. But there it was, and – really – his great reveal was no surprise at all. I wrote the four words in block capitals and stared at them: Eliot's last message.

IT WAS MY BROTHER.

Friendly Advice

The doorbell rang. I looked through the peephole and saw Elaine Clover standing outside.

She was the person I most wanted to see, but I wasn't sure I wanted to let her in right now. This wasn't the right time. But I knew I had no choice. She might well have seen me through the window and I needed to talk to her. So I called out – 'One minute!' – hastily gathered up Blakeney's pages and tucked them away in a drawer. I slid a couple of dirty dishes into the dishwasher, grabbed my glasses and phone, and took one quick look around the room. I was still in the house in Muswell Hill and I'd been doing my best to keep it tidy in case Rob and Steve happened to come back. It was much roomier than my flat, with high ceilings, cornices and lots of original features, but its main showpiece was a kitchen that might have been delivered by a spaceship. I'd never seen so many knobs and buttons, blenders and processors, multiple ovens, cupboards and drawers. Practically the only device I'd used in the week I'd been there had been the kettle.

I opened the door. 'Elaine!' I said. 'I'm glad to see you.'

'I've just been to your flat. There were decorators there. They told me you'd moved out and I had to persuade them to give me this address. What's happened?'

'I was burgled.' I didn't want to go into it all, not with her.

'Oh my God! One thing after another! Are you all right?'

'Not really. Do you want to come in?'

We embraced and I showed her into the kitchen. It's funny how that's always the room of choice. Nobody actually lives in a living room any more – if they ever did. I noticed that Hugo had sprinted out of sight the moment he heard the bell and realised that he would be doing that for the rest of his life.

'I should have called ahead,' she said. 'But there are things I've got to tell you and I didn't want to do it over the phone.'

'Have you driven all the way here?'

'No. I've got a lunch in Hampstead and I thought I'd take a chance that you were in. If I'd missed you, I could have browsed in the bookshops or something. Did you know that Charles and I met in Hampstead?'

'I didn't.'

'I was living in a shared house in Frognal Lane.' She looked at me wistfully. 'That was a long time ago.'

'Would you like a coffee?' I asked.

'Please. White – no sugar.'

I found the percolator and made coffee for both of us as we talked around the subject that had brought her here. She looked as immaculate as ever – her clothes, her jewellery, hair that looked fresh from the hairdresser's. She really was a lady who lunched. I knew that, by contrast, I was a wreck. But I was entitled to be.

Finally, we were sitting together. I'd carried over a box of tissues and placed them between us, as if one or both of us might need them. 'So what's happened?' I asked.

'Tell me what Charles said to you,' she countered. 'When we spoke on the phone, you said he'd given you new information.'

'It was nothing that will help me,' I said gloomily. 'He'd spoken to Eliot about the death of his grandmother . . . that was all.'

'Poor Eliot! It's just so horrible. Every day I wake up, I can't believe he's dead. With Charles, I'd known him since he was a child.' She drew a breath. 'Emma Wardlaw came to see me yesterday.'

I felt a rising sickness in my stomach. I was glad we'd come to the crunch. I needed this to be over. But I was also afraid. My heart was beating so hard that I could feel its rhythm in every part of my body. 'What did she say?'

'They're going to arrest you, Susan. Very soon.'

I nodded, dazed. 'She told you that?'

'She said that they'd found fresh evidence in your flat. And they've had another witness report of your car being in Trafalgar Square . . .'

This was the first thing she'd told me that I didn't know. 'How did that happen?'

'A phone call.'

'Another anonymous tip-off?'

'I don't know. I suppose so. You can't drive from one side of London without being seen.' She realised what she'd just said. 'I was there when you arrived, Susan. You can tell me the truth. Did you drive . . . ?'

'Why are you even asking that, Elaine? Why would I lie to you?'

'The police are convinced you killed Eliot because he fired you and – I've got to tell you this – they're not going to find it very difficult to prove in front of a jury. If it goes that far.'

'That's what DI Blakeney said. He said there wasn't a jury in the country that wouldn't convict me.'

'He's right. But . . .' She hesitated. 'I could lie for you if you want. I could tell them I saw you coming out of the station.'

I looked at her hopefully. 'Would you do that for me, Elaine? Would you really perjure yourself in court?'

'If you wanted me to.'

I shook my head. 'No. I couldn't do that . . .'

'I'm so frightened for you, Susan. You have no idea what prison is like. You've seen what it's done to Charles. He's older than you, he's a man and he was strong when this all began, but I'm not sure you'll be able to survive it. First the humiliation. The arrest and the trial. The media hounding your family, writing lies about them, never leaving them alone. You must warn Katie and her children. Their lives are going to be torn apart.'

'You're scaring me, Elaine.'

'The system is vile. It's inhuman. I watched Charles being ripped to pieces and I can't bear for it to happen to you. I don't think you'll be able to survive one week in a women's prison. Every time I visit Belmarsh, it makes me sick. Charles often says he wishes he'd taken sleeping pills or thrown himself under a train before he was arrested. He says that it would have been easier for him in the long run. His life was over anyway.'

'Is that what you're advising me to do, Elaine?' I looked around me and noticed a rack of knives on the counter next to the fridge. They were Japanese, made by Gyuto. Damascus steel with maple wood handles. Typical Rob and Steve. They'd told me the blade would cut as easily through meat as through bone and that you wouldn't feel the difference. 'Are you saying I should kill myself?'

She reached out and gently laid her hands on mine. 'I could never do that,' she said. 'But as a friend, I must tell you that what's going to happen to you could be even worse than death. If you'll take my advice, you'll go far, far away. Don't let them put you in prison.'

'But if I try to run away, it'll make me look guilty.'

She leaned back. 'You are guilty, Susan. That's what they think.'

I stared at her, in shock. 'I have nowhere to go.'

'Then maybe you should find . . . an easy way. Avoid hurting people who are close to you. Don't put yourself through all this pain.'

I pulled out a tissue and wiped my eyes. 'I don't know,' I said. 'Maybe you're right.'

'I only want what's best for you, Susan.'

'I know that. But there is one thing I don't understand.'

'What's that?'

'You've just been to my flat. The decorators told you I was here. But how did you know where I lived in the first place?'

She looked stunned — as if it was the most absurd, irrelevant question I could have asked. 'Eliot told me,' she said at last.

'Why?'

'I don't remember. I wanted to know where you lived and he told me.'

'But why would you want to know that?'

She smiled, confused. 'I don't know what you're getting at, my dear.'

'Detective Inspector Blakeney said something very interesting to me just a few days ago. We were talking about the break-in at my flat. It wasn't a burglary, Elaine. Someone trashed the place and tried to kill my cat. It must have taken them a while, so he asked me who knew I wouldn't be at home that day. And there was something else. I didn't drive to the party, but someone still reported seeing my car in Trafalgar Square – and was even able to read part of the licence plate. It must have been someone who knew what car I drive.'

'And who would that be?'

'Actually, it might be you. Nobody else knew about my MG. Not Eliot, not Roland Crace, not Jonathan, no-one. When I visited Marble Hall, I parked in the car park. When I saw Dr Lambert, I had to leave the car round the corner from his house. But you've seen it lots of times. When I went to Gillian's, you saw me arrive.'

Elaine looked at me and spoke with total sincerity. 'I promise you, Susan, I never told anyone what car you drove.'

'That's not quite what I mean,' I assured her. 'You were also the only person who knew I was going to be in Belmarsh Prison – because you helped arrange it. I didn't tell anyone else. And that was when my flat was ransacked.'

'Susan, are you suggesting—'

I held up a hand, stopping her. 'You telephoned me when I was at the station,' I said. 'Where were you?'

'I was at home.'

'In Parsons Green.'

'Yes.'

'Well, that's definitely a lie, Elaine. Don't you remember? Somebody rang the doorbell in the middle of our conversation. Your doorbell plays a few bars of a piece of music by Bach. It's Charles at the piano. But the doorbell I heard was a very ordinary one. In fact, I think it was identical to mine.' I hurried on before she could interrupt. 'And there was another funny thing. When the doorbell rang, you lowered your voice. Why would you do that if you were in your own home – or anywhere else for that matter? But while you were there, smashing and tearing up everything you could get your hands on, you were disturbed by an Amazon delivery. There was a package on the floor, waiting for me when I got back. That was why you spoke more quietly. You didn't want the driver to know you were there.'

'Susan – this is madness. You don't know what you're saying.'

'You wrote "KILLER" on the wall. That was clever. It made everyone think I was being blamed for Eliot's death and it also made it more likely that I was the one who was responsible. I was to blame. But you were there to plant the watch, just as you had planted the piece of cloth and kicked in the grille of my MG earlier. You must have left the party shortly after Eliot and found him lying in the road. I have to say, it must have taken quite a mind, an incredible reservoir of hate, to turn what had happened into an opportunity. But that was when you got the idea. You decided to use his death to frame me. Punish me, the same way Charles has been punished . . . at least, that's how you saw it. And Charles is in on it too, isn't he? The two of you, working together. Why else would he have agreed to see me? He made it clear how much he hates me, but when I was with him, he couldn't stop himself. He told me that I was going to get a taste of my own medicine. That's what the two of you planned. The only trouble is, you've overreached yourself, Elaine. Coming here and telling me to slit my wrists in the shower or jump under a train. Did you really think that was going to work? Did you really think I was going to sit here and let you watch me die?'

She said nothing, but as I watched her, an impossible transformation came over her face. It was like a special effect on the cinema screen as layer after layer of her personality was wiped away, revealing the Fury beneath. It was the eyes that gave her away. The hatred that she felt for me – deep, vengeful, all-consuming – had finally been released, welling up from the very depths of her being. It was extraordinary, really. Nothing had changed. Her expression was frozen in place. Yet everything had changed.

'You were lying from the very start, weren't you,' I said. 'When we met at Causton Books, you pretended to be my friend because you were working out how to trap me. Did Eliot know too? Was he part of it?'

'Eliot knew nothing.'

And there it was. The admission. Game over.

'It doesn't matter anyway,' she went on. 'Nobody is going to believe you. As far as the world is concerned, we didn't have this conversation. I wanted you to feel what I felt, Susan, when you took Charles away, ruined our retirement, stole our last years together. I wanted you to understand what your high-mindedness, your cruelty, your intransigence did to us.'

'Charles killed Alan Conway. He tried to kill me.'

'I wish he'd succeeded. You bitch! He had done so much for you. If it hadn't been for him, you'd never have had a career in publishing. He took you in and gave you everything you wanted and you never showed him a shred of gratitude. Did you ever think about me and my daughters? My grand-children? Did you ever think about what you did to us?'

'I did nothing to you, Elaine. It was Charles.'

'Charles made a mistake, that's all. Two mistakes. He pushed that stupid author off the tower – well, he deserved it – and he trusted you.'

'Do you know who killed Eliot?'

'I don't care who killed Eliot! And no. I didn't see anything – but if I had, I wouldn't say. I heard a screech of tyres as I came out of the party, but I didn't see the car. Eliot was already dead. That was when I knew providence was on my side and that I could pay you back the way you so dearly deserved. I took a scrap of his clothing and his watch and some dust from the road and after that it was all so easy. You can tell the police anything you like, my dear, but they're not going to believe you. You can put a knife in yourself or you can wait for someone to do it to you in prison. Either way, you're finished. You're dead.'

She got to her feet and that was when I did something so stupid, looking back on it now, I honestly believe I deserved everything that followed. It had gone so well, but right then the cold-bloodedness of what she had done, the madness of it all, got through to me. She had said she'd wanted to be my friend and I'd believed her. More than that, by reporting Charles to the police, I felt I'd done her harm and therefore in some way I owed her. What a fool I'd been! For a brief moment, I was furious with both myself and her.

'It's not going to work, Elaine,' I called out to her.

'Go to hell, Susan.'

I pulled my mobile phone out of the tissue box, where it had been all along, and held it up for her to see. 'I've recorded every word of this conversation, Elaine. You talk about traps, but the moment you came through the door, you walked into mine. All I wanted was to hear it from your own lips – and you've spelled it out very nicely. I think you're the one who's going to need a lawyer. Now get out of here.'

She didn't move.

'Give me that,' she said.

'No. I'm giving it to the police.'

'You tricked me.'

'That's right. Just like you tricked me!'

'Give it to me!' She moved incredibly quickly. She had been standing near the counter and even as she spoke, her hand had whipped out and grabbed one of the Japanese knives. Suddenly I was looking at ten inches of razor-sharp steel.

'Don't be stupid, Elaine,' I said, doing my best to keep my voice steady, glancing around the room for anything I could use to defend myself. 'People will have seen you arrive. Your car is parked outside. If you hurt me, you're going to be the one who ends up in prison.'

'Give it to me!'

There had been a second transformation. It was only now that I realised Elaine wasn't just vengeful, she was seriously out of her mind. What was left was this crazed woman in Dior and Estée Lauder brandishing a hideous carving knife in a way that was both improbable and terrifying.

'Think of your daughters, Elaine. Think of your grand-children. Don't you want to see them again? Go home. We can forget about this . . .'

I was lying. Elaine had perverted the course of justice, obstructed the police and God knows what else. Nobody was going to give her a free pass and perhaps somewhere inside that broken mind of hers she knew it. She let loose a stream of swear words, screaming them as she moved towards me, and I was so paralysed by what she had become that I didn't realise what she was going to do until it was almost too late. I saw the knife above her head. I saw her bring it down in a vicious, scything motion. But it was only when the blade sliced through my upper arm and chest, cutting open my dress and the flesh beneath, that I understood I was in mortal danger and unless I reacted very quickly, I was going to die.

'Give me the phone!' she screamed, her voice like nothing I had heard before.

I backed away, aware of blood coursing down my arm and seeping through my clothes. There was no pain yet. That would come later. I tried to stop her. 'You don't know what you're doing, Elaine. Stop this! This is crazy!'

Somehow, I'd had the presence of mind to pick up a chair and I held it with the legs pointing towards her, using it to keep her away from me. She was slashing with the knife, left and right, left and right, eyes staring. I saw it sweep inches away from my face, just out of reach. My blood was splattering the white Carrara marble floor. And still she was screaming, a hysterical, meaningless cacophony. By this stage, all she wanted to do was kill me and to hell with the consequences. There was nothing I could say to her. The rising flood of grief and rage had finally burst its banks.

She lowered the knife and charged towards me. I chose the moment to thrust forward, pinning her between the four legs of the chair and propelling her backwards into a larder cupboard, which happened to be open. There was a crash of breaking wood. Spice bottles and storage jars cascaded onto the floor and exploded all around her. She lashed out with her left hand and I lost hold of the chair. It was sent hurtling to one side and now there was nothing between Elaine and me. She saw her opportunity, rushing towards me with the knife. I backed away, almost slipping on my own blood. I couldn't stop her. It was over for me.

I heard an explosion of wood and glass and saw the window on one side of the room disintegrate as a metal cylinder – which I would only later recognise as a dustbin – smashed into the room. It came within an inch of hitting me and for a terrible moment I thought someone else had joined in the attack, that somehow Charles had got out of Belmarsh and had arrived in time to help his wife. But it had been used as a battering ram, not a weapon, and a second later, Detective Inspector Ian Blakeney climbed through the hole that had been made and imposed himself between me and Elaine, his face flecked with blood from the fragments of broken glass.

'Drop the knife, Mrs Clover. I'm a police officer.'

Elaine stared at him.

'Put the knife down. Now!'

The madness had already left her. As she realised what she had done, she burst into tears, howling like an animal. Her hand fell and she dropped the knife, which broke on the marble floor. Blakeney was unarmed. It was only his personality that was keeping her at bay.

'I want you to kneel down and put your hands behind your head, Mrs Clover. I don't want to hurt you.'

Slowly, dazed, still sobbing, she did what he had said.

He looked at me. 'Susan, do you have a phone? I want you to call 999 and then hand it to me. Can you do that?'

I no longer had the phone! I must have dropped it when I picked up the kitchen chair. For a terrible moment, I wondered if Elaine had managed to destroy it after all. Not that it would really matter. Not after what Blakeney had witnessed. He was standing over her, his eyes fixed on her. I felt something pulling at my dress and remembered that it had a pocket. The phone was inside. I must have slipped it in there without realising what I was doing. I did as he asked. I dialled the number and when it was answered, I handed it to him.

That's all I remember. After that, like a character in a Victorian novel, I think I must have passed out.

Explanations

The next twenty-four hours were confused. I was taken to the wonderful Royal Free Hospital in Hampstead and I had to stay in overnight, but the knife wound was less serious than the amount of blood had suggested. Elaine Clover had managed to draw a line about an inch deep across my arm and chest and although I would carry a thin scar for perhaps the rest of my life, at least she hadn't cut into an artery. The wound hurt much more after it was dressed, but that was a good sign, the nurse said cheerfully. There's no healing without a little pain.

Detective Inspector Blakeney came to see me the following morning, alone. He sat on a chair some distance from the bed and I felt a strange sense of embarrassment, propped up in my hospital nightie. I didn't like him seeing me like this. Even so, I was glad he had decided to visit. There were explanations I wanted to hear, starting with how he had come to throw a dustbin through the front window of a house that did not belong to me. Heaven knows what Rob and Steve were going to say. I might have pushed our friendship over the edge.

'Perhaps I shouldn't admit this,' Blakeney said. 'I was driving up from Finsbury Park and I decided to call by the house . . .' he shifted uncomfortably on his seat '. . . to see if you'd looked at the pages.' He went on hurriedly. 'You see, I've never shown anyone my work before – let alone a professional editor – and I couldn't get it out of my head. I was up half the night, worrying about what you'd think.'

'What do *you* think?' I asked.

'Well, I've tried to capture Alan Conway's voice . . .'

'You've done more than that. I thought it was terrific. The writing was wonderful, and perhaps even more importantly, the ending makes complete sense. Robert Waysmith was the killer! Of course, I shouldn't have been surprised – it's what you do – but I'm still annoyed I didn't see it myself.'

'That's very kind of you . . .'

'I mean it. And thank God you turned up when you did!'

'Yes.' He nodded. 'I was at the door when I heard screaming coming from the kitchen. I looked through the window and to begin with I couldn't believe what I was seeing. There was Mrs Clover coming at you with a knife and you had your back to me, so I couldn't see if you'd been hurt. All I knew was that I had to get in there and stop her. I thought about ringing the bell, but there wasn't time. Then I saw the dustbin. I picked it up and threw it at the window.'

'Thank you,' I said. 'I think you may have saved my life.' There was something about those last three words I really disliked. They were such a cliché. But there was no other way to describe what he had done and they were certainly true. 'You know that it was Elaine – the piece of cloth, the grille of my M G, the Rolex watch. She was punishing me for what she thought I'd done to her husband. It's all on my phone. I recorded her. She told me everything.'

'You'd managed to work that one out then.'

'Yes. I should have just let her walk out of the room and think she'd won – but I was stupid. I showed her my phone and told her I'd made a recording. It's exactly the same mistake I made with Charles when he attacked me at Cloverleaf Books. Why couldn't I keep my big mouth shut?'

'You're being unfair on yourself, Susan. It was a natural reaction after everything she'd done to you. You wanted to show her it was over. You just didn't realise she was going to turn into—'

'Mrs Bates in *Psycho*.' That was what he was probably thinking too, although he'd never have said it, not officially. 'Well, I hope that means I'm not a suspect any more,' I said.

'I think I'd already come to that conclusion,' Blakeney agreed. 'I told you from the start I didn't think it was very likely that you had killed Eliot Crace—'

'Very likely . . .?'

'We had to pursue every line of inquiry, Susan. Anyway, it's over now. I have your phone. Mrs Clover is in custody.'

I shifted position and felt my injury protest. 'Can I ask you something which may surprise you?' I said. 'Are you going to have to prosecute her? Despite what she did to me, I don't think Elaine is a bad person. I think she needs help. What happened to her – what I put her through – made her lose any sense of perspective. I feel sorry for her.'

'First of all, Susan, you did nothing to her. Her husband was a murderer and even if you'd stayed silent, there was no way he was going to walk away from what he'd done – the burnt-out office and all the rest of it – so put that thought out of your head. As for Elaine Clover, I'm afraid it's out of my hands. She tried to kill you. I saw it with my own eyes. And while she's been wasting our time with her lies and contrivances, let's not forget that the real killer of Eliot Crace is still out there, sitting pretty.'

'Roland Crace.'

'We'll come to that . . .'

'It was my brother,' I said. I had to let him know I'd worked it out.

'Yes.' He smiled. It was something he didn't do very often. 'You really liked what I wrote . . . the style, I mean?'

'I'd say you're a natural-born writer – and it's put a thought in my mind. Do you think you could write another twenty thousand words connecting what happened after Alice Carling was found dead with the chapter you wrote?'

'Why?'

'Because then we'd have a book that we might be able to publish.'

He shook his head. 'That's a terrible idea.'

'Tell me about Roland Crace. Are you going to interview him again?'

'I already have and I'm afraid I'm going to have to disappoint you. I spoke to him yesterday evening and confronted him with what Charles Clover told you when you visited him in Belmarsh. Roland admitted that he, his brother and his sister did indeed conspire to kill their grandmother – if you can call three kids meeting in an empty cottage a conspiracy. He remembers the three of them making a potion which included the cough medicine that Eliot had stolen from the family doctor and he accepted that it might have contained some quite toxic substances, too, including crushed berries taken from a yew tree. If Miriam Crace had drunk it, there was every chance she could have died, although I'm not sure the lemon and ginger pick-me-up would have been enough to hide the taste. Not with all the other stuff that was in there. She'd have known something was wrong.

'But that wasn't what Roland intended anyway. He knew that Julia had taken the bottle of so-called poison into her room and he was just scared that she was going to use it. Her grandmother had humiliated her in front of the entire family – something about her weight and a party dress. Roland had spent half his life protecting both his siblings and that was what he did then. He sneaked into her room and stole it, but he didn't go anywhere near his grandmother's room. That's his story, anyway. He went to the bathroom at the far end of the corridor and poured it down the toilet—'

'Unaware that Eliot had seen him leaving.'

'Exactly. He's adamant that he didn't kill her, and I think I believe him. As far as I can see, someone else in the house learned what the kids were up to and they snatched the opportunity to feed the old woman with real poison. I have ordered an exhumation, by the way. I'm afraid we have no choice now but to dig her up.'

'So Eliot got it wrong!' I said. 'It's tragic, really. All his life, he thought his big brother was a murderer, but he kept it secret because of the love between them.'

'But then Roland had an affair with his wife.'

'And the book was his way of getting back at him.'

'I'm afraid so.' Blakeney paused. 'When are they letting you out of here?'

'They want the doctor to have one last look at me but I should be home by midday. And by home, I mean my own place. I'm afraid my friends won't be too pleased with me – or with you, for that matter. That was their front window you smashed.'

'Do you want me to apologise?'

'Not at all. I've never been happier to see anyone in my life.' Except, I thought, for Andreas when he fought his way through the flames to pull me out of the Cloverleaf office after Charles had set it on fire.

Blakeney got to his feet – but before he left, he had one more thing to say. 'You know who the real killer is, don't you? You've worked out who killed Miriam Crace all those years ago and Eliot Crace now.'

I couldn't help smiling. 'How do you know?'

'Well, don't take this the wrong way, but it's the way you're sitting there. It's the first time I've seen you looking pleased with yourself.'

'Well, I think I deserve it. And you're right. I think I have the answer.'

'Are you going to tell me?'

'Not right now, if you don't mind, Detective Inspector. I've had a rough twenty-four hours. But if you'll answer something for me, I might be tempted to give you a clue.'

'Go ahead.' He perched by the window.

'I'm speaking out of turn and I'm not out to cause anyone any trouble, but I've got to ask you if your sidekick, Detective Constable Wardlaw, was telling me the truth.'

'You know she'd hate the word *sidekick*.'

'I'm delighted. I'll use it the next time we meet.'

'What did she say?'

'It was when she delivered those pages you sent. Basically, she said you were pretending to be my friend but it was all untrue. Behind my back, you were convinced I had killed Eliot and you were just hanging around in the hope I'd say something that would give me away.'

Blakeney had shown no expression while he listened to this. It was a while before he spoke.

'She said that?'

'Yes. I repeat, I don't want to get her into trouble, but it would be good to know where I am with you. It seems to me that Emma Wardlaw had it in for me from the moment you and I met and I wonder why.'

'I'm sorry, Susan. Wardlaw's not such a bad person when you get to know her. She's smart. She's honest. We've worked together for a long time. But – I'm telling you this in confidence – eighteen months ago, she got divorced. It was unpleasant. There's a child involved. And it's done her head in. She hasn't taken to being a single mum and she doesn't know where she stands. If she reacted to you that way, and I'm not for a minute excusing her, it's probably because she was worried about any feelings I might have for you. She's quick off the mark when it comes to that sort of thing and she was afraid you might get in the way.'

'Feelings?'

'Let's just say, she didn't want us to be friends.'

There were plenty of other questions I could have asked right then, but I let it go. 'You want a clue,' I said.

'If you'll be so kind.'

'Well, you were the one who gave it to me, so I suppose that makes us quits. It was in that notebook you found at Eliot's house. He wrote down a lot of things that turned up in the solution to who killed Margaret Chalfont. Lola performing as Mata Hari, for example. And there were two notes that set me thinking. Kenneth Rivers being treated for arsenic poisoning was one of them.'

'I rather suspect that it was arsenic that killed Miriam Crace,' Blakeney said.

'I agree. But it was the other clue that gave everything away. Eliot wrote a question. "*Why did Bruno leave?*"'

'I'm not even sure who Bruno was.'

'He's a tiny character in the book. He never even appears, but some of the characters talk about him. He was the gardener at the Chateau Belmar. There was also a Bruno at Marble Hall. He was Miriam Crace's chauffeur and I only know about him because Leylah mentioned him to me when we had drinks at the Savoy. But here's the thing. When Eliot was writing his book, there was a sort of schizophrenia going on in his head. He was thinking about his own family and his childhood at Marble Hall – and at the same time he was creating a parallel world with Lady Margaret Chalfont and her family at the Chateau Belmar. And I think, when he wrote that question – *Why did Bruno leave?* – he had forgotten which one he meant.'

'Bruno the gardener or Bruno the chauffeur.'

'The gardener didn't leave. Cedric talks about him in Chapter Eighteen.'

'So Eliot must have been thinking about his grandmother's chauffeur.'

'There was something he knew, or half knew. That's why the name crops up twice. And it suddenly struck me, I don't know how, that it was the key to the whole thing.' I was suddenly exhausted. I sank back into the pillows. 'But that's all you're getting for now, Detective Inspector. There are still a few things I need to work out.'

He moved to the door and opened it. But before he left, he turned to me. 'Could you do me a favour, Susan, and call me by my first name?' he asked.

'I'm not going to do that until the case is over.'

'And when that might be?'

'I'd like to see Jonathan Crace and Roland. And I also need to speak to Julia. She teaches under the name of Julia Wilson at a school in Lincoln – she said it was called St Hugh's. Do you think you could get hold of her for me?'

'Yes.'

'And then let's all meet at Marble Hall. We have to go back to where it all began.'

Back to Marble Hall

It felt odd, returning to Marble Hall in the back of a police car with Wardlaw driving and Blakeney next to her, but they still hadn't released my MG – it was now being used as evidence against Elaine Clover – and I didn't fancy the train. We turned into the gates and drove through woodland. For the first time, I noticed the ruined cottage where three children had once hidden themselves away, pretending to be a secret society called the Rogue Troopers to plot the murder of their grandmother. I leaned forward as the main house came into view, its ivy and gabled windows, its wings and towers all bolted together as if in homage to every Golden Age mystery. It all felt completely right. This wasn't just the end of a journey but the laying to rest of any number of ghosts.

The car park was empty. DI Blakeney had insisted that the house should be closed to the public while we were there and although Jonathan Crace had grumbled – the loss of even a single day's revenue was a blow to him – he had been forced to comply. The Little Parlour Tea Room was dark. The gift shop was selling no gifts. The entire house had an unwelcoming feel that no tourist would have noticed but which made it truly authentic for the first time since the death of Miriam Crace.

Frederick Turner was waiting for us at the main entrance and as he limped towards the car, more worn out than he had been the last time I came here, who else could I think about but Frédéric Voltaire? I had met Frederick most recently at the party and he had seemed more conciliatory, but I wondered how he would greet me now. I remembered how offended he had been by what he saw as my attack on Miriam Crace and how he had virtually thrown me out. I didn't think he'd be happy that I'd returned.

I was in the company of two police officers, though, and that made a difference, and as for Frederick, he was there in an official capacity – to open the door and show us in. He was reserved but polite, addressing himself more to Blakeney than to me. 'The others are waiting for you in the dining room. I'm afraid the kitchens are closed, but there is coffee in in the room. If there's anything else you need, please let me know. This way . . .'

As he showed us through the silent house, the lights off and the rooms all empty, it occurred to me that this was how Frederick had lived for the last seven years, still trapped in the same building where he had been brought as a child. He'd once joked that he might come back to haunt the place, but in a way he already did. Everyone else had gone. Miriam was dead and now Eliot was too. What must it be like to endlessly walk these corridors and stairways as the only living memory of what had once been? Every day, when the tourists left and the ticket sellers and the other ladies went home, he would be here on his own, making his way up to the suite of rooms that he still occupied on the second floor. And what then? A box set on Netflix? A pile of books? A ready-prepared dinner-for-one heated up in a microwave? It would have driven me mad.

He showed us into the dining room, which I had already visited but which had made little impact on me when I first saw it. This time, I wondered if Eliot hadn't used many of its features as inspiration for the *petit salon* where the Chalfonts had taken their breakfast. There were the same double windows, the antique rosewood dining table, even a grandfather clock. I noticed a painting on the wall: a vase of tulips, which, though clearly not painted by Cézanne, could have been the inspiration for the masterpiece that Eliot had described. There was an unpleasant smell in the air, a mustiness that I'd somehow missed the last time I came here. Perhaps it had been less apparent when the place was filled with tourists. It was the smell of loneliness, of a lifestyle long forgotten.

Three people were waiting for us.

Jonathan Crace was at the head of the table. Of course. Where else would he have chosen to sit? Today, he was wearing a blue blazer and striped tie. They went well with the ginger hair and the signet ring. Roland Crace was next to him, already avoiding my eye and looking nervous . . . as well he might. The last time we had spoken, I had accused him of cheating on his own brother and he had thrown me out of Eliot's house. At the other end of the table, keeping her distance from her brother and her uncle, Julia Crace didn't look at all happy about being dragged down here from Lincoln. I wondered how Blakeney had managed it. Had he threatened to arrest her if she failed to show up?

None of them was pleased to see me. For the moment, they said nothing. But I could tell that Jonathan Crace was furious. He must have been informed that I'd had nothing to do with Eliot's death, but I'm sure he still saw me as the architect of all his misfortunes.

Frederick Turner hovered at the door. 'I'll leave you to it,' he said.

'I think you should stay with us, Mr Turner,' Blakeney said. 'You were here from the very start and I'd have said you were very much a witness to what happened.'

'Are you sure?' Frederick glanced at Jonathan as if asking his permission to remain.

'If the police officer wants you to stay, you might as well sit down,' Jonathan snapped. 'By the way, the coffee is revolting. I don't suppose you can make some more?'

There were two coffee flasks and a plate of biscuits on the table. I was reminded of my initial meeting at Causton Books. That could have taken place a century ago.

'Yes. I can go to the kitchen—'

'I think we can manage without coffee, if you don't mind, Mr Crace,' Blakeney said, not hiding his distaste. The way Jonathan had spoken, he could have been addressing a waiter or a servant. He closed the door as Frederick reluctantly took his place at the table, keeping as far away from everyone else as he could. Wardlaw and Blakeney sat next to each other. I took a place opposite Julia.

'Why is she here?' Roland asked, his voice utterly flat and unfriendly. He meant me.

'I know it's unorthodox,' Blakeney replied. 'But it was Ms Ryeland who asked for this meeting. Given that she was working with Eliot and was unfairly accused of his murder, I felt she had a right to a hearing.'

I expected Wardlaw to show her disapproval but Blakeney must have had a word with her because for once she kept her thoughts to herself.

'Forgive me.' Jonathan Crace didn't sound remotely apologetic. 'Are you telling me that you've made us come all this way simply to listen to this woman complain about the way she was treated?'

'No, sir.' Blakeney looked as angry as I felt. 'There's rather more to it than that.'

'Does she know who killed Eliot?'

'Yes. As a matter of fact, I do,' I said. I couldn't hold back any longer. I looked him straight in the eye.

'So why don't you tell us?'

'Eliot was killed by the same person who murdered Miriam Crace.'

Jonathan swallowed, as if he had accidentally eaten something unpleasant. 'My mother was not murdered,' he said. 'Dr Lambert lives down the road, he'll tell you—'

'He'll tell us what you paid him to say twenty years ago,' I interrupted. 'That she died of mitral stenosis. But you know that's not true. She was poisoned.'

'I think you should be very careful what you say, Ms Ryeland.'

'What? Or you'll threaten me with those very expensive lawyers you're always going on about? I think we've gone past that, Jonathan. And you can call me Susan, by the way.' I was already on the edge of losing my temper. He had a way of making 'Ms' sound like an insult.

'Well, I wish to place it on record that I never paid Dr Lambert a single penny—'

'You need to be aware that Dr Lambert has made a statement in which he contradicts you, Mr Crace,' Blakeney said, and I loved the deliberately cold and officious tone of his voice. 'As a result of our inquiries, we have interviewed him under caution and he has admitted receiving a quite considerable sum of money from the estate to say that your mother died of natural causes, even though this was clearly not the case. You will be aware that we have requested an exhumation, which will be taking place later this month.'

Jonathan took the knock and tried to pretend it hadn't hurt him. 'That wasn't me,' he insisted. 'If it happened, I knew nothing about it.'

'I'm afraid he's given a very different version of events, sir. He also has documentary evidence. The money was paid to him in the form of a cheque and it's your name on the dotted line.'

I must admit it was delightful watching Jonathan squirm. A lot of the colour had left his face. 'I was protecting my mother's legacy,' he said at length. 'I did nothing wrong.'

'That is not the case, sir. You were perverting the cause of justice—'

'It was twenty years ago.'

'But it was still a crime and it may well be that charges will be brought against you.'

'How was I to know?' Jonathan insisted. For a moment, he sounded almost tearful. 'Her heart could have stopped at any time.' He regained his composure. 'Why would anyone want to kill her?' he demanded.

'If you'll let me speak, I'll tell you,' I said.

'All right.' Jonathan slumped in his chair. 'Get on with it, then.'

'Do you have to be so rude?' I wanted to ask him. 'What have you ever done in your entire, miserable life that entitles you to talk to me like that?'

But I didn't. Instead, I began.

'You might like to know that your mother was almost certainly poisoned by arsenic,' I said. 'Her husband, Kenneth, had a lifelong interest in taxidermy. He was a taxidermist himself, but he also bought animals that had been killed and stuffed years before. You may not be aware of this, but taxidermists once used arsenic-based insecticidal soaps to clean the insides of dead animals. They say that if you pick up a specimen that's more than fifty years old, you should always wear a mask and gloves. You can quite easily kill yourself and that is, in fact, what nearly happened: Kenneth became seriously ill. Dr Lambert described treating him for lesions and warts, which are both symptoms of arsenic poisoning, and he prescribed something called dimercaprol, which I've looked up on Google and it turns out it's the classic cure. Speaking personally, I think taxidermy is disgusting, but the point is that anyone could have sneaked into Kenneth's workshop and scratched enough arsenic out of a stuffed owl and a couple of hedgehogs to kill everyone in the building.'

'Why am I here?' Julia asked. 'Why do I have to listen to this?'

'Don't you want to know who killed your grandmother, Julia?' I asked her.

'Not really. I'm just glad she's dead.'

562

'You're here because you may have information that helps us, Miss Crace,' Blakeney explained.

'I don't know anything.'

'But you and your two brothers talked about killing Miriam,' I reminded her. 'You wanted to poison her.'

'That was just a game. And we didn't know anything about arsenic.'

'That may be true. But after Eliot was caught trying to steal poison from Dr Lambert's medicine bag, the entire house knew what you were thinking. And somebody realised that you'd given them a fantastic opportunity. They could poison Miriam with arsenic and, with a bit of luck, nobody would even notice. If they did, it was you children who would get the blame. Either way, they'd be in the clear.'

'Why would anyone want to kill her?' Roland asked. 'Grandma was eighty-three years old. She was ill. She was going to die anyway.'

'That's the question everyone asked in your brother's book,' I said. 'Why would anyone want to kill Lady Margaret Chalfont? But there was one person in this room who had every reason to kill Miriam.' I turned on Jonathan Crace and rather enjoyed seeing him trying to avoid my eye. 'She was threatening to sell the estate to American interests. I think you'd have happily killed her to prevent that.'

'It was all words. She would never have done it.'

'You say that now. Were you so sure of it then?'

'Are you saying I killed my own mother so that I could take over her legacy?'

'No, Jonathan. I'm just saying you could have. Just as

ANTHONY HOROWITZ

Roland and Julia could have killed her to stop her taunting and teasing them. I know you like to pretend this isn't true, but you know perfectly well that your mother was so vile that simply to meet her was a good enough reason to want to kill her – your lawyers probably hated her too.

'But the actual reason Miriam Crace was murdered was very human, very understandable. It's nothing that anyone has ever considered, but it's been in front of us all the time.'

I turned to Julia.

'I met your aunt Leylah for a drink and she said something very strange. It's been on my mind ever since. She was telling me how everyone in the Crace family was a liar. Jonathan had lied about the death of his daughter. Gillian had lied to Eliot. And then she said: "*Freddy lied about his car accident – you should ask Julia what really happened.*" I remember the exact words. So let me ask you now. In what way did he lie to you?'

'What has my accident got to do with anything?' Frederick interrupted. It was the first time he had spoken since he had sat down.

'I don't know what you want me to say,' Julia complained.

'Just tell me what happened.'

She answered before he could. 'We were driving through west London. Uncle Fred – that was what I always called him – was taking me to the airport. We were in Kensington High Street and there was a red traffic light. I didn't realise what was about to happen until it was too late. He drove straight through it and a lorry, crossing the junction, smashed into us. It hit the driver's side of the car, which was why he was the one who was more injured. I got away with a broken collarbone and cuts and bruises.'

'I told you about this,' Frederick said. 'I wasn't concentrating. I had flu.'

'No. That's not true.' Julia had finally answered my question. 'I know that's what you told everyone, but you weren't ill. You were fine. You just weren't looking where you were going. You didn't see the light was red.'

Frederick stared at me balefully. 'This happened a long, long time ago,' he complained. 'It was my fault and I was the only one who was badly hurt. Why bring it up now?'

'Why did you lie?'

'I didn't! Well . . . maybe I did. I felt dreadful about what had happened. Julia broke her collarbone. She missed her flight. What was I meant to say? That I was asleep at the wheel?'

'You could have told her you were colour-blind.'

Nobody spoke. Everyone was staring at Frederick.

'Confusing red and green is one of the most common symptoms of colour blindness,' I went on. 'Drivers who are colour-blind have to be aware of the *position* of each light. They don't think red, yellow, green. They think top, middle, bottom.'

'So what? So what?'

'Are you right-handed or left-handed, Frederick?'

'Why do you want to know that?'

'Please answer the question, sir,' Blakeney cut in.

'I'm left-handed,' Frederick admitted.

'I already know that,' I said. 'When you were at the party, you were holding a champagne glass in your left hand. Your right hand was in your pocket.'

'My mother was left-handed.' It was Jonathan who had spoken and it was the first useful thing he'd said.

565

'I know that too,' I went on. 'When I was doing the tour of this house, I went into her office and saw her collection of twenty-three left-handed pens. She was also colour-blind. After Eliot went on *Front Row*, a journalist called Kate Greene wrote an article in the *Daily Mail* in which she mentioned that Karim and Njinga were both colour-blind, *like their creator, Miriam Crace*. You all know that being colour-blind and being left-handed are major genetic traits. Eliot told me that Frederick changed after his accident. He became angry and more distant. I think that was because he'd realised the truth.' I paused. After everything I had been through, I wanted to enjoy the moment. 'Miriam Crace was his mother.'

Both Jonathan and Roland Crace looked shocked. Julia was simply intrigued. Frederick had lowered his head, trying to hide his expression.

'Frederick told me that he came to Marble Hall in 1961, when he was almost six years old,' I said. 'That means the year of his birth was 1955. He had spent the first five years of his life in the St Ambrose Orphanage and Children's Home in Salisbury, which had Miriam Crace as its patron. He believed that his mother was a Traveller called Mary Turner and that his father was an itinerant worker – which would explain his mixed heritage. I imagine you've already checked that out, Frederick. You know it's not true.'

Frederick didn't reply.

'The year 1955 was also an important one in Miriam's life. That was when she came back from a six-month stay at a clinic in Lausanne, following a nervous breakdown caused by overwork. I think we've all guessed that there was no breakdown. There was an unofficial biography of Miriam written by a man called Sam Rees-Williams but never published. He claimed that she was promiscuous, that she had sexual affairs with both men and women and that this put her marriage under strain. He wrote that her visit to Lausanne was a trial separation from her husband, Kenneth, but he got that bit wrong. I think she was pregnant. Just like Alice Carling in Eliot's book, she had a Roman Catholic background. She couldn't have an abortion. It would have been unthinkable to have a child out of wedlock. So she gave birth to the child abroad and when she got home, she put him in her own orphanage and left him there for five years.'

'Who was the father?' Blakeney asked, but I think he already knew.

'That's a very good question,' I said. 'All along, I've been puzzled as to why Miriam, who seems to have been a world-class racist, adopted a mixed-race child at a time when attitudes were much more conservative than they are now. I asked Leylah about this. After all, Leylah had been the subject of racist abuse herself and there was that business with those two new characters in the books – Karim and Njinga. It was Leylah who told me about Miriam's chauffeur, a Black man called Bruno. According to Leylah, Miriam adored him. She told me there was even a photograph of him on the piano – and the moment she said that, I should have twigged. I mean, he was her driver. Not her husband!

'Unless, of course, he was also one of her lovers. This was 1955, let's not forget. Miriam's career was exploding. She was a married woman. When she gave birth to a mixed-race child, she must have believed that catastrophe was staring her in the face, that if she was found out, her rise to fame and fortune might be over. Why did Bruno leave? That's what Eliot asked in the notes to his manuscript, and the answer is that Miriam couldn't risk having him anywhere near her. She fired him or persuaded him to take a job elsewhere and then, once she'd got rid of him, she adopted their son and brought him to live in Marble Hall.

'It's a sad story. We have to look at it from Frederick's point of view. His whole life has been an enigma. He's never met his real father. He was adopted by this wonderful, famous author, but she never treated him like the rest of the family. He was given a room up in the attic and sent to the local state school. Miriam was his adoptive mother, but he wasn't even allowed to call her that. Later on, he was packed off to accountancy school to become the family's bookkeeper, and when that didn't work out, he was sent back to Marble Hall to be a glorified tour guide. Eliot called him a second-class citizen and that's exactly what he's always been.

'Do you think Frederick never wondered why he was being treated like that? Do you think he never asked himself why he was so different? Well, the answer came after his car accident. He already knew he was left-handed. Now he realised he was colour-blind.

'Just like Miriam.'

Frederick looked up. He'd had enough. I saw that at once. He just wanted this to be over.

'It was after the accident that I started asking questions,' he said. 'And you're right, Susan. It was easy to discover that Mary Turner had never existed and that my documents at the orphanage had been falsified. Then I made the connection with Lausanne. It was a prenatal clinic – nothing to do with stress or mental health. But, you know, I didn't need proof. I think, in my heart, I'd always known. A son will always recognise his mother even when that mother has lied to him every single day of his life.'

He drew a hand over his one good eye, fighting for control.

'My first thought was to tell the world what I'd found out, what a devil she was, what a monster. I knew all about the sex scandals too. Kenneth Rivers told me. He was my one friend in that house and I think he half suspected the truth about me. Maybe he saw something of her in me. I could have brought her down that way too – but what good would that have done me? I'd have lost everything. The family would have rejected me. And if I destroyed her reputation, we'd lose the money too . . . the books, the Little People! What would you have done if you'd been me? She sent my father away! She made sure I never met him and he never found out I existed. I finally managed to track him down, but I was too late. He was dead. He died on his own, in poverty. She ruined his life the same way she ruined mine.

'I knew I had to kill her. She was dying anyway, but I wouldn't be able to live with myself if I didn't pay her back. A mother . . . doing what she did to her own flesh and blood? I'd have loved to have strangled her. I'd have loved to have cut her throat. I thought about smothering her in her bed. But when I heard about the grandchildren and Eliot stealing medicine from Dr Lambert, that was when I knew it had to be poison. At the end of the day, I didn't care how she died so long as it was by my hand.

'So . . . you're right. I used arsenic that I scratched out of the feathers of one of the birds that Kenneth had bought as part of his collection. It was a kingfisher in a glass case. We'd always been told that we must never touch it and once I'd cut it open, I soon found out why. Of course, I couldn't be sure if it would work, but if it didn't, I'd try again.

'I didn't need to worry. It worked first time. You know, I think it was the only time in all the years I spent at Marble Hall that I felt complete. I had to laugh when Jonathan bribed Dr Lambert to issue a false death certificate. Natural causes! He was so scared that the truth about that bitch would come out that he helped cover up her murder.'

'You also killed Eliot Crace,' Blakeney said.

Frederick nodded. 'I was sorry about that. It wasn't something I wanted to do. But I had no choice.'

'You made a mistake,' I said. 'At the party, Eliot shouted to everyone that he knew who had killed his grandmother and that he had seen them go into her bedroom. He said he could see them right there, at the party. But he wasn't talking about you, Frederick. He was talking about his brother, Roland. Still you followed him out. You had a car. You ran him down.'

'It was his own fault. He shouldn't have boasted like that.'

'He wasn't boasting, Frederick. He was in pain. Like you.'

Frederick shrugged. 'I had to stop him talking. What else was I meant to do?'

Jonathan, Roland and Julia were frozen, unable to take in what had just occurred. In their different ways, all three of them had played a part in the events that had led to Eliot's death. Blakeney and Wardlaw got up and closed in on Frederick.

'You're going to have to come with us.' Wardlaw put a hand on his arm.

But I couldn't leave it there. 'I am so very sorry, Frederick,' I said. 'You were treated horribly and I can try to understand what you did when it comes to your mother. But Eliot was never a part of it. He was a victim as much as you. And killing him was unforgivable.'

'You're right, Susan.' Frederick Turner looked at me with the saddest smile I'd ever seen on a man. 'But you know what? I don't think he was so happy being alive. Maybe I did him a favour.'

They led him away. I watched them go. Then, without saying anything to anyone in the room, I followed him out. I wasn't sure how I was going to get back to London, but I didn't care. I just wanted to get into the fresh air and walk away.

It was finally over. I'd named the true killer and closed the investigation, but right then I felt only sadness. Two lives taken but so many more lives destroyed. That was the legacy of Marble Hall.

ONE YEAR LATER

Nine Lives

We had the launch at Hatchards, Piccadilly, one of my favourite bookshops in London. They have a round table in the room where you come in, next to the cash tills, and they had completely covered it with copies of my new book: *Pünd's Last Case* by Eliot Crace and Ian Black.

Why 'my' new book? Well, a lot had happened in the year since Frederick Turner was arrested and a huge scandal had exploded around the Little People and everything to do with Miriam Crace. I'm afraid there was no longer going to be any Netflix series. Suddenly, charity shops were piled high with unwanted copies of the books. Marble Hall had temporarily closed to the public while the estate reconsidered the family profile. I heard rumours that it had been privately sold to a Russian oligarch. I felt a little sorry for the Daphnes and the Enids who had worked there, but otherwise I couldn't help feeling that the house had got what it deserved.

As for me, I was now the head of my own publishing company, Nine Lives Books, named after Hugo, who was very much his old self. Perhaps I should have mentioned that Steve, who had lent me his house in Muswell Hill, was a successful investment banker and once he had got over the damage done to his property during my brief tenancy and had accepted that it wasn't my fault, we'd started talking and he'd decided to back me in a new enterprise. I had a tiny office in the back end of Farringdon, four members of staff and a roster – so far – of three books. But against all the odds, in a world dominated by multinationals, we were doing rather well.

After the storm broke and I'd watched the Fall of the House of Crace, I moved into action. I had already decided that I'd had enough of freelance editing and that it was time to go into business for myself. Once you've been a commissioning editor, no other job in publishing feels quite so worthwhile: finding and nurturing new talent, developing a book and watching it take shape – the content, the cover, the distribution, the reviews – and at last spotting its first appearance in the *Sunday Times* Top Ten and Nielsen BookScan.

To start with, I had forced my way into Michael Flynn's office at Causton Books and persuaded him to let me buy the rights to Eliot's book. Actually, I had blackmailed him. There were a whole lot of stories swirling around in the press and he knew how badly he'd behaved towards me, caving in to Jonathan Crace's demands to get rid of me for no good reason. And what had he got in return for all his efforts? He'd spent a fortune on two new editions featuring the Little People that would never see the light of day and as far as he was concerned, the less said the better. I promised to keep quiet if he let me have what I wanted. An unfinished manuscript, a whodunnit with no solution, was a small price to pay for my silence. He squeezed a small sum of money out of me, just to save face, but I knew that I'd paid a fraction of its true value.

I also had the ending! I had managed to find the extra twenty thousand words I needed to bulk out the last section. The cover looked terrific, quite art deco, a silhouette of Atticus Pünd walking between two bending palm trees, with the Chateau Belmar behind. I'd sent out advance copies to a variety of authors and critics and we'd had great feedback. Shari Lapena and Kate Mosse had provided cover quotes.

The second book from Nine Lives would be out in a couple of months' time. I'd managed to track down Sam Rees-Williams, the author who had written the biography of Miriam Crace. It had been commissioned by HarperCollins, but when they'd decided against publishing it, the rights had reverted to him. He had been utterly disheartened by what had happened and he had never written another book, but I visited him in Oxford – he was working as a security guard at the Pitt Rivers Museum – and persuaded him to have another try. He went back to his original manuscript, made the necessary changes and updated the ending. We'd given it a new title: *Miriam Crace and Her Little Shop of Horrors*. Of course it had to have the word 'little' in there somewhere.

Commissioning the book had been a commercial decision. I knew there was enormous interest in Miriam Crace and that a new biography couldn't be better timed. But I'll admit that I wasn't sorry to be getting back at Jonathan Crace and his nephew Roland for all the harm they'd caused not just me but many of the people around them. At the same time, I felt a certain protectiveness towards other members of the family who had never asked for any of this. I'd talked it through with

Sam and we'd agreed to go easy on Julia, Leylah, Edward and his wife, Amy (whom I'd never met), mentioning them by name but largely keeping them out of the spotlight. The main thrust of the book was Miriam herself and she deserved everything she got.

After that, I was planning to publish a crime novel in time for Christmas, the first in a projected series. It was being written by a detective with an insider's knowledge of life in the police force, writing under the same pseudonym he had used to complete *Pünd's Last Case*.

Ian Blakeney had become Ian Black. He was still working as a detective inspector and had chosen not to use his real name. He had investigated the murder of Eliot Crace and he had finished Eliot's book, adding the extra twenty thousand words I needed. I knew that this turnaround would have made for an interesting interview on *Front Row* – for one – but he felt uncomfortable with his new-found fame and we both agreed that anonymity was the best policy. He had already decided to retire in a few years' time and he was as surprised as anyone to have fallen into this new career.

I saw him now, standing in the background while the white wine and canapés were served. The same sort of crowd who always turned up at book launches seemed to be enjoying themselves at this one. My sister, Katie, was close by and Ian had his two children, Tom and Lucy, on either side. They were very proud of him, but he was standing there in his jacket and tie, making no secret of the fact that he couldn't wait to get home.

He and I were together and had been for eleven months.

We weren't married and I wasn't living with him yet, but

we saw each other most evenings and weekends. We went to concerts and the theatre, he cooked or we went to restaurants, we talked books. We were planning a trip to Central America. We felt as if we'd known each other much longer than we really had and I knew in my heart that this time it was for keeps. Katie loved him. Tom and Lucy were about the same age as her children and together we made a family much happier and healthier than the Craces and the Chalfonts had ever been.

I'm not saying that you are only complete if you have a job and a relationship, but unfortunately this was what I had learned from the moment I moved back to Crouch End. I needed them both and I'm afraid all the charms of Hugo, along with the two goldfish, Hero and Leander, hadn't been nearly enough for me. I had Ian and I had Nine Lives. My first book was out and I had never been happier.

I glanced at it, lying on the table. *Pünd's Last Case*. I had gone back to the original title because I felt I owed it to Eliot, but this time I was determined it would be exactly that. I'd finished with Alan Conway and his famous creation. From the moment they had come into my life, almost thirty years ago, they had caused me nothing but trouble. But as I stood there, I knew I'd finally put them behind me. I had made a resolution as far as Atticus Pünd was concerned and this time I was going to keep it.

Never.

Never again.

Acknowledgements

This is the third outing for Susan Ryeland and Atticus Pünd and you wouldn't be holding it in your hand if it wasn't for Lesley Manville, the brilliant actress who has played Susan twice – and will return when we shoot this one. On the last day of shooting *Moonflower Murders* in Crete, she mentioned that she would like to come back one more time and, in that moment, this book sparked into life. I want to thank her and Tim McMullan (a graduate of *Foyle's War* and a perfect Atticus) for encouraging me to do my best work. Eleventh Hour Films produced both seasons and will produce the third. I'm grateful to Jill Green and Eve Gutierrez and also to Susanne Simpson at WGBH/PBS for their huge input.

As always, I am very fortunate to be with Penguin Random House, who are much nicer and more supportive than Causton Books who appear in these pages. The full cast is listed below but I want to say a special thank you to my tireless editor, Selina Walker – and also to Venetia Butterfield and Joanna Taylor. I was under a lot of pressure to finish the book and to adapt it for TV, almost simultaneously, and they were very helpful to me when I most needed it.

I must thank Eileen Marino who generously bid in a charity auction on behalf of the National Literacy Trust (one of my favourite charities) and who now finds herself vilified in The Landscape of Criminal Investigation.

My long-suffering agent, Jonathan Lloyd, continues to tell me only what I want to hear. I also want to thank two of my foreign publishers. Jonathan Burnham at HarperCollins NY often guesses the endings of my books – but didn't guess this one. And Iris Tupholme at HarperCollins Toronto is a vital part of the triumvirate that gives me first-draft notes.

At home, I was helped as always by my assistant, Tess Cutler, who manages my life, and also keeps the world at a safe distance. I am looked after by a family that seems to be expanding all around me and I am endlessly inspired by Nicholas, Sophia, Cassian, Iona, Boss and Chase. My wife, Jill Green, remains the number one influence in my life, the first person to read my scripts and my most perceptive critic.

Finally, as always, a thank you to the booksellers who stock this book, who remember the title when customers forget it (*Moonflower Murders* was surprisingly problematic) and who have such a profound knowledge of what their customers want. A special shout-out to Helen at The Open Book, Richmond, which is just round the corner from me. I'm quite sure this book will be in the window. And you might even find me browsing and buying books inside.

PUBLISHER
Selina Walker

EDITORIAL
Joanna Taylor
Mary Karayel

DESIGN
Glenn O'Neill

PRODUCTION
Helen Wynn-Smith

UK SALES
Alice Gomer
Emily Harvey
Kirsten Greenwood
Jade Unwin
Phoenix Curland

INTERNATIONAL SALES
Anna Curvis
Barbora Savolova

PUBLICITY
Klara Zak
Olivia Thomas

MARKETING
Rebecca Ikin
Sam Rees-Williams

AUDIO
James Keyte
Meredith Benson